dragonfly

Also by Julia Golding

dragonfly

JULIA GOLDING

Marshall Cavendish

Marshall Cavendish Corporation

99 White Plains Road

Tarrytown, NY 10591

www.marshallcavendish.us/kids

Library of Congress Cataloging-in-Publication Data

Golding, Julia.

Dragonfly / Julia Golding. — 1st Marshall Cavendish ed.

p. cm.

Summary: When Tashi, the rigidly formal sixteen-year-old Fourth Crown Princess of the Blue Crescent Islands, reluctantly weds roguish eighteen-year-old Prince Ramil of Gerfal, their religious, cultural, and personal differences threaten to end their political alliance and put both countries at the mercy of a fearsome warlord.

ISBN 978-0-7614-5582-0

[1. Duty—Fiction. 2. Interpersonal relations—Fiction. 3. Princesses—Fiction. 4. Princes—Fiction. 5. Fantasy.] I. Title.

PZ7.G56758Drc 2009

[Fic]—dc22

2008033012

Printed in China (E)

10 9 8 7 6 5 4 3 2

ɪɪɪ𝚌 Marshall Cavendish

For Joss, as always

As kingfishers catch fire, dragonflies draw flame.
GERARD MANLEY HOPKINS

N
W   E
S

ice archipelago

the
crescent islands

kai

rama

sapphire
ocean

lir-salu

phonilara

the
known world

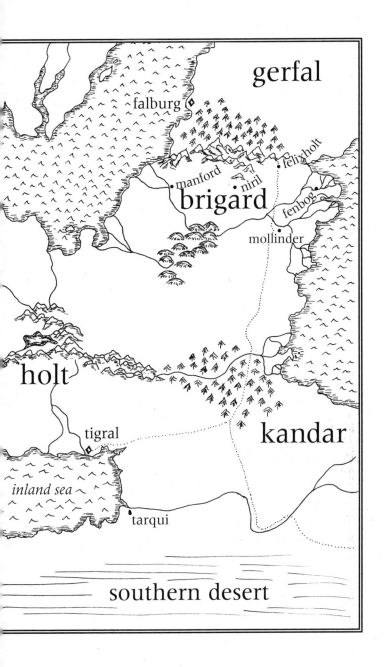

Chapter 1

The Fourth Crown Princess of the Blue Crescent Islands had sixteen rituals to observe from the moment of waking to when she broke her fast. These included getting out of bed on the right-hand side; turning to the east to bow to the sun; submitting to having her hair groomed with forty strokes from a silver-backed brush by the Under Mistress of the Royal Chamber; and—

Princess Taoshira paused. *What have I forgotten? Goddess rot the Etiquette Mistress's rule book, I know there's something else.*

"Your fingerbowl, Your Highness," intoned the Senior Mistress of the Chamber, holding out a bronze basin.

Fingerbowl! Why do I always forget the fingerbowl? Taoshira rinsed her fingertips delicately and dried them on a white linen towel.

Probably, chimed in another voice in her head, *because when you were at home—before you were chosen as princess—you had to wash your hands under the pump in the yard, jostling the serving girls for your place in the line.*

Taoshira, or Tashi as she used to be known to her family, almost smiled at the recollection—then remembered that the Crown Princess was not allowed to show emotion until she had said the Four Blessings, the true beginning of the day in the Royal Palace, and accompanied the words with the appropriate gesture.

"Eternal Goddess of Mystery, give our people wisdom" (*touching her head*);

"Gracious Mother of Mercy, look upon our people with compassion" (*right hand on heart*);

"Kind Sister of Healing, bless all who are ill" (*hands outspread*);

"Joyful Child of Hope, prosper our work this day" (*fingers arched, thumbs touching in a triangle*).

The four attendants gathered in her bedchamber gave the required response in unison: "As the Goddess wills."

Tashi was relieved that was over. She liked the morning prayer to the four faces of the Mother Goddess but had not yet got used to the fact that she was now an official priestess for the entire nation. If she forgot to say it—or even fluffed the words—her people believed that dire consequences would be felt throughout the land. It had been very different mumbling the same prayers to herself up on the hills of her family's estate on Kai, the northernmost of the islands that made up the Blue Crescent, named for the curving shape of the isles in the Sapphire Ocean. In those days, as a faithful Kaian, she had said the words with only her goats to hear her as the sun broke over the jagged crests of the

Marine Mountains. She had never dreamed that she would be snatched from that life as abruptly as a kid is plucked from the ground by a bird of prey. From insignificant daughter of an impoverished matriarch, she had become one of the four most powerful women in her world.

Tashi stood with arms outstretched as the Assistant Under Mistress of the Chamber removed her night-gown. That was another thing that had taken a lot of getting used to: standing stark naked in front of her attendants with only her long fair hair to veil her while they went through the ceremonial dressing. Over the last four years, from blushing furiously she had progressed to thinking of other things while they fussed over her. The ceremony had its set order: first placing on the white silk under-robe, then the sleeve-less orange tunic of the Fourth Crown Princess, next the flamboyant embroidered gown (today was one of her favorites—the dragonfly design), and finally the orange sash.

Four items of clothing. Her life was ruled by that number. It had decided her fate when the last Fourth Crown Princess had met an untimely death at the age of twenty. The Blue Crescent Islands always had four crown princesses, one from each isle of Rama, Lir-Salu, Phonilara, and Kai. It had been the princess from the smallest and most northern island that had died, so the priests and priestesses of Kai had gathered to iden-tify the next candidate. Their choice was restricted to all eligible twelve-year-old girls of matriarchal families.

Normally, the choice fell on the greatest and most wealthy households, but it seemed that in Tashi's year something had gone awry and she—the youngest daughter of a family whose claim to matriarchal nobility was largely on paper—had been chosen. Her family had long since ceased to be noticed at court, their wealth dwindling until they had become hill farmers in an obscure province.

There had been no question that she would accept the role. Tashi had known that her family would benefit hugely from having their daughter at the seat of government—and she also shared the belief that the Goddess's hand was behind such decisions, no matter how imperfect her human agents. Though Tashi had wondered many times over the years that had transformed her from free-living goat herder to a key part of the most formal court in the known world, whether the Mother had not chosen her for a bit of light relief from her three co-rulers. She sometimes felt she was more court jester than ruler as she struggled to submit to her new life.

Only to herself would she admit that the ceremonies and duties were driving her mad; and yet she was committed to repeating the same pattern day in, day out for the rest of her life, for the good of the nation.

The Etiquette Mistress, one of the highest ranking officials in the court, arrived even before the breakfast.

"Now, Crown Princess, shall we resume our lesson on the right degree of bow to give the Gerfalian ambassadors?" she asked, opening her scroll at the correct place.

"As the Goddess wills," replied Tashi, keeping her face inscrutable.

Ramil ac Burinholt, Prince of Gerfal, had risen before the sun for the hunt. The dawn had found him and his friends riding pell-mell through the Royal Forest, leaping fallen trees, whooping with excitement as they picked up a trail. Ramil loved the reckless speed of the chase and rode like the wind when the mood took him. His mother had originally come from the hot deserts of the far south, princess of a dark-skinned people known as the Horse Followers. His friends always said it was her blood in him that caught fire when he and his stallion, Leap, set off on one of their mad careers through the forest, leaving all the others behind. The professional huntsmen just shook their heads in despair and let the young Prince go, knowing from experience that he would return when it suited him, having caught nothing.

At one with his galloping horse, Ramil entered a state of pure happiness. The greens, oranges, golds, reds, and browns flashed by as Leap streaked through the trees. Twigs snatched at Ramil's clothes but were unable to catch him. The rush of air was cool on skin. Harness jingled and leather creaked in a tuneful counterpoint to the rapid thud-thud of the hooves. Leap's footing was sure; he was fresh, ready to run for as long as his rider wished. It was their great game, their moment of release from stable and council chamber.

Having covered a mile in this fashion, Leap barely slowed for the stream that crossed their path, jumping it in one bound. Once on the other side, he pulled up by a thicket of hawthorn and snickered to his rider.

"What's the matter, boy?" Ramil asked, patting his mount's sweat-stained neck.

Leap shook his black mane and snorted, shifting his hooves nervously.

In the joy of the ride, Ramil had almost forgotten the purpose of their outing this morning, but he trusted the stallion's instincts, not to mention his sense of smell. He reached for one of the short spears strapped to his back.

"We're close, are we?"

Ramil strained his hearing, listening for the tell-tale sound of snuffing or movement in the undergrowth. The ancient trees of the Royal Hunting Forest were particularly gnarled and squat in this part, as if like old men, they had stopped growing taller and started put-ting on weight round their middles. Dark-green holly and brambles swallowed up the space beneath the oak canopy. Plenty of places to hide; very hard to see. He nudged the horse forward. There! Definitely some-thing moving through the bushes. Ramil shifted his grip on the spear and held it ready over his shoulder.

Twigs snapped aside as a boar erupted from the undergrowth. Stubby tusks lowered, it charged towards the horse and rider. Leap side-stepped deftly, moving to give Ramil a clear shot with his spear. The boar passed them and reached the bank, trapped between huntsman and water. With gritty spirit, it wheeled round to face the spear, small black eyes glaring. Ramil rose in the stirrups, paused, and then let the weapon drop.

"Lucky for you that my friends were not here, brother," he addressed the boar. Replacing the spear in its holster, he spurred Leap forward, jumping back over the stream, leaving a confused boar in sole possession of the bank.

"Fine prince I am." Ramil chuckled, apologizing to Leap with a pat. "But we have meat and he was magnificent—a fine sire for lots more boars just like him, don't you think?"

A horn sounded in the trees to the east, summoning the stray Prince to return to the hunt. Ramil and Leap trotted back at peace with each other. As they neared the old road, three young lords on fine horses joined them.

"There you are, Ramil!" called Hortlan, the Prince's cousin. "So what have you caught?" He gave Ramil a huge grin, already knowing from the empty space on the pommel that the chase had been fruitless.

"I had him. I was this close!" replied Ramil, holding up a gloved hand, finger and thumb indicating the distance. "A massive boar, enough to feed the whole household for a week!"

"And?" Hortlan mocked, giving no credence to his cousin's description.

"He charged and I—" Ramil began to laugh, both at himself and at his friend's expression of scepticism. "And I ran for it."

"Now that I don't believe!" Hortlan slapped Ramil on the back. With his long light-brown hair and blue eyes, Hortlan was as unlike his curly black-haired, dark-eyed cousin as one could get. "A Burinholt run from a little hairy pig? Never!"

Ramil shrugged. "All right, all right, I made that part up."

"And the boar too, if you ask me," muttered Lord Yendral to the trees, but loud enough for all to hear.

"Ramil the Unblooded, that's what we should call you. Bane of every hunt," quipped Lord Usk, son of the Gerfalian Prime Minister. A big-framed youth, he had the reddish-brown hair of his Brigardian mother. "My father should propose a law to keep you in the castle come winter. We'll all starve otherwise."

Ramil bowed in his saddle. "Thank you for that vote of confidence in me, my friends. Come, let us take back the tale of my heroic deeds to the castle and dine on fresh air and spring water in my honor."

Ramil always insisted on grooming his own horse, so he waved away the stable boys waiting in the courtyard for the huntsmen's return. The stables were his favorite part of the royal palace, built within the walls of the old fortress, the castle keep. The first King Burinholt had established his throne in dark days when the Gerfalians were little better than raiding barbarians. The core of his old coastal stronghold reflected these times: a simple round tower, a landmark to ships at sea, built on a motte, with the rest of the castle sheltered in the bailey. Times had changed for the kingdom: no enemies had come knocking at the door for so long that the palace had spread down the hill in more elegant and much less defensible buildings. A splendid feasting hall now sat on a low promontory opposite the original tower; its high windows and vaulted roof, decked with beautiful stone pinnacles, was in clear view of every house in the valley. Ramil knew that his people thought of the feasting hall as the center of power, but he preferred to think of the modest round keep as the true heart of the kingdom. It was where the King and his family still lived, simple in their tastes and dress when not on show.

Ramil hummed a folk song to Leap as he groomed him. He loved the deep colors of the horse's coat. Unless you were this close, you would call him black but Ramil knew he was really a deep blue—the color, his mother had claimed, of the night sky over the desert. Leap, a birthday present, was one of the last links to her since her death seven years ago. She had died giving birth to his little sister, Briony, a honey-skinned creature with round scared eyes, an exchange for the vibrant Queen Zarai of Gerfal. The entire nation had mourned Zarai. Ramil had found it hard not to hold his mother's death against the little girl, her only fault being that she had been born.

Ramil wondered if he over-compensated by being too kind and polite to the young Princess, rarely if ever showing her the rough-and-tumble, easy love of a brother. She had always treated him with suspicion as if she sensed his resentment. They spent little time together, but still he felt as if he had let down his mother by somehow failing to love his sister enough.

"I know, I'll teach her to ride," Ramil told Leap. "I'll get a nice docile pony and take her round the palace park tomorrow. She's half Horse Follower too: maybe that will set things right between us."

Happier with himself, he slung the grooming equipment into a bucket, gave Leap a final stroke on the nose, and headed back to his rooms. As he entered the dark archway leading into the keep, he was intercepted by one of his father's servants.

"Your Highness, His Majesty requests your presence in the council chamber immediately," intoned the elderly man with great self-importance.

Ramil sniffed at his sweaty hunting clothes, muddy brown breeches, and leather jerkin.

"Not like this, surely?"

"Immediately, Your Highness; those were his very words."

With a mild curse, Ramil retraced his steps, crossed the courtyard separating the keep from the feasting hall and entered a long, low building to the right of the grand entrance. His feet echoed in the cloister, disturbing the scribes at their desks in the administrative heart of the kingdom. Seeing who was passing, they all stood and bowed. So used to this treatment, Ramil did not notice them bend, no more than he questioned the breeze through long grass.

King Lagan ac Burinholt was sitting at the head of the table in the White Stone Council Chamber when his son clattered into the room. And he was not alone. Ramil saw at once that most of his ministers and three foreigners were with him. King Lagan frowned when he noticed the state of his offspring, covered in mud and distinctly windblown, wearing clothes that little distinguished him from the stable boys. A well-built man with brown hair silvering at the temples, Lagan always appeared in simple but impressive robes when meeting foreign dignitaries. He did not want them to forget that Gerfal, with its riches of mines and forests, was amongst the most prosperous of the known nations. Today's robes of green velvet were edged with gold. Underneath he wore a loose fitting black tunic and completed the ensemble with a circlet of gold in the shape of intertwining branches.

Ramil did not need to be told that the servant had been overly eager to hurry him into the royal presence. A stop at the palace baths would have been advisable. But, a prince to the core, he decided it was best to pretend nothing was the matter.

"Father, I came as soon as your message reached me," he said, going down onto one knee on the white paved floor.

"So we can see," the King said dryly. "Ambassadors, may I present His Royal Highness, Ramil ac Burinholt." Ramil bowed to the three ladies at his father's right hand, all from the Blue Crescent Islands from the look of their elaborate embroidered robes, veils and white-painted faces. They stood in unison and folded in the low bow due to royalty, even mud-stained young princes.

"Ambassadors, your presence does our court great honor," Ramil acknowledged them, wondering secretly what on earth had brought these envoys from the other end of the known world. The Islands lay far to the west, a long sea voyage around the lands of the Spearthrower's empire. A dangerous journey not to be undertaken lightly, thanks to the depredations of the warlord's imperial Pirate Fleet.

The King rose, giving the signal for all to do likewise.

"Ladies, now you have seen my son, let us reconvene this time tomorrow, giving you a chance to recover from your arduous voyage."

The ambassadors bowed again, this time a shade lower as fitting for a monarch.

"Ramil, come with me." Lagan beckoned his son to follow him into the retiring room behind the king's dais.

Perplexed, Ramil trailed after his father. Lagan dismissed the servants, threw a log on the fire, and sat down in an armchair with a grunt of contentment. Compared to the White Stone Chamber, it was a comfortable room, much like an old slipper after the pinch of formal footwear. Ramil felt more at ease in his muddy clothes and slumped in his favorite chair.

"Wine? Kava?" Lagan offered his son a drink from a tray set ready on a low table. Ramil accepted a cup of the dark, bitter kava that had been his mother's preference.

"Sorry about that," Ramil said awkwardly, gesturing to himself and then into the hall. "The messenger made it sound as if I had to come at once."

"A wise king never hurries without knowing to what he goes," said Lagan, quoting from the *Book of Monarchs*, one of Ramil's least favorite texts from his days in the schoolroom.

"Yes, but the wise son jumps when his father whistles," Ramil countered.

Lagan laughed. "How true. Never mind all that now: I have something very serious to discuss with you."

"Would it have to do with the ambassadors, by any chance?"

Lagan nodded and sipped his wine. "You won't have failed to notice that Holt has been regarding us with less than friendly eyes of late."

Ramil nodded. The coast had been raided by so-called pirates—really privateers working for the warlord of Holt, Fergox Spearthrower. There had been several skirmishes along the border between Gerfalian troops and men from Holt's latest conquest, Brigard. War had not yet been declared but it was already being fought.

"The Blue Crescent Islands have also had their fair share of attention from the warlord. In our different ways, we represent the next logical conquests for Holt."

"But that'll never happen," Ramil objected. "Gerfalians will never let Spearthrower invade. We'll fight his armies street by street, field by field—"

Lagan held up his hand. "I know, Ram, I know. But I also know that the Brigardians had a brave army, as well equipped and trained as ours. They did not give in easily, but yet they fell."

"They were starved into submission. Fergox cut them off by sea—that's what broke them."

Lagan sipped his wine. "I'm glad to see you've been paying attention at council. I will never again say that your glazed look is because you are daydreaming. But you are right. Fergox exerts his power by both land and sea. We might be able to match him with our armies, but we will never be the equal of the Pirate Fleet. That's why we need an alliance with the Blue Crescent."

Ramil nodded. It made perfect sense. The Crescent navy was famed throughout the known world for its strength as a fighting force. Used mainly to defend the waters of the Sapphire Ocean, the four Crown Princesses could call on at least a thousand ships with highly skilled crews who also trained as land-based fighters. These marines were a remarkably versatile force, even more surprising in Ramil's view because half of them were female. Women did not train for combat in Gerfal. But the Islands were a long way away and though Gerfal and the Blue Crescent were not enemies, neither were they exactly friends. Their cultures were worlds apart.

"So how are we going to make this alliance? I can see we will benefit from their navy. What do they get from us?"

"Initially, raw materials and promise of military support in the event they are attacked. We do not know which country Fergox is going to strike first, but we both have an interest in seeing the other survive. And there's something else too."

"Oh?" Ramil was feeling tired after his long morning of riding. He yawned. For all the threats to Gerfal, his father appeared to be on top of everything. He had little to do but approve the sound preparations for their defense. "What else?"

"A royal alliance."

"What?"

"In short, you."

All tiredness vanished. "No! I'm not marrying one of their matriarchs. I don't want a white-painted she-witch as a wife."

Lagan frowned. He had expected his son to react like this, which was why he was holding this meeting in private. Prejudice against the strange people of the Blue Crescent ran deep in Gerfal—indeed the King was not too keen on them himself.

"Not a matriarch. The match is to be with one of the Crown Princesses."

"But that's no better," thundered Ramil. "She could be anyone—the most recent one was dragged from the gutter if the stories are to be believed."

Lagan sucked his teeth, waiting for his son to finish his outburst.

"There's no royal bloodline—just a series of nobodies dressed up in stupid costumes! Heaven's sake, Father, they prize poetry and paper-folding over swordsmanship. I doubt a native of the Blue Crescent Islands has ever sat on a horse. They're all for boats and canals, not roads and carriages like a civilized country!"

"You're being ridiculous, Ramil. The waterways of Rama are among the wonders of the world."

Ramil was annoyed with himself, recognizing he'd gone completely off the point with his sweeping attack on Crescent culture.

"Look, Father, put yourself in my shoes. You know as well as I do that marriage to one of them would be a living death. They are so formal they have sixty things to do before and after belching. God knows what you have to do before kissing a Crown Princess!" Ramil shuddered at the thought. "Don't do this."

"We have no choice. It is the only way our two countries can be brought to trust each other—we need the Blue Crescent if there's to be a throne for you to inherit."

Ramil tried a different tack. "I thought the Crown Princesses didn't marry."

"This one does."

"Which one? They're all near ninety, aren't they?"

"You exaggerate, Ramil."

"So I'm to marry one of four but I'm to have no say in the choice, not even to say which I'd prefer?"

"Correct. This is a marriage of state, not a farm boy picking a milkmaid at a barn dance."

Ramil bunched his fists. "I'm not going to do it, Father."

"You will do it for Gerfal. You will do it to show that you take your responsibilities seriously."

Ramil stood up abruptly, with half a mind to storm out. "You can talk. You always said you married Mother for love."

Lagan threw another log on the fire. "I married selfishly. I weakened Gerfal by choosing your mother."

"She was a princess—"

"Of a people that counted for very little here in the north. If I hadn't met her at the Great Horse Fair, I would've been married to Fergox's sister, did you know that?"

Ramil shook his head.

"I ducked out of the match, I admit. Junis was not the woman of my dreams. I knew my father was planning the wedding so I took the decision out of his hands and married in a ceremony in the desert before he could stop me."

Ramil suddenly understood. "So is this why you have not told me any of this before? You were afraid I'd bolt and hitch up to the first likely looking woman?"

"Yes. You are very much like me, Ramil. I was afraid you'd make the same mistake."

"But your marriage to Mother was not a mistake. You were happy—you had me and Briony—"

"We were happy, yes, but Gerfal was not. Think what might have been if I had allied us to Fergox by marriage: we wouldn't now be fearing for our future. But if you do your duty, you give Gerfal a good chance of surviving free of the warlord. Indeed, even better: you stand to expand our own power westwards—we could see Burinholts on two thrones."

Ramil seethed with anger—he felt like a sheep herded into the shearing shed, about to lose the comfortable fleece of dreams and pleasures that had so far made up his life. "But you forget the elections they've got there."

Lagan waved his hand airily. "Practices can change. Those elections are open to abuse and have been manipulated by Fergox. Why do you think an insignificant girl was chosen as the new Crown Princess? He's bribed some of the priesthood—he's weakening the rulers. When the Crescent Islanders realize this, they will want to put a stop to it, drag the Islands away from the vagaries of elections into the modern age of strong hereditary leaders. To men."

Ramil considered his father's words carefully before replying. "So what you are really asking me to do is to marry this crone to cement an alliance while all along we're planning to take over?"

"Not a crone. I have already said we will only accept a woman of child-bearing years. And yes, we can offer the Crescent Islands strong leadership when the time is ripe."

"Can I refuse?"

"If you refuse, I will open negotiations with Fergox for a suitable match for you. I understand his sister is still unwed. The Inkar Yellowtooth will no doubt accept a fresh young man like you in her bed."

"You are joking!"

"Sadly, I am not. I wish to spare my people a war we cannot win. Without the Blue Crescent, the only future is as a vassal state of Fergox. He would ask just such a sacrifice of us—a pledge of our loyalty."

Ramil was overwhelmed by a desire to start the day again; go back to the forest but this time forget to come home.

"So I have no choice?"

"No, I'm sorry, but you don't."

"The wedding—when, where?" Ramil snapped.

"The details are yet to be decided. Go and take a bath."

Lagan dismissed his son with a sigh. Ramil stalked out with his shoulders hunched. It grieved the King to know that he had just shattered his relationship with his only son. He remembered exactly what it had felt like to have his father behave as king rather than loving parent. His father had never treated him the same after his marriage to Ramil's mother, and his beloved wife had barely been received at court until the old king died. He feared Ramil would now hold a similar grudge against him.

Once the Prince had gone, the King rang a bell. The chief of his guard came in.

"See that Prince Ramil does not leave the castle until further notice," ordered Lagan. "Make sure he does not visit the stables on any pretext."

If the guard thought the order strange, he did not say. He bowed and left quickly to organize a twenty-four hour close watch on the young heir to the throne.

Chapter 2

Tashi was the last to arrive at the Hall of the Floating Lily, the seat of government in the four isles and one of her favorite places in the palace. The roof opened out from a central dome in the shape of an inverted water lily, petals becoming cream-colored pillars turning blush-pink where they joined the mosaic floor. The patterns on the ground reflected the rich culture of the Blue Crescent: the ever-present motif of the water lily, perfect beauty floating on the water like the Islands themselves in the Sapphire Sea; the dragon of eternity chasing its tail; the leaping dolphin, legendary friend of the first Mother; the dragonfly, the herald of the Great Goddess herself, catching fire with a fragment of her glory.

Tashi approached her fellow rulers with a carefully measured step. Marisa of Phonilara, the First Crown Princess, was already sitting on her throne—the Throne of State, which was carved like a ship in full sail—her white robe spread around her so she looked like an old wrinkled figurehead. The Second Crown Princess,

Safilen of Lir-Salu, a fine-looking woman in her fifties, was just taking her seat on the Throne of Plenty—a magnificent piece decorated with images of the harvest of land and sea. She swept the folds of her green robe, embroidered with golden sheaves, so that they rippled gracefully to rest on the floor. The Third Crown Princess, Korbin of Rama, followed her, sitting down swiftly on the Throne of Justice. Her face was set in a frown, fingers stroking the blue sash in her lap in a subtle sign of irritation. Her chair was cast from bronze, its back shaped like the blade of a sword. Korbin was the closest to Tashi in age, being only twenty-nine. The last place, the Throne of Nature, was built of plain wood. It was no better than many a chair in a matriarch's hall but its simplicity was to remind the four rulers that the riches of the land and sea, the civilization their ancestors had built here and the ocean they had come to dominate, were all founded on the natural gifts of the Islands. Without the blessings of the Creator Goddess, none of this would exist.

So why, wondered Tashi for the hundredth time as she approached the seat of unyielding wood, *does the most junior Crown Princess get to sit on it?*

Tashi bowed to her sister rulers and took her place, spreading her dragonfly robes in an elegant arc around her feet to mirror Safilen's gesture.

A bell rang in the roof, signalling that the government was in session.

Marisa rose to her feet. "Sisters, the first matter for our consideration are the preparations for our defense against our enemy, Emperor Fergox Spearthrower. Our messenger birds from the embassy in Gerfal have brought a reply to our proposal of alliance. King Lagan agrees."

Tashi joined in the round of polite applause from all in the room. She had known that the First Crown Princess, responsible for foreign affairs, had spent months conducting these delicate negotiations. Tashi remembered the rough-looking ambassadors she had practiced bowing to only the month before. Their tunics and trousers had seemed very out of place amongst the robes of the Blue Crescent court, their loose long hair almost wild compared to the modest veils customarily worn in the palace. And the Gerfalians had all been men.

"King Lagan agrees that our alliance must be cemented by ties that cannot be easily broken. He proposes a royal marriage with his only son and heir but has rejected my suggestion that this should be with a daughter from one of our leading matriarchal families. His Majesty is clear that only a Crown Princess will do. Though it is against our practice, I reluctantly agree with him. Extraordinary times demand extraordinary measures. Prince Ramil must marry an equal to show that the two nations join as equals."

Tashi did not at first understand what Marisa was saying—it was so unexpected. Crown Princesses were allowed to marry, but only as a private matter, kept away from the court. The Second Princess was well known to have been married happily for twenty-five years, but few had seen her husband, rumored to be a priest in one of the lesser temples. But a public—a state—marriage was unheard of, a major break with tradition. Tashi was not the only one to be surprised; all the councillors gathered on the benches around the thrones looked perplexed, a very extreme show of emotion for the notoriously controlled court of the Blue Crescent.

Safilen rose to speak.

"Sister, I understand the wisdom of alliance, but marriage to one of the four, that will have results none of us can predict, change the entire balance of power in this court."

The First Princess acknowledged the justice of the remark with a nod. "Of course, I know this, but we can also predict that this court will not exist in a few years' time if we do not forge alliances now. What will Fergox Spearthrower make of our customs and our laws? Nothing. He will desecrate the temples of the Mother and put us all to the sword, Crown Princesses and commoners alike, if his behavior in other countries is anything to go by. I propose a change, yes, but nothing as radical as he would force upon us."

Korbin rose.

"If what you say is correct, sister, then the only matter that remains is which one of us shall be chosen to represent our country in this alliance?"

Tashi raised her fan to hide a smile. The Third Princess

made it sound as if marriage was a sporting competition. In importance and age, Korbin was clearly the front runner for the task.

"King Lagan requires the wife to be of child-bearing years so that narrows our choice," continued the First Princess with the merest glint of amusement in her eyes. "Our ambassadors describe Prince Ramil as (forgive the undiplomatic language; I asked them to be frank) 'an uncouth boy of eighteen.' We must vote as to which of our two younger sisters should take up this burden."

Two younger sisters. Tashi suddenly woke up to the fact that she was being seriously considered for the marriage.

"The one chosen should be prepared to spend much of her time away from court. Her role will become that of a roving ambassador between us and Gerfal."

Marisa did not have to spell it out, but Tashi knew what that meant. If the Crown Princess was away from the Islands, she would lose much of her power, miss the government sessions, reduce her influence with the people. Tashi glanced at Korbin's severe face: she too was quickly counting the cost.

But I can't do it! Tashi thought in a panic. *I'm barely accepted as it is. A strange marriage would just about be the end of me, demote Kai further in importance, signal the end to my training and education. Added to that the fact that I don't want an "uncouth boy."*

"We will vote in the usual way," announced Marisa.

Each princess picked up the four voting sticks that sat on an arm of each throne—white, green, blue, and orange.

"Blue or orange?" intoned the First Princess. "Begin."

As described in the Law of Voting, second scroll, paragraph one, each ruler chose her stick. A bell sounded. One by one, four sticks were cast onto the tiled floor between the thrones, falling on the lily mosaic designed to be a reflection of the dome above.

"The decision is taken," Marisa declared.

Tashi stared at the floor in disbelief. Three orange sticks and one blue lay at her feet. The three older princesses had all voted for her.

"But I can't—" she began.

Her three co-rulers looked at her in astonishment. No princess ever raised a personal objection in open court.

Tashi stood and bowed. "Forgive me, sisters. What I meant to say was 'As the Goddess wills.'"

She walked out quickly, knowing she was breaking precedent by leaving before her elders, but she couldn't stay there after what they had just done to her. Once in the corridor she broke into a run, gathering up the heavy brocades of her robes in clenched fists. Little Kai, unimportant island of the union, sacrificed to please some distant king and to keep the other three safe. She could scream. It should've been Korbin: she was older, fully trained as a diplomat, more than ready for marriage, representative of the largest island, Rama, so less likely to lose her influence. So many reasons pointed to her.

But they had all voted for the youngest, least important, most dispensable princess at court. An insult to the Gerfalians if they realized it.

And an insult to me too, Tashi realized. They probably thought a goat herder would be a good match for the "uncouth" barbarian prince.

Tashi stormed into her bedroom, shut the door in the Etiquette Mistress's face, and threw the bronze fingerbowl out of the window. It made a satisfying clang as it hit the pavement below.

She flung herself on her bed. She'd do her duty but Goddess help Prince Ramil if he expected any more from her than that. If he did, she would make his life very unpleasant.

The point when Ramil completely lost his temper was when he was refused entry to the stables. He had intended to fulfill his promise and take his little sister riding, but a guard stopped them both at the entrance.

"I'm very sorry, Your Highness, but the King has ordered that you are not to be allowed in here." The guard, a jovial man for whom Ramil had often bought a drink in the inn by the castle gate, was now looking very sober and very serious.

Inside their loose boxes, the horses neighed, sensing the presence of their favorite rider at the door.

"Ram, where is the pony?" whispered Briony, clutching her brother's hand nervously.

"The pony is in the stable, but apparently I'm not able to fetch it for you." Ramil could feel his temper getting the better of him. "The Princess—is she allowed in?" he snapped.

"Of course, Your Highness." The man lowered his spear.

"And if I order a groom to bring the pony here, will I be allowed to take my sister into the park?" Ramil asked acidly.

"No, Your Highness, I am ordered to keep you in the castle."

Ramil turned to his sister. "Sorry, Briony, lesson cancelled. Run back to your nurse."

Leaving Briony bewildered by this sudden change of plan, he strode out of the courtyard, heading for his father's chambers. King Lagan was closeted with the Prime Minister, Lord Taris, a map spread on the table in front of them, dotted with tiny figures of men and ships.

"So, I am to be a prisoner in the castle, am I, Father?" Ramil asked, not stopping for the courtesies of greeting.

Lagan pushed a division of soldiers towards the mountain passes crossing to Brigard.

"It is my wish to keep you close by until the marriage takes place," Lagan answered calmly.

"That is outrageous, Father! You are treating me like a criminal!"

Lagan sat back and regarded his son astutely.

"Would you give me your word that you will not desert us?"

"Of course, I—"

"Would you swear it on the good name of your mother?"

"I . . . " Ramil faltered.

"Exactly."

Ramil twisted his riding gloves in his fingers. "Do you think she would've approved of this, Father?"

Lagan picked up a model of a cavalry officer thoughtfully. "No, I know that she would not. She would've saddled your horse for you and bribed the guards to let you leave."

"So why are you doing this to me?" Ramil cried in despair.

"Because she would have been wrong. Sometimes the head, rather than the heart, has to rule."

Ramil could have screamed with fury. His particular heart had become a fiery ball of loathing.

"I hate you, Father."

"Do not say that," Lagan replied wearily. He had had just such a scene with his own father and his punishment for his choice then was to have to live through it again today. "I am trying to save Gerfal. I'm saving you from yourself. If you ran from your duty, believe me, you would never forgive yourself."

Ramil was burning to throw something, to hit his father even. "You talk about duty, Father, but you forget that I can show no duty if I cannot choose. How will you know whether or not I would act as becomes a prince of Gerfal if you do not allow me the chance to make my own mistakes or even make my own right choices? How can I ever be fit to rule Gerfal like this?"

Lagan nodded his approval. "You argue well, my boy, but the time to give you that opportunity is not now. Later, I promise, you will have plenty of freedom to show you are fit to rule."

"But—"

"I cannot risk the nation's happiness on your experiments in rule."

"All right then. Shut me in the dungeon—show the people just what you think of me."

Anger flashed in Lagan's eyes. "You are being insolent, proof that I was right to confine you!"

Ramil gave a hollow laugh. "Unfair, Father; very good maneuvering, but unfair. Do not try to blame me for your injustice towards me!"

Lagan rose, assuming the full dignity of his position, his green robes sweeping the floor. "Consider, Prince Ramil, in your pride and your selfishness, that I could be wrong to you but right for our people. Tell me, in my place, would you put the happiness of your own child over your duty to your nation? Tell me, what would you do?"

Ramil glared at his father. "I would trust my son."

He left the chamber, slamming the door behind him.

The crown barge glided up to the palace mooring accompanied by the quavering pipes of the royal orchestra. Streamers fluttered gently from the prow—orange in honor of the passenger who was to take this journey to the sea. Tashi was bringing nothing with her. All her belongings and ceremonial robes had been packed by others and sent ahead. They didn't feel like hers in any case. She'd struggled for years to make herself into the Fourth Crown Princess, but the marriage decision had driven a breach between her two selves. The princess was an empty shell, a collection of words, actions, and drapery; Tashi was far away, hidden somewhere inside herself, watching it all with disdain.

The other three Crown Princesses stood beside her as the priests went through the ceremony of farewell.

"I have asked the Etiquette Mistress to write a new set of rituals suited to your life as a traveller, sister," said Korbin haughtily.

"As the Goddess wills," murmured Tashi.

"We would value frequent messages from you," said Marisa, "and will expect the nuptial visit of you and your consort in the spring."

Tashi nodded, not trusting herself to say anything on the subject of consorts.

"A word in private, sister," Safilen spoke gently, taking Tashi's arm. The other two rulers watched in surprise as she led Tashi aside. The courtiers tried to ignore this break with precedent, keeping their eyes to the barges gathering in a flotilla of orange ribbons. The sun glanced off the network of canals that crisscrossed the plain before the palace, making the water dazzle liquid gold. Swallows swirled in the sky above the jade-colored roof of the palace.

The Second Princess drew Tashi into an arbor covered in a vine, grapes dangling in ripe clusters. She cupped Tashi's pale face in her hand and looked deep into her green eyes.

"You are unhappy, sister."

Safilen said it as a statement, not a question.

Tashi blinked, feeling tears spring into her eyes. No one had mentioned her emotions since she arrived at the palace. It was as if she had been stripped of the desires, hopes, and fears of youth and slowly become a machine created to rule. Now, just when she needed to be at her most hardened, the Second Princess was talking about feelings.

"You think we voted for you because you are the most junior among us? That you do not matter?"

Tashi nodded.

Safilen dropped her hand from Tashi's face and instead took Tashi's fingers in hers. Another unparalleled sign of sympathy.

"I cannot answer for my sisters, but I voted for you because I thought you deserved a chance of happiness. You struggle—we all struggle—with the role the Mother has given us. My life has only been bearable because of my husband. I wish that for you too."

Crown Princesses never, ever mentioned their private life. Another custom shattered.

"But if I marry, I want someone from our own

people—someone who loves me. Not an uncouth prince marrying me because his father says so!" Tashi blurted out.

The Second Princess's eyes twinkled. "Uncouth sounds . . . amusing. And besides, we could not send the Third Princess, could we?" She nodded over to the grim face of their co-ruler, whose forehead was pinched in a frown. "What life for a poor eighteen-year-old boy would that be?"

Tashi lifted her sleeve to hide her gaping mouth. A joke from the Second Princess? That was definitely not in the Etiquette Book either.

Tashi spent the slow voyage to the naval port thinking over the Second Princess's words. Her body sat in the Throne of Nature on the open deck so that all her subjects could see her, but her mind was far away, speculating about the motives behind her co-ruler's kindness. The Second Princess was from Lir-Salu, the second smallest island. In many ways, Lir-Salu had the most to gain from Kai's decrease in influence, but Tashi could not shake off the impression that Safilen had been sincere in the wish for her happiness.

Am I going to distrust everyone or believe that, sometimes, I will meet friends? Tashi asked herself. *Do I want to end up like Korbin, frowning at all I see, or like Safilen, content and still human?*

She had to take the risk for her own sake, and for Kai.

Tashi signalled to a scribe.

"Please send the following to my sisters. 'I, Fourth Crown Princess, hereby delegate in my absence my voting powers to Second Crown Princess. I trust she will think as I would have of the beloved people of Kai in all matters concerning the rule of our Islands.'"

The message was despatched by carrier pigeon. Tashi watched the bird soar over the canal locks that the barge had already passed through on its journey to the sea. She wondered if she was being a fool. Had Second Princess merely calculated that inexperienced Tashi would react gratefully to her show of concern? As representative of both Kai and Lir-Salu, Safilen would augment her influence at court as rival to both her co-rulers.

Be quiet, Tashi snapped at her cynical side. *Let me at least think that I have one friend at court. Don't spoil it for me! Sometimes the heart has to rule over the head.*

Tashi had seen maps of the Known World but never comprehended its vastness until this voyage across the Northern Ocean. Gerfal lay over a thousand miles away, beyond the Empire of Holt, beyond anything that Tashi found familiar. The Blue Crescent navy could not land at any Holtish port, of course, so had to sail far to the north to the islands of the Ice Archipelago for supplies midway through the journey. Fortunately, the winter had not yet frozen the seas, but Tashi woke to darkness each morning in her state cabin and had to say the Four Blessings well before the sun rose. Ice covered the inside of her windows, froze her breath and made icicles on the rigging, which crashed to the ground each day when the sun, feeble and low on the horizon, nudged away the darkness for a few hours. The people of the Archipelago were suspicious but not hostile, providing furs, meat, and fresh water to the twenty ships in Tashi's escort. They encountered no challenge from the Pirate Fleet. Any scout ships soon disappeared back to Holt when they counted the strength of the Crescent navy.

By late November, just as the seas further north were locking the Archipelago away for the winter and the sun no longer rose, the fleet turned south for Gerfal. They arrived to be greeted by a flotilla of the much inferior Gerfalian navy and were escorted to the port of the capital, Falburg. The Gerfalian sailors could only whistle with amazement at the size and firepower of the Crescent ships with their white square sails and ferocious figureheads of dragons and bulls embellished with gold paint. The Islands alone knew how to manufacture gunpowder, and the smallest of the Crescent ships had at least twenty cannon, the largest over a hundred. The marines were armed with long rifles, a technology unknown on the mainland. There, the crossbow was the main long-distance assault weapon.

The flagship of the fleet moored at the dockside to receive the representatives of King Lagan. Tashi sat once more on the Throne of Nature, brought out on deck for the purpose. She was dressed in her most elaborate gown, figured with leaves and wild animals in honor of the forested land of Gerfal. Her face was painted white, her eyes outlined in kohl, her hair hidden under a veil of green silk. An orange sash clinched her waist and fell to the deck in a swirl of color.

Lord Taris, Prime Minister of Gerfal, knelt before her. Behind him knelt a stocky young man with red hair, introduced as his son, Lord Usk.

"Your Royal Highness, on behalf of the King and all his people, I welcome you to Gerfal," Lord Taris said in Common Tongue, the shared language of the Known World.

"Thank you, Prime Minister," said Tashi, following the script written for her by the Etiquette Mistress. Though she was fluent, she felt awkward speaking Common. "I bring greetings from my sisters, the Crown Princesses of the Blue Crescent Islands, and I bring gifts." She nodded to a line of servants waiting with the appropriate presents—wine, silk, parchment, and salt. She took the topmost sheaf of paper and quickly folded it into the dragonfly, her personal symbol, and handed it to the Prime Minister. "A gift for Prince Ramil ac Burinholt." A person from the Blue Crescent would understand this as a sign of great favor and trust, equivalent to saying that you place your life in their hands, but the Prime Minister had obviously not been briefed correctly on this aspect of her culture for he fingered it nervously. The Crescent sailors stirred, wondering if he meant to show disrespect.

"Er . . . thank you, Your Highness," the Prime Minister said, passing it to his son. "We will make sure he receives it." He did not like to add that the Prince should have been here in person to greet her, but had gotten so drunk the night before on hearing that the fleet had been sighted, that he was incapable of standing. "If you would care to alight from your vessel, I have a carriage waiting for you."

Tashi drew in a breath. A carriage? No doubt pulled by one of the famous Gerfalian horses she had read about. She couldn't wait to see it.

"Thank you, Prime Minister." Her excitement entirely hidden from her hosts, she nodded and her attendants hurried forward to pick up her chair. According to the Etiquette Mistress, a crown princess's feet were not to touch Gerfalian soil until she had had a chance to say the prayers suitable for arriving in a foreign country. Four burly attendants carried her down the gangplank and stopped in front of the carriage. Tashi saw with a shiver of delight that not one but six white horses were waiting to pull it. She then realized there was a hitch: her throne would not fit in the cushioned interior of the carriage; she would have to descend.

But what about the prayers? she wondered. *I'll have to do them now.*

Nodding to her chief priest, she waited for him to strike the bell so she could begin the long prayer of thanks in her native language, uncomfortably aware that she was keeping Lord Taris standing on the dockside with no explanation.

"As the Goddess wills," she intoned at last.

Rising, she accepted Lord Taris's hand to step up into

the carriage. To her surprise he got in beside her, with Lord Usk sitting opposite, so close that their knees were almost touching. The breach in royal protocol was staggering. She wondered if they knew that the Crown Princesses only ever travelled in their own compartments. Apparently not, for the Prime Minister kept up a constant commentary as they rode through the streets of Falburg, pointing out places of importance, remarking on the commerce and customs of the city. Tashi pressed her lips together. No one spoke to a crown princess unless invited to do so. She could feel her cheeks blushing under her white paint, and she concluded that either the Gerfalians were more barbarous than she had heard or he was deliberately mocking her age and inexperience. Her silence only seemed to make him more talkative. He even tried to include his son in the conversation, claiming the young man was a great friend of her husband-to-be.

Hardly a recommendation for my favor, thought Tashi to herself. *He is probably as uncouth as his prince.*

Lord Taris pointed out the feasting hall up on the promontory overlooking the city. Its walls shone white in the sunlight; orange and green flags fluttered from the roof. Tashi allowed it to be an impressive sight, but alien to one used to the waterways and curved roofs of the Islands. These battlements and stone pinnacles looked very forbidding, conjuring up images of the claws and teeth of wild beasts crouching for the kill. She had been told that the people of the continent were warlike but she had not expected their buildings to be so too.

"We have arranged a welcome banquet, Your Highness, for this evening," the Prime Minister continued, trying to ignore the cold silence in the carriage. "Is that to your liking?"

Tashi nodded. "As the Goddess wills."

"We say 'God willing' here; you'll have to get used to that, I'm afraid. I understand you conceive of your Creator as female?"

Tashi's eyes widened. Blasphemy after insults: it was too much!

"We have made arrangements so you can carry out your religious duties undisturbed," the Prime Minister ploughed on. "There was some opposition, as you might imagine, but we have secured a small temple in the palace grounds for your own private use."

And I'm supposed to thank him? Tashi fumed. She tapped her fingers on her knees, a sign of severe displeasure if he had known how to read her moods.

The Prime Minister sighed with relief as they passed under the palace gateway. The carriage drove up to the steps to the Crown Princess's apartments where her servants, who had gone ahead of her, were waiting. He helped her descend, then watched her disappear into the building without a word. He turned to his son.

"Well, what do you think?"

"I think we've got a problem," said Lord Usk, stuffing the dragonfly into his pocket.

Dragonfly

Confined to his rooms, Ramil had woken with a terrible hangover and decided to get rid of it by returning to drinking. Hortlan and Yendral were trying to dissuade him, but Ramil was too depressed to care.

"Ah, Lord Usk!" he called in greeting as his friend came back from his trip to the port. "How is my sweet, my darling, my flower of the Blue Crescent?"

Usk tugged at his tunic, pulling out a crumpled paper object. "She asked me to give you this. It's a . . . actually, I'm not sure; it looks like some kind of bird."

"Ah, my dove flew across oceans to give this to me!" Ramil scooped up the fragile paper dragonfly and kissed it dramatically. He cast it into the air. It fell in circles to the floor, blunting its point. "Clever girl—look, it flies! Have a drink, Uskie." He slopped some beer into a tankard for him. "So, speak up, what's she like?"

Usk took the drink, glancing nervously at the other two. They went still, sensing that the news was not good.

"She's . . . well . . . not very talkative."

Ramil hit his forehead with the palm of his hand. "They've sent me a mute—how kind!"

"No, she can talk. She's just . . ."

"Just what? Beautiful? Intelligent? Witty? Everything a man could desire?"

"Formal."

Ramil refilled his own tankard and took a deep draught. "To formality—that well-known quality in all good wives!"

"But she's young. She might warm up a bit when you get her . . . you know . . . on her own," continued Lord Usk, trying to make the best of it.

"How young?" asked Lord Hortlan, also looking for a bright side. They all knew their friend was doomed.

"About sixteen, seventeen maybe. It's hard to tell under all that face paint."

Yendral began to laugh.

"What's so funny, my lord?" growled Ramil.

"That is wonderful—just wonderful—they've sent you the new one," Lord Yendral said, shaking his head.

"What's so special about the new one?" asked Ramil grumpily.

"Don't you remember the scandal? She's the farm girl—the one Fergox bribed the priests to choose, if the rumors from Holt are to be believed."

Ramil threw his tankard at the opposite wall. It chipped the plaster and left a brown stain splattered on the whitewash. "A peasant! I expect you could smell the pigsty, couldn't you, Usk?"

Lord Usk shook his head, nudging Yendral to stop winding up Ramil. Usk was shocked by the bitterness in Ramil's tone: the Prince was usually the last person to be cruel to another. "No, she seemed very refined as far as I could tell. Remember, Ram, these Blue Crescent people assume the dignity of their elected position. Her background doesn't matter; she's a Crown Princess."

"You sound like your father," muttered Ramil mutinously. "You can say that it doesn't matter: you're not the one who has to marry her." He looked for his tankard, then remembered he'd thrown it away. "Marl! Bring me more beer!"

The serving man appeared in the doorway, fumbling with his apron.

"I'm sorry, Your Highness, but His Majesty says you're to be sober for this evening. He asks your lordships to take the Prince to the royal baths and scrub some sense into him."

Yendral stood up. "Consider it done. Come on, let's get this pitiful prince of ours fit for his princess."

"Roll me in the mud. That's what Her Highness is used to," shouted Ramil as they dragged him down the corridor. "*To market, my sweet, to buy us a pig, home to our farm to make it grow big,*" he warbled.

"Can't you shut him up, Yendral?" implored Usk. "What if the Crescent people hear him?"

Lord Yendral took out a handkerchief and stuffed it in the royal mouth. Together the three friends manhandled Ramil all the way to the baths, only letting go when they passed him over to the merciless care of the muscular attendant.

Tashi felt very lonely sitting in her rooms going through the rituals with only a few attendants to spectate. In the palace on Rama she had always known that her sisters were performing the same service at exactly the same time in other parts of the palace, as were the priests and priestesses in the temples throughout the Blue Crescent. It had felt like one great service, all for the Mother. As the only one performing these rituals for thousands of miles, probably at a different time as even the sun was strange here, she found her voice sounded very thin and weak, the bell insignificant, the responses feeble.

The evening service complete, the Etiquette Mistress displayed the gown she had selected for the banquet: white silk, decorated with golden dragons. Tashi nodded her agreement. She didn't really care for it, but then again she didn't care what she looked like. No one would mind as this was not about her at all: it was about the joining of two nations, not a girl and a boy. Her hair was hidden under a sunburst gold headdress and veil, her face paint retouched.

"You are ready, Your Highness," declared the Etiquette Mistress, noting with quiet approval the composure of the Crown Princess, whom she had always considered too free with her emotions. "You do honor to our people," she added with a rare touch of warmth.

The Royal Chamberlain led the way to the feasting hall where the Gerfalian court was already assembled. Tashi peeked over his shoulder at the open door and saw that there were hundreds of strangers all waiting for her. She felt terrified. And one of them was to be her husband. They all seemed the same to her—the bearded men with long wild hair and strange clothes, the women with low-necked gowns that clung to their shapely forms, leaving little to the imagination, so unlike the fair-haired, pale-skinned people of her own court. If a woman ventured in public like one of these Gerfalians, she would be considered half-dressed; an unshaven man would be censured by the priests.

"Her Highness, Taoshira of Kai, the Fourth Crown Princess of the Blue Crescent Islands and dependent territories," announced the Chamberlain.

The room fell silent. Tashi walked smoothly up the central aisle, keeping her eyes locked on the man at the center of the long table in front of her. She reached the bottom of the dais and bowed as befitted one ruler greeting another.

"Your Majesty," she said in Common.

"Princess Taoshira, you honor all Gerfal with your presence." King Lagan came down the steps to greet her, kissing her hand in Gerfalian style. Tashi had been warned to expect this so did not flinch at the contact. "Please be seated at my side."

He led her to her chair. Tashi noted with pleasure that it was of equal magnificence to his own. She swept her gown into an arc as she sat. A dog promptly flopped down on it, drooling on the priceless fabric. King Lagan bent and stroked the beast.

"My favorite hound," he said in explanation. "Do you like dogs, Princess?"

Warming to this fatherly man, Tashi was about to tell him about her own dog, the one who helped her keep her flocks safe on Kai, but then remembered her status.

"I love all animals created by the Mother," she replied, giving the answer the priests had taught her.

"What, even wasps and wolves—and pigs?" A young

man snorted on her other side.

Tashi turned to him with a frown. He looked different from the others—his skin was darker and his black hair tightly curled like a Southerner. She wondered if he was some kind of entertainer, a court jester perhaps. He was very sloppily dressed and had already spilt something on his red velvet tunic.

"Yes, even those, for they all have their place in the Mother's plan for her world," she said in a haughty tone that the Third Princess would have been proud of.

King Lagan was looking thunderous but he struggled to keep his temper. "Princess, may I introduce my son, Prince Ramil, to you."

Tashi faltered. "*This* is Prince Ramil?"

"Yes, this *is* Prince Ramil," the young man repeated, giving her an insolent smile and tapping his chest.

"Ramil!" warned the King.

"Oh, I apologize, Princess. I am hopeless at these sort of introductions." Ramil seized her hand and kissed it quickly. "You-honor-us-with-your-presence," he gabbled.

Tashi was aware that all eyes were upon them. She wanted to slap the boy for his behavior but instead clasped her hands in her lap. It was worse than she had feared: he was unspeakably rude and not even trying to be pleasant to her.

"Thank you, sir," she replied quietly, trying not to show that she was upset. "Your welcome to a stranger displays all the qualities I have come to expect of Gerfalians."

Ramil frowned. If he was not mistaken, the little peasant had just reprimanded him.

"And your present to me on your arrival—apologies that I was unable to attend, by the way—shows all the generosity of your people." He pulled a sorry-looking piece of paper out of his pocket. To Tashi's horror, he spread it flat, obliterating her model, and made a crude paper dart. "Here, accept this with my dutiful best wishes." He dropped it in her lap.

"What's this?" said King Lagan, picking up the dart and looking at it in confusion.

"A love token, Father," said Ramil, tucking into the plate of meat in front of him.

"Strange token, my boy. There's nothing written on it."

Ramil merely smiled and shrugged. "The Princess understands. It's a Blue Crescent tradition."

Tashi swallowed and dug her nails into her palm to control herself. She feared she was going to burst into tears in front of all these barbarians. The gold trimmings of her headdress trembled.

"I am sorry, Your Majesty, but I find I am tired after the long voyage. I will retire. Please enjoy the feast in my absence." Tashi rose to her feet and swept from the hall before anyone could stop her.

Everyone jumped to their feet to bow as the Princess made her escape. King Lagan narrowed his eyes at his son.

"What?" said Ramil innocently.

Chapter 3

The King and his ministers were holding an emergency meeting. The Crown Princess had refused to leave her quarters for the last week, and preparations for the wedding were making no progress as the Blue Crescent delegation was withholding its cooperation.

"What has got into the girl?" asked the King. "She said she was tired. She can't still be tired!"

Prince Ramil sprawled in his chair, feeling quietly pleased with this development. Perhaps his father might be having second thoughts about the advisability of the union.

"Your Majesty, I have spoken to the Etiquette Mistress," replied Lord Taris, "and, after much prevarication, I persuaded her to explain the situation. It appears our greetings turned out in Crescent culture to be a catalogue of insults to the Princess."

"Insults! But you met her yourself! We held a feast in her honor. What more could Her Highness want?" King Lagan stroked his favorite hound's silky ears to calm himself. His country was on the brink of disaster and all because of some white-faced girl who was keeping to her room in a tantrum. He wanted to box her ears. Didn't she understand what was at stake?

"I fear we got it wrong from start to finish. The worst insult apparently was offered by Prince Ramil himself."

The King rounded on his son. "What did you do?"

Ramil sat up indignantly. "Nothing. You were there. *She* sent me this stupid paper bird. How about that for insults!"

"That 'stupid paper bird,' Your Highness, was her personal sign, the dragonfly," said Lord Taris.

"Didn't look anything like a dragonfly," grumbled Ramil.

"To hand your symbol to another is to entrust them with yourself—the fragility of the paper expressing the delicacy of each person's soul."

"Oh." Ramil started to have an inkling of what he had done.

"Your son took this gift, flattened it out, and made it into a paper dart."

"Ramil!" growled the King.

"I didn't know!" he protested. "What was I supposed to think? She came thousands of miles and gave me a squashed paper model."

"Actually, the squashing was my fault," admitted Lord Usk, his blushing cheeks clashing with his coppery hair. "It was very neat the way she made it, but by the time it reached Prince Ramil, I'd . . . er . . . sat on it."

King Lagan buried his face in his hands and groaned. "So we have a stranger in our midst, a princess, but also, let us remember, a girl of sixteen. She's come to do her duty by giving herself in marriage to my son, behaving with decorum beyond her years, and what do our young people do? They snub her, sit on her gifts, then fling them back into her lap."

Ramil and Usk looked at each other guiltily.

"Suggestions?" rapped Lagan.

"Send her home," mumbled Ramil.

The King scowled at his son.

"I think we owe her an apology," said Lord Taris. "Your Majesty, if you could perhaps speak to her?"

"I'll talk to her, but Ramil is the one who should apologize."

Ramil felt hot under the stares of all the ministers. He knew that Hortlan and Yendral would tease him unmercifully for crushing his future wife's gift like an ill-mannered oaf. But it hadn't been his fault. He'd warned his father that the two cultures were completely incompatible.

"Of course I'll say sorry," Ramil said grudgingly. "I did not intend to insult her."

"No? I am surprised to hear that." Lagan felt like shaking his son. He sat there so sullen and uninterested in the business, almost as if it were someone else's betrothed they were talking about. He acted as if he had no inkling of the true seriousness of the situation. Gerfal could not afford the failure of this union. "I'll seek an audience with Her Highness and then perhaps,

Ramil, you can make your own peace with her in a suitable setting, away from the confines of the court. Do something that shows that you *do* have a good side. Sometimes I need reminding you have one too!"

"The Princess shows an interest in the horses, Your Majesty," interjected the chamberlain as the King and his son exchanged stony glares. "She apparently visited the stables early this morning."

"That's it!" Lagan thumped the table. "Take the girl riding. Show her you can be considerate, if you try."

"So I'm allowed out again, am I?" Ramil said, folding his arms across his chest.

"Even you, Ramil, would not abandon a foreigner in the forest. I trust you to show her the courtesy of a host," Lagan replied, moving on to the next item on the agenda.

Tashi was in a terrible state. She realized she had to face the Gerfalian court again, but now that she had hidden in her rooms for a week it was doubly difficult to come out. She felt humiliated—and knew she was a failure. Wrapped in one of the furs bought in the Ice Archipelago, she paced the private terrace in front of her chamber, staring down on the city below her with unseeing eyes. She already hated it here and suspected that the people despised her. Even in the stables, the servants had all gazed at her like some curiosity in a menagerie. No one lowered their eyes respectfully as she passed.

On her desk lay the many drafts of the letter announcing her decision to return home unmarried. She hadn't plucked up the courage to send it yet, but she knew with a fierce certainty that she could not abide to be married to that sneering boy who'd insulted her so publicly. All who had travelled with her were whispering about it behind her back. She understood that scuffles had broken out down at the docks between sailors from the two navies. If she stayed much longer, she'd end up causing a war, not bringing about an alliance.

The Etiquette Mistress appeared at her elbow.

"Your Highness, the King wishes to speak to you. He is waiting outside and asks if you are at leisure?"

Tashi felt a momentary panic: she couldn't refuse to see the King though she would've liked to. She smoothed her robe. There was no time to change into more formal attire. She was wearing barely any make-up apart from the everyday kohl around her eyes. At least her hair was decently covered.

"Tell the King I will receive him now," Tashi said stiffly.

The Mistress departed and returned swiftly with the King. He strode towards her, arms outstretched.

"My dear princess! It grieves me that we have offended you."

Tashi flinched back but, before she knew it, found herself hugged to his chest and patted on the back.

"You have been so brave to travel all this way and we failed you. My son is heartily sorry for the incident with the paper dragonfly. He had no idea of its significance and thought you were playing a joke on him."

Tashi disentangled herself from his robes. "A joke, sir?"

"Come, sit by me." King Lagan slapped the seat beside him. "Damn chilly out here, isn't it?"

He was swearing and talking about the weather now. Tashi did not know what to do.

"Don't be scared: I'm not going to eat you, if that's what you're thinking," continued the King. Without all that make-up and glitter, he could see that she was a pretty little thing. And so young. It made him sad to think that she'd come to the other end of the world to marry his inept son when she should be growing up peacefully in her own home. Another sacrifice. He pulled her gently to the seat beside him. "There, that's better, isn't it?"

Tashi nodded, finding it easier to do as he asked than explain why it was inappropriate for a Crown Princess.

"We got off on the wrong foot last week, but I would like us to start again. I think it wise for you to get to know Ramil away from everyone. He's a good boy really."

Tashi supposed she could forgive a father for blind prejudice but she could see no redeeming feature in the Prince.

"He's offered to take you riding, if you would like that."

"Your Majesty is very kind, but I do not ride."

"What! Not ride! Well, then there's a treat in store for you. Ramil is an excellent rider—gets it from his mother, Zarai, a princess among the Horse Followers. He'll have you in the saddle and away before you know it. He's a very good teacher."

Tashi did not trust Ramil to come within a foot of her, let alone teach her to ride, but she did not know how to refuse this attention without seeming rude.

"I would not dream of taking up the Prince's time. If I am to learn to ride, I would be happy with one of the ordinary instructors."

"Time? Why, there is nothing more important than him spending time with you. Say nothing more on the subject. Tomorrow morning, just after nine, he'll be waiting for you in the stables."

King Lagan rose and patted her again on the shoulder.

"I hope to see you at dinner, my dear. Good afternoon."

Tashi watched him leave, in a state of shock. He'd patted her several times—no man had touched her like that since her father said goodbye to her on Kai four years ago. He'd called her "my dear" as if they were already kin. Clearly he did not respect her, regarding her as a wayward daughter to be cajoled into accepting his son's grudging attentions.

She returned to her desk, folded up the latest missive, and slipped it into the tube for the carrier pigeon. It was no good. The alliance could not go ahead. Her embassy had failed. Let the Third Princess take her place if she wished. Tashi was going home.

Ramil waited in the stables with Leap and a white mare he had selected for the Princess. Whisper was a gentle animal, suitable for a novice. Ramil's spirits lifted now that he was back among the horses: at the very least he'd get beyond the walls, even if it was with his ball-and-chain of a princess dragging behind him.

He heard feet on the cobbles and turned to see the Princess approaching with two attendants, her painted face ghostly in the dark of the stables. She was wearing a ridiculous gown covered with dragonflies. Was that a reminder of his mistake?

"Your Highness," Ramil said with a bow.

"Prince Ramil," she replied, giving him the merest bend in reply, a serious slight if he had known. Her attendants glared at him.

"I have taken the liberty of selecting a suitable mount for you. Her name's Whisper. A good horse. Very dependable. She'll treat you gently." He glanced at her attire again. Was she really expecting to ride in that? "Do you wish to ride astride or side-saddle?"

The Princess looked puzzled. "I do not know."

She really did know nothing about riding, thought Ramil incredulously.

"I suggest you try side-saddle until you can order more suitable clothes."

He whistled to a stable boy and ordered the appropriate tack. Tashi meanwhile was making friends with Whisper, stroking her nose timidly. Tashi felt she was falling in love with her already. She held out high hopes for this ride, even with the unpleasant company, having promised herself this one treat before announcing her decision to the Gerfalians that she was returning home.

"Princess, are you ready?" asked Ramil, holding out a hand to help her step on the mounting block. "One leg goes there, the other there. Yes, that's right."

Tashi shook out her skirts, feeling nervous now that she was perched up on Whisper's back. What if she fell? She had an image of herself sprawled in the mud in front of a laughing Ramil.

"I'll take the leading rein," explained the Prince. "All you have to do is stay in the saddle."

Ramil leapt onto his own mount and urged the stallion forward in a stately walk. The two horses made their way through the crowd of spectators that had gathered in the courtyard. Tashi kept her eyes lowered, trying to ignore the good-humored cheers and whistles of the stable boys. Ramil glanced sideways at his guest. It was impossible to know what she was thinking: her white face was blank of expression. She was like one of Briony's porcelain dolls. Fragile. Cold. He wondered what he would have to do to get a smile from her.

Ramil kicked Leap to go a bit faster and they began to trot down the paved street leading to the gate. Now he got a reaction. She had bitten her bottom lip, face furrowed in concentration.

"The Royal Forest is very beautiful, even at this time

of year, Your Highness," Ramil said, trying to make conversation.

Tashi did not reply. She was trying to work out how to stay on and was not listening.

"Perhaps Your Highness would like to go a little faster?" Ramil asked slyly.

Still nothing. They'd reached the sweep of parkland that led to the eaves of the forest. Ramil had been shut inside for months. The temptation was too great.

"As you wish, Your Highness." He urged Leap into a gallop. The Princess gasped and clutched the pommel of her saddle as Whisper followed. She looked terrified, or was it just that ridiculous face paint?

"Don't you love the speed?" Ramil called over his shoulder.

They crossed the meadow and passed under the trees.

"Stop! I order you to stop!" called the Princess. Her knuckles were white as she gripped the saddle; she was sliding all over the horse's back with no conception of how to stay on.

Ramil threw back his head and laughed. He couldn't imagine anyone not enjoying a fast gallop across country. "If we are to be married, you must learn not to order me around. I don't like it. Let yourself go for once, Princess. Enjoy yourself!"

He spurred the horses on. Branches seemed to reach out and grab Tashi. She was convinced now that this mad boy was trying to kill her. But it was no time to stand on her dignity. She had to end this before she broke her neck.

"Please, Prince Ramil, please stop!" she screamed.

Immediately, Ramil slowed the horses to a gentle walk, then a full stop. He knew he'd gone too far. It was the poor girl's first time in the saddle: he should never have scared her like that. He cursed himself for being a hard-hearted idiot. Then he heard something slither to the ground. The Princess was standing on the forest floor, trying to unhook her skirts from the saddle where they had become entangled. Ramil dismounted to help her.

"I'm sorry," he said, trying not to laugh at the absurd sight of the prim Princess fighting her own robes. "I'm not normally like this. I've just been shut up for so long in the castle and I—" He stopped. The girl was actually crying. He'd wanted a response—insults, laughter, something human—but he hadn't wanted this.

Now that she was back on the ground, Tashi's self-control had crumbled. The one thing she'd been looking forward to in this hellish place had been turned into a nightmare.

"I hate you. I hate Gerfal. I hate everything about this place." Tashi sobbed, ripping her underskirt to free it. "You don't have to worry about how I'll treat you after our marriage, because the alliance is off. I'm going home."

She started to stride away, heading in completely the wrong direction, deeper into the forest.

"Princess! No!" Ramil ran to her side and seized her arm.

"Let go of me, you barbarian." Black stains of kohl ran down her cheeks. She looked quite wild.

He let go, hands held up in surrender. "All right, all right! I was only trying to tell you that you are going the wrong way. The castle's over there."

With as much dignity as she could muster, Tashi swept round. Ramil watched until she was out of sight, torn as to what he should do. He had got his desire: the marriage was cancelled; but he knew he had behaved very badly. He would never have dreamed of treating an ordinary Gerfalian girl like that. He thumped his head on the saddle, making Leap start. What about Gerfal and the alliance? He should go after her and this time make his apology sincere.

"Princess, Princess, wait!" He caught up Whisper's trailing reins, remounted Leap, and urged the horses after her. She couldn't have gone far on foot.

Suddenly, a net fell from the branches on top of him. Ramil struggled to free himself, but felt the net tighten. He was yanked from the saddle, falling to the ground with a thud. He could do nothing. This was supposed to have been a romantic excursion so he carried no weapons, not even a knife. The net pressed his arms to his waist. Was this the Princess's revenge for his behavior? Had some of her men followed them and decided to teach him a lesson?

"Put him in the cart," growled a deep voice somewhere behind him. Ramil was dragged along the ground, then heaved into a cart, a canvas thrown over the top of him. He shouted for help, but felt a sword point at his throat.

"Make another sound and I regret I'll have to cut

your tongue out," the man hissed. He gave Ramil's cheek a shallow cut with the blade. "There's a reminder for you."

The cart heaved into motion, heading into the forest.

It was dark when the canvas was taken off Ramil and he was removed from the cart. From the network of branches overhead, Ramil saw that he was still in the forest, somewhere far in, he guessed, as nothing looked familiar. A circle of wagons was drawn up around a campfire. He had expected a gathering of grinning Crescent sailors, prepared to remind him of his manners to their ruler; what he had not expected was a bunch of circus performers, travelling with their entourage of animals.

"What the—" he began.

He received an elbow in the stomach, cutting off further protests.

"Be quiet!" growled the strong man, the size of a troll from one of the Gerfalian folk tales. He gripped Ramil by the scruff of his neck. "And get in there, lad."

He shoved the Prince into a foul-smelling, high-sided wagon. Ramil lay on his back in the straw at a loss to explain what was happening. The daring of these circus people was breathtaking. They'd abducted a member of the royal family not a mile from the castle. How could they expect to get away undetected? They'd be hanged from the battlements when the King's guard caught up with them.

As his eyes adjusted to the darkness, he realized he wasn't alone. A girl in a white nightdress was hunched in the shadows in one corner, her eyes wide with fear, but she wasn't looking at him. Cautiously, Ramil turned his head and realized that he was sprawled not five feet from a snow tiger. Ramil stifled his urge to yell. Fortunately, the beast was occupied by a large haunch of venison, doubtless poached from the Royal Forest, and had not yet considered the newcomers as dessert. Ramil picked himself up on his hands and knees and crawled towards the girl.

"Well, this is interesting," he said lightly, trying to act as if this was an everyday situation for him. He owed it to one of his subjects to at least play the part of prince.

The girl hugged her arms to her sides but said nothing. Ramil looked at her more closely. There were signs that she had been roughly handled: her face was scratched and her wrists bruised. He felt indignant for her. How dare these criminals ill-treat a Gerfalian girl! There were strong laws against such behavior.

"Don't worry, miss, I'll think of something to get us out of here. If they've harmed you in any way, I'll make sure they are brought to justice." He reached out to reassure her but she flinched away. He decided to put it down to her natural suspicion. "It's all right. I'm Prince Ramil. They probably don't realize who they've kidnapped. I'll make sure my men rescue you too when they come for me."

She still said nothing.

"I suppose our first problem is what to do about him." He nodded over at the tiger.

"It's chained." The girl broke her silence but her accent was funny, not Gerfalian at all.

He stared at her. No robes; no face paint. It couldn't be—

"Do I have you to thank for this, Prince Ramil, for a further assault on my dignity?" the Fourth Crown Princess asked bitterly. "Even for you, this goes beyond ill manners. It is an outright declaration of war. You have your men bind me, strip me of my robes, my veil, throw water over me, and lock me up with a tiger!" She sounded near hysterical. "Did you find out that I had informed my sisters of my intention to return home? Did you have my messages intercepted too? Is this some kind of punishment?"

Tashi swallowed a sob. She knew better than to expect any consideration from this evil boy. He probably thought this saving-the-Princess-from-the-tiger would rescue the alliance, but she was not fooled. She'd spent the last few hours in a cage with a hungry cat, albeit one chained at the far end: she would never forgive him.

"But I thought . . . I thought it was you and your people who had ambushed me!" protested Ramil. He shook his head, trying to clear his thoughts. "But if not you, then who?"

The Princess turned her back on him. Ramil retreated to the corner nearest the door, watching her shoulders heaving as she wept silently. There was something terrible in the sight. He suddenly understood how the past few days must seem to her—a foreign country, insults, and now this. She was still his responsibility because she'd been kidnapped on Gerfalian land, a place where she had every right to expect protection and respect. Even if he disliked their culture, he had learned how important the ceremonial robes and trappings were to the Crescent people; and here she was stuck in a cage like a wild beast, wearing only a thin, plain dress. It was all wrong for her to look like a plucked peacock.

"I'm sorry, Princess. I'm really, really sorry that this has happened," Ramil said sincerely.

Tashi turned her eyes on him briefly: he was staring at her. "Don't look at me," she said in a whiplash of a voice. The foreign Prince was seeing her without her robes of state, her hair uncovered; she felt practically naked. "Isn't it enough that I'm suffering without you seeing me like this?"

Ramil looked away, unclasped his scarlet cloak and held it out to her.

"Take this. You must be cold."

Tashi took it warily from his hand, thinking this was all part of the plot and he was trying to win her over by his show of concern. But as she watched his face for some indication whether her guess was correct, some smug expression or smile, she noticed that the Prince had a cut on his cheek, dried blood streaked on his skin. A doubt crept in. What if this was not some ill-judged plan of his? What if he was a victim too? That made their position far, far worse. There would be no grand rescue staged by the Prince to impress her, no triumphant return to the castle.

"I've got to know something, sir," Tashi began.

"I promise I'll tell you if I know the answer." Ramil was watching the tiger now that the Princess was out of bounds. The creature had eaten its fill, relieved its bladder in a powerful, stinking jet of urine, and now settled down to sleep. It seemed little bothered to be sharing its cage with two humans.

"Are you really not responsible for this? Swear on all that you hold sacred that you are not."

Ramil put his fist to his chest. "I swear on my mother's good name that I knew nothing of the abduction. But what about you? I thought at first that you had organized it."

"Me!" Tashi exclaimed. "What could I possibly gain from arranging for you to be . . . to be caged?"

Ramil shrugged. "Revenge. Satisfaction for insults. I don't know—maybe you just find it funny."

Tashi looked horrified at the suggestion.

"It's all right, Your Highness, I do not need you to swear your innocence to me. I will not accuse the Blue Crescent Islands of an act of war. I have a higher opinion of your honor than you do of mine. No, I think responsibility lies elsewhere: we share a common enemy." Ramil lay back on the straw and closed his eyes. "Either that, or it's a joke in desperately bad taste by my friends to throw us together."

"You think this is possible?" asked Tashi, bewildered.

Ramil sighed. "No, that last suggestion was a joke of

my own." Was he never going to find the right note of conversation for this girl? She took everything so seriously.

Then again, she is shut in a tiger's cage with you. Perhaps your joke was ill timed, grumbled his more regal side.

King Lagan spent the day in a pleasantly optimistic mood. Ramil had galloped off with his young guest and not returned—a sign that they must be getting on well enough to prolong the ride. He couldn't imagine Princess Taoshira staying more than a polite hour if she were not enjoying herself. Walking through the corridors of his palace, Lagan began to whistle. He was remembering his own rides with Ramil's mother, Zarai, when he was that age. The forest had been magical, allowing them intimacy and informality away from the rigors of court life. It was a place where two young royals could remember that they were also girl and boy. There had been a particularly comfortable bank of moss near the stream. He rather hoped Ramil had found it.

As evening approached, the chamberlain sought an audience with the King.

"Your Majesty, the Blue Crescent delegation is concerned that the Princess has not yet returned."

Lagan looked up from his pile of state papers. "Can they allow the child no privacy?"

The chamberlain decided not to answer that question.

"It appears she has to fulfill an important religious ceremony every evening and her absence is regarded as most inauspicious."

Lagan threw aside his pen. "Inauspicious, eh? Well, perhaps we'd better send out the guard with some torches to search for them. Tell the delegation not to worry. I expect they got a little lost or forgot the time. Let me know when they get back." Lagan rather liked the idea of challenging the little Princess about her tardiness to see if he could raise a blush under all that silly white paint.

The guard returned at midnight, having found no trace of either Ramil or the Crown Princess. Lagan was forced to revise his opinion that their absence was innocent. He had a creeping conviction that his son had done something extremely stupid. First time out of the castle: had Ramil bolted? But then what of the Princess? Surely he would have returned her safely. It was common courtesy to do so. Ramil may have many faults, but Lagan did not think lack of chivalry to a lady in his charge was one of them.

He summoned the Blue Crescent delegation to the White Stone Council Chamber so it could witness and participate in the efforts to discover the young people. The Islanders sat ranged on the far side of the table from his ministers, their hostility and suspicion like a blistering heat in the room. Lagan realized that they put the fault for whatever had happened squarely on the Prince's shoulders. He could hardly blame them; his son had done nothing to inspire their confidence, quite the contrary. Whatever the truth, it was the responsibility of Gerfal to sort it out.

The Chief Warden of the Forest was also present. He reported that the young Prince and Princess had been seen galloping into the forest that morning but his wardens had kept aloof as ordered. No one had noticed them after that.

"Why did no guard accompany the Princess?" snapped the senior priest in the Blue Crescent delegation.

Lagan wondered if he could explain to this hard-boiled old man the idea of a romantic ride for two under the greenwood boughs. He decided not to attempt it.

"Prince Ramil does not habitually take a guard when riding in the forest." Not least because no guard could keep up with him when he was in the saddle. "He was following usual practice. The perimeter of the forest is patrolled by wardens and my own soldiers. It has always been regarded as safe anywhere within five miles of Falburg."

" 'Usual practice'—'always regarded'—it appears to us that Your Majesty's judgment has been proved in error,"cut in the Etiquette Mistress, snapping her fan shut.

Lagan ignored the slight to his wisdom. "Such are our customs, madam. However, this is getting us nowhere. We must send out all available men. I want the Royal Forest searched all the way to the mountain passes. Every village, every traveller, every cave, den or hiding place is to be examined." He turned to the delegation. "Would you like to send your own men to participate?"

The chief priest nodded. "I have five hundred sailors awaiting my orders."

"Good. Send them to the chief warden here and he will distribute them among the teams."

The council meeting broke up. Lagan retired to his private room and filled a wine glass with a shaking hand. He was hoping that his son had proved honorable and that none of this was his fault. Desertion now, coupled with losing the Princess, would mean war with Taoshira's people—there was no doubt about it. Twenty Crescent ships were in possession of his main harbor, in a prime position to bombard the city and destroy the capital. But if his hope proved to be correct, then that meant Ramil was detained against his will. His son was in danger.

Chapter 4

Many hours after nightfall, the door of the cage was opened and a tiny man appeared with a lantern.

"You're to get out now if you want food and a wash," he announced in a squeaky voice.

With a glance at each other, Tashi and Ramil got up. The Prince jumped down first, then offered his hand to help Tashi to the ground. She let go quickly, wrapping his cloak more securely around her shoulders as she surveyed the scene before them.

An odd collection of some twenty people were eating a late supper around the campfire. A giant of a man with a big bushy beard was playing cards with three wiry-looking individuals; acrobats, Tashi guessed. An old woman sat by the pot, her hair in long grey ringlets. She had a scarlet scarf tied around her middle and gold rings in her ears. Her clothes were ancient and patched but she was in possession of a fine pair of new boots. Tashi's boots. Sensing the Princess's scrutiny, the old woman gave her an implacable stare. She then tapped her pipe on the heel of her left boot and chuckled. Tashi dropped her gaze to her own bare feet.

A handsome man with long dark sideburns strode forward. He had a fur cape thrown carelessly over one shoulder, brilliant red tunic, and knee-length brown boots that had seen better days. Tashi glanced resentfully at Prince Ramil's footwear and wondered why he was still in ownership of them when hers had been taken.

"Prince Ramil, it is an honor to welcome you to our fireside," declared the man with a flourishing bow, ignoring Tashi. "I apologize for the abruptness of our invitation but my master said we were to bring you with all speed."

Ramil tapped his hands angrily by his sides. The man had a Brigardian accent and had already revealed that he knew full well who his prisoner was. Any hope that this was a mistake was extinguished.

"You will be hanged for your actions unless you release the Princess and myself immediately," Ramil said curtly.

The man put his hand to his brow. "It pains me to refuse a royal command but I am acting under orders from my superior. For the moment, I suggest you make the best of it and join me by the fire. You must be hungry—thirsty too, I expect. Come. It will be necessary to return you to your less than luxurious quarters in a short while, so make the most of this brief reprieve."

Seeing the sense of this, Ramil turned to allow the Princess to precede him to the fire. In the light, he saw for the first time that she had the most striking mane of long fair hair.

"Oh no, not her," the man said, taking a step to separate them. "I do not allow Western demons to sit with my people. She can eat on her own."

"Then I eat with her," announced Ramil, roused to anger on the Princess's behalf.

"No, you dine with me." The man produced a knife and felt its edge, drawing blood on his thumb. "A Gerfalian prince is a worthy companion but a Blue Crescent woman is hardly human. They feel nothing, have you not noticed?" He waved at Tashi. "See, she says nothing—does nothing. We took her robes and she did not complain. We threw her in with Kosind and she did not scream. It's unnatural. Leave her."

The man hooked the Prince's arm in his and began to drag him away.

"I will stay with the Princess!" Ramil struggled to free himself.

Tashi turned her back on the fire, feeling so weary of these Easterners. She hardly cared for the man's insults. How could such a one understand her? There was no need for the Prince to risk injury on her behalf. In any case, she preferred to eat alone.

"Go with him, Prince Ramil. I am content."

Tashi sat cross-legged on the ground, too far from the campfire to benefit from its warmth. Looking up at the stars, she realized how late it was and she had not yet said the evening service. The Mother would understand but Tashi knew she should delay no longer.

Preparing herself, she rose to her knees and began quietly to say the words, miming the action of the ringing bell as none was available. At first, no one noticed her humble ceremony, but then the little man who had fetched them from their prison came over with a bowl of food. He put it down but she continued without a pause, her hands sketching circles in the air before her. This amused him so he fetched some of his friends from the fireside: the strong man, Gordoc, and the tiger tamer, Pashvin. The tamer prodded Tashi with his whip but she did not break off her prayer.

"See, it's as Orboyd says, less than human." Pashvin chuckled, sitting down to watch.

The big man leant forward and fingered a strand of Tashi's long blonde hair.

"Pretty color," he murmured.

"See if you can make her squeal," suggested Tighe, the dwarf.

Gordoc grinned and put his mouth to the Princess's ear. "Boo!" he whispered.

Tashi closed her eyes. These men were no more than flies buzzing in a room, beneath her regard. She had to complete the last prayer or her people would suffer.

Pashvin lifted the heavy hank of hair from her back and blew on her neck. Getting no response, he let go and shrugged.

"She's no flesh and blood woman," he concluded.

Tashi came to the final blessing, giving the response that usually fell to her attendants. "As the Goddess wills."

It was at that moment that Gordoc decided to stroke

her hair. Tashi emerged from her prayer to feel a large hand on the back of her head. Without thinking, she swung round and slapped the big man hard on the side of his face, then jumped up and stalked away. Pashvin rolled around on the floor, howling with laughter.

"Maybe she's . . . half human," he said through gasps.

Gordoc set off in pursuit. "Aw, come back, my pretty one, I meant no harm."

The altercation caught the attention of Ramil, Orboyd, and the others by the fireside. Seeing Tashi pursued by the giant man, the Prince leapt up. Swiftly, Orboyd kicked Ramil's feet from under him and shifted the grip on his knife to prick him in the ribs.

"Settle down. He won't harm her. Let him have his fun," Orboyd ordered.

Ramil tried to get up a second time but the circus leader kicked him back again with an exasperated sigh.

"Anyway, why should you care? It was no secret that you didn't want her. You've no liking for these Blue Crescent women any more than I have. I wager neither of us would say no to a handsome Eastern girl, but these fair-haired witches don't please a man."

Ramil rolled onto his knees.

"But I can't let you treat her like that. She's my guest. Any insult to her is an insult to the ac Burinholt royal family!"

"I'm sorry you feel like that, Prince, because it's no use getting all hot and bothered about her. She's no longer your problem. Lads, sit on our guest here."

The three acrobats moved so quickly that Ramil had no chance to escape. He found himself pinned to the ground by their combined weight.

"I was going to have to tie you up anyway. We're expecting company and unfortunately we need to gag you." Orboyd produced a silk handkerchief and knotted it around Ramil's mouth. Next he roped his hands and feet. "Put him back in with Kosind and cover him up," he ordered the acrobats.

Carried like a rolled carpet, Ramil was put in the cage. His ropes were fixed tightly hand and foot to rings on the floor, and finally he was buried under a layer of straw. Uncomfortable though he was, he was tormented by fears for the Princess. If they treated him like this—a person they considered an equal—what would they do to someone they considered a witch?

Gordoc cornered Tashi by the magician's wagon. She knew it was no good screaming. Who would help her? Ramil was useless—she expected nothing from him. She gripped the sides of the wagon behind her and closed her eyes tight, wishing the man away. She felt a big hand touch the side of her face, just where she had struck him, then move to stroke her hair. She shuddered.

"See, I just wanted to touch your hair. Like gold, it is. Please don't run away. You can trust me to protect you. Come back and eat your supper. I'll tell the others not to tease you." He took her hand and towed her after him. A few of the campers looked up in interest as they returned to the fire.

"Catch the witch, did you?" called out Orboyd.

Gordoc grunted. "You're not a witch, are you, Princess?"

Tashi shook her head.

"She's just scared of us."

Orboyd laughed. "Scared of you, more like."

Gordoc smiled proudly at his princess. "Oh no, I've given my word I'll not let you lot harm her. She knows she can trust me." The big man picked up her bowl and thrust it at her. "Here, eat. You have to go back in with the other one in a moment so you'd better get that down you."

Tashi ate quickly, trying to hide her movements by letting her veil of hair flop forwards, but Gordoc brushed it back, out of her way. He then led her to a tent so she could wash and use the privy, then guided her back to the wagon. Orboyd was waiting, holding a rope and scarf.

"I'll do that," said Gordoc. "There now, that's not too tight?" Once Tashi was bound and gagged, he scooped her up in his arms, climbed the steps back into the cage, and placed her gently on the floor next to Ramil. "Make not a sound now and I'll let you out of here as soon as we've got to safety." He scattered the straw over her like a blessing.

The night seemed endless to Tashi. Lying on the wooden floor, pricked and near suffocated by straw, she tried to come to terms with what she was experiencing. None of her training had prepared her for this. No one here saw any of the things in her that her own people believed; she was not respected, listened to, or loved. So what did that make her? A demon, according to Orboyd. But she knew she was loved by the Mother; she couldn't be evil, even if other people fixed such labels to her. A pretty pet to the big man who had sensed her fear? But Tashi, raised in a land of matriarchs, revolted at the idea.

I suppose I'm left with me, whoever that is these days, she thought bleakly.

Ramil could hear the Princess breathing next to him but was tortured by the fact that he could not speak to her, not even to ask if she was unharmed. He owed it to her at least to think of some way of escaping. They were still in Gerfal, heading down to the mountains that formed the border with Brigard. The alarm must have been raised by now and his people would be combing the land for them. It was inconceivable that a caravan such as this would be missed before it reached the border.

At dawn he heard the sound he had been expecting all night: the approach of horsemen.

"Ho there, travellers!" called a Gerfalian soldier. "We have orders from the King to search all vehicles on the roads this day."

"But of course," said Orboyd at his most generous. "We are a peaceful group with nothing to hide. Conduct your search and welcome."

Ramil writhed in his bonds but he was so tightly bound and gagged he could do nothing to alert them to his presence. He heard the tramp of feet and good natured banter as the soldiers passed the time with the circus people.

"Found anything?" asked Orboyd casually from outside the wagon.

"No," replied the soldier. "What's in there?" He thumped the side of the wagon.

"Our tiger, Kosind. You're welcome to go in." Orboyd lifted the canvas on the front of the wagon, letting in the daylight. The tiger rose on its haunches, stretched and yawned.

The soldier peered into the cage. "It stinks in there!"

"That's wild animals for you. Shall I fetch the key?"

The soldier shook his head. "No, that will do."

Orboyd dropped the canvas back down.

Ramil cursed the soldier. Sweat was running off him as he pulled on his ropes. This was their last chance!

Then he heard a thud. Tied less tightly, the girl beside him had enough freedom of movement to hit her head and heels on the floor in a regular beat—*Thud-thud-thud! Thud-thud-thud!*

"What's that?" asked the soldier suspiciously.

"Tiger's tail thumping. Means he's hungry," replied Orboyd coolly.

The girl changed the rhythm—*Thud-thud! Thud-thud!*

"I think perhaps we had better take another look at that hungry cat of yours." The soldier took a firm grip on the canvas.

"That is a shame." There was a hiss of breath and the

sound of a body falling to the ground. "I do so hate shedding blood this early in the day," said Orboyd.

Further away, another man shouted but his scream broke off abruptly.

A short while later, the door to the wagon flew open. Ramil's bindings were yanked free and he was dragged, still half-covered in straw, down the steps and out into the clearing. Tashi was dumped beside him. In front of them lay the bodies of a Gerfalian forest warden and a Crescent sailor.

"Look what you made us do!" raged Orboyd, his hands still red with the warden's blood. "We were trying to do this the kind way—no one getting hurt, just a quick dash for the border and goodbye. We are peaceful people and you made us kill these men!"

Ramil now noticed that the dwarf, Tighe, was wiping a bloodied knife on a rag. It seemed that he had been responsible for despatching the sailor.

"I cannot have this. You must play by my rules or there'll have to be more killing." Orboyd seized the whip from the tiger tamer. "Which one of you made that noise? I've got to punish you or you'll force me to kill again and I don't like it!" He ripped the gag off Tashi, then Ramil. "I hope, Your Highness, it was the witch. I don't want to lay a finger on you if I can help it."

"It was me!" Ramil said quickly.

"He lies. It was me," Tashi said, appealing with a look to Gordoc.

The big man strode forward. "You're not harming

the girl!" He snatched the whip from Orboyd's hand and threw it back to Pashvin.

"You forget yourself, Gordoc. I say who gets punished and who doesn't!" thundered Orboyd, going eye to eye with the giant.

The old woman strode over, still wearing Tashi's boots, and spat at the ground in front of her. "You're wasting time, Orboyd. Now you've killed these men, others will be after us. We've got to get to the border by nightfall. There's time enough for punishment when we get to Brigard."

Orboyd broke away from Gordoc. "All right, Minka, all right, we'll settle this later. Hide the bodies. Set the horses loose. Gordoc, put our guests back in the cage and tie them up properly this time."

The bodies of the warden and the sailor were not found until the evening. Ramil's and Tashi's riderless horses were discovered not long after, trotting back towards the castle. King Lagan heard the news with dismay. It seemed clear that Ramil and the young Princess were victims of some terrible crime. He regretted now that he had doubted his son even for a moment. Were their bodies waiting to be found too? Fearing the worst, he ordered the search to be intensified. Every wagon was unpacked, every traveller questioned; all that is except for the cage belonging to one very hungry-looking tiger. The border guard had peered inside and decided that no one could be in there and live. Besides, the circus people were friendly folk, free with their food and wine, in no rush to pass over the border to Brigard. They did not act like fugitives with something to hide.

Once in Brigard, the neighboring country recently conquered by Fergox Spearthrower, Ramil and Tashi were untied and taken out of the cage. The mood of the circus people lightened now that the immediate danger of discovery had passed. They were travelling through spectacular mountain scenery: soaring peaks, snow-covered slopes, and thick forests of pine trees. They had to climb high to cross the range. The air was icy but the weather fine. Gordoc insisted that Tashi ride beside him for protection, snugly wrapped up in his fur rug. Ramil could see her now in the wagon ahead of him, her long fair hair streaming down her back in a ripple of gold.

He'd had no opportunity to talk to her—not that they had anything to say to each other—for he was now the travelling companion of Orboyd. The circus leader had taken the precaution of chaining his guest to the wagon, but then proceeded to treat him like a favored friend, chatting about Brigard, the fluctuating fortunes of his little band, his plans for the future. He regarded Gerfalians as natural friends to the Brigardians, lamented the political circumstances that temporarily put them at odds, looked forward to the day when those differences would be settled by Gerfal bowing to the inevitable and submitting to Fergox. He referred often to his master and hinted that Ramil would be seeing him soon.

"Who is your master?" Ramil asked frequently. "A Brigardian noble with a grudge against Gerfal?"

Orboyd refused to be drawn. "I'm under orders not to say. But I assure you he will treat you as befits a royal prince of noblest lineage. And one day, when you are King, I will be able to point to you and say 'that man rode on my wagon.'"

Ramil thought it best not to mention that if he lived to be King he'd make sure that Orboyd was caught and tried for his crime against the royal person, so he was unlikely to live to enjoy his association.

"And the Princess? What does your master want with her?"

Orboyd shrugged, not very interested in that question. "Don't know. Hostage perhaps? He doesn't like the Blue Crescent Islanders, but then who does, except perhaps their mothers?"

"Gordoc appears to like the Princess," Ramil suggested quietly. He was sick of hearing such derogatory remarks about the Islanders from Orboyd, not least because they were uncomfortably like his own comments made back in the palace.

"Oh, Gordoc." Orboyd snorted. "He's soft-hearted. Nursed an abandoned leveret this spring only to cry buckets when he stood on it. I wouldn't pay much attention to him."

Tashi, meanwhile, sat beside the giant, letting his friendly talk wash over her. He let her mumble her prayers at the appointed time, did not mock or try to startle her. He just occasionally stroked her hair as if he could not believe its color and had to test that it was real.

She spent the time meditating on her anger. The

murder of those two men in the forest had shocked her deeply. She was angry with her abductors, but most of her rage was directed at all Gerfalians, and one in particular. No one need have died if they had done their job of guarding her properly. How like Prince Ramil's people to let the caravan over the border without even a proper search! The prince had been useless as she anticipated and now seemed quite content to sit fraternizing with Orboyd when he should be doing something before they got too far from Gerfal. What it was exactly she expected him to do, she didn't know, but something, anything!

"Gordoc, do you know where we are going?" she asked hours later.

The giant almost dropped his reins, so surprised was he to hear his little travelling companion speak. She had a nice voice too—soft and gentle.

"We're going to meet him," he replied. "That's all I know."

"Who's him?"

"The master."

"Do you know his name?"

"Aw, little one, I can't tell you that." Gordoc passed her an apple.

Tashi twisted it in her fingers. "Can you tell me if he is a big master, like King Lagan, or a little master, like Orboyd?"

Gordoc chuckled. "You're trying to catch me out, aren't you? Well, he's nothing like Orboyd. Much, much bigger. But never you mind, you'll meet him soon enough."

Ramil persuaded Orboyd to let him join the Princess for a short time that evening as they made camp. When he approached her spot by the tiger wagon, he found she no longer ate alone. Tighe, Pashvin, and Gordoc sat around her with their bowls, watching her like an audience, even exchanging critical observations about her performance of the ritual.

"She did that one beautifully," remarked Tighe as Tashi made a sinuous gesture with her hands.

"I thought yesterday's was a little more pronounced," Pashvin noted with the air of an expert. "Today's is more subtle."

"She does everything beautifully," breathed an enraptured Gordoc.

Ramil sat down quietly and waited for her to finish. He admired her concentration with all these onlookers. Finally, he recognized the Crescent words of completion, having heard them often enough from the delegation.

"As the Goddess wills," he muttered in Common.

Tashi folded her hands in her lap.

"Do you mock me for praying, Prince Ramil?" she asked.

"No, I thought I was being polite." Did she have to be so hostile? he wondered.

"I was told by your prime minister that you say 'God willing.'"

"We do, but I was trying to . . . oh, does it matter?"

Ramil felt exasperated: he'd extended the olive branch only to have it snapped.

"Actually, it does matter," Tashi said simply. She was feeling more at peace with the world now that she had done her prayers. "My beliefs are important to me and if you are treating them with respect that . . . well, that's an improvement."

Was it possible? Had a glimmer of a smile just appeared on her lips? Ramil thought.

"Now, you're laughing at *me*, Princess," said Ramil. "You think me an ignorant boor."

"You are an ignorant boor, Prince Ramil."

Gordoc's mouth was hanging open. "She speaks so well, doesn't she, Pashvin?"

The tiger tamer nodded, fascinated by the exchange.

"Was that a joke at my expense, Your Highness?" Ramil asked.

"I thought you were the expert on jokes. You tell me." Tashi picked up her bowl and began eating.

"When you put it like that, then I suppose, no, it wasn't really a joke because it's true." Ramil stretched out on the grass. "I'm a disgrace to my name. Been drunk half the time ever since I was told I was to marry you. Managed to insult you and all your countrymen from the moment of our first meeting—if not before. Add all that up and I suppose it does equal ignorant boor."

His honesty pulled on a thread in the knot of anger inside her, loosening it a little. She hadn't expected him to see himself so clearly.

"I'm sorry you hated the idea of marrying me, Your Highness. I wasn't that keen on marrying you either," she admitted.

"I can imagine," Ramil said dryly.

Their eyes met for the first time in understanding.

"It seems as though that will no longer be a problem for either of us. Someone has other plans," she said.

"So it would appear." Ramil rose. "Princess." He bowed and returned to the fire.

Through her eyelashes, Tashi watched him go. Perhaps he was not all bad. She remembered that he had tried to take the punishment for her yesterday and given her his cloak. He did appear to be attempting, as far as it was in his nature, to be polite to her. Added to that, he was the closest thing she had to an ally in the camp if they were to get free.

Escape? Was it possible? She thought about the road they had come down today: a harsh road through the mountains. Even if she did slip away, she'd not get very far on foot before she was caught. Still, she'd have to try as soon as an opportunity offered. Whatever lay at the end of this journey was unlikely to be good news for her or her people.

Chapter 5

From his vantage point on Orboyd's wagon, Ramil had been eyeing the circus horses for some miles now. He knew that he would have to make an attempt to escape before they left the mountain passes. He could ride swiftly, use the difficult terrain to his advantage, get back over the border without being overtaken. The leggy grey at the back of the string looked the most promising but Ramil had a nagging doubt about the gelding's stamina. He might do better on that solid-looking piebald, particularly as the first part of the journey would be uphill.

The only problem was the Princess. She couldn't ride and she would slow him down. He knew that he had to leave her behind if he stood any chance of succeeding, and yet—

Your duty is to Gerfal, the Prince told himself. *And if you want to help the Princess, you'd do better escaping to fetch an army than riding blindly into Brigard just to keep her company.* He still felt rotten that he had to make the decision to abandon her. It wasn't very heroic.

The caravan stopped for the noon meal. Ramil wandered casually over to the horses. He could feel Orboyd watching his every move so he tried to look as aimless as possible. The piebald pricked his ears forward and snorted, smelling the horse-knowledge on the human. Ramil stood forehead to forehead with the beast, searching for that shared peace that was the beginning of all rider and horse partnerships among his mother's people. The circus folk and Tashi stopped their preparations for the meal to watch.

"What are you doing to my horse, Your Highness?" Orboyd asked suspiciously.

Ramil stood up straight. "Ever had trick riding in your circus, Orboyd?"

The chief shook his head. "No, but I've seen it down south."

"Perhaps you should think about it. Shall I show you?"

"You, a prince, show us trick riding? Now that I have to see!" Orboyd laughed.

Ramil shrugged good-humoredly. He intended to display some of the skills every cavalry officer in Gerfal learned as a cadet. If the circus folk thought these trick riding, that was all right by him.

Orboyd strode forward and untied the piebald. "The name's Flea."

Ramil quickly saddled up and began a warm-up circuit of the meadow where they had stopped the wagons. It had been absurdly easy so far. No one else was mounted. There was nothing to stop him galloping away. What he needed now was a distraction.

"Go on then, Your Highness, show us what you can do!" called Orboyd, watching him with his hands on his hips. As Ramil completed a circuit, he noticed that the chief had a crossbow at his feet. Perhaps Orboyd was not as careless as Ramil had thought. He wouldn't get far with a bolt lodged between his shoulders.

Rising first into a crouch, then into a standing position, Ramil continued to gallop Flea round in circles. His perfect balance brought a smattering of applause.

That's nothing, thought Ramil. *Wait until you see this.*

Placing his hands on either side of the saddle, he slowly turned upside down, now riding in a headstand. Next he rode cross-legged facing backwards, then hanging upside down under the horse. He was enjoying showing off but all the while he was alert for his opportunity.

Suddenly, the display was interrupted by a shout from Gordoc: "Where's the Princess?"

The attention of the circus folk snapped away from Ramil. Orboyd grabbed his bow from the ground and began firing off questions and orders.

"Where's the witch? Didn't you tie her up when we stopped, you fool? Find her!"

The men scattered in all directions. Ramil couldn't believe his luck: the Princess had provided him with the perfect distraction. Swinging up to a secure seat in the saddle, he urged the horse forward and galloped up the mountain road.

"Stop him!" yelled Orboyd, realizing his second prisoner was on the loose. Ramil ducked. A crossbow bolt whistled overhead and quivered in the trunk of a pine tree. He was out of range before Orboyd had a chance to reload.

The road switchbacked steeply up the mountain. Ramil pushed the horse as hard as he dared, sending stones clattering back down the cliffside. He could see the caravan stranded in the meadow behind him—the men running about in confusion, hurrying to saddle horses to come in pursuit of him, others searching for the Princess. He muttered a quick prayer for her protection. She stood little chance of escape unless she was good at concealing herself, but he could do nothing for her.

As he turned the last corner to the top of the ridge, a terrified, piercing scream rent the air, echoing off the mountainside. Startled, Ramil reined his horse to a stop. Down in the meadow below, a man in scarlet was dragging a girl along by her hair.

Orboyd raised his eyes to the figure on horseback high up on the road above.

"Prince Ramil," he shouted, "if you take one step further, I'll kill the Blue Crescent witch, I swear I will!" He shook his captive viciously.

Ramil hesitated. He could see his pursuers were closing in, their horses making good speed up the slope. He had to leave now if he wanted to escape.

Gordoc strode into the meadow, pushing his way past the men who'd recaptured the Princess. "Give her to me!" he bellowed. "Don't you dare hurt her!"

Orboyd did not take his eyes off Ramil. "Boys, sit on him."

The three acrobats leapt on Gordoc's back and wrestled him to the ground. He yelled in fury but could not dislodge them.

"Don't make me kill her, Prince. I'm a peaceful man!" Orboyd shouted. He twisted his fist more tightly in Tashi's hair and brandished his knife.

Ramil closed his eyes and cursed. He'd seen the results of Orboyd's love of peace: two bodies in the Royal Forest. There was no choice. It was one thing to ride off leaving her to take her own chance, it was another to be knowingly responsible for her death. He nudged Flea round, walking him back down the path. As he did so, four riders galloped round the bend and tugged him from the saddle. Tying his hands in front of him, they forced him to run behind them back down the road.

The camp was eerily silent when Ramil stumbled into the meadow. Gordoc was collapsed against the wheel of his wagon, sobbing. There was no sign of the Princess. Orboyd marched up to Ramil and struck him hard across the face, still clutching the hilt of his knife.

"I thought we had an understanding! I told you to play by my rules and no one gets hurt!"

"I will not apologize for trying to escape. It is my duty as a prince of Gerfal to make the attempt," Ramil said proudly, but his heart was in the grip of fear. Where was the Princess? Why was Gordoc crying? Orboyd hadn't killed her after all, had he?

"And now I'll be in trouble because I was supposed to deliver you both without damage." Orboyd cursed and shoved the knife back in the sheath on his belt.

"What have you done with the Princess?" Ramil's tone was menacing, but he'd never felt more powerless.

Orboyd ignored him. He turned to the rest of his band. "We're leaving. Hitch up the wagons. As for you, Prince Ramil, as you have so much energy for escaping, you can walk." He seized the end of the rope tying Ramil's hands together and lashed it to his wagon. "We'll see after thirty miles if you still think it a good idea to steal one of my horses."

Tashi's eyes fluttered open and closed again. She was confused, for a moment thinking she was back on board the flagship as everything around her was rocking and swaying. She plucked at her covers and found, not the fine spun woollen blanket off her bed in the royal cabin, but a matted fur. Memory came back in painful fragments. Ramil had been showing off on that horse, acting more like a circus boy than a prince of the realm, but she'd used the distraction to slip into the wood. Unfortunately, she'd not got far before Gordoc noticed she was gone. Recalling how she had scaled trees to get away from trouble as a child, she had tried climbing one of the pines by the roadside. She'd seen Ramil ride by without so much as a look behind him and realized that he had a much better chance of success than she had. Still, she had managed to lodge herself up in the branches, hoping it would not occur to the circus people that a princess would climb trees. But her white dress had given her away. She was seen almost immediately by the acrobats. They had jumped onto each other's shoulders and pulled her down as easily as harvesters picking an apple. Then Orboyd had stormed over and started beating her; he appeared in his anger to have lost all self-control. She thought he was going to kill her. He had dragged her back to the meadow on her knees, shouted to the Prince to return, then—

Then what?

Tashi touched the bandage on her head. She must have been knocked out. She didn't know if the Prince had escaped or not. Had he come back or had he ridden on? He'd probably have gone on, got out of this madness and be well on his way to the border by now. She wished him luck.

In the grip of a low fever, Tashi lay on the pile of furs. As the miles rumbled by, she watched the accoutrements of the fortune teller's art sway around her—a glittering ball, a dried snake skin, hanks of unidentified hair, a string of bones. To her eyes, it seemed barbaric, like something from a winter fireside story of witchcraft and evil spirits. Had she fallen into one of these tales? Had the Mother abandoned her to the evil ones?

Tears leaked from the corners of Tashi's eyes as she tried to remember her prayers. Too weak to do the ritual properly, she cried her prayer silently as she had done as a child when she'd woken from a nightmare. But it was no use. The Mother had never felt more distant, more unloving.

For the next few days the circus wound its way down to the plains of Brigard. Ramil was exhausted with walking, almost asleep on his feet for much of the time. Orboyd had stopped speaking to him, appearing to regard the escape as a personal slight on his hospitality. Mountain scenery gave way to craggy hills, rough grass, and poor pasture. They passed more people: shepherds with faces tanned like old leather, messengers on fleet-footed horses, farmers travelling to local markets. Ramil found it odd to see life going on as normal for all these Brigardians. The locals spared a puzzled glance for the dusty young man stumbling on behind the lead wagon, but were really more interested in catching a glimpse of the tiger, or seeing the acrobats limber up. Living in a land under occupation by Fergox Spearthrower's armies, it was usually best not to ask too many questions.

Ramil noticed that the number of soldiers on the roads increased the further into Brigard they travelled. He racked his brains to remember the detailed maps he'd seen of this part of the world. The nearest town of any significance was Felixholt, a semi-fortified settlement commanding the head of the valley. In friendlier times, it had been a frequent destination for Gerfalian merchants, but since the occupation, Brigard no longer welcomed traders from outside Spearthrower's empire. Stuck out on the northernmost edge of the warlord's lands, Felixholt must be suffering; market days would now be sad affairs.

The cart rose to the top of the last hill before the

valley and Ramil received an unpleasant shock. The pastures around Felixholt were covered with tents— a canvas city to house an army. He had little experience of warfare but he could tell that this wasn't just a contingent to maintain the occupation; this was an invasion force. Gerfal must be next on Fergox's list of targets. Ramil cursed his evil fortune. He now had an even more pressing duty than escape: he had to get a message to his father—his country had to be warned.

The circus was waved through all checkpoints on the way to the town. It was no comfort to find that they were expected. As Ramil stumbled nearer, he saw the high stone wall that enclosed the holt. On the peak stood a nobleman's modest castle overlooking the brick and thatched dwellings of the townsfolk. Not a grand place, but today a vast imperial flag flapped over the tallest tower. Staring at the banner with sinking heart, Ramil realized that his assumptions about the abduction were all wrong. If the flag meant what he thought, the motivation had been political, not greed for a ransom.

When the caravan approached within a bowshot of the walls, the big wooden gates of Felixholt opened and a party of some sixty cavalrymen on tough shaggy horses clattered out, forming two rows on either side of the road. All the soldiers looked battle-hardened, stern-faced, and few were unscarred. They wore red leather armor and carried round shields and short spears. Many had long plaited beards threaded with scarlet cord—the sign among Fergox Spearthrower's elite troops of the number of heads they had collected in the Empire's wars. Ramil began to have a clearer idea as to who might be commanding this army. Though his despair deepened with the knowledge, he stood up straighter as became a prince of Gerfal, even a captive one.

The wagons stopped. Orboyd got down and stood bareheaded before the gates, evidently waiting for a sign before continuing into the town. Then the riders began to thump their spears on their shields in a steady beat. A single horseman on a magnificent blue roan stallion trotted down the steep road from the citadel. He was in no hurry, raising a hand to the people hanging out of the windows to watch, then resetting his gold-trimmed purple cloak over his shining mail shirt. There was no haste for Fergox Spearthrower because he knew the world would wait for him.

Orboyd knelt in the dirt of the highway, as did all the circus folk. Only Ramil was left standing. Fergox reined in his horse ten paces from the wagons and dismounted. He had a sturdy frame, short grizzled grey hair, and a fighter's face: crooked nose and hard blue eyes. He was clean shaven, needing no beard with scarlet threads, for everyone knew how many men he had killed over the years.

"Report, Orboyd. I understand you were successful." Fergox's voice was harsh but penetrating. Even the soldiers at the back of the guard of honor could hear every word.

"Yes, master. Your spies were able to tell me exactly

when and where to find them and Gerfalian security was weak."

Fergox smiled, a chilling expression from him. "They have become complacent, thinking that no one dare strike at the heart of their kingdom. They will not be so lax again. You've done well." He offered Orboyd his hand to kiss. "The spymaster will pay you double for your service to the Empire. But first you must present me to our guests."

Orboyd bowed himself backwards from Fergox to reach Ramil. He untied the Prince and led him forwards. Ramil did not resist, preferring to walk with dignity to being dragged before his enemy.

Fergox shook his head and tutted. "What's this, Orboyd? Why is Prince Ramil ac Burinholt tethered like a bullock to your wagon? That is no way to treat royal blood."

"But, your lordship, he tried to escape—"

"I expected no less of a prince." Fergox regarded Ramil with approval. "Still, perhaps it was as well to punish the cub."

Ramil clenched his fists. A prince of Gerfal, a cub? Fergox spoke as if the ac Burinholts were already under his dominion.

Fergox gave Ramil a curt nod in greeting. "Prince Ramil, I have ordered suitable quarters to be made ready for your accommodation. We have much to talk about but doubtless you would first like to rest yourself after your journey."

Ramil had to speak. "No, I first demand to be

released. There is no war declared between Gerfal and Holt. Bringing me here as a prisoner—abducting me in my own lands—these are scandalous acts, unworthy of a noble. I demand—"

"Tush, tush!" Fergox waved Ramil away as if he were a bothersome child having a tantrum. "We are beyond all that now, surely you realize that, Prince Ramil? Seizing you *was* my declaration of war. There will be time enough to discuss all this later." He turned away from Ramil, dismissing him. "But what of the Princess? Where is she? You did bring her, didn't you, Orboyd?"

The circus man tugged at his collar. "I did, sir, but she hurt herself when trying to escape."

"He lies," Ramil said angrily. "He beat her senseless."

Fergox's face darkened.

"That's not it at all," Orboyd protested, rushing to excuse himself. "The boy didn't see anything. You know, sir, what these Blue Crescent infidels are like, so cunning, so wicked. The witch used her spells to slip away and . . . and fell out of a tree."

"Where is she?" snapped Fergox.

"In the wagon over there," Orboyd said quickly. "She's received the best nursing from us despite her evil ways and is nearly fully recovered."

In an ill-humor now, Fergox slapped his gloves into his hand and strode over to the fortune-teller's wagon. He leapt up the step at the rear and threw the canvas aside. Light streamed into the darkness, striking a mass of golden hair spread out on a shabby sheepskin.

Tashi woke abruptly to see a dark figure of a man silhouetted in the entry. She raised herself on an elbow, trying to make out who it was.

"Gordoc?" she asked hoarsely. It had been hours since anyone had given her water.

The man kicked the furs aside and knelt beside her. It wasn't Gordoc, or anyone from the circus. He was a complete stranger, but he was looking at her with intense blue eyes. Then he reached out, touched her hand and raised it to his lips.

"My little Tashi," he said, letting her hand fall gently back onto the covers.

Tashi's heart gave a wild skip of joy. He knew her true name. "Have you come to save me, sir?"

He nodded. "Yes, I've come to save you. This whole journey has been merely a step on the path to your salvation."

Tashi lay back on her bed, feeling at peace for the first time in months. "The Mother sent you. She hasn't abandoned me," she whispered.

The man shook his head. "No, not the Mother. She is a blasphemy; she does not exist, just a fair mask put on by evil powers. You are deluded and misguided but soon all that will be behind you."

"No," gasped Tashi, hugging the covers to her chest. "That's not true!"

She flinched as he ran a finger down her cheek, his expression hungry. He must have been a demon sent to tempt her to despair. Her fever could not yet have broken; this was a horrible dream.

"Rest, Princess, there is much you must do for me. I need you well and looking your best." He nodded, pleased with what he saw. "My Tashi. My agents chose well for me when they had you elected."

He jumped back out of the wagon, letting the canvas fall back into place. Tashi touched her cheek, the skin still burning where he had caressed her. How did he know her name? What did he mean when he said that his agents had chosen her? She was chosen by the Goddess, by the priests of Kai, not by a man from the East with a cruel mouth.

The wagon trundled up the cobbled streets. Tashi could hear the jingle of bridles, hooves, and people shouting in the streets.

"Come see the Prince!" they called.

She closed her eyes. So Ramil had not even managed to get away. Could the boy not do anything right?

"Orboyd's caught a witch too!" someone shouted.

The cry was taken up and passed from house to house. "A prince and a witch! A prince and a witch!"

Tashi lay quietly on her bed, thankful that she was hidden away. She couldn't understand how these people confused her beliefs with witchcraft. Where she came from, witches were said to dabble in dark powers, exerting their will over others to harm them. But she had touched no one, barely spoken, tried to be as self-effacing as possible and yet still they said these terrible things about her. What had she done to deserve it? The wagon drew to a halt and the canvas side was lifted.

She sat up to find Orboyd standing over her. It was the first time she had seen him since he had struck her and she could not repress a shiver of fear.

"We're here," he said curtly. "Gordoc, carry her inside."

Her one-time protector made the wagon creak as he clambered aboard. He knelt beside her, reached to touch her hair but stopped himself.

"I'm sorry, little one, I broke my word. I didn't stop them hurting you," he said sadly. "But come now, here we part. Let me carry you inside. You'll be well looked after from now on."

Tashi caught a glimpse of Ramil being led into an archway in the castle courtyard as she was taken through a doorway on the opposite side. Gordoc followed an old maid up the spiral staircase to a room at the top. The woman unlocked the door and ushered them into a comfortable bedchamber, a copper bath already full of water in front of a fire. The hangings were rich but, to Tashi's Blue Crescent eyes, too loud and busy, depicting the confusion of the hunt and war. They clamored from the wall like a fanfare of trumpets, not the subtle whisper of the silks hanging in her chambers back in Rama. Gordoc placed her in an armchair.

"Farewell, Princess," he said with a bow.

"Thank you, Gordoc. You've been . . . .been kind," Tashi said, sorry to see him go. When he was around, she had always been sure of having someone to speak up for her, even if he couldn't protect her.

Gordoc bowed again and shuffled out, leaving her alone with the maid. The woman was watching her nervously.

Tashi sighed. "What's your name?" she asked, used to the hostile stares of these Easterners.

"Mergot," the woman said, adding no "my lady" or "your highness." Tashi let it pass.

"And who is your master, Mergot?"

"Lord Gunston, but that weren't him you saw earlier." Mergot began to unbutton the back of Tashi's filthy white shift without so much as a "by your leave."

Tashi resigned herself to this treatment. Clearly she was expected to bathe and hopefully change into some fresh clothes. She felt weak but had no objection to the plan, so she allowed Mergot to continue.

"So who did I speak to earlier?" She had thought him a demon conjured up by her illness, but it appeared he was flesh and blood, which was far more terrifying. Shakily, Tashi took Mergot's arm and stepped into the bath.

"Only Lord Fergox Spearthrower himself, him that's going to save you." Mergot's voice was proud.

Tashi had been preparing herself for bad news, but this was far worse than she had feared. The Emperor himself! What price would he demand from her people for her return? "But I don't need saving *by* him—I need rescuing *from* him."

Mergot laughed as if Tashi had just cracked a joke. "He said you'd be confused. He told me you weren't really evil, not like the other three witches. That's why

I offered to look after you when none others wanted to. They said you'd curse them, but you won't spell an old woman like me, will you?"

"I know no spells," Tashi replied quietly.

The maid clucked sceptically and poured a basin of hot water over Tashi's hair. With rough fingers, she washed away the dirt of the journey. The bathwater was filthy by the time she had finished.

"There now," Mergot said, wrapping her in a towel and drying her like an infant. "You're to rest tonight. Our lord will see you tomorrow, he said, if you're strong enough."

Too exhausted to argue, Tashi nodded, pulled on the clean nightgown and climbed into the bed. Mergot bustled round the room for a few more minutes, then left, carrying off Tashi's dirty clothes in a bundle. The sheets smelt sweet; the bed was warm. Tashi heard the key turn in the lock, then fell asleep.

Chapter 6

Ramil had also bathed and changed but, unlike Tashi, he was expected to dine with Fergox that evening. An armed guard escorted him down the dark, cramped corridors of the old castle keep to Fergox's private chambers: no one here was taking any chances that he might escape again. Ramil found the ruler of most of the known world reading by the fire, the leather-bound book looking oddly small in his strong fists. Fergox threw it aside on his approach.

"Are you a scholar, Prince Ramil?" he asked, waving Ramil to a chair opposite him.

A servant carried in a small table and began to set it for supper.

"I can read, sir," replied Ramil, "if that's what you mean."

Fergox smiled and tapped the cover of his book. "A soldier's answer. The ac Burinholts never prized learning. Your scholars are much undervalued. That will change."

Ramil swallowed his bitter retort. Fergox was already reordering the kingdom he had not yet conquered.

"You are probably wondering what I have got planned for you," Fergox said in a friendly fashion, pouring two glasses of red wine. He sounded like a benefactor planning the career of a favorite ward.

"It had crossed my mind, yes," Ramil answered sardonically.

"Ha!" Fergox raised a glass to him. "I like you. Plenty of spirit. I always rather admired the Burinholt dynasty."

"You have a strange way of showing your admiration: kidnapping me, locking me up with a tiger, dragging me all the way from the border."

Fergox raised an eyebrow in interest. "My man locked you up with a tiger, did he? What, you and my little Tashi?"

"Who?"

"The Princess Taoshira."

Ramil nodded, wondering at the familiarity of tone.

"That was very imaginative of him. I suppose there was no other way of smuggling you across the border. Orboyd is really one of my most useful spies."

The servants entered with the dinner. Produce from all over Spearthrower's empire had made its way to his table. Ramil did not recognize some of the dishes but had no desire to display his ignorance so ate everything without question.

"But back to the subject of your future," Fergox said, pouring some more wine. "I am in your debt, Prince. It was a lucky turn of fortune when your father and the old witches negotiated your match to little Tashi. You cannot imagine how much easier it made my plans, for it brought the Blue Crescent Princess so close to my snares. I was going to have to lure her from her island somehow but you did it for me." Fergox reached out to a globe by his side and gave it a languid spin. "And it has all turned out far better than I could have hoped. As you may guess, the Blue Crescent is none too pleased that *you* let the Princess be taken." He gave a rough laugh at Ramil's scandalized expression. "And some, thanks to the whispers circulated by my men, think you are to blame. Rumor has it that, rather than wed her, you killed her in the forest and ran for the border."

Ramil put down his knife and fork, his appetite fled.

"There will be war between your two countries come spring. Your father will be only too relieved to receive my offer of alliance. It will appear to him most . . . timely."

"You are trapping him so you can take Gerfal without a fight?"

"Of course. I do not want to squander my men on your little kingdom when I have my sights set on the much bigger prize to the west. He'll need my armies to defeat the Blue Crescent forces. The price will be acknowledging me as overlord."

"Why not crush Gerfal, like you did Brigard?" Ramil tossed back his wine angrily.

Fergox gave him a cold smile. "What would be the point? I have a large empire to control. If I can achieve my aims without wasting resources on unnecessary battles, then I will do so."

"And what about me?"

The warlord refilled Ramil's glass. "I will tell your father that you came here to seek my aid against those Westerners. I received you as a cousin with open arms, welcomed you into my household, took your unwelcome bride off your hands and even offered you one of my blood as your wife instead to cement the alliance."

"He'll never believe it," Ramil said defiantly, hoping his father would not think him capable of such treachery. This story made him out as a traitor to Gerfal, bringing war upon them by ill-treating a princess.

"Perhaps not, but that won't matter. This is the public story; what he knows in private is neither here nor there. By spring he will have no choice but to accept it or end up fighting on two fronts." Fergox smiled at Ramil's expression. "Don't look so sad, Prince Ramil. You will still have your throne. It could be much worse."

"A throne, but no power." Ramil drained his glass, trying to rid himself of the foul taste in his mouth.

"Some power," corrected Fergox. "And, if you please me, my favor."

Ramil resisted the temptation to tell the Spearthrower what he could do with his "favor."

"And what of the Princess Taoshira, my unwanted bride as you called her?"

Fergox cocked his head quizzically, his eyes calculating. "Do you care what becomes of her, Prince Ramil?"

"She was under my protection, my guest—"

Fergox nodded, as if this explained everything. "Ah yes, Gerfalian chivalry, I had forgotten. I have no plans to harm her, if that is what worries you. Quite the opposite: I intend to give her an important role in shaping the future of her country."

"And that is . . . ?"

Fergox picked up the book he had discarded and brandished it at Ramil. "Did you know that the Blue Crescent Islanders do not believe in God?"

"They believe in a Goddess."

Inspired by his subject, the warlord's eyes lit up with religious fervor. "Exactly. They are in thrall to a demon, an abomination. They let women rule them, their sons do not inherit, they live in the darkness of ignorance. Princess Taoshira is going to bring them to the light."

Ramil shifted uneasily in his chair. "And how is she going to do that?"

Fergox turned his attention back to his food and speared a piece of venison. "By turning to the true faith, of course. Holin the Warmonger, the Father of all other gods, has shown me the way."

Ramil had heard of the Holtish name for the supreme being. Spearthrower introduced worship of this bloody deity in every country he conquered. Images of him had been set up in temples, a warrior priesthood introduced, icons painted, many bearing a striking likeness to Fergox. It had become the most powerful religion in the world, attracting willing and reluctant adherents every day.

"And how will you persuade her? From what I have seen of the Princess, she is very devoted to her own faith."

"Pah!" Fergox spat out a bit of gristle. "She's young.

She'll listen. When I bribed the priest on Kai to choose her, I made sure they picked someone from a family free from the influence of that foul court. I know she's had four years of it, but she is not beyond redemption. Those other three witches will be burned at the stake when we conquer the Islands, but my Tashi will ride in to Rama at my side to institute the new religion."

"What do you mean 'by your side'?"

Fergox looked up at the earnest young questioner and winked. "I also asked them to pick me a comely wench. She's to be my wife." He scratched his chin, thinking about it. "Number five, but the prettiest armful of the lot. Number one wife is becoming a bit of a scold, thinks she's superior to the rest. I think I'll execute her when I return home." He picked up a pen and scribbled a note in the margin of his book, as if making a memorandum to unleash the imperial axeman on his unfortunate spouse.

Ramil tried not to imagine what it would be like to be number five wife to Fergox. He wouldn't wish that on his worst enemy, let alone the little Islander. Could the warlord be dissuaded from the plan?

"But you surely will not hope to defeat the Blue Crescent navy? You won't be able to walk in and take over!"

"You forget, Princeling, that the navy will be at the other side of the world bombarding Gerfal. I think we will have no trouble just walking in, as you put it. You're not eating. Is there something wrong with your meal?"

Ramil shook his head. The problem was the company.

"And if the Princess does not convert, what then?"

Fergox gave a heartless smile. "She'll discover I can be very persuasive."

The next morning, Tashi was surprised to find that her ceremonial robes had been restored to her. There was a new white shift in place of the one that had got ruined on the journey, but the orange tunic, dragonfly robe, and orange sash were lying on the clothes press, cleansed of any stain.

But not my boots, she thought with a sigh. *I don't think I'll ever see them again.*

Having no one to wait on her, Tashi went through the rituals, even remembering the absent fingerbowl as she mimed washing her hands. She then struggled into her clothes, feeling sure the layers must be all uneven at the back and the sash badly fastened. She stroked the heavy brocade with its turquoise and gold dragon-flies, admiring afresh the skill of the craftswoman who had made it many years ago on the orders of a previous princess. It really did make her feel royal when she wore it. A mirror stood in the corner. She walked over to inspect herself. It was odd to see the old Fourth Crown Princess staring back. She'd almost forgotten what she looked like.

Mergot came in without knocking. She hesitated near the doorway, no longer so sure now that the girl was dressed up in the strange clothes, looking so foreign. She held out a green veil, stick of kohl, and a pot of white make-up, not daring to come nearer.

"You're to put these on," she said, placing them on the floor and retreating. "I'll be back in an hour to fetch you."

Tashi sat in the window and carefully applied her make-up, obscuring her individuality under the mask of the ruler. She supposed that the return of her robes amounted to an invitation to appear in her official capacity. Perhaps it meant that Fergox was going to treat her as a state prisoner and grant her the privileges that went with that status, giving her the chance to contact her sisters and open negotiations. She threw the veil over her hair and pinned it in place. She was ready.

Bare toes peeped out from under the robe. Almost ready.

True to her promise, Mergot reappeared an hour later, accompanied by four guards. They made the sign against evil, two fingers to their forehead, as Tashi stood up to receive them.

"My lord asks if you are fit enough to walk downstairs," Mergot muttered, not looking at her.

"I am," Tashi said simply.

"Then follow me."

The guards made way as Tashi emerged from her bedroom. They walked in pace with her down the steps and across the snow-covered courtyard. The frosty bite of the stones hurt her feet but she kept her face impassive, trying to remember she was a Blue Crescent princess and proud of it. Physical discomfort was nothing. Emotions were to be hidden. Ice cold and strong, she told herself, that was what she had to be for her people.

All who had gathered there—farriers, servants, soldiers—stopped what they were doing when the foreign Princess appeared among them. Their eyes were fearful; many reached for the hilts of their weapons. Tashi almost laughed at the irony: they were scared of her! A girl of sixteen with no weapons or special powers, a prisoner in the land of her enemies far from home, and yet they still trembled as she passed.

Mergot led her to the threshold of the great hall of the castle and stopped.

"You are to go in there," she said, pointing.

Tashi bowed her head in acknowledgement and pushed the door open. It swung back to reveal the great hall of the castle, decked in imperial banners. Fergox sat on a throne at the far end, surrounded by his senior officers and nobles. Soldiers stood to attention on both sides of the room. A group of red-robed priests, heads shaved leaving only a topknot on the crown, waited about halfway down, holding an icon of the Spearthrower's war god. Standing at Fergox's right hand, looking very uncomfortable, was Prince Ramil. He gazed at her and shook his head slightly, a gesture that was both a warning and regret.

Tashi had no choice but to enter. She took a breath and began the long lonely walk down the chamber. The paving stones were worn, as if many supplicants had passed this way over the centuries. Her robes swished softly, almost the only sound in the room. She reached the foot of the throne and stood without bowing, waiting to see what Fergox would do.

"Princess Taoshira," announced the warlord, "Holin, the Warmonger, has smiled on you. He sees the purity of your heart and knows that you are not beyond redemption. Renounce your old faith and kneel to his image, and you shall go free."

Tashi swayed as if he had struck her: this was the last thing she had been expecting. A demand for a ransom or treaty, threats and bargains: she had been prepared for all these, but an order that she recant was startling and offensive. Seeing her surprise, Fergox smiled and beckoned the priests. They moved in behind Tashi, pacing forward to the beat of a solemn low chant. Unnerved, she turned to find the icon elevated in front of her, the frowning god with his spear and axe looking down on her like Fergox's angry twin. The chief priest struck his staff on the ground.

"Pay homage to Holin!"

Tashi faced Fergox and clasped her hands in an appeal. "Lord Fergox, I am a ruler of my country and should be treated with the respect due to my rank. I stand here as a helpless prisoner. You should not abuse your power over me with insults to my faith."

Fergox descended the step and took her shoulders. He pulled her round to face the priests again.

"Come now, my little princess, all you need do is kneel and this will all be over," he said in her ear.

Tashi shook her head. "I cannot do what you ask, sir."

He frowned. "I feared as much." He nodded to the priest and raised his voice. "The delusion remains. The girl must be cleansed before she can accept the truth. I entrust her to you and your brethren." He gave Tashi a little shove between the shoulder blades.

"But, sir!" Tashi cried. "I am a state prisoner! You cannot treat me like this!"

Fergox continued to walk back to the throne, not even paying her the courtesy of looking at her as he spoke. "You are an infidel in need of salvation. I can treat you as I see fit." He sat down. "It's for your own good."

Two acolytes seized Tashi's arms. The chanting grew louder, swelling around her so that her protests could no longer be heard. The chief priest snatched off her veil and orange sash and cast them into the fireplace. He then ripped off her dragonfly gown and orange tunic, tearing the priceless fabric as he did so. When Tashi was clad only in white, he put round her shoulders a long black robe.

"The mark of the penitent," intoned the chief priest to his audience.

He held up a cloth to be blessed by sacred water sprinkled from a gold cup.

"The falsehoods of the demon goddess will be wiped from your heart as we wipe the mark of her from your face." Tashi tried to duck but the two acolytes pinned her arms to her sides. With rough movements of the cloth, the chief priest removed the white paint from her face. "You return to us as a humble petitioner for the mercy of the all-powerful Warmonger."

"No!" Tashi shouted. She wanted everyone to hear that she resisted this and would until her last breath. "No, no! I am the Mother's servant. I am—"

The chanting grew louder.

"You will come to our temple to seek enlightenment," announced the chief priest. "You will dwell there to be schooled out of your errors until you are ready to avow publicly your repentance."

"I won't!" Tashi sobbed. "I won't! You can't make me!"

The body of priests bowed to Fergox and filed out of the chamber, forcing Tashi along in their midst. Silence fell as the doors closed on them.

"Well," said Fergox, jumping to his feet and rubbing his hands as the dragonfly robe smoldered in the fire, "I thought that went very well." He clapped Ramil on the back. "She'll make an excellent penitent. I am looking forward to forgiving her."

The priests placed Tashi in a cell in the temple crypt. It was freezing cold but they appeared to think that earthly comforts would impede her conversion. She curled up in the corner, hiding her face under the sleeve of the robe, aware that many people were coming and going by the grating in her cell door to stare at the foreigner. Her heart was filled with bitterness and shame. She realized now that she had only been allowed her robes so she could be ceremonially stripped of them before the eyes of Fergox's court. She had unwittingly played into his hands by coming dressed as the Fourth Crown Princess.

I should have gone as barefoot Tashi in rags, then perhaps they would have spared me, she thought miserably.

But no, that seemed unlikely. Fergox was set on defeating her, forcing her to submit to his bloodthirsty god. There was no question of sparing her.

And would she bow to this god eventually? The Mother seemed to have abandoned her; did it matter whom she worshipped now?

She groaned softly, then bit her lip to stop any further betraying noises. Yes, it did matter. Not for the Fourth Crown Princess, not even for the Blue Crescent Islands, but for Tashi. Fergox had taken away everything she'd had since she was twelve—respect, power, position—but she would not let him take away the girl who had said her prayers to the sun each morning, accompanied only by her goats.

Tashi shivered, hearing sniggering at the door. It was easy to make such proud statements; so much harder to live by them. She rubbed her cold feet, trying to bolster her resolve.

I have known a mother's love and so surely the great Mother of us all is worth serving even when she appears to have turned her favor away?

That wasn't enough, not nearly enough against the humiliation she was suffering. What else could she use to protect herself against despair?

A true believer goes on believing even when all else is lost.

It's the last thing I have to hold on to. If I let go of that, then I have lost my soul. I've killed Tashi.

But grim determination didn't stop her feeling wretched. Nor did it stop her tears. She did not care what the onlookers thought. She was still, after everything, only a young girl. Only human. She hoped they would remember that.

Alone in his chamber, Ramil fumed, pacing up and down. He had watched that whole sorry farce unwillingly—a naked sword poked in his back by the guard behind him. It had been made very clear to him that if he spoke, or even tried to leave, the guard would run him through on Fergox's orders.

Ramil thumped the wall. The poor Princess had walked to her doom without any idea what lay in store. She had been humiliated before everyone, but at least she had not gone quietly. He mentally applauded her defiance. Under that Blue Crescent reserve there was a fine, spirited girl. He wondered how he had not noticed back in Gerfal. But what must she be thinking and feeling now, holed up somewhere with those priests? He was desperate to do something for her, to let her know that she had a friend in the castle. It would do no harm to his own pride to explain that he had been forced to watch her ritual shaming. He could not bear her thinking he collaborated in it with Fergox.

Ramil looked around his room for inspiration and

noticed the desk under the window. A sheet of paper lay ready for any letters he cared to write. Pushing the inkpot aside, he picked up the paper and set to work.

"Princess, Princess!"

Tashi raised her head to the door. It was getting dark and even colder. She felt as if her feet and hands had turned to ice. But no one all day had called her "Princess." "Witch," "demon" and other even worse names, but not that.

"Who is it?" she asked tentatively.

"Ramil."

Tashi was not sure she was pleased to hear his voice. He'd seen what had happened and made no effort to stop it. Her cheeks flushed at the memory.

"To what do I owe the honor?" she replied, taking refuge in sarcasm.

"I . . . I wanted to give you this." He held out something white. "It's all right. I got permission from the priests to be here. I told them I was going to rescue you from evil ways. I don't think I and the red brethren had quite the same thing in mind, but they agreed I could see you nonetheless."

Stiffly, Tashi got to her feet and moved to the door. The only light came from the lantern out in the corridor where he stood. It was very hard to see what he had in his hand.

"Go on, take it," Ramil urged.

She reached out and took a tiny paper model.

"What is it?"

"A dragonfly." Ramil sounded sheepish. "I'm not very good at it. Yours was much better but it was the best I could do."

The crude dragonfly quivered in her hand.

"Thank you." Tashi found that she was crying again. Before this journey, she hadn't wept for years, and now she couldn't stop the tears coming. "I am very touched that you thought to do this for me."

"Come here." Ramil stretched his arm as far as he could to brush the tears from her face. His thumb gently traced the line of her cheekbone. She really was very pretty, he realized. "I just wanted to tell you that you were magnificent in there. And you have never looked more royal to me than now."

She shook her head.

"No, Princess, I mean it. And what is more, I regret every stupid thing I've said and done in your presence. I'm to blame for this and I promise you, Your Highness, that I'll think of a way of rescuing you. If you'll let me, of course."

Tashi leant her face against the door, comforted by his hand just touching her cheek. "I don't understand what I've done—why he is doing this to me," she said bleakly. "Is he making the same demands of you?"

"Not exactly," admitted Ramil. "He's using us to make our countries go to war and then he is going to take them over. Me, well, me he wants as a puppet prince married to one of his Spearthrowing daughters,

God help me, and you he wants to present to the Blue Crescent Islanders as his bride."

Tashi shuddered, revolted by the thought of Fergox touching her again, let alone marrying her. "But I can't, I don't . . . he thinks I'm an infidel."

"He believes you'll convert. He wants to use you to smooth the way to the change of state religion in your home."

"I'd rather die first."

Ramil nodded. It was exactly as he expected. "I promise I won't let it happen."

Tashi gave a sad laugh.

"I know you don't think I have it in me, but I'm going to get you out of here. It will just take time and planning. We can't rush into it like we did on the road; we'll work together, not separately. I came tonight to beg that you will not give up hope."

"I'll try not to, Prince Ramil."

He raised her hand to his lips and kissed it. "Call me Ram. It's what my friends all call me."

"In that case, I'm Tashi." She paused. "But that's not what my friends call me back home."

"What do they call you?"

"The Princess Taoshira, Fourth Crown Princess of the Blue Crescent Islands and dependent territories. We're very formal, you know."

Ramil smiled. "I've noticed. And I also think, Princess Taoshira of the rest of it, that you are making a joke."

Tashi nodded, her face wrinkling into an answering

smile. "But you can call me Tashi. It's my family name. I don't feel very much like the Princess Taoshira right now."

"Thank you, Tashi." Ramil dug in his pocket. "Oh, and I should have given this to you when we first met. I hope it's not too late." He handed her a second paper model. Tashi took it from him, looking puzzled. "It's a horse."

She put her hand over her mouth to disguise her amusement. "And very like it is too, sir."

"It's my personal sign. It's me."

Tashi stopped laughing. "Oh, I'm sorry. I must have offended you—"

He put his finger gently to her lips. "No, no, you forget, I am not an Islander but an ignorant boor. We do not take offense easily. Just look after it for me, will you? And remember, I'm coming back for you."

She appreciated the sentiment but knew better than to expect so much. "Good night, Ram," she said sadly. "And Goddess bless you."

Ramil saluted. "Farewell, Tashi. God be with you."

Chapter 7

King Lagan's spies returned with disturbing news from Brigard. A young man answering the Prince's description had been seen tied to a circus wagon and forced to walk miles. The same spies had reported no sign of the Princess.

The King debated the news with his chief advisers long into the night. Could it be Ramil? Lagan supposed he should be thankful that it sounded as if his son was alive, but how had he been smuggled across the border and why? Had he been betrayed by the Blue Crescent people? Had the Princess arranged for him to be abducted and then disappeared to make it look as if she had nothing to do with it? Lagan found his age-old distrust of the strange Westerners resurfacing. Why was his son the one being dragged to a humiliating fate in Brigard and their Princess nowhere to be seen? She could even now be hidden aboard one of their vessels, using this as a chance to declare war on Gerfal. After all, you never really knew what those white-faced women were thinking.

The next reports from his spies in Brigard added further to the alarm and confusion.

"Your Majesty," said the forest warden, kneeling before the King in the council chamber, "I have ridden far into Brigard disguised as a farmer and return with a harvest of grave news. Fergox Spearthrower is massing his armies all along our border. Reports from Felixholt, Niril, and Manford tell the same tale: soldiers are arriving from all over the Empire and digging in for the winter. It is likely they mean to make an assault on us come the spring thaw."

"We have feared this for some time," said King Lagan, glancing at the stern faces of his ministers gathered around him. "And we are prepared."

While trying to appear confident before his subjects, Lagan thought privately that his divisions, strung out in a thin line along the Brigardian border, were unlikely to be able to withstand this attack. If only the alliance had gone ahead, he would have a navy to defend his coasts and troops to spare for the border where the blow would fall first. But now, he had to prepare for an attack from the sea as well as by land.

"And, Sire, I bring other news," the warden continued, looking uncomfortable.

"Is it of my son?" Lagan asked eagerly, sitting forward.

"Yes, Sire. A merchant friendly to us in Felixholt told me that his royal highness had been seen. He is a guest of Fergox himself in the citadel."

"A prisoner, you mean?"

"My informant was not certain. He only knew that Prince Ramil had been present at the testing of someone he called 'the Blue Crescent witch.' I think he meant the Fourth Crown Princess."

Lagan sat back. "Testing? What does that mean?"

"According to my man, she was denounced as a heretic, stripped of the symbols of her rank, and is now a penitent in the houses of the priesthood of Holin the Warmonger."

Lagan closed his eyes briefly, remembering the innocent face of the girl he had talked to on the terrace. He regretted now that he had suspected her. She too was caught in Fergox's trap. But how had she got there and what part had his son played?

"And my son was present at this ceremony?"

"Apparently so, Sire."

"Willingly?"

"I do not know."

The councillors sat in silence while the news sank in. They all knew that Ramil had despised his intended bride, but to take her to Fergox for such treatment would be unforgivable. And how did that balance with the story that Ramil himself had been dragged to the Spearthrower's court?

"Your Majesty." Lord Usk was on his feet. "I beg leave to go in search of Prince Ramil."

"And I," added Hortlan and Yendral.

Lagan sighed. He knew how they felt. If he did not have to attend to the affairs of the nation, he would jump on a horse and go and find his boy himself.

"I understand your concern, my lords. God knows, I feel it too, but I need all my young warriors with me at this time. An army stands between us and Ramil if the reports are correct. You would be riding to your deaths. Your duty now lies with the men of your houses and lands. We will soon have a fight on our hands; every one of you has a part to play in defending Gerfal."

"But, Sire!" protested Usk.

Lagan raised his hand. "I appreciate your zeal for my son but there is nothing you can do. I will not believe he stays of his own free choice: he is a prisoner of war. I fear we will hear all too soon Fergox's conditions for his release."

"What of the Blue Crescent delegation, Your Majesty?" asked Lord Taris. "Should we tell them this news?"

King Lagan tapped his fingers on the arm of his throne. He was facing war with the most powerful naval empire in the world all because of a misunderstanding. He needed some brilliant stroke to avoid it, but what? Some gesture of good faith, a pledge of his son's honor. (Ramil had to be innocent, he had to be!)

"I have little doubt that the Blue Crescent will have their own informants in Spearthrower's court. They will hear this news eventually. Far better if we show our friendly intentions by revealing it now. Summon the delegates and—" Lagan ran his hand across his brow, weary and grief-stricken. It was hard to think like a king when he was full of the worries of a father "—wake the Princess Briony. I will require her to be present at our meeting with the delegates."

An hour later, the Etiquette Mistress and Chief Priest were sitting opposite the King. A tousle-haired princess perched on his knee, half asleep, a robe over her nightgown and her favorite doll on her lap. Lagan hugged her fiercely.

"You'll have to trust me, Briony," he said in a low voice. "You'll come to no harm."

Briony, who hadn't been worried before, now felt alarmed. She stared anxiously at the strangers opposite, wondering what was going on.

At a sign from the King, Lord Taris presented the delegation with a copy of the written report by the Gerfalian spies. Lagan gave them a chance to read it, then spoke.

"You will see that our information is far from complete."

"*Your* information," snapped the Etiquette Mistress, incandescent with rage, "says that your son witnessed this sacrilege but did nothing to prevent it!"

"What could he do, a prisoner himself?" Lagan asked, keeping his tone even.

"We do not know that he *is* a captive!" said the priest angrily. "Your spies' reports are at odds. Prince Ramil made no secret that he disliked this union. How do you know that he did not plan this?"

"I trust my son." As Lagan pronounced his conviction, he recalled Ramil's words said in anger only a few weeks ago. Like a cloud shifting from the face of the sun, he felt his private doubts dispel. Ramil could be foolish and downright annoying, but he wasn't so base as to plot against the Princess and the wishes of his own father. "And as a proof of this trust, I offer you my only remaining child, the Princess Briony, to be a pledge of her brother's honor."

"Father!" exclaimed Briony, squeezing his arm in shock.

Lagan held her small hand reassuringly. "I entrust her to you in the knowledge that you will treat her as one of your own until such time as the Princess Taoshira is restored to you or the full truth of these terrible events is revealed."

The Blue Crescent delegation were visibly taken aback by the magnitude of the gesture on the part of the Gerfalians. After a brief whispered exchange, the Etiquette Mistress rose and bowed.

"We accept that the father has had no part in the affront to our nation, but it remains to be seen whether the son lives up to his sire's greatness," she said. "We will treat the Princess Briony with all the honor that should now be shown to the Princess Taoshira but is denied her; your daughter will receive comfort and freedom while our beloved Crown Princess receives taunts and a prison cell. Come, Your Highness." She held out a hand to the little girl; Lagan pushed Briony gently off his knee. "In view of the change in our circumstances, we will no longer trespass on the hospitality of your court but accommodate ourselves aboard our own vessels."

The Blue Crescent delegation swept out, carrying a scared little princess with them. Lagan sat stony faced as his councillors whispered among themselves. He had spent both his children now in the service of his country and had nothing left. If this did not stop the war with the Westerners, then he could only fight with small hope of survival.

Tashi woke the morning after Ramil's visit feeling stronger. Tucking the paper models in the wide pockets of her black robe, she performed her rituals, then paced the cell to keep the cold at bay. After her public trial, she hoped that the priests would leave her alone to private contemplation. She could bear the incarceration, cold and comfortless though it was, as long as she did not have to go through further humiliation in front of other people.

Her hopes were dashed when a young priest came to fetch her.

"You are expected to attend morning worship in the temple," he announced, keeping his eyes averted as if he thought she would bewitch him with a look.

"But I do not worship your god," Tashi replied, her back to him as she leant her forehead against the wall for comfort, finding the stone more sympathetic than his hostile looks.

"You will come." He nodded to the temple guards who stepped into the cell. They surrounded her, swords pointing to her throat.

Brimming with impotent fury, Tashi walked into the corridor. The priest led her out of the crypt and into the temple itself. She'd had no chance to look at it properly when she had been brought this way the day before; now she saw that a once plain and simple building had been redecorated in honor of the new god of the Empire. Bright frescoes of war covered the walls, gleaming with scarlet, gold, and black. The altar shone with the polished metal of the shields and weapons of fallen foes. A huge icon of Holin hung over the table, draped in swathes of red cloth. The priest directed Tashi to kneel on the stone floor in front of the congregation, who were seated in relative comfort on wooden benches. Her anger had burned itself out and was now replaced by fear, as she wondered what new humiliation they had in store for her. Keeping her eyes lowered, she sensed the presence of hundreds of people, all gathered eagerly for the service. The front rows were occupied by the rich, wrapped in furs and velvet against the chill air. Fergox would doubtless be somewhere close, sitting at the front in the place of honor. Her neck flushed as she remembered what Ramil had said about the man wanting to wed her. If this was how Fergox wooed his wives, then marriage to him was worse than any prison sentence.

A cymbal clashed and a drum began to beat. The senior priests filed in bearing the weapons of their god: swords, pikes, bows, axes, spiked maces. Junior acolytes followed, clashing wooden sticks together in time with the drum. The congregation rose to its feet, but Tashi remained kneeling, her hands clasped loosely in her lap. In unison, the people began to chant the hymn of praise to Holin. She could hear Fergox's voice booming the words out behind her.

"Praise to the war god, glorious in victory,
Crushing his enemies all over the world,
We offer ourselves in perfect obedience,
Spilling our heart's blood and bending our knees."

The chief priest, a withered-looking man with a pinched, thin face, halted behind the altar and raised his arms, displaying hundreds of tiny white scars. He took a knife and in the sight of everyone made a shallow cut on his forearm.

"Honor the Warmonger!" he cried.

"All honor to his name," responded the congregation.

Tashi watched in fascination as he let the blood drip onto the white cloth spread out on the table. He then chose two weapons from the altar and handed them to a pair of priests waiting eagerly on either side of the table. He gave one the mace, the other a sword. Neither was given a shield. The two men turned to face the congregation. Tashi could see the steel caps on their boots.

"See how we fight for Holin!" they shouted in unison.

To Tashi's horror, they then swung at each other, sword angling down at the knees of the opponent, the mace bearer going for the head. The combat was only paces away from her. She could feel the rush of air as weapons slashed and robes whisked. The priests dodged skillfully; so far no one had landed a blow. Tashi began to hope that this was just an elaborate dance pattern to celebrate battle without causing injury, but then the mace bearer crashed his weapon into the skull of the swordsman, who had not moved quickly enough. Tashi flinched as bone split and she was sprayed with a mist of blood. The victim fell onto the floor in front of her, so close she could have touched his head. The victor yanked out the mace to the applause of the audience. He shook it in the air and then presented it to the chief priest to take pride of place on the altar. The dead man was left lying where he fell. Tashi was shaking, sure she was about to vomit; she inched back to avoid the blood pooling on the steps until she felt a firm pressure on her neck. It was Fergox. He had risen and was now standing behind her.

"Stay where you are!" he ordered.

Stooping down, he dabbled his index finger in the blood, then wiped it on the forehead of the victorious priest who knelt before him to receive the mark of honor. Seeing Tashi's look of horror, Fergox smiled, reached out and smeared some on her cheek. Revolted, she made to wipe it away.

"Leave it!" he said, slapping her hand down. "Blood spilt bravely is better than white paint of falsehood." Leaning closer, enjoying her fear of him, he slowly daubed her other cheek.

Tashi trembled, close to tears, as Fergox watched her reaction with a mocking expression. She could feel the blood drying on her cheek, pulling on the skin, but she dare not touch it.

Fergox turned from her and raised the victorious priest to his feet. He then lifted the man's fist in a punch of triumph.

"See how we fight and die for Holin!" Fergox shouted.

The crowd cheered and the priests struck up a chant.

"Give your offerings of blood, gold, and service," the chief priest cried in ecstasy.

The priests divided into two columns and began moving among the people with bowls. Most of the congregation poured out the contents of their purses, but some of the most zealous adherents sliced their hands with a knife and let the blood fall into the basins, prompting applause from the onlookers. As the priests brought the offerings to the altar, one paused by Tashi and held out his bowl. Eyes on her clenched fists, she shook her head, and he continued on to the front without a word.

The rest of the service seemed interminable to Tashi as she tried to regain some control over herself, some calm to counterbalance the panic and revulsion she felt. Songs were sung to the accompaniment of drums and blaring horns; a long recitation of the martial virtues expected of the perfect warrior was read out by a temple guard; the chief priest spoke at great length about the evils of foreign gods and the superiority of Holin. All Tashi could see was the dead man sprawled before her, receiving no honor because he had committed the sin of being beaten.

Finally, at the end of the ceremony, the chief priest held up a hand for silence.

"Now we come to the Choice. One here among us has followed the demon goddess all her life but today, Holin, in his mercy, has given her this chance of salvation." He nodded to two assistants. They stood before Tashi, the one on the right hand holding warm clothes and a loaf of bread, on the left, a birch rod. "Choose service to Holin and your trials will be over; refuse and your mortification will continue until you are cleansed of your errors." He paused, then asked, "Penitent, who is the Supreme God?"

Silence fell in the temple. Tashi closed her eyes, wondering if her voice had fled. She had to say something.

"I am the Mother's servant." Her voice was surprisingly loud in the hushed temple.

"Blasphemy!" shrieked the priest. The crowd murmured and hissed at the kneeling figure in her black robes. "Take the witch back to her cell!" he ordered.

Two guards seized Tashi roughly under her arms and towed her back the way she had come. Behind her, the chanting began again as the priests hurried to purify the temple after the pollution caused by her words.

Once back in her cell, Tashi dashed to her water jug and rubbed frantically at her bloodied cheeks. She felt dirty long after she had cleaned the marks off.

Please, she begged the Goddess, *please may they leave me in peace!*

She was not to get her wish. The chief priest and his

entourage followed on the completion of the service. He bore the birch rod in his hands, his expression unforgiving. Tashi backed against the wall, feeling the priests' hostility like a physical blow as they crowded into her small room. The chief priest curled his lips in disgust and threw the rod at her feet.

"You've chosen the way of discipline. You will learn to fight and submit as becomes a warrior of Holin."

Tashi held out her empty hands. "My religion is one of peace. I will not fight."

He ignored her. "Your trainer will remain with you. Everyone fights eventually."

With a swirl of red robes, he was gone, leaving a single priest behind. Glancing up at him fearfully, Tashi saw that it was the man who had so efficiently wielded the mace to kill his opponent. He now wore a robe fastened with a linked belt and a breastplate made of gold, spoils of his victory and a sign that he had graduated to the highest level of warrior-craft. About fifty years old, he had the scarred face and hands of a professional soldier. He regarded his pupil for a long silent moment then pointed to the rod.

"Pick it up," he ordered, drawing from the fold of his robes a similar instrument.

Having no idea what to expect, Tashi scooped the rod up from the floor. She had decided to obey any order that did not conflict with her principles.

"Penitent, all Holin's followers must learn to fight for him and to submit to him as a good soldier does to his commander. You will quickly feel the penalty of refusing an order from me, your master, if you refuse to give battle when told to do so. Therefore, I say, 'Fight!'"

The warrior-priest launched himself at her, swinging the rod down in an arc like a sword slash. Instinctively, Tashi raised her arms across her face. The blow whipped across the back of her hands. She yelped.

The priest gave a cold smile. "I think you understand now. I will keep on attacking until you fight back." He raised his rod again, expecting her to launch her counter-strike.

"I will not fight for your god," Tashi retorted, turning quickly so that the next blow fell on her back. The sting made her gasp.

"That is blasphemy." The man bent the rod in his hands, his eyes glittering with battle-fire. "The Warmonger wants strength and blood from his followers, not weakness and cowardice."

"Then I won't follow him."

The third blow hit her ribs with a crack.

"You must fight back or I will beat you until I have no more strength to raise my arm."

Tashi believed him, but either she let him break her body or crush her will. She took a step forward, held her rod between her two hands and snapped it over her knee. She threw the pieces to the ground.

"I am fighting back, sir, in the only way my faith allows."

He raised his arm to strike again but Tashi did not flinch this time.

"I did as you asked: I fought, but still you would hit me?" she asked, steeling herself for the blow.

The priest slowly lowered his rod, his expression one of reluctant admiration. "You have strength, witch, but it is in the service of the wrong god. I will return tomorrow to continue our lessons," he said, tucking the rod away in his belt.

Ramil had decided that he stood the best chance of escape if he ingratiated himself with Fergox. If he could earn the man's trust, it was likely the guard on him would be relaxed sufficiently for him to slip away and make his preparations. To do so, he would have to start acting as if he accepted that he was a guest rather than a prisoner. On hearing from the two soldiers who were his permanent escort that Fergox usually spent the morning sparring with his warrior priests, Ramil went in search of his host. Their information had been correct: Fergox was duelling in the practice courts adjoining the temple, an arena surrounded by a wooden barrier. As Ramil approached, he could see warriors testing their skills on the sawdust-covered floor. Fergox was in the very middle, stripped to the waist, sweat running down his back, a few cuts to his torso, but he was getting the best of the fight. With a skilful swipe of the sword, Fergox had his opponent on his knees, blade pointing to his windpipe.

"Submit to me, and thus to the Great Holin," Fergox panted. There was a hungry look in his eye, as if he hoped to have the excuse to finish the thrust.

"I submit," said the priest, letting his blade fall to the ground with a clatter.

With a tight laugh, Fergox dropped his sword and stepped back.

"Honor to the Mighty Holin," he chanted.

"Honor to his name," replied the man, completing the ritual. He looked immensely relieved to be walking away with his life.

Fergox reached for a towel held out by one of his servants, wiped his face with it, and slung it around his neck. He then saw Ramil leaning against the barrier.

"Good morning, Prince Ramil. I trust you slept well?"

Ramil bowed. "Indeed, sir."

"Would you care to fight?" Fergox gestured to the rack of weapons inside the court—swords, spears, mace, and staff. "I like to practice with at least three partners each day to keep up my skills."

Ramil vaulted over the barrier. "I do not pretend to match you in experience or strength, my lord." It did not suit his plans to risk getting injured just to show off his swordsmanship. "Would target practice be an acceptable competition between us?" He chose a short spear, the sort he carried when hunting back in Gerfal. "Perhaps you would care to show me the skill that earned you your title?"

Fergox nodded. "I have no problem with that, Princeling." He picked a spear and gestured to a row of straw men-targets against the wall at the far end of the arena. "A killing strike wins—head or heart."

They walked together to take up their positions

opposite the dummies. Fergox felt the sharpened end of his spear thoughtfully.

"I hear from the priests you visited my little penitent."

Quelling any sign that would betray his nervousness on this subject, Ramil nodded. "Yes, I went to reason with her but found her unmoved."

Fergox lifted the spear to his shoulder and took a few swings to loosen his arm and neck muscles.

"She's putting on a good show for the people. Prettily stubborn. A sudden conversion would not be half so impressive."

He launched the spear and it struck the central dummy in the head.

"A fatal blow," he said with a satisfied smile.

Ramil warmed up, then cast his missile, imagining the dummy to be Fergox. It flew hard and fast, piercing the straw man in the heart.

"Excellent!" Fergox clapped him on the back. "Your family should be proud of you. Best of three?"

Ramil was about to agree when a red-robed priest appeared at Fergox's elbow. He muttered a swift report out of Ramil's hearing, bowed and retired. Fergox turned back to his young challenger with one of his chilling smiles.

"I do apologize, Prince Ramil, but we will have to postpone our contest. I am called away to our not-so-penitent penitent. She has excelled herself this morning and I must congratulate her."

He walked out of the practice courts, leaving Ramil to wonder what he meant.

The door to the cell opened for the third time that day. Tashi took up her post against the far wall, her fingers clutching the stones apprehensively.

"Ah, Tashi, Tashi, you are remarkable!"

Fergox Spearthrower stood before her, arms outstretched in a benevolent gesture. He was bare-chested, covered in cuts, and had a towel round his neck. She could smell the sweat of combat on him from the other side of the room.

"You've found your own way to fight. I like that. It suits a female follower of Holin: passive resistance, scorn of pain and punishment—excellent."

"I didn't do it for your Warmonger," Tashi said, her eyes lowered.

"Ah, but everything you do is done for Holin. You cannot help yourself." Fergox smiled and crossed the cell to embrace her. "You were worth the money." He pressed her to his chest and kissed the top of her head.

Tashi pulled away. "What do you mean? Worth what money?"

He ran his hand over her hair, trapping one lock in his fingers. "You don't understand, my poor, sweet girl. You're only here because I paid the chief priest on Kai one hundred thousand gold heralds to pick you. I made you what you are. If it hadn't been for me, you'd still be herding goats." He tickled her under the chin with her hair.

"No." Tashi shook her head, pushing his hands off her. He was leaning over her, trapping her against the wall, smiling his horrible smile that said he knew everything about her, how she felt, how she thought. "I don't believe it."

Fergox chuckled. "Must I show you his signature on the receipt, little penitent? I doubtless still have it somewhere in my treasury."

"No." Her protest this time was feeble. She sagged against the wall, feeling as if he had removed all strength from her. Was it possible? Was she his creature? It would explain the sudden death of the previous princess and the oddity that someone as insignificant as her had been chosen. But if that was true, it meant the end of everything she believed in.

"I wouldn't let it worry you, Tashi. You made a very fine princess and will be a beautiful wife for an emperor when the time comes." He patted her consolingly on the cheek. "I'll leave you to your penitence. Don't take too long about it, will you? The disciplines get very nasty after a few weeks of resistance and I'd hate to think you'll suffer so unnecessarily. You'll submit in the end. Everyone does give way to me."

He ran his finger down the side of her face and then touched her lips. "Just say the words, Tashi, and you'll be out of here and in a warm chamber lying in a bed with silk sheets."

She turned her head away, too devastated to speak. She felt his hand removed and heard the noise of the door closing. Alone again, she slid down the wall to the floor, feeling as if her whole world had crumbled around her.

Chapter 8

The Midwinter festival approached. Snow built up on the pitched roofs and would periodically fall in little avalanches into the castle courtyard. The stones around the well were slick with ice, the chain dripping icicles. The white mountains would have been beautiful if Ramil had not felt they looked like the bars of his prison. He fretted with each day that passed that escape was becoming more difficult as the weather closed in. Heavy snowstorms now often blocked the road to the castle. Teams of soldiers labored to keep the pathways between the army camp and the citadel clear. Fergox was using the winter to harden and train his troops. Many of them were from the warmer countries of the south and were not accustomed to the bitter weather. As he tramped through the castle, Ramil often came across young men with dark skin like his own cowering around the campfires, doubtless wishing they had never signed up for the warlord's army.

Though seemingly at a loose end, Ramil had not been idle. He had already hidden two bundles of clothes and provisions in a quiet corner of the castle, enough he hoped to see a pair of fugitives far along the road. But the most difficult challenge remained. He had to have a horse capable of carrying two. Ramil had not forgotten the princess's incompetence in the saddle: she would have to ride with him. That would mean stealing one of the nobles' horses from the stables, rather than one of the army mounts, a tricky feat as they were well guarded. Somehow he had to achieve this and get the princess away before anyone noticed. How he was to do this was beyond him at the moment. Every time he saw her, she was hemmed in by priests. They had started to bring her to the practice courts each morning to offer her the various weapons of combat. A regular crowd gathered to see her snap the arrow or throw aside the sword, but not before she had usually taken several blows from her trainer. It was a cruel game that everyone, apart from Tashi and Ramil, appeared to enjoy.

Two days before the Midwinter feast, a messenger arrived at Felixholt with the news that Fergox's sister, the Inkar Yellowtooth, and her army from Kandar, an eastern province of Holt, had been sighted. Fergox took Ramil up to the top of the tower to watch for her approach.

"Now my armies are all gathered," Fergox announced. "Junis is the last to arrive as usual. She likes to keep her little brother waiting—she's the only one who dares." He chuckled and slapped Ramil on the back. "I think you'll like her, Ramil. A fearsome warrior. She'll give us good sport on the practice courts tomorrow."

Ramil took the offered spyglass and saw the banners of the Inkar Yellowtooth crest the last hill. A soldier with an iron helmet, two plaits of grey hair, and a leaf-shaped shield rode in the vanguard.

"There she is!" Fergox said. "Let us go down and meet her." He whistled for his groom to saddle his blue roan. "I don't want her complaining that I slighted her."

The elite troops were rushing to mount up to provide Fergox with a guard of honor. A groom led forward Fergox's horse and a stout mare for Ramil. Fergox slipped on his gloves, eyeing the prince speculatively.

"I believe I can trust you to attempt no foolishness, young prince, if I allow you a mount?"

"But of course, my lord. I have long since given up hope or desire to flee," Ramil said meekly. "Where would I go with the snows deep in the mountain passes and your army encamped on the road?"

"Quite so. I'm glad you understand. We have been getting on well; I would hate to make the conditions of your stay here less comfortable. Come, let us see what the old girl makes of you."

The guard of honor trotted off in advance, Fergox and Ramil following at an easy pace. They arrived at the town gates just as the Inkar galloped up, her banner fluttering behind her.

"Junis!" cried Fergox, nudging his horse towards his sister and embracing her from the saddle.

The Inkar raised her visor revealing a keen-eyed face with a wolfish grin. Her front teeth lived up to her nickname, abnormally long and yellow. "Fergox, I came as promised."

Her brother gripped her forearm. "I only asked you here to share the spoils. Our little war will soon be over and we can return south. But I am pleased to see you arrive in time for Midwinter."

"I'm not one to miss a feast, brother. Now tell me, where are your two bargaining chips? I'd like to see them."

Fergox gave a grin to match hers. "I thought as much. Let me introduce you to Prince Ramil ac Burinholt." He waved his arms to where Ramil was waiting quietly on his mare.

Ramil bowed in the saddle. "Lady," he said politely, though he had never seen anyone less ladylike in his life. He had just been wondering what kind of marriage his father might have had with this fearsome woman if that alliance had gone ahead. He could see why his father had run for the desert.

Junis urged her horse forward and gave Ramil a frank inspection. "Not much of Lagan about you, is there, Prince Ramil? I suppose you get your coloring from your mother?"

"Indeed, my lady, I look much like she did."

Junis turned back to her brother. "Has he tried to escape?"

"Of course," replied Fergox.

"Good. Any use with the weapons?"

"An accomplished warrior."

"Excellent. I look forward to seeing more of our young guest. And what about the other?"

"With the priesthood." Fergox gestured to his sister to ride on. They trotted side by side with Ramil just behind, listening to every word.

"Still not broken in yet?"

"Not yet."

"You're being too kind, Fergox. You should just declare her a convert, marry the wench and have done. Who cares what she really believes once she's your wife?"

Fergox frowned. "I will not take an infidel as my bride. Holin would be most displeased."

Junis was unimpressed. "All this fuss over one girl! Take her as a concubine then. That will send the message to the Blue Crescent Islands that their surrender is inevitable."

"That is not the plan, Junis," Fergox said sternly. "Remember, I have worked towards this moment for years and will not throw it away on a hasty gesture. I need a public renunciation of the goddess from the girl. She must be the one to bring her people to the true faith. Don't underestimate me, Junis; we are making progress with her."

The Inkar laughed, shaking her head in disbelief. "I don't know, Fergox. When did you get so . . . so political?"

Fergox smiled at his sister's look of disdain, his anger subsiding. "In my old age, it seems to me that spreading the faith of Holin Warmonger is even more important than conquest."

Junis gave a sceptical snort. "But the god of battle demands blood, not weasel words."

"And blood he will get—the blood of thousands of new believers shed willingly in his service. Think how he will reward me—my empire spread across the known world united by worship of Holin, an impressive legacy to leave my dynasty." Breaking away from the dream, he swung towards his sister, thumping her on the arm. "But you, you are just as you've always been, Junis. Admit it, you have always had the soldier's attitude, wishing to run complications through with your sword if they get in the way."

"Is there any other kind of attitude, brother?"

"Not in your lands perhaps. Come, let us go somewhere warm. We have plans to discuss and a barrel of good, strong beer to broach."

The last few days had passed like an evil dream for Tashi. Something had snapped inside her since Fergox told her about his bribe. Doubting herself, her resistance had become habit rather than deeply felt. Indeed, she had been sucked dry of any feeling except despair. She could see no escape from her suffering, not even Ramil's promise to help, as she did not believe he had it in him to pull off a successful rescue. In any case, she was an outcast, cursed, a fake, not deserving of help. She had begun to hope that some lucky accident on the practice courts would put an end to her misery, but so far her trainer had refrained from any action that would produce serious injury.

At the end of each session her trainer made her kneel in the sawdust as he asked her to name the supreme god. Since Fergox's visit, she now replied, "I do not know," before being led away. And it was true. She no longer knew. This was happening to her for one of three reasons, she concluded: because the Goddess was inferior to Holin and powerless to stop him; or she had only ever been a delusion; or, worst of all, she had abandoned Tashi, in which case she was her Mother no more. The one and only Goddess, the creator of the universe, had shut out Fergox's false princess, cut Tashi off from her people. Who now could Tashi serve, cursed creature that she was?

The eve before Midwinter, Tashi saw that there was a newcomer to the practice courts. A woman with long grey hair was sparring with Fergox, laughing wildly and slashing at his shield with a curved sword. Their bout was attracting all eyes, even Ramil's; he was leaning over the barrier watching the battle with a grim smile. Tashi's trainer signalled for her to stay back.

Fergox smashed the blade from his sister's hand. It flew into the air and spiralled into the dust.

"Do you submit?" he shouted.

"Not likely!" cried Junis, catching him with a blow from her shield so that the ruler of most of the known world fell on his rump. He leapt up and chased his sister round the ring, threatening her with the flat of the sword. She finally turned and gave a sweeping bow.

"I yield, brother. I am pleased to see you have not gone soft over the past year."

He bowed in reply. "I would not dare, knowing what you would do if you once got the better of me."

The Inkar picked up her weapon. As she did so, she noticed the black-robed figure standing with a priest at the other end of the courts.

"Yours?" she asked her brother.

He nodded. "Yes, the little penitent."

Junis snorted and strode over to Tashi.

"You, girl," she said abruptly, "I hear you are putting the priests to a lot of trouble."

"That is not my intention," Tashi replied, wondering who this terrible-looking woman was.

"Pitiful answer. Show some backbone, girl. If you intend to resist, at least don't apologize for it. Here, priest, let me take the girl's lesson."

"But, my lady—" protested the trainer, glancing to the warlord.

Fergox intervened. "It's all right, Training Master, I give my permission." He drew his sister aside. "I don't want her damaged, understood? I'm still planning to wed her."

"Pish!" Junis sniffed. "She's not as fragile as she looks. We women never are. Right, girl, it's time you learned to make proper use of a sword." She thrust a heavy blade into Tashi's hands. The girl could barely lift it. "Raise it into the guard position like so." Junis held her own sword out in front of her, its point rock steady.

"I don't want to fight you," Tashi said in a voice little more than a whisper. This woman's presence seemed to crush her, making her feel small and insignificant.

"See, I told you." Fergox laughed. "She's as stubborn as a mule. Come, the troops are assembled for us to review them." He strode off, calling for his clothes.

Junis sheathed her sword and waited for him to go. But instead of following, she took Tashi by the shoulders.

"We've waited on your whims long enough. Come on, girl, fight!" She shook Tashi hard, making her teeth rattle. "Wake up! In Spearthrower's empire, you fight or you die!" She pushed Tashi away and drew her blade again. "Unlike your teachers, I'm not going to miss when I aim at you. What will you do now, Blue Crescent Princess? Die like a dog or fight like a hero?"

Junis raised her sword, her expression merciless. Closing her eyes, Tashi gripped the hilt of her own blade, determined not to flinch from the blow. She heard Junis grunt as she swung—she heard the whistle of air—but then a pair of arms clasped her from behind and lifted her sword to block the downstroke. The blades clashed together, the Inkar's fierce swipe skidding off to the ground.

"Perhaps your ladyship would prefer to do battle with someone who wants to pit his strength against hers," Ramil said, pushing Tashi gently behind him. He levered the blade from her frozen fingers and then tested its weight by twirling it in the air.

Junis glanced at the pale-faced girl who had fallen back to take shelter behind the barrier and then at the dark-skinned boy who was grinning roguishly at her.

"Hah! You're right! It would be much better sport to

see what Lagan's boy is made of." She swung at him but Ramil was ready for her, meeting her stroke with a high defense. Circling round, she probed his guard with a flurry of quick passes. He defended them swiftly and efficiently.

"I see the Gerfalian sword trainers have not neglected their prince," Junis noted with approval, stepping back.

"I have much still to learn, my lady," Ramil replied, taking the chance to go on the attack. His opponent was strong and crafty and a match for his height; he would have to use his superior agility to outwit her if he wanted to win the bout. He dealt her a complex pattern of thrusts and cuts that kept her backing away, but then a momentary doubt crossed his mind, giving her the advantage again. Would it be better to lose to ingratiate himself with the old she-warrior? Or maybe she'd like him better if he won? That certainly suited his mood. He returned to attack, wielding his sword with fluid skill that would have made his old teachers proud. Junis was forced onto the back foot and finally disarmed with a twist of Ramil's blade.

"Do you submit to me, and thus to our Father God?" Ramil asked as was the custom on these courts.

Panting, Junis replied, "I submit. And, by Holin, well fought, young Prince! You would give my brother a hard time—there's a match I'd like to see."

Ramil bowed. "I would not presume to challenge him, my lady."

Junis lifted her tangled locks off her neck to cool

down, catching sight of Tashi watching nervously from the sidelines. She pointed her blade at Prince Ramil. "There, girl, that's real fighting! As for you, pale-faced witch from the western islands, you disgust me. I do not know why my brother wastes his time on you. Take her away. Come, Prince, let's go drink to Midwinter cheer."

The high point of the Midwinter holiday was the feast in the banqueting hall. Entering the packed chamber, Ramil saw that the walls had been decked with greenery, the floor covered with fresh rushes, a huge meal prepared by the castle kitchens. Everyone was busy with the celebrations: this night, Ramil decided, would offer the best hope of escape.

"Young Prince!" called the Inkar from the top table. She was dressed rather incongruously in a rose-pink gown with plunging neckline showing her wrinkled throat and battle-scarred chest. "Sit by me." She patted the seat beside her. Ramil made his way through the crowds and took his place.

"Midwinter greetings, my lady," he said.

"Fie upon you!" Junis roared with laughter. "Are they so meek in Gerfal that men and women merely exchange words at Midwinter? In my lands, we are not so bashful." She leant forward and kissed him heartily on the mouth, then slapped him on the back. "See, that's how we do it."

Ramil repressed the urge to wipe his mouth on the

back of his sleeve. It had been like being kissed by a camel.

"I . . . er . . . I am honored." He dragged the words up from somewhere.

"So you should be. I don't make a habit of kissing men. Only a favored few."

He wasn't reassured by this but attempted to change the subject. "More wine, your ladyship?" He took a gulp of his own glass to remove the taste left in his mouth.

"Why not? Where in Wrath's name has my brother got to?"

Her query was answered by the appearance of Fergox at the doors to the chamber. The room fell silent as he moved between the tables to take his place. To Ramil's surprise, Tashi followed him like his shadow, head down.

Junis groaned. "He's got that poxy milksop in tow. What do you think, Prince Ramil? Has she bewitched Fergox? I've never known him to make so much fuss about a girl before. Usually weds them and has them nursing his little warriors before the year's out. But this one—no, he even cares what's in her head, not just what she looks like. He wants a real conversion from her."

Fergox took his chair and pointed to a spot two paces behind him for his prisoner to stand. He held up his arms.

"Welcome to our feast. Everyone is invited to share the food on my table tonight: friend and foe, master and servant, faithful and heretic, for one night we make no distinction. Midwinter cheer to you all!" He drained his gold tankard and threw it into the crowd for any lucky man to catch. A fight broke out between two bare-armed guardsmen vying for the prize, resulting in one losing his front teeth and being stretchered out. The victor drank his health from the tankard to the cheers of the onlookers. Fergox roared with laughter and applauded.

Junis tugged his sleeve once he was seated. "Why did you bring her?" She jerked her head at Tashi who was now sitting on the floor being examined by two friendly dogs.

"What's it to you, sister? I like her, that's all you need to know." He heaped his plate with red meats. "She's got those lazy priests of mine earning their keep for once. Besides, I want her to know what she's missing with her obstinacy. She could be here like our young prince, a guest of honor at high table, not sitting with the animals at my feet."

Ramil's cheeks flushed. He hoped Tashi had not heard. She had her face buried in the silky coat of a red setter. He thought her choice of company was better than his, snuffles from that snout far more appealing than kisses from the Inkar.

The entertainers entered with the Midwinter cake. They scattered among the tables, performing to those who called them over. Ramil was not surprised to see some familiar faces. The acrobats from Orboyd's circus flip-flopped down the central aisle; Minka perched on the benches telling fortunes to fresh-faced soldiers and hopeful girls; Gordoc arm-wrestled with all challengers and bent iron bars on demand, making short work of the thickest metal.

Ramil used the distraction provided by the circus folk to leave his place and crouch down beside Tashi.

"Midwinter cheer, Princess," he said softly.

She looked up to return the wish but found she couldn't. Instead, she shook her head.

He shifted one of the dogs to sit down. "At home, we celebrate with a hunt in the forest, followed by story-telling and songs in the hall. I tell my good jokes and everyone laughs. My father tells his bad jokes and every-one still laughs. Privilege of being king, I suppose."

He saw a smile flicker on her lips, then fade. Encouraged, he continued.

"My sister gets really excited about the presents. Did you meet her? She's like me but well behaved. Anyway, this year she was getting a pony from Father and me. I hope he remembers to give it to her—I chose it myself." He frowned for a moment, wondering what kind of Midwinter they would be having in Falburg palace. "The best part comes at midnight when we put out all the lights and fires all over the palace as a sign that the old year has died. The king snuffs out the last one—it's very dramatic as we all wait in darkness. Then I get to light the first candle of the new year. The flame is passed from person to person, put to every hearth in the palace, so we all share that one light and hope." He paused, finding his throat strangely constricted. He'd been trying to cheer her up, but succeeded in making himself acutely homesick.

Tashi stroked the setter. "In the Blue Crescent Islands we have a special ritual for New Year's day," she said, picking up his theme. "We release pigeons at dawn to take messages to all the noble houses around the islands. When I was still at home, before I was a princess, I used to love it when our bird arrived. You couldn't start the feast and the music until it came and we all got very hungry waiting. Kai's a long way from Rama so we were always the last to eat."

Ramil smiled. "And what was the message?"

"It's always a special poem, a mada. It must have four lines and four-eight syllables. We hold a competition each winter and the best one is chosen for the New Year. It's usually in praise of the Mother." Tashi's brief pleasure at the memory soured on the mention of the Goddess. "I don't know what they'll do this time. It's the role of the Fourth Crown Princess to select the winner. See, I got all the vital jobs." She combed her fingers through the setter's ears, picking out a burr and throwing it aside. "I don't suppose they're missing me; they'll just rewrite a few rituals and carry on. They'll probably start looking for a new candidate to take my place when they hear how I've betrayed them."

Ramil didn't like this new tone in her voice. "You haven't betrayed them, Tashi. You've been strong. You're resisting Fergox the only way you can."

"But I can't defend the Goddess anymore—I'm not

worthy. I wanted that woman to kill me yesterday, did you know that? I'm a joke—just a goat girl made into a princess by a warlord. It doesn't matter what happens to me now. I couldn't go back to being the Fourth Crown Princess even if I do get out of here, not now that I know what I am." She stared down at the filth on the floor below the bruised rushes. "You'll stand a much better chance if you escape alone. You should go soon—go without me."

"No." Ramil covered her hand with his and gripped it. "I'm leaving tonight if I can, but you are coming with me."

She shook her head. "Do not throw away your one chance. I'm not worth it. The Mother has turned her face from me—I'll only bring you bad fortune."

"Don't say that: it's not true! Look, if you stay, Fergox will use you to overthrow your own government. Surely you can't let that happen? You'll eventually be forced to become his fifth wife. Do you really want that?"

"Of course I don't. But as I seem to be cursed, maybe I'll bring a curse upon him." She sighed. "Ram, can't you see it doesn't matter anymore what I do, but you, you're still needed at home. You go. If my people are still there, tell them the truth. Let them rejoice that Fergox took me away before I could do any more damage to my country."

"No, I refuse that mission, Princess. See, you are still ordering me around like a ruler—it's in you, it's what you are meant to be, no matter what others are telling you. I've given my word that I'll only escape with you by my side. So forget about yourself for a moment: if you care anything about me, about the fate of my country and yours, you are coming with me or I don't go."

"But, Ram—"

"You've got my little horse still?"

She nodded.

"I believe that in the Islands it is understood that when you accepted it, you took responsibility for my soul. I'm holding you to that, Tashi."

"You've been talking to my little penitent for a long while, Prince Ramil," called Fergox, throwing a bone to the dogs. "What are you discussing?"

"Midwinter customs, my lord," replied Ramil, letting go of her hand.

"And is it the custom in Gerfal for a prince to sit with the dogs?" Fergox filled his plate with more meat.

"No, sir," replied Ramil, rising from the floor. "It is our custom to have songs, stories, and dancing."

"Dancing!" Junis shoved back her chair with a scrape. "There's an idea for a cold winter's evening. Come, little Prince, teach me some Gerfalian dances."

Without waiting for an answer, she hooked Ramil by the elbow and marched him into the center of the room, snapping her fingers at the minstrels. "Play!" she barked, gripping Ramil in a bearlike hug.

Fergox chuckled and patted his knee. "Join me, Tashi. This will be most amusing. My sister has taken a liking to the Prince, poor lad. He'll soon wish they were back on the practice courts rather than on the dance floor—she'll do him more damage here than there." Tashi did not move to obey the summons. Fergox frowned. "Come here or do I have to drag you?"

She got up and perched uneasily on his knee.

"See, nothing to be afraid of, is there?" Fergox murmured, putting his arm around her waist. "I'm just wishing you Midwinter cheer." He kissed her hand. "Now, you wish me Midwinter cheer back."

"Midwinter cheer, sir."

"A cold greeting if ever I heard one. Never mind; next year, when we're seeing in the New Year together on Rama, celebrating the dawn of an enlightened age of worship of the supreme God, there'll be plenty of opportunity for warmth. You'll like that, won't you, Tashi? Of course you would: every woman desires to be wife to the most powerful man in the world!" He didn't wait for—or seem to require—an answer, so certain of his own irresistible attractions. "Off you go, back to your cell." Fergox pushed her up and signalled to the guard to take her away. "I can't have you sitting here all night or my people will think you've been hard at your spells again. My sister's already convinced you've bewitched me. Though it seems young Ramil has been the one charming her." He roared with laughter as the red-faced Ramil clumped by with Junis in his arms, attempting to teach her the steps of a dance. "Midwinter cheer, my little penitent!"

Chapter 9

R amil let Junis believe she had drunk him under the table.

"Another one, sweetheart?" the old woman crowed as he slid from his chair pretending to pass out. She poked her brother in the ribs. "A good boy but can't hold his drink!"

Fergox saw that his sister had reached the rowdy stage of drunkenness. Any moment now she would be picking fights with everyone, including him, or singing scurrilous songs that would make the toughest soldier blush.

"Come along, Junis, I'll see you to your bed," he said, getting up unsteadily. He only now realized how much wine he'd consumed. The boy had been very free with the jug.

"Can't I take him with me?" groaned the Inkar as she staggered to her feet.

"Leave him be. He'll not be happy tomorrow morning when he wakes. You can have him later if you still want him."

The brother and sister swayed off together through the mass of snoring, sprawling bodies slumped on and under the tables.

When they had gone, Ramil picked himself up cautiously. He stank of the wine he had slopped down his front but was stone-cold sober. He knew he had just missed a fate worse than death. The thought of spending the night with Junis was enough to make him foreswear the company of women forever.

He picked his way through the dregs of the festival to the big man sitting morosely by the fire.

"Gordoc, Midwinter cheer to you," Ramil murmured. He hoped he would find the strong man sober enough for the task he had in mind for him.

Gordoc raised his sad grey eyes to Ramil's face. The Prince felt a twinge of conscience: should he ask the man to help him when in all likelihood he would suffer for it?

"Prince, Midwinter cheer to you," Gordoc said in a very uncheerful voice. There was no trace of drink about him. It appeared he had not been in the mood to participate in the festivities.

"Did you see the Princess?" Ramil probed gently.

"Aye, I saw her. They said they were going to look after her but she's hurting bad. I can tell." He tapped his chest. "She's hurting in there."

For a simple man, the giant had a very clear sight of people, thought Ramil.

"Yes, she's hurting—and it won't stop unless we get her out of here." Ramil paused. If Gordoc was going to give him away, this was the moment when he would call the guard. Instead, he gripped Ramil's arm.

"You can do it? You can save the Princess?"

Ramil nodded. "I can do it, but I'll need your help." He glanced around the room. No one was watching. The guards were distracted, flirting with some girls in the entrance. He would not find a better moment. "Come with me now. I need you to break the Princess out of her cell and get us a horse. Once that's done, I'll take her far, far away."

"You'll take her where she can be happy?" Gordoc rubbed his big hands through his wiry brown hair wearily.

"I hope so—I'll certainly try."

Coming to a decision, Gordoc stood up. "I don't understand about these wars and things. I'm a good Brigardian and they say you're my enemy, but you make more sense to me than my friends. Little girls should not be beaten by red-robed devils. They should be looked after—made to smile again. If you can do this, Prince Ramil, I will be in your debt."

Ramil tried to hush him. "Quiet now, we don't want the guards to hear us. Let me lean against you. Pretend you're helping me stagger out."

Gordoc did better than that. He slung the Prince over his shoulder and strode from the room. Ramil's guards looked up as they passed.

"Where're you going with him?" one asked, his arm around an attractive serving maid.

"Taking him to his bed on orders of the master," Gordoc replied.

The guard waved him on, more interested in the charms of his female companion than the snores of a drunken boy.

Once outside, Gordoc stamped over the snow-covered courtyard to the temple doors.

Ramil thumped his back. "Put me down!"

Gordoc dropped him at the entrance to the temple. It was deadly quiet inside. The smell of recent blood-shed hung in the air; a single light flickered on the altar throwing ghostly shadows on the icon of Holin.

"Who goes there?" challenged a guard.

Gordoc did not bother with a reply. He thumped the guard once on the head. The man crumpled like an unset jelly turned from its mold. There was no going back now. They had attacked a guard and would have to go through with this.

"She's down here!" Ramil whispered, leading the way to the crypt.

He could hear Gordoc's breath coming in quick, angry bursts. "They put my pretty underground?" he asked outraged. "With no sun, no light? Buried her with the dead?"

Ramil thought it wise to stoke up the man's indigna-tion. "And no blanket on these cold nights. Even Kosind the tiger has been treated better than the Princess."

They reached her cell door. The corridor was empty. Ramil tapped lightly.

"Tashi, it's time," he said.

They heard movements on the other side and a pale face appeared at the grate.

"Ram? And Gordoc, is that you?"

"Yes, my pretty. Stand back."

Tashi fled to the other end of the cell, guessing what was about to happen. Gordoc charged at the door and crashed into it with his shoulder. The door groaned, creaked, and on the third kick, burst open, the lock dangling from the splintered wood. Gordoc immediately entered and knelt before her.

"You're free. Run away now and be happy."

Tashi dropped to her knees and hugged him. Ramil realized he had never seen her willingly touch another person before—it was a huge gesture on her part.

"Gordoc, thank you. But you mustn't get into trouble. You must run too!"

She was right, thought Ramil, they couldn't leave the big man behind—he'd be identified by the guards and punished. That meant they would need at least two horses.

"Come, let's go," whispered Ramil. "Someone may have heard us."

The three fugitives ran down the corridor, through the silent temple and out into the courtyard. Gordoc held Tashi's hand, helping her up the stairs and then carrying her over the snowy ground so that her bare feet would not suffer. Ramil led them to the stables by a back way he had scouted through the servants' quarters, picking up his bundles from their hiding place as he did so.

"Right," he said in a low voice, pulling them into the

shadows by the stable doors. "This is where it gets difficult." He peeked out. Two guards stood on duty. They looked fed up but very sober, having had to miss the feast to do this task. "We've got to get past them."

"Difficult?" said Gordoc. "I think not."

Before Ramil could stop him, the big man had broken cover, making straight for the guards. They pointed their spears towards him.

"Midwinter cheer, my braves!" he bellowed, holding out his arms.

"Midwinter cheer," they replied uncertainly, glancing at each other.

"Bad luck to be on duty tonight," Gordoc called, sweeping them up in a brotherly embrace, an arm slung around each man's shoulders.

"Someone has to do it," said one, lowering his spear.

"Aye, we drew the short straw," added the other.

"That you did."

So swiftly that Ramil missed it, Gordoc clashed the two men's heads together. They ricocheted to the ground, out cold.

"Where do you want them, Prince?" Gordoc asked.

Ramil ran forward and pushed open the stable door. "In there," he said, pointing to an empty stall.

Gordoc picked up the two men and placed them carefully on the straw. He grinned at Ramil. "See, not so difficult."

Tashi crept into the stable and took Gordoc's hand again, seeming to find comfort in the giant's strength. Ramil quickly ran his eye over the horses on offer.

"Well, I suppose we might as well go for the best." Stepping up to Fergox's blue roan, he held out a hand and caressed the horse's nose. "Will you carry two, my friend?"

The stallion snorted, liking the sound and smell of this human. Ramil quickly opened the loose-box door and placed Fergox's best saddle on him. It was no time to worry about deepening their offense by stealing a horse and tack.

"And now for you, big man," Ramil said. "I think there's only one mount here that will carry you." He saddled the Inkar's grey warhorse, trained to carry a warrior in armor. "I hope you can ride."

Gordoc nodded. "I rode as a lad—until I got too big."

"That will have to do. We'll lead the horses out by the postern gate. It's the least heavily guarded. Follow me." He beckoned to the other two.

They paused at the corner of the stable block before coming into view of the gate.

"How are we going to get past these guards?" Tashi asked, shivering in the cold. "More Midwinter cheer?"

Ramil shook his head. "There are always at least six on the gate—two for the portcullis, two inside, and two outside. I'm afraid that trick won't work again. We need to get them together so no one has a chance to raise the alarm."

"How are we going to do that, Prince?" Gordoc asked in his not so very quiet whisper.

"I'm still thinking about it. To be honest, I'm surprised we've got this far."

Tashi smiled to herself. That was more like the Ramil she knew: slapdash, rushing in unprepared. The efficiency of his rescue had been impressive, but out of character.

"I think I can flush them out of their hiding places," Tashi said softly, remembering the scared looks she had always attracted as "the Blue Crescent witch."

Ramil chewed his lower lip, calculating how many he and Gordoc could take out between them. He had a sword borrowed from the practice courts. The giant needed no weapons but his hands. They had to fight six men while protecting the Princess and two horses— it was going to be tough. But he couldn't let her take the risk, even if she could do as she said. "No, it's too dangerous. Stay here," he ordered.

"Not as dangerous as being caught," she whispered.

Tashi slipped from Gordoc's side and stepped out into the open before Ramil could catch her. Raising her arms in front, she began running through the ritual of the fingerbowl in her own language. She kept her eyes fixed on the soldiers as she flicked imaginary water at them.

The men leapt to attention when they saw the black-robed figure drifting towards them.

"The witch!" one gasped. "How did she get out?"

Tashi moved on to the forty strokes of the silver brush, waving her hands from her hair and out to the soldiers.

A guard lowered his pike, jerking it in her direction as if she was a wild animal that he was trying to drive off. He was shaking in his boots. "She's spelling us! Get back, witch!" His companion panicked and thumped on the gate, summoning reinforcements. The two guards from the portcullis rushed through the postern, weapons levelled at the pale girl who was now twisting and turning in the steps known as the Dance of the Dragonfly, a favorite game of children in the islands.

"Dragonfly, dragonfly, dance over the pool. Dragonfly, dragonfly, catch me a fool!" she chanted, making the trapping motion that children used to pick the next "dragonfly" in the game. The men flinched back as if feeling a blow. Two more guards arrived from outside. One had an arrow already in his bow. He aimed at her, the point quivering in his terror. They didn't notice the giant creeping in the shadows behind them.

"Stop her!" the guard squeaked, but no one dared touch her. The archer lost his nerve and loosed his bowstring, the arrow embedding in her thigh. Tashi sank to the ground, clutching her leg. Before the soldiers could move to recapture her, there came a grunt of fury from the gateway and two guards fell to Gordoc's fists. Ramil attacked from the flank, running one man through and slicing the throat of the archer. Gordoc threw a fifth man against the wall, then punched the other one in the face before he could mount a defense. Ramil felt like vomiting as he saw the blood he had spilt splattered on the snow. He had never killed a man before, but he knew there was no time for squeamishness. He ran to quiet the horses as Gordoc picked up the Princess.

"We must ride quickly and see to her wound once

we are clear of the castle," Ramil said hoarsely. There was no point trying to hide the bodies: they would lose too much time and the bloodstained ground told its own story. He swung up into the saddle and took Tashi from Gordoc, settling her in front of him. Gordoc pushed open the gates and stood back to allow Ramil to gallop through first. He then mounted the Inkar's grey warhorse and spurred it on, looking like a grown man on a child's pony. Together they clattered down the cobbled road to the main gate.

"Make way!" Ramil shouted as guards stepped out into the road. "Messengers for the Spearthrower!" Most jumped back but one brighter man realized that something was amiss when he saw the fair-haired passenger. He swiped at Ramil with his spear, only to be kicked in the head by Gordoc. A horn sounded up in the citadel. With dread, Ramil knew they were galloping towards trouble at the main town gates. These were bound to be defended now that the alarm had been raised.

As he feared, a group of soldiers waited with drawn swords and pikes, the front row kneeling in the road to stop their flight. Ramil had not, however, reckoned on the warhorses. Trained for combat, the stallions kicked out and reared, fearless of the blades, stamping a way through the line of unfortunates who had been on duty. Gordoc reached from the saddle and lifted aside the heavy bar locking the gates from the inside. With a roar he hurled it at the reinforcements rushing from the guardhouse, knocking them over like ninepins.

The way clear before them, Ramil spurred his horse

onwards. The blue roan streaked down the road, taking them beyond bowshot from the wall. Heading north, the two horses ran towards the mountains for a mile, passing through the checkpoints before the sleepy soldiers had a chance to react. Horns and bells sounded in Felixholt as the garrison mobilized, soldiers shaken from their drunken stupor. Taking advantage of a quiet stretch in the trees, Ramil steered his horse off the road and took to the countryside, looping round to head south. He had long since decided that this was their only hope of escape. North was where Fergox would look for them and was where he was massing his troops. The warhorses plunged through the woods and broke out into open fields. Ramil could hear the snorts of the grey working hard to keep up so he knew Gordoc was still with them.

"Run, boy, run!" he urged his mount as the first flake fluttered from the sky.

The horses galloped on into the night, twin tracks in the white fields soon filled by the blessing of a heavy fall of snow.

Two hours later, Ramil judged they could risk a brief rest. Their steeds could not go much further at this pace, burdened as they were, and he was worried about Tashi. He could hear her breath coming in pained gasps as she pressed her hand to her wound to staunch the bleeding. He spotted a wooden barn situated quite far from a farmhouse. There were no lights—it seemed as if the inhabitants were asleep. It would have to do. Signalling to Gordoc, he directed his horse to slow to a walk.

"Can you hold yourself in the saddle, Tashi?" he whispered.

She nodded.

Throwing the reins to Gordoc, he slid off the horse and crept to the side of the barn. It was not unknown for farm workers to sleep in such buildings. He had to hope this farmer was kinder to his men in winter. He unbarred the door and peered inside. The smell of cows hit him: a whole herd was sheltering on the ground floor. Climbing up into the hayloft he paused, waiting for his eyes to adjust to the poor light. It was empty of inhabitants, apart from a cool-eyed owl up in the rafters. He returned quickly to his companions.

"All clear. We have about an hour or two, I guess, until the farmer stirs—longer maybe if they were celebrating Midwinter tonight. Let's see to the Princess and the horses."

The cows made no fuss as Ramil led the horses to their trough for a well-earned drink and a share of the fodder. Gordoc carried Tashi up to the hayloft and laid her on a pile of straw. Ramil joined him. They both looked down at Tashi who had her eyes closed, fighting the pain.

"And what was all that about, Your Highness?" Ramil muttered angrily as he assessed the wound. The arrow had passed through her robe and into the fleshy part of her leg. From the limited amount of blood, he guessed it had missed the major artery but it had done enough damage. He ripped the cloth away from the shaft. "I told you it was too dangerous but you had to dance around like that and scare us all!"

"You should've listened to him, my pretty," Gordoc said sorrowfully. He put the leather strap of his belt between her teeth for her to bite down. Ramil knew he was going to make the wound worse drawing out the arrowhead, but they could not leave it there to fester. Better to be quick.

Tashi cried out as he tugged the barbed points free; it hurt even more than when the arrow had first entered. Her leg began to bleed again. Ramil ripped up the black robe to put pressure on the wound, then bandaged it tightly. The sharp pain receded, leaving a dull insistent ache.

"Sloppy shot," Ramil remarked, able to smile now that the worst was over. "Hit nothing vital. And now I've ruined your robes, you'd better put these on." He pulled some warmer clothes out of his bundle: shirt, leggings, thick jacket and scarf. "Sorry I couldn't find any shoes your size, but there are some woollen socks that'll do while we ride."

Gordoc helped Tashi lift herself up so she could slip the leggings on under her robe, then the two men turned their backs as she changed into the shirt and jacket. The effort almost made her swoon as every movement reawakened the pain in her leg, but she knew it was worth it once she began to feel warmth. She lay back on the straw gratefully, covering herself with the remnants of the penitent's robe.

Ramil knelt beside her and brushed her hair off her forehead gently. His heart twisted with concern: she looked so pale and fragile. "Rest now, Your Highness. We've got to be gone before the sun's up."

Tashi nodded and fell immediately into a deep sleep, feeling safe for the first time in weeks.

Moving before dawn, the three travellers spent the rest of that day riding through the barren countryside of Brigard, steering due south. Ramil and Gordoc spoke only briefly, the attention of both devoted to putting as much distance between them and Felixholt as they could. Tashi said nothing at all, sunk far into herself, allowing the others to make decisions for her. Fortunately for Ramil, Gordoc knew the land around these parts well, having travelled them many times in the past with Orboyd's circus.

"We should make for the Fens," he advised. "It's a wild place. Fergox's rule is felt only weakly there. We'll be able to hide until she is fit to ride further."

They reached the outlying regions of the Fens by evening, entering a strange empty landscape with stands of tall bulrushes and networks of ditches, slow going for the horses. The wind cut through their clothes with a biting edge.

"We can't spend the night outside," Ramil told Gordoc. "Do you know somewhere we can stay?"

The big man wiped a droplet from his nose with his sleeve. "Aye. There's a windmill not far from here. The keeper used to let the circus stop in his yard. He may let us stay if we pay him well."

Ramil shook his head. "I've no money, and I doubt the priests left Tashi with any gold."

Gordoc chuckled and patted his pockets. "But I, young Prince, have my winnings from last night on me. You can thank the weak-armed soldiers of the Spearthrower for that."

The windmill sat at the head of a drainage ditch, a dark cross against the night sky, its purpose to pump the water from the low-lying fields reclaimed from the fens. The keeper was a surly man with a hunched back, shrivelled up like a blighted leaf. He greeted Gordoc but spared not a word for Ramil or Tashi, sensing they meant trouble.

"I don't want to know," he said, biting the coin. "You can stable your horses here tonight, eat and sleep under my roof, but you're to be gone by sun up. No names, no faces. If you're caught, you were never here."

After seeing to their horses, Ramil joined Tashi by the fire in the little room allocated to them. Gordoc was supping with the miller, feet up on the table. Ramil admired the strong man's ability to seize his chance to relax when it was offered. As for himself, he was still jumpy, expecting their pursuers to be knocking down the door at any moment.

"How's the leg?" he asked Tashi, passing her a bowl of bean soup and a hunk of bread.

"Fine," she said quietly.

"You've just had an arrow pulled out of your thigh and you say it's fine!" Ramil marvelled. Blue Crescent people were so understated, it beggared belief.

"All right, it hurts." Tashi put the soup aside untouched.

"You have to eat." Ramil took a spoonful of his own meal, his empty stomach growling.

"I'm not hungry."

"I don't care if you're hungry or not; you have to eat or you'll slow us down."

Tashi closed her eyes, refusing to listen to him. His restless energy and positive attitude dropped like a stone into her well of despair, causing a ripple before vanishing.

Ramil tapped her arm, annoyed by her passivity. "Look, I'm going to need some help here, Your Highness. I may have got you out of the castle, but we're still in the middle of Fergox's empire, hunted by all his troops by now."

"I told you to leave me behind."

"And I told you that I was going to rescue you." He now knew how the Inkar had felt; he wanted to shake Tashi himself. "Listen to me: you've been through a terrible ordeal. Fergox has meddled with your head, told you stuff that's not true, confused you. Are you going to believe what he said, or what you've spent your whole life trusting?"

Tashi shivered. "I can't explain it, Ram. I think I've lost my beliefs completely. My faith was like one of those bogs out there—I thought it was all green and pleasant until I tried trusting myself to it, then I fell through." She clutched her hands together in a tense, desperate knot. "I'm drowning."

Ramil, who had never stopped to ask himself what

he really believed, tried to imagine what it was like to be her, a person whose whole life had been governed by an acute sense of her Goddess. He guessed a little of the emptiness and the fear that Tashi was feeling. He thought he'd saved her from Fergox, but now he realized he'd only brought part of her with him. If he was to do his job properly, he would have to help her escape this too, unlikely though he was as a defender of the Blue Crescent faith.

"You think this just because he told you he bribed the priests?"

She nodded.

"Well, I've known for ages that he did that—the rumors have been around for years."

"Is that supposed to make me feel better?"

"No, it's supposed to make you realize that, once you were made into the Crown Princess, how you got there no longer mattered to everyone else."

"It matters to me—it will matter to my people."

Ramil ran his fingers through his hair in exasperation. "Look, I don't know very much about your faith but if it's anything like mine, I'd be wondering if the Supreme Being cannot use even a man like Fergox in his or her plans. You might be where you are now because your Goddess exploited the Spearthrower's greed. Maybe she wants you here."

Tashi opened her eyes. His dark gaze was fixed on her, full of compassion.

"Do you think that's true?" she whispered, hardly daring to allow herself to hope.

"Oh, Tashi, I don't know." Ramil rubbed his face, not feeling up to this deep discussion, though he knew it was vital. "I've never claimed to know what's true when it comes to the big questions of religion. I'm just an ignorant boor, remember."

She smiled at the reminder of her own rash words. Ramil felt an urge to kiss her sweet, sad lips, but instead reached out and took her hand.

"What I do know, Tashi, is that it is possible and preferable to the alternative explanation that Fergox is in control of all our destinies. And I suppose the only way to find out who is right is to live our lives as if we do have faith in our Father—or Mother in your case. It seems to me that in the end your Goddess and my God are two sides of the same Creator."

Tashi knew she had reached a turning point. She could continue on to despair, following the path pointed out to her by the Spearthrower, or she could listen to Ramil and walk the way of faith with nothing but hope to guide her. She knew which she wanted to choose, if only to spite Fergox. Not the most admirable reason, but it would have to do for now.

"Thank you, Ram. I take back what I said about your being ignorant. I think you are wiser than me."

"So you'll help us in this mad jaunt of ours through occupied lands, fleeing all the soldiers of the Empire?"

"I wouldn't miss it for the world," she said, picking up her bowl.

Chapter 10

The Fens in winter were a strange place, home to wild birds with eerie calls that sliced through the thick freezing mists curling off the water. The reeds were frosted white, pale ghosts of their green summer selves. The channels were edged with wafer-thin ice like lace on a lady's gown. Black eels could be glimpsed rolling in the muddy water beneath, their skins shining with an oily sheen. The riders had to pick their way through the paths, often trusting themselves to unsafe causeways and bridges as they headed deeper into the marshy lands. They saw only a few people, most of whom travelled by flat-bottomed boats, going about their secret business away from the highways of Fergox's empire. Wherever the three travellers could, they avoided being seen, hiding in the rushes until the waterpeople had passed. Finding shelter at night was the main problem as they had now gone beyond Gordoc's knowledge of these lands. After the mill, they had risked spending the dark hours in a fisherman's empty hut, horses and humans crowded together for warmth. The rotten hull of an upturned boat hosted them the third day from Felixholt, but by the fourth they were in the empty flats of the true Fens and were facing a night in the open.

Ramil looked down at the golden head of the girl sitting in front of him, who was wrapped in scarf, cloak, and his own arms, but still she shivered. He wondered if she would survive a cold night outside. Her wound was healing slowly and she winced with the pain any time she moved her leg. Luckily no fever had set in—perhaps it had been too cold for that.

"We'll stop early tonight," Ramil announced. "Build a shelter and a fire."

Gordoc nodded. "Aye, Ram. We have to keep her warm."

The level space between two stands of rushes offered as good a campsite as any they would find for miles. A willow tree wept in one corner forming a natural barrier against the snow falling gently from the sky. The clouds were iron grey like an old bruise.

Tashi accepted Gordoc's help to dismount. "I'll go and bathe my leg," she said, limping out of the clearing, carrying with her a broad strip of cloth.

"Don't go far!" warned Ramil.

"I won't—I can't," she called over her shoulder.

Together Ramil and Gordoc gathered some dead branches littering the space beneath the willow and began to build a fire. The horses stood patiently under the tree, cropping the meager winter grass that poked through the thin layer of snow. The blue roan shook his mane. Ramil looked up.

"What's the matter, Thunder?" he asked the horse. He'd given the stallion that name because his coat reminded Ramil of a stormy sky.

The stallion shifted his hooves, his twitching muscles betraying that he was nervous about something.

"I think there might be trouble," the Prince told Gordoc in a low voice. "Which way did Tashi go?"

Before the giant could answer, there was a shout from the eastern edge of the clearing. Five men leapt out of the rushes, whooping and wielding pikes. Ramil dived for his sword, still on the saddle, but was knocked back by a blow from the butt of a pike held by a tall red-haired man. He tumbled to the ground, a boot pressed to his throat. Gordoc was roaring with fury, hemmed in by four men prodding him with the points of their weapons like a wild bear baited by huntsmen.

"What are you doing in our lands?" demanded the red-haired leader. He and his fellow bandits were dressed in strange clothes, muddy brown and green like the landscape, allowing them to creep up unseen upon their prey.

"They must be spies!" snarled a swarthy man, jabbing Gordoc in the stomach.

"Those horses—and the saddles—that's imperial gear," announced a third, jerking his head at the two stallions.

"Speak!" barked the leader.

Ramil struggled onto his knees, nursing his chest where he had been struck.

"We stole them," he said, taking a guess that the Spearthrower's men were not welcome in this company.

"They lie," said the swarthy one. "They smell of Fergox and his thugs. They've got this far. We'll have to kill them or they'll take back news of us to the occupier."

"I fear you are right. Sorry, lads, but we live in dangerous times and it is better to be safe than sorry." The leader drew a knife from his belt and yanked Ramil back by the hair, exposing his throat to the blade.

Just then a stone sailed out of the rushes close to the river bank, hitting the red-haired man square on the forehead. He was felled like a tree put to the axe. A second stone followed, striking the swarthy man in the back. He yelled and sprang round, giving Gordoc a chance to grab him in a crushing hug. Ramil scrambled to his feet and drew his sword. Tashi limped out into the open, her cloth sling weighed down with another missile. The three remaining men retreated, holding their pikes out in front of them.

Ramil grinned at her in amazement. "I thought you didn't fight," he said, circling round to stand beside her.

"I don't fight for the Warmonger, but I'll fight for my friends," she replied, swinging her sling with intent. "You learn a thing or two as a goat girl."

"Thank the Mother for that." Ramil turned his attention back to the red-haired man who was coming round. He placed the point of his sword at the man's throat.

"Now, let's start again, shall we?" he said politely. "We're not from Fergox—not in the sense you mean. In fact, we are even less anxious than you to meet with his spies or his soldiers. We were just intending to make a peaceful camp and go on our way before you rudely interrupted us. Now it seems only fair that you tell us who you are and why you felt obliged to slit our throats without giving us a fair hearing?"

The red-haired man groaned and sat up. He then noticed the girl with her long fair hair and immediately cringed away.

"The witch!" he cried, touching two fingers to his forehead to ward off evil.

Tashi felt a flash of annoyance. "Let's not start all that again!" she said tartly. "I'm not a witch. I'm just a foreigner with different colored hair who speaks another language. I didn't strike you down with a spell. I hit you with a stone picked up from the riverbank. You should know because you can feel the lump it left on your thick skull!"

The man shuffled back a pace on all fours. "But you escaped from Felixholt by witchcraft, they say."

"I escaped thanks to the cunning and strength of my friends and a bit of play-acting on my part." She walked off to the edge of the clearing in disgust. "I hate Easterners," she muttered to the horses, burying her head in Thunder's mane.

Ramil smiled at the haughty back of the Princess Taoshira, relieved that she had regained some of her spirit. "But at least you will believe us when we say we do not wish to place ourselves in Fergox's tender loving care again as we've taken so much trouble to escape. Now you know who we are, tell us who you are."

The red-haired leader raised his hands in a gesture of surrender. "I'm Melletin Fernson. You've run into a patrol of the Fenland Resistance."

"Resistance? To the occupation by Holt?"

"That's right. The last unconquered corner. Fergox does not yet hold sway over this part of Brigard, though he likes to claim it is all his. We only cling on here because he doesn't know too much about us. That's why we were going to silence you."

Ramil let the euphemism for killing him pass. There would be time enough to settle that score if things went well. He lowered his sword. "Then, friend Melletin, we are on the same side. I am Prince Ramil ac Burinholt, this is the Blue Crescent Princess you've heard about, and the giant there squeezing that unpleasant fellow to death is our loyal friend, Gordoc Ironfist. Hey, Gordoc!" Ramil called. "You'd better let him go."

The swarthy man dropped to the ground, gasping for air.

"Now the niceties of introductions are over, perhaps you would be so kind as to conduct us to some shelter. The lady here has been wounded and could do with a proper healer, if you know one." Ramil held out a hand to pull Melletin to his feet.

Melletin rubbed his forehead. "She's not the only one. I can take you to our camp. But I'm afraid we cannot offer luxuries fitted to a prince."

"My friend, last night I slept in a boat, the night before that in a hovel, so I'm sure whatever you have will be an improvement."

Following in the footsteps of Melletin and his band, Ramil and Gordoc led the horses with Tashi mounted on Thunder. They travelled deeper into the Fens. It was easy to see how the resistance might be able to survive out in these wilds. No army could march through on this boggy ground in formation and it would be relatively easy to pick off the enemy's forces in swift raids from the rushes. Hundreds of men could simply be made to disappear and no one would ever know their fate. Even the Spearthrower's favorite subduing tactic of slash and burn would not work here where there was more water than fuel for fires.

They arrived at the camp at dusk. Tashi was relieved to see that it was a more substantial place than she had anticipated, consisting of semi-permanent domed tents made from hides stretched over bent poles. Each dwelling had its own chimney and garden plot. Melletin led them to his tent, one of the largest in the settlement.

"Please enter and take your rest. I must report our arrival to my commander and seek approval for my decision to bring you here. I'll also send a doctor for the lady." He gave Tashi a wary look, but whether that was because he still thought her a witch or because he remembered her skill with the sling, she didn't know.

Tashi was left alone in the tent while Ramil and Gordoc saw to the horses. She stretched out with a sigh of pleasure on the cushions spread on the cheerful home-woven rugs. The tent smelt of fresh rushes on the floor and wood smoke. Melletin's things were spread around untidily. There was a neat little stove in the center with a pipe leading outside. Tashi held her chilblained hands up to the warmth, feeling them tingle as they defrosted.

She heard a polite cough at the door. Tashi turned to find a man with long white hair and a neatly trimmed beard waiting for permission to enter.

"Please come in," she said, half-rising.

"No, no, don't get up," said the man briskly, plumping his bag down on the floor beside her. "I'd be a poor doctor if I made my injured patients leap to their feet on my arrival."

"The wound's not so bad now."

"Let me be the judge of that, young lady," the doctor said sternly. "Now let's have a look at it."

Shyly, Tashi drew aside her clothing. Alert to her embarrassment, the doctor began talking again to take her mind away from his examination.

"My name is Norling, Professor Tadex Norling, formerly of the University of Molinder, our old capital, now chief medical officer of the new capital of all true Brigardians, fondly known as Fenbog."

"I'm honored, sir, to have your attention," Tashi said, guessing that this was quite a comedown for the august professor of medicine.

"God in his wisdom has seen fit to return me to my professional roots. Who am I to argue with Him?" He unwound her makeshift bandage and gave a disgruntled hum. The wound was still oozing blood and clearly giving the patient much pain.

"What did this and when?"

"An arrow, four days ago."

"I suppose some fool ripped the head out without waiting to have it removed properly?"

"We were in something of a hurry to avoid more of these in our backs."

"Humph. You're lucky you came to me. It should have been stitched immediately, but I'll do my best. I'm afraid you'll have a scar for the rest of your life."

"Small price to pay, sir, for what I avoided in running away."

The doctor threaded a needle he took from a clean pack. "And what was that?"

"An unhappy marriage—"

He gave a world-weary sigh. "There're plenty of those, my dear."

"To Fergox Spearthrower."

"In that case, you got off very lightly indeed." He glanced up at his patient. "This will hurt, I'm afraid."

The doctor was impressed: she uttered not a moan as he stitched the wound.

"Good girl. You only needed four," he announced, snapping the thread.

"Only four. That's very auspicious," she said dryly. "Thank you."

"I'll remove them in a few days. Keep the wound clean and let me know if anything changes."

"Yes, Doctor."

He looked her over again, noting her thinness and signs of recent ill treatment. "I'd say what you need most is rest and good food."

"I like that prescription."

"I don't suppose you want to say where you got those?" He pointed to the bruises on her arms, legs, and chest. He leant closer. "If the men you are with have been violent towards you, I can help. We have laws against that kind of thing here."

Tashi gave a strained hiccup of laughter. "You are very kind. No, my companions have treated me with the greatest possible respect and tenderness. I got these because I'm a witch, apparently, and wouldn't fight the priests of Holin."

Professor Norling sat back on his heels and tutted. "Disgraceful. Sometimes I despair of my fellow countrymen. Their minds are nests breeding superstition and fear. I have a salve that will help those heal. Rub it on twice a day and they'll be gone by tomorrow night."

Melletin returned with Ramil and Gordoc.

"I apologize, my lady, but the commander deems it necessary to see you immediately," he said.

Professor Norling shook his head. "My patient needs rest. She certainly shouldn't go traipsing around the camp: I've just this moment finished stitching her up!"

Melletin grimaced. "Perhaps you might like to explain that to the commander. Rather you than me, Professor."

"How is she?" Ramil asked anxiously.

"She would be much better if some idiot hadn't torn out the arrow," Norling replied, throwing his equipment back into his bag. Ramil looked abashed. "But she'll do very well now as she's fortunate enough to have the best doctor in Brigard to look after her."

"And the most modest," Tashi slipped in, keeping her face straight.

"I'll carry her to this commander of yours," said Gordoc, cutting through the difficulties with his usual clear-sightedness. He wrapped Tashi in a blanket and picked her up. "Lead on."

Melletin guided them through the maze of wooden pathways connecting the camp. The ground was so wet it would soon turn into a quagmire without the boards, he explained. Professor Norling tagged along behind the party, still muttering about doctors never being listened to or respected in this uncivilized hole.

The commander resided in a tent double the size of the others, divided into several rooms. Melletin showed them into the first of these, the public area, and then disappeared through a flap to inform his leader of their arrival. Ramil began to feel nervous. It was all very well persuading a patrol by force to take them in, but how would the commander look upon their presence? It surely wouldn't have escaped his attention that Fergox would be ripping Brigard apart to find the two fugitives.

A man of medium height and heavy build pushed the flap aside and strode into the room. Dressed smartly in the same green and brown colors of his patrol, he had curly dark-red hair and a hooked nose. No one could look into his face and make the mistake that here was a man to mess with. He gave a perfunctory bow.

"Prince Ramil ac Burinholt, Princess Taoshira, welcome to Brigard," he said, taking a chair behind a table. "Please be seated." Melletin came in with some camp stools and set them on the rugs in front of the commander's desk.

Professor Norling bustled forward. "Your Grace, my patient cannot perch on that thing. She needs a proper chair at the very least."

The man rose and picked up his own chair, bringing it round to Tashi.

"Will that do, Tadex?" he asked, taking a stool for himself.

Norling nodded and retired with his professional dignity intact to the pile of cushions at the side of the chamber. Gordoc placed Tashi in the chair, then stood behind her, arms folded.

"Thank you for your welcome, sir," said Ramil, taking his seat. "May we know who addresses us?"

"I am Nerul ac Mollinder, the Duke of Brigard, one of the last surviving members of the ruling family."

Ramil stood up and bowed. "Your Grace, I am honored to meet you. We thought your family had been wiped out by the Spearthrower."

Nerul spat at the mention of Fergox. "The last duke, my uncle, and his sons were killed in battle. My mother and father were hanged on the battlements of our castle in Mollinder when the occupier rode in to enjoy his triumph. The rest of my relatives are either dead or slaves. Only my brother and I slipped through the net like two of our fenland eels."

"I grieve for the old duke and your family. My father always spoke most highly of him," said Ramil.

A slim red-haired man entered from the private quarters carrying a roll of parchment. From the strong resemblance between the two men, Ramil guessed this was the younger brother, but whereas Nerul gave the impression of authority and strength, this man was handsome and elegant, his movements graceful—the courtier to the commander.

"My brother, Merl ac Mollinder," Nerul said in a businesslike tone.

Merl bowed, inspecting the newcomers. He gave Ramil and Gordoc a brief glance, but his gaze lingered on the Princess. Tashi lowered her eyes, not liking his frank interest.

"So, against the odds, you escaped the Spearthrower and stole his and the she-wolf's warhorses," Nerul said, his fingers laced together on the desk. "My spies carry all sorts of incredible tales about the pair of you—and your giant." He nodded at Gordoc. "You will not be surprised to hear that Fergox and his sister are none too pleased. I understand that before you said your farewells to him, you were both destined in your different ways to join the Spearthrower dynasty."

Ramil nodded. "Therefore you will understand why we were so anxious to put some distance between us and our suitors."

"Quite. But what of the Princess here? You are very quiet, Your Highness."

"I have nothing to say, Your Grace," Tashi replied, still feeling Merl's gaze on her. Each time she glanced up, he was watching her with a strange look in

his eyes. Not fear, thank the Goddess, but specula-
tion.

"My spies tell me you endured the ungentle persua-
sion of the priests of Holin and refused to convert. The
townsfolk are convinced you have demonic powers
and that the escape was down to your evil arts," Nerul
said, examining her face for her reaction.

"Then the townsfolk are gullible fools." Tashi folded
her hands together, taking the demure stance of the
Fourth Crown Princess in the Hall of the Floating Lily.

"But it is useful to Fergox for them to believe this as it
makes his lapse in security less glaring. He wants no hint
of weakness about his rule. He argues that no one can
protect themselves against a demon on horseback." Nerul
drummed his fingers on the table. The girl gave nothing
away. "He has vowed to burn you at the stake in the town
square when he catches you, you know, Princess."

"At least he no longer wishes to marry me. I should
be thankful for small mercies."

Nerul frowned. "But what should I do with the pair
of you, that is the question. If Fergox gets wind of you
being here, he will no longer ignore our presence in
this damp corner of his world. He has written us off as
too difficult, content to box us in and cut off our lines
of communication when and where he can, but with
you here, that all might change."

"There is a hundred thousand herald reward for
your recapture, Princess," Merl added in his soft,
smooth voice. "Only fifty thousand for you, Prince,
I'm afraid."

"I'm deeply offended," muttered Ramil, trying to catch Tashi's eye and make her smile. He was less worried now that he'd met Nerul as he felt certain that here was an honorable man. Whatever Nerul decided about them, it would not be to betray them to the enemy.

Nerul stopped drumming, having come to a decision. "Your arrival here is obviously a problem for us, but I would prefer to see it as an opportunity. I have before me representatives of the last two free nations— the next targets on Fergox's list. Before you sits the head of a resistance movement that spreads far beyond this sorry-looking bog. I have relations with similar groups throughout the Empire, even in Fergox's capital, Tigral. Fergox thinks he is invincible. He keeps on expanding his rule but forgets about the people he has walked over. His slaves are so badly treated they have little to lose and much to gain if they were to rise. We will not remain crushed by his war machine, but we need arms and allies. Together we may be able to knock him from his throne once and for all."

Ramil had no hesitation. "I know I speak for my father when I say that any assistance we can offer your resistance will be yours for the asking. All I need is a method of communicating with him and I am sure he will fulfill my words with deeds."

Nerul turned to the Blue Crescent Islander. "Princess?"

"Your Grace, you will know that I share the rule of my lands with my sisters so am not empowered to undertake alliances without their agreement," Tashi said formally. "Also my current status is under question since my abduction. I have no idea what steps have been taken either to restore me or to replace me."

"Perhaps I can help you there," Nerul said. "I have an excellent source in King Lagan's court who keeps me well informed. The Blue Crescent were going to declare war on Gerfal but were convinced by King Lagan that he was innocent in the matter of your abduction. The Princess Briony is guest on your ships as a pledge of good faith. But as to what is happening in your court at home, I have no idea, I'm afraid. I have insufficient funds to buy information from an Islander and I have never yet succeeded in placing one of my own spies on Rama, more's the pity."

"No, that would be difficult," Tashi said, allowing herself a small smile of satisfaction. It was very hard indeed to imagine an Easterner successfully infiltrating the court, not least because they would look like a duck among swans and be caught out at the first ritual. "If I am still recognized as the Fourth Crown Princess, I promise I will ask my sisters to look favorably on your request."

"We could use your help at sea. That has always been our weak point. No rebellion can survive starved of supplies. Speaking of which, I have been most deficient as a host. You have not eaten or drunk anything since your arrival and we must repair the oversight. Come with me. We were about to have supper and it's already laid in the room beyond."

As they relaxed after the meal with a glass of wine and a handful of hazelnuts, Nerul looked thoughtfully at Tashi.

"I think, Princess, that we should best keep it a secret that you have joined us—secret from our own people, I mean. As you are no doubt all too aware, some of them entertain strange ideas about the Islanders and no one is above temptation. A hundred thousand heralds might test the loyalty of even my most faithful men." He looked over at Melletin, who with Professor Norling had joined them for supper. "Did you tell your men to keep their mouths shut?"

Melletin nodded. "I told them you would separate them from their manly pride if they squeaked so much as a word."

Nerul grinned. "That's the least I would do to them. And I trust everyone in this room knows how to keep a secret?"

Melletin and Norling murmured their assent.

"But won't they realize?" Tashi asked. "I don't exactly blend in." She gestured to her hair. No one in the East had such fair hair; the lightest color being a mousy brown.

"I'm afraid it will necessitate a disguise on your part, Princess. If you would consent to wear the clothes of one of our ladies, you could dye your hair. Professor, do you have something the lady could use?"

"Yes, yes, that's very simple. What color do you fancy?" Norling rifled through his bag.

"I suggest red," said Merl with a lingering look at Tashi. "Then we can say she is a distant cousin who has returned from her education abroad. This will both explain the accent and account for her escaping Fergox's purge."

"Then red it is. It will wash out, of course. I brewed it myself for our spies." Norling placed on the table a vial of dark liquid.

Merl snatched it up before Tashi could take it.

"As we cannot risk allowing a maid to see you as you are, perhaps you would allow me to assist you, Princess? We have a wash tent through here."

"I . . . er . . . I . . . " Tashi tried to think of a polite way of refusing.

"It is no trouble and I'm sure you understand the necessity of not being seen about camp as you are," Merl continued smoothly.

Ramil fumed as he watched Tashi being led further into the family rooms of the tent. Nerul gazed after the pair, his expression thoughtful.

"It seems my brother has taken a shine to our guest," he said, stretching his muscular arms above his head and yawning.

"The Princess Taoshira is . . . was my betrothed," Ramil said hotly.

Nerul gave him a sharp look. "Is or was?"

Ramil rubbed the back of his neck awkwardly. He no longer knew. "Our marriage plans were interrupted by our unexpected jaunt to Brigard."

"Oh? My sources tell me that she had called the alliance off just prior to her disappearance," Nerul said lightly. "It seems to me that the young lady is free to choose her own partner now."

Chapter 11

Merl ordered his servant to bring hot water and leave it outside the wash tent. Draping a towel over Tashi's shoulders, he poured a warm jugful over her hair, whisking it expertly from her neck and letting it drip into the basin. She wondered where he had learned the skill of washing a woman's hair but did not dare ask. Neither of them spoke as he massaged in some perfumed soap, his fingers lingering as they brushed the nape of her neck. Tashi felt goosebumps all down her spine and prayed that he would not notice her response to his touch. Rinsing the suds from her hair, he then applied the dye. The water turned orange-red in the bowl.

"The professor is an expert in dreaming up these disguises. A very useful ally," Merl said, breaking the silence as he wrapped a towel around her damp hair. "I'm in charge of our spy network in Mollinder and, thanks to the professor, we are able to give our agents a new appearance when needed. He even has a dye for skin to make you as dark as your friend, Prince Ramil, though I would hate to see that on you. Your skin is beautiful—the color of milk."

Tashi knew that her cheeks were definitely not the color of milk—more the color of raspberries. No man spoke to a woman like this in the Islands. Courting was done by the exchange of poetry and hints. Merl was about as subtle as a brass band.

"Too much flattery, sir," she replied, shifting to finger-dry her hair in front of the stove.

Merl took a comb and began to untangle her locks. "You cannot have too much flattery, Your Highness. I speak only the truth. I fear you have been neglected if you think my praise excessive. A beautiful woman should hear such words from all her admirers. There!" He stepped back. "Now all you need are some clothes. I have sent for some to be laid out for you in my chamber. Allow me to show you where that is."

He offered his arm and led her to his room. On the bed was a long green gown, scoop-necked in Eastern fashion.

"I'll leave you to change," he said, kissing her fingers.

Tashi slipped out of her shirt and pulled the gown over her head. It fell in a full skirt from her hips and was cinched by a belt embroidered with white lilies. She guessed it must have once belonged to one of the ladies of the ac Mollinder family. Pacing to the mirror, she presented herself for inspection, amazed and confused by the transformation. She was used to seeing herself in the many layers of the Blue Crescent robes; now she stood in a gown that clung to every curve of her body. Her neck felt exposed. She knew from Fergox's court that this was normal for a lady in these lands, but it made her self-conscious. And her hair: it now rippled over her shoulders, shining with a copper flame.

Merl coughed outside the door. "May I enter?"

"Yes, I'm ready," Tashi replied, though she felt far from prepared to meet anyone just yet.

Merl stood in the doorway and paused dramatically, holding out his hands.

"You are a vision of loveliness, Princess. You were beautiful in your rags; you are radiant in your riches. My little cousin indeed."

"I'm not sure," Tashi said, putting her hands to her cheeks. "It's not how an Islander would dress."

"Exactly. You're an honorary Brigardian now. Trust me, you will do very well."

He escorted her back to where the others were waiting.

"May I present her ladyship, the copper lily of the ac Mollinder family."

The men rose on her entrance, Ramil wide-eyed, Gordoc beaming proudly, but Nerul looked sad.

"It was my mother's dress," he said softly, leading her to a cushion beside him. "But I think she would be pleased to see you wearing it, cousin, as it becomes you so well."

Ramil was not pleased when Merl made the suggestion that the Princess, as suited her role as family member, be provided with quarters in the commander's tent.

"Surely you see, Prince, that it will be easier to hide your presence among us if we separate you?" Merl said smoothly. "We can say you are a mercenary soldier come from the southern desert. Our giant here is Brigardian so no one will wonder that he joined us."

As much as Ramil hated the idea of leaving Tashi to be sweet-talked by a man he had decided was an unbearable flirt, he could think of no sensible protest to raise against what was a sound plan.

"Will you be all right, Tashi?" Ramil asked, which was his way of enquiring if she minded being abandoned to Merl's assiduous attentions.

"I'll manage," she replied, amused by Ramil's sullen expression. She knew that Ramil had never desired her as a woman—he'd been quick enough to make his distaste plain back in Gerfal—so she thought he was being merely protective of her. That he might be jealous did not cross her mind.

"You clearly have ways of getting news from Gerfal, Your Grace," Tashi said, turning to her host. "Is it possible to pass a message to my people and to King Lagan to tell them we are safe?"

"There are Brigardian exiles in Falburg who keep me informed of court gossip," Nerul explained. "We have a number of ways of communicating but in winter most news comes via the fishing fleet as the mountain passes are closed. You can certainly send a message that way."

"And could we return by sea?" Ramil asked eagerly.

Nerul shook his head. "Your chances of success are slight. The Pirate Fleet searches every vessel and is being very thorough since your escape. Coded messages may pass where people cannot."

"Pehaps Prince Ramil might be able to hide himself amongst a crew?" suggested Merl. "But I'm afraid the Princess would stand out—there are no women on board those boats."

Ramil was not going to let the Brigardian noble separate him from Tashi so easily.

"I gave my word to the Princess that we would escape together so I will not abandon her in Brigard. If I did this, her people would probably declare war—and rightly so—as Gerfal is to blame for allowing her to be abducted in the first place. No, if we travel to Gerfal, we go together. But not by sea, it would seem."

"Not by sea," echoed Nerul. "But there is still much that can be done as we wait for word from your father. Fergox will not sit still while the snow falls. This is the time of preparation before he unleashes his forces. We should make that interval as difficult for him as possible."

"Upset Fergox?" Ramil lay back on his cushion and grinned. "I like the sound of that. Count me in."

Tashi felt at ease in the tent room that had been given over to her. For the first time in Brigard she was in a space both comfortable and simple. Her bed was a canvas stretched over poles, warm and soft with ample cushions and sweet-smelling blankets. Hangings woven with golden flax and marsh flowers decorated the walls, making the chamber feel as if it belonged to this landscape, a hidden corner of the Fens. More dresses had been found for her and a fur-lined cloak, but best of all a pair of snug-fitting leather shoes.

Left alone to perform her rituals in the privacy of her room, she found new peace in saying the prayers. In prison, the rituals had become a distressing process which she forced herself to complete out of duty. Then had come the dark days of doubt, when every word felt like a curse upon her. Now trusting, as Ramil had suggested, that the Goddess's way still lay before her even if it was leading her down strange paths, she relaxed and lingered in the beauty and tranquillity of the ancient liturgy. She began to see new depths to the movements, understanding that the gestures were not just punctuations to the speech but prayers themselves, like a symbolic dance.

Sitting back after having completed the morning ritual, Tashi dwelt upon the lessons she was learning. Her experience of faith had not been so pure or simple since her hillside prayers as a child.

This must be good, she thought, *this must be what the Goddess is teaching me*. Remembering how she had fretted in the palace on Rama, burdened with the demands of her office, she could see herself far more clearly now that it had been taken away from her. She had tried so hard, too hard, to be what others expected her to be, that she had forgotten that the only one she had to please was the Goddess. And one thing Tashi now knew was that the Goddess did not care for the ritual but what was inside the heart of the believer who performed it.

"Thank you for the lesson, Mother," Tashi murmured, "but did you have to go to such extremes to teach me?"

No answer—but it was not an empty, angry silence like before in Fergox's prison. Nature continued calmly on its business outside, the reeds rustling, the wind whispering, and children laughing in the distance.

"I suppose that means that you had your reasons, Mother." Tashi concluded her prayer time by putting her palms together, then pushing them out and dropping her hands to her knees. She bowed low so that her forehead touched the rug. Opening her eyes, she found that she had not been so private as she thought. During her meditation, someone had placed a sprig of winter greenery on her pillow. Threaded through it was a thin gold chain with a tiny key on the end. Having seen this around the camp on flags and uniforms, Tashi guessed this was the ac Mollinder family symbol.

So was it a gift, or part of her disguise—perhaps both? Tashi stood before her mirror and fastened it around her neck. The chain was long, the charm disappearing down the front of her dress, resting on her breastbone.

Leaving her chamber in search of breakfast, Tashi found Merl waiting for her at the table. His eyes fell on the necklace and he gave a smile, making no comment.

"Now, fair cousin," Merl said when she had finished eating, "would you like me to show you the delights of our camp? That should occupy, oh, half an hour of your time."

"Thank you. I would like that. But I would also like to make myself useful. Is there any task I can do?"

Merl gave her his most brilliant smile. "I would like nothing better than to have you beside me as a help-mate. Indeed, I have much tedious work for the pen and you would free up a man for fighting if you would do this."

"Then that is settled. I will help you with your intelligence work."

"And now, for your tour of our little dukedom."

Merl proved to be an entertaining and informative guide. He showed her the armory and the forge where the smiths were hard at work, bare-chested in the freezing weather, hammering new blades and shoeing the resistance's horses. They stopped in the communal kitchens—tables under a pavilion and open-air stoves—to taste the bread offered by an apple-cheeked cook. At the school for the camp children, Professor Norling stood at the blackboard in front of the oldest pupils. Their math lesson was most unconventional as he had them working out the amount of explosive required to take out the supports of a local bridge.

"An interesting topic," Tashi remarked in a low voice.

"You should see the practical," Merl commented dryly as he led her away.

The last area he took her to was the stables. Outside, the fighters were honing their skills in armed and un-armed combat. Again Tashi was impressed to see women among the fighters. Her own army comprised half men and half women, but she had thought the Easterners did not allow their females into battle. She expressed this view to Merl.

He laughed. "That is true in normal times, but we are not a conventional army. Our women number among our best and most effective agents, getting into the houses of some of our key targets."

"You use them as assassins?" Tashi watched enviously as one dark-haired girl not much older than she was floored a man twice her size.

"Yes. They can also cause havoc in markets and barrack cookhouses, places where it is harder for a man to go unnoticed. And as messengers they are invaluable."

Tashi spotted Ramil among the men practicing with swords. He glanced once in their direction but then ignored them, redoubling his attack on the unfortunate man who had volunteered to be his partner.

"Ramil knows how to wield his blade," remarked Merl, watching him critically.

"Yes, he bested the Inkar in the practice courts. She thought him a match for Fergox," said Tashi, admiring the Prince's elegant pattern of strikes.

"He should perhaps ease up a little though," said Nerul, striding up behind them. "I do not want one of my best men in the infirmary." He bowed to Tashi. "Good morning, cousin."

"Good morning, Your Grace."

"I have a messenger leaving for the coast today if you would like to send word to your people. Merl here will show you our codes."

"Thank you."

Merl held out his arm. "Let us return to our desk, cousin, and I will induct you into the delights of the codebook."

The following days, Tashi spent much of her time with Merl, reading correspondence, summarizing reports for Nerul, and generally managing the information coming into the resistance headquarters from all over Brigard and beyond. Merl made sure she saw all communications concerning the search for her and Ramil. Fergox had despatched hunters over the surrounding areas, concentrating on the paths to the mountains and to the coast. He was reported to be increasingly frustrated by the lack of information or sign of his fugitives. The soldiers who had been on duty and survived the escape attempt were the least fortunate for they had been executed the following day and their bodies now hung on the battlements as a warning to others. Spies said that the Inkar Yellowtooth had killed a man on the practice courts in her fury at the loss of her favorite horse.

Tashi said a prayer for the soul of all those who died, even though they were her enemies. She hoped the Inkar's victim had not been her trainer who, though stern, had always been fair to her under the rules of his faith.

Sifting through the papers, Tashi began to enjoy her work, finding she had an aptitude for translating codes back into Common. Concentrating hard on a defined task like this took her mind off her precarious position and made her feel useful—a pleasant change from the last few months. She also expanded her knowledge of parts of the Empire to the south of Brigard: the warmer climes of the forested Kandar, the Inkar's domain given to her by her brother after his first conquest; the slave plantations of the lands around the Inland Sea and the heart of the Empire, the capital Tigral. She even read despatches from those who had travelled all the way to the edges of the Southern Desert, an ungovernable land inhabited by a nomadic people called the Horse Followers, the tribe from which Ramil's mother had come. They were no friends to Fergox, but kept themselves hidden in their desert, beyond the march of any army foolish enough to attempt to cross that waterless expanse. As yet, they stood apart from the resistance, wishing it well but considering it none of their business.

The only shadow over her days in Nerul's tent was the continuing campaign by Merl to win her favor. He was witty, kind, complimentary and Tashi was not impervious to the charm of being gently wooed by a handsome man. Yet she found it all very confusing, not certain of her own part in this game. In the Islands, his behavior would have been an affront; here it seemed that gifts and sweet-talking were an accepted part of life between men and women, not even necessarily meaning courtship. He presented her with a ribbon for her hair and tied it on himself; he caressed her fingers on handing her papers, leant over her as she worked so that his breath tickled her neck. He'd even once kissed her playfully to congratulate her on her first mistake-free translation. She had been stunned at the familiarity, wondering if she should protest, but he had moved on quickly to another subject as if it had all meant nothing. It was most perplexing.

After seven days of this treatment, she decided to go to her friends for advice. As Easterners, Ramil and Gordoc should be able to tell her how to respond to these approaches. She sought them out in Melletin's tent after dark one evening, taking care not to be seen by anyone as she crossed the camp. Her luck was in: they were alone, tending their weapons, checking straps and sharpening blades.

"May I come in?" she asked shyly, leaning on a walking stick.

Gordoc jumped up. "Princess, of course you may join Old Gordoc and Ram. We've been wondering what had become of you." He guided her to the cushions. "We thought you'd quite forgotten us."

She shook her head. "Of course I hadn't but it would look strange for a cousin of Nerul to spend too much time with mercenaries. I have my family's reputation to think of."

"How's the leg?" Ramil asked tersely, not looking at her.

Tashi thought his manner cold but put it down to their being affronted by her failure to call on them earlier. "Much better, thank you. The stitches have been taken out. I think I'm fit again, though Professor Norling still wants to cosset me a while longer."

"So what have you been doing closeted with Merl all week?" Ramil enquired, polishing his blade vigorously.

She raised an eyebrow. "How did you know about that?"

"The camp gossip. They're talking of how he's hardly left your side."

She rubbed her ankles, pulling her knees to her chest. "Actually, that is what I wanted to talk to you about."

"Oh, yes?" Ramil's tone was still hostile.

Tashi turned to Gordoc's more friendly face. "I'm a stranger to your ways and I wondered if you could tell me about . . . well, you know . . . how men and women treat each other here."

Ramil dropped his sword with a clatter. He grabbed it up again swiftly.

"What do you want to know, my pretty?" Gordoc asked, his expression one of puzzlement. "Do you want me to scare Merl off—thump him for you? Just tell him your Uncle Gordoc will have words with him if he offends you."

"No, no, I don't mean that." Tashi smiled. "He's not insulted me—at least, not by Eastern standards, I suppose." She wrinkled her nose.

"What's he done?" growled Ramil.

"Well, first there's the gifts—flowers and jewelry, mainly. What should I say when he gives me things?"

" 'Thank you' usually does the trick," said Gordoc

bluntly. "That's what the girls I know do. They put them away for a rainy day."

"So it doesn't mean anything if I accept them?"

"It means you are encouraging his attentions. Do you want to encourage him?" Ramil asked, mustering all his self-control. She was free to be romanced by whoever she liked, he reminded himself, though he really wanted to tell her to throw the gifts back at the red-haired, fox-faced flirt.

Tashi shrugged. Ramil now noticed she had a new chain around her neck—a costly one by the looks of it.

"I don't know." She sighed. "I want to be nice to him. I'm grateful for all that he's done for me."

"And what else has he done?" Ramil couldn't keep the suspicion from his voice, but Tashi did not seem to notice.

"Well, he pays me extravagant compliments all the time—"

"That usually means nothing," Ramil advised. "Not that they aren't deserved," he added hastily.

"Don't you start!" Tashi laughed. "But the thing that worries me most are his kisses."

"Kisses!" Ramil jumped up and strode to the other side of the room.

Tashi frowned. "Is that very shocking? I thought it might be but I wasn't sure."

"What kind of kisses?" Ramil sounded as if someone was strangling him.

"Oh, just light ones on my hands and neck a couple of times, once on my lips."

205

"And did you kiss him back?"

"Ram! Of course I didn't! What do you take me for? I just wasn't sure what was allowed and what wasn't. He always does it in a very respectful way."

"It's never respectful to kiss a girl on the lips, Tashi," Ramil warned her. "He's taking advantage of your ignorance."

Tashi bit her lip. "Oh."

"But if you like him, my pretty, it is not wrong to kiss," Gordoc said fairly, stretching out on the cushions with a reminiscent smile.

"It would be very wrong back at home. We never touch our admirers and only accept poems and paper flowers," Tashi told him.

"Kissing is nice. It's fun," Gordoc continued. "But you must not let him do any more unless you want to bed him."

"Gordoc!" Tashi was now blushing bright red, as was Ramil. "I didn't come here for that kind of advice."

Gordoc looked confused. He propped himself up on his elbow. "Where I come from, Tashi, men and women bed each other first, then wed when they have children. No one wants a barren wife. Merl may wish to find this out."

Tashi got up. "I'm not . . . that wasn't what I meant." She got up, fastening her cloak with clumsy fingers. "Forget I asked."

She limped out quickly. Gordoc raised an eyebrow at Ramil who was still standing on the other side of the tent.

"Did I say something wrong?" he asked.

Chapter 12

Lady Egret, a Brigardian noble in exile, begged an interview with King Lagan three weeks after Midwinter.

"Must I see her?" he asked Lord Taris with a groan, clearing a space on his desk for a new file of army reports.

"If it was any other Brigardian I would say no," replied the Prime Minister, "but Lady Egret is not one of the troublesome ones and has more sense in her little finger than most of them do in the whole of their bodies."

"I could do with some sense myself," mused the King. "We're facing an invincible army and an impossible fight and still I have absolutely no intention of surrendering. All right, send her in."

King Lagan rose to greet the tiny elderly noble who entered supporting herself on an ebony walking stick.

"Lady Egret, it is a pleasure to see you," he said in a kindly tone, directing her to a chair. "How can I help you?"

The old lady settled her black shawls comfortably and handed her stick to Lord Taris.

"I have a confession to make, Your Majesty," she said briskly.

"Oh?" King Lagan smiled. He could not imagine this grandmotherly person having anything very shocking to say.

"Yes, and you will not be pleased with me. It is time I outed myself as a spy."

"A spy?" exclaimed Lord Taris. "For who?"

"For whom, dear, whom," she corrected him. "For the resistance movement in Brigard, of course."

King Lagan relaxed. The resistance movement was no threat to Gerfal and he doubted very much she had been in a position to pass them any vital information.

"I'm afraid I've kept them abreast of all council deliberations thanks to my sources in the palace," she continued, oblivious to the reactions her words were causing in her two listeners. "That, of course, will cease from this moment. I hope from now on our coopera-tion will be frank and aboveboard, particularly when I give you this." She handed over a letter. "I received it this morning and only just decoded it."

Lagan took the paper in trembling fingers. "It's from Ramil," he said hoarsely, reading it through quickly. "He's escaped—as has the Princess—by Thorsin, I knew he had it in him!" He scanned it all the way to the bottom, absorbing the request for assistance for Duke Nerul. Overcome with joy and relief, he knelt, seized the old lady's hand and kissed it fervently. "Lady Egret, you are a jewel."

She smiled fondly at him and tapped his head with her finger. "Tush, tush, Your Majesty, you'll turn this poor woman's head if you go on in that fashion. Your boy's well, that's the main thing. He and the lass have given Fergox something to cry about, stealing his horse and everything." She chuckled. "The girl's sent a message to her people too. I will deliver it immediately." She cocked a quizzical eyebrow. "That's if you are not going to arrest me as a spy?"

"Arrest you, my dear lady? I want to marry you for bringing me that news!"

"Sorry, Your Majesty, but Lord Egret wouldn't be pleased if you did that." Smiling, she rose and walked out, her stick clicking on the marble tiles.

Lord Taris had now read the letter through.

"I take it, Your Majesty, we intend to help the resistance?" he asked.

"Absolutely, we are fighting the same war after all." Lagan smiled and stretched his arms, feeling one of his heaviest burdens had fallen from his shoulders. He no longer had to tiptoe around Fergox in fear of reprisals on his son. They now had a straight fight before them. Lagan rubbed his hands together, beginning to see all sorts of possibilities with Nerul's men behind enemy lines. "Find out what we can do, will you? Ramil mentions arms and support from the sea."

"We could do with Blue Crescent aid for this, sir,"

Taris said. "I wonder what Princess Taoshira has written in her communication."

"We should've asked the old girl. Track her down and see if she is at liberty to tell us, will you? At the very least, I hope it means I will get my Briony back again. I know, I'll hold a party for her—and take her on a pony ride—I think that will be quite in order, if I can be spared from my official duties for the afternoon."

"You're the King," Taris reminded him with a smile.

"But you're my conscience, Taris, you know that."

"Then your conscience says we should keep his highness's current location secret, but an announcement of his escape is most desirable. Therefore, a party is quite in order—if not essential—for the morale of the nation."

"Excellent. I really should promote you, old friend. Only trouble is, there's nowhere to go but down from your office."

"I am well aware of that, Your Majesty."

Lord Taris bowed and went out to spread the good news in the court.

The wagon train was making heavy going of the road from Tigral to the furthest corner of Fergox's empire where his armies were massing. The winter weather was no help, and the soldiers had experienced endless trouble: broken bridges, badly signposted crossroads, unexplained diversions, poor workmanship from farriers, causing the cart horses to shed their shoes a mile down the road. Anyone would think that the people of Brigard were trying to impede the work of the army. Surely they hadn't forgotten so quickly the war that had crushed them and the bloody public reprisals? The commander of the supply wagons made a mental note to suggest to Fergox that the populace be reminded forcefully that they were under occupation and should give all cooperation to their new masters.

"Can't wait to be back in Holt," complained the commander, riding his horse at the head of the procession. Twenty carts rumbled along behind him, full of food and arms for the Felixholt garrison. "Got a nice little girl tucked away in the Dovemarket at Tigral. She thinks soldiering is all fighting and heroics and don't believe me when I tell her it's grunt work for idiots."

His second-in-command riding beside him nodded as he chewed on a piece of dried meat stolen from the supplies.

"My boys are the same—all mad to be soldiers and won't listen to me," he remarked. "Still, we're nearly there now, sir. There're some good inns in Felixholt and the priests are allowing extra fights to the death in the Wargod's ceremonies—soldiers against prisoners. Should be worth seeing."

Just then the bridge on the road in front of them exploded in a cloud of dust and a deafening report. Fragments of wood and stone rained down on the soldiers. Horses screamed and reared in panic.

"Draw your swords!" yelled the commander, mastering his mount and galloping back down the line. His second was lying in the mud, struck through the eye by flying shrapnel.

Resistance fighters in green and brown emerged from the bushes on either side of the road. Arrows flew out of the trees, picking off the men in the wagon driving seats. Soldiers fell to pike and sword before they had time to raise their own weapons. The commander found himself face to face with a dark-skinned rebel on a fearsome warhorse, far superior in height and skill to his own. Their swords met but he knew within seconds he was out-classed. He felt fear, then pain, then nothing.

The fight was short and bloody. Nerul had instructed that they should take no prisoners and allow no one to escape to carry news of the attack to Felixholt. The supplies and men were simply to vanish from the road. Melletin took command of the wagons, ordering his men to roll them onto some rafts constructed for the purpose. They were quickly poled away by the watermen into the reeds, their stores to be used to supply the resistance and feed the needy people of the region. The heavy horses were led off to stables in out-of-the-way farms. The bodies of the enemy dead were stripped and then thrown into a pit some distance from the road for mass burial. It was ugly and brutal work. Ramil was revolted by the bloodshed but he knew it was necessary. These wagons were the lifeline of Fergox's army—an army that would kill all who stood in their way. As rider of the fastest horse, he and a handful of others were sent in pursuit of those who had fled. This felt particularly horrible work, cutting down men who were trying to escape. But if they carried word of the resistance to Fergox, the reprisals locally would be merciless as the population would rightly be assumed to be harboring enemies of the Empire.

The last man down, Ramil dismounted and vomited into the reeds. He would never again make the mistake of thinking that battle was glorious.

Tashi had known nothing about the raid. By the rules of the resistance, such things were kept strictly to those who were involved, so she was surprised to find Melletin's tent empty when she called by late that evening. She hadn't dared come back before now; her cheeks still flushed as she remembered Gordoc's ham-fisted attempt to advise her. She'd spent hours agonizing that Ramil would be thinking worse of her and finally could stand it no longer. She had to come and see him just to check that he was still her friend.

Finding no one at home, she decided to wait for a few minutes. She made herself comfortable by the stove, throwing on a couple more logs to warm the place up for the men when they returned.

"My pretty!" Gordoc stood in the doorway, beaming at her. He was wet and covered with mud and other stains, looking quite wild.

"Are you all right?" she asked anxiously.

"Yes, yes, just a little tussle out on the road. Nothing for you to worry about." Gordoc strode to a washstand and began to clean himself up. The water turned pink as he rinsed his hands.

Tashi got up to pour fresh water into the basin for him. "Where did you get hurt? I can't see a wound."

"Nor will you, Princess. I'm afraid that's not my blood but the other fellow's."

"Oh." Tashi tried not to think too much of what his great fists had just been doing. She'd seen him fight before, of course, but that had somehow felt different. "Where's Ramil?"

"Finishing up the job."

"You mean he's fighting too?"

"Like a tiger."

Tashi sat down to wait with Gordoc. An hour passed and the giant began to get restless. Tashi's mind was whirling, imagining all sorts of horrible fates for their friend. He could have been captured, killed, thrown from his horse in the dark . . .

The flap to the tent opened and Ramil stepped in, his face grim.

"Thank the Goddess!" Tashi exclaimed, rushing towards him. So relieved to see him alive and well, she wanted to hug him but was too shy to do so. She hovered awkwardly an arm's span from him.

"What are you doing here?" Ramil asked. He knew the words sounded ungracious, but she was the last person he wanted to see, sullied as he was by the deeds of that evening.

She stepped back, interpreting his mood as coolness towards her. "I just stayed to see that you were safe. I'll go now."

He caught the edge of her cloak as she passed. "No,

214

I don't mean it like that." He wanted to break down and cry on her shoulder, tell her how ugly and disgusting killing was, how men died hard deaths, calling for their loved ones, but he couldn't. He was doing it to protect her from all that. He couldn't tell her the truth.

But Tashi could see the misery in Ramil's face: it made her heart ache. She glanced up at Gordoc. The big man was tactfully retreating to the sleeping quarters, sensing that Ramil did not need an audience right now.

"What's the matter?" she asked softly, placing a hand on his arm.

His shoulders heaved in a racking sob.

"Oh, Ram." She pulled his head down towards her chest, allowing him bury his face and cry himself out. Then when the sobs had stopped, she let him rest there, gathering himself to face her.

He pushed her gently away. "I've made you all wet."

"It's no matter."

"I'm sorry."

"Don't apologize—and don't explain. I can imagine what you've seen—what you've had to do. There is no shame in grieving for the horrors of war."

Ramil collapsed onto the pillows, exhausted by the events of the day. Tashi refilled the basin and washed his face and hands with a cloth like a mother tending a feverish child. He watched her through half-closed lids, marvelling that anything so beautiful could be near him now and not be revolted. He noticed that he had left a smear of blood on her skin.

"Here." He took the cloth from her and reverently

wiped the stain from her collarbone, but then his fingers hooked the necklace. He lifted it clear of her bodice, the charm dangling between them. An ugly mood flooded him. "One of Merl's presents?" he asked bitterly.

Tashi nodded, blushing.

"I notice that he doesn't go on any of these raids. The duke's little brother stays tucked up in his office with you. I don't suppose he cries all over you, does he?" Ramil knew she had done nothing to deserve it—had shown him tenderness and compassion—but he couldn't stop himself. He felt so hurt, he wanted someone else to feel the pain too. "No, I remember, he kisses and caresses you." Tashi jerked back as if he had slapped her. The necklace snapped, the broken ends left dangling in his fist. "I'm sorry. I should never have said that. I'm all wrong tonight." He took her hand, poured the chain into her palm and closed her fingers upon it. "You should leave me."

"I don't understand you, Ram," Tashi said, close to tears herself. "What have I done to make you despise me?"

He shook his head, unable to answer. It wasn't what she'd done—it was what he had just done out on the road.

"I'm trying to fit in with your ways." Tashi rubbed her eyes with the back of her wrist. "But I don't know how to talk to you, or how to treat other men—every step I take is a mistake."

Ramil felt doubly wretched now that he'd made her cry. "No, Tashi: you're good and pure and innocent. You just make me feel ugly and twisted and dirty beside you. I only hope Merl deserves you."

Ramil got up and left the room before she had a chance to reply.

Ramil woke late and rolled out of his bed with a groan. He still felt depressed by the events of the night. Inspecting himself in the rusty mirror as he shaved, his eyes had a haunted look.

You only did what you had to do on the raid. What you need is some hard exercise—something to drive away this gloomy mood, he told his reflection. He lacked the courage to turn his thoughts to what he had said to Tashi.

He turned instead to the practice fields by the stables and began to warm up, stretching, jumping, running. A number of young soldiers were already lining up to take on the Southerner, as they called him. Ramil had become the new champion to beat, but today was not to be their lucky day as he was burning with anger, channelling it into ferocious swordsmanship. No bout lasted more than a few minutes.

Just as Ramil was taking a breather, Merl walked by leading a pretty white mare, Tashi mounted sidesaddle on its back. Ramil could see that she was listening intently as the Brigardian explained the use of the reins and bit. She didn't notice Ramil watching her. Merl made a joke and she laughed, patting the horse's neck. She looked relaxed and very pleased about something.

Gordoc arrived beside Ramil, spouting puffs of white breath into the bracing, cold air.

"Look at him!" Ramil said. "Now he's got her in the saddle, impressing her with his teaching skills!"

Gordoc stared at his friend and scratched his unshaven chin. "What is wrong with that? She looks happy. We want her to be happy, don't we?"

"Yes, but not with him."

Suddenly lots of things made sense to the giant. He put an arm around Ramil's shoulders.

"You are jealous, my friend."

"No I'm not."

"Yes, you are. You think that Merl is going to snatch her from under your nose."

"I'm just worried he'll take advantage of her. He's got a reputation around the camp for getting girls into trouble and you heard how naive Tashi is."

"You are not very good at lying, Ram. Your interest is not brotherly concern. You, my friend, are in love with her yourself."

"I'm what?"

"In love." Gordoc picked up a weight and began to exercise his bulging biceps. "But you make a terrible lover."

Ramil flushed. "Do I?"

"Yes, you confuse her," he continued. "You treat her coldly and make her feel in the wrong. You give no gifts. You haven't even tried to kiss her. Merl does it all much better. He makes his feelings plain. If you don't hurry up, he'll have tumbled her before you get a chance."

"I don't think she would allow anyone to tumble her, as you call it," muttered Ramil uncomfortably. "She is a lady."

"Well, I don't know much about ladies, but it seems to me they are girls all the same. I don't know any woman who could hold out long under that kind of attack." Gordoc nodded to Merl, who had now got his hand on Tashi's leg under the pretext of adjusting a strap.

"I'll kill him," growled Ramil.

"That would not be wise, my friend, as he is your ally in this war. If you are so worried about him, you should start your own campaign to win her affections. You cannot expect her to read your mind—she is no fortune-teller able to see into the secrets of men's hearts. You have to show her."

"And how do I do that?"

"Do you noble folk always make things so complicated? Is it not obvious what a man should do with the woman he loves? Mind you, if you try anything, as Tashi's protector I'll have to thump you." He grinned at Ramil. "No exceptions."

Ramil pondered Gordoc's advice and decided he should take it—apart from the last gem. He needed to open his counter-attack with something subtle—something she would appreciate. Then he remembered what she had said about courtship in the Islands consisting of poetry and paper flowers. With no paper at hand, he tried composing a poem in his head, but gave up when the only rhyme he could think of for "Tashi" was "ashy." Inspiration struck, however, when he passed some women weaving baskets out of reeds. He begged some materials and sat down among them. The weavers became interested in his experiments to fold the reeds into something resembling a flower. One of them took up the challenge and came up with a successful pattern, then taught it to him. They cackled and joked as he left them, wishing him well with his sweetheart.

Ramil reached Nerul's tent but found that the riders had not yet returned. He left the reed rose on her pillow and slipped away without being seen.

"I think you've made an excellent beginning," Merl complimented Tashi as he led the mare back to the stables. "Are you sure you've not ridden before?"

"We don't have horses on the Islands," she explained. "It is our custom to travel by water and ox-cart. I have ridden once before though. Prince Ramil was supposed to be teaching me."

"Oh yes, and what did he do?"

"Galloped me off into the forest—it was all too much too soon."

"How thoughtless." Merl held out his arms for her to dismount. "I hope you don't think that of me?"

Tashi tried to ignore the subtext to his remark. "No, you've been very patient." She slid down, but he did not step back, keeping his arms around her.

Merl tipped her chin up with his finger. "I've been more patient than you know, Tashi. Ever since I saw you, I've been wanting to do this." He bent down and kissed her long and hard on the mouth. She tried to push him away but he was crushing her to his body, curving her backwards. Tashi felt surprise, then panic, then fear. Finally, he let go.

"There, that wasn't so bad, was it?" he said lightly, running his hands over her waist and hips. "I know you've been wanting me to do that. All those smiles and pretty thank yous for my gifts and all the while a lover's kiss waiting at the corner of your lips to be collected."

"But I haven't . . . I didn't mean . . ." Tashi couldn't find the words, horrified that he could have taken her responses as encouragement. Part of her mind knew that she had every right to be outraged at the liberty he had taken, but somehow he had made it into her fault and her main feeling was now one of guilt. She had unintentionally led him on. Whatever he thought, she had to get away from him.

"I'm sorry if I have behaved inappropriately," she began, annoyed to find she sounded like a schoolgirl apologizing to a teacher for misbehavior.

He was watching her with an amused smile, still far too close.

"You must remember that I am a stranger to your ways," she whispered.

He took her hand and kissed the palm. "You are no stranger. I feel I know you very well, my darling."

"Please don't call me that."

"I'll call you whatever you wish." He was now kissing the tender skin on her forearm.

"Please don't, Merl. I can't accept these . . . these attentions. It's not right."

He let go of her, frowning. "Are you saying, Tashi, that you don't like me?" He tapped her on the nose. "I think you have been teasing me, little cousin. And you'll have to make it up to me sooner or later. Today I'll let you off. But I'll be back to collect the penalty." He leant forward and gave her another, more restrained kiss. "Don't forget: you owe me."

Tashi ran back to her room, tore off her cloak, and threw her shoes into the corner. Ramil had told her last night that she made him feel dirty; well, that was exactly the effect Merl had on her. She could not stomach the idea of spending another moment alone with him. No wonder Ramil couldn't bear to be with her! Collapsing on the bed, she heard something crunch beneath her. Feeling the pillow, she pulled out a battered rose made from reeds. A little plaited "R" hung from the bottom. Curling up and hugging the flower to her chest, she burst into tears, feeling very foreign and very confused.

Tashi's solution to the problem of Eastern men was to withdraw as far as possible into being the Fourth Crown Princess. She did not approach Ramil at all but walked with her eyes lowered as she went about the camp. She could not avoid Merl, but she maintained a strict distance, keeping her face impassive and her movements guarded. He seemed amused by her reaction and tried to thaw her new reserve but she ignored him, presenting her work on his desk with a wordless bow and spending most of her time in her room. She refused his invitation to take more riding lessons.

"The Princess isn't happy again," Gordoc remarked to Ramil, seeing her pass the entrance to their tent one day.

Ramil said nothing. He had noticed that this new behavior coincided with his attempt at a love token. He could only assume it was not welcome.

The first time he saw her properly was the evening when news from Gerfal finally arrived. Nerul summoned them to a council in his tent. Tashi kept them all waiting, making her entrance at the last moment in a sweep of skirts and an elegant bow. She sat on Nerul's chair as if it were a throne, her hands folded in her lap. Ramil raised an eyebrow at Gordoc. The big man was looking even more puzzled because he had never been treated to the full Princess Taoshira act before.

Nerul cleared his throat. "I have messages to deliver to you both, Your Highnesses. Your father, Prince, sends his warmest congratulations on your escape. He fully endorses your suggestion that Gerfal support the resistance and will be sending arms and supplies as soon as possible. He says you are at liberty to choose your own course from here on as he places full trust in you to decide in the best interests of your people."

Ramil smiled. He knew his father was sending a coded apology for having doubted his judgment in the autumn.

"And as for you, Princess Taoshira, you will not be surprised to learn that your people also rejoice at your freedom. The correspondent, one entitled the Etiquette Mistress, regrets that they are not empowered to offer full assistance to either us or Gerfal as this would be tantamount to a declaration of war on Fergox Spearthrower. That decision rests with all four Crown Princesses in concert. However, she takes into account your instructions to defend aggressively their ships presently at anchor in Falburg harbor." Nerul looked up. "By that, I guess, you have told them to protect the sea approach to the Gerfalian capital?"

Tashi nodded. "It was the best I could do on my own authority. They have rules of engagement to respond if attacked. Fergox cannot get past them without provoking my ships to open fire."

"That is very good. Unfortunately, it may not be enough. Foiled in his plan to force an alliance upon Gerfal by causing a war between your two countries, the Spearthrower has determined on a full assault on Gerfal as soon as the snows melt. King Lagan is aware of this and knows he faces an impossible defense without powerful allies. And I believe, Your Highness, one of your last acts before your abduction was to call the alliance off?"

The Fourth Crown Princess inclined her head. "Yes, I did."

Ramil looked down at his nails.

"Then Gerfal will fall and Fergox triumph once more." Nerul threw the letters on the desk in contempt.

In the silence that followed, Tashi felt everyone in the room was thinking that she was to blame for this. She even thought so herself. If she hadn't been so hasty to run away from marriage with Ramil, negotiations could have continued for their mutual self-defense. It was too late to call back the messenger bird. The only answer was to return to the Blue Crescent Islands herself and argue that the alliance should go ahead even without the marriage. She owed it to kindly King Lagan, to the people of Gerfal, to Ramil.

"I now regret my actions and will do all I can to repair them. I will return to my sisters and beg them to send our navy to aid you," Tashi said steadily, knowing what she was proposing was highly dangerous and probably impossible, but she had to do something. "I will leave immediately."

Merl crossed the floor and put a hand on her arm. "Tashi, Tashi, you can't possibly know what you are saying. You'll be caught—dragged off to Fergox again. We couldn't bear that—I couldn't bear that."

The Fourth Crown Princess brushed his hand off and froze him with her glare. "I am well aware of the risks, my lord. I am not a heedless girl to be told to sit quietly in a corner while others take action, but a ruler of my country with a responsibility to our friends and allies."

She turned to Nerul, knowing that he would understand this. "I am grateful for the shelter you have given me these past weeks, Your Grace, and would value your advice how best to proceed. To return home by the south means I will have to travel in lands strange to me. Perhaps your network will be able to assist?"

Nerul rose and bowed, impressed by the girl's determination. "I place it at your disposal, Princess."

"And obviously, I will accompany the Princess," Ramil said firmly. Tashi opened her mouth to protest but he continued, "If you do not let me travel with you, Princess, then I will follow. You will not deny that this political alliance concerns me closely. My father has left me to be my own judge and it is clear to me that I can best serve my country by ensuring your safe return to your court. I ask nothing else." He held her eye, his expression stubborn.

"And the Princess is going nowhere without me," said Gordoc, crossing his arms on his chest, daring her to refuse him.

The Fourth Crown Princess arched her fingers and pressed them to her lips, trying to stop her outward control from collapsing. They had just offered to follow her into mortal danger. But she knew that she stood a much better chance with them by her side so, though her instinct was to protect them, her duty was to accept.

"I thank Prince Ramil ac Burinholt and Gordoc Ironfist for their generous offer. I will leave tomorrow at dawn and would be grateful for their company." She rose and swept out of the room.

Merl followed her. He burst into her room without asking leave to enter. She had her back to him, head in her hands.

"Tashi, I thought we understood each other!" he appealed to her, grabbing her elbow to swing her round. "I want you to stay here with me—never to leave my side."

"Please do not touch me, Merl," she said, trying to pry his fingers off her arm. "I do not have the luxury of considering my own or your feelings on this subject."

He seized her other arm, holding her tightly. "You can't go. You'll be killed."

"It is my duty to try." She looked down, trying to prevent any of those signals that apparently so confused him.

Merl's handsome brow was pinched with concern. "Send a messenger—send Ramil. There is no sense in risking yourself. You are too precious—let others go in your place."

"I will not send others on a journey I would not undertake myself, least of all Prince Ramil. Only I can reinstate the alliance. Please let me go. You have no right to touch me like this. You're hurting me."

"I have the right of a lover who will not let his lady be parted from him." He bent forward, seeking her mouth, but she twisted away.

"I do not want you as a lover, sir. I have never wanted you. Let me go!"

Her cry brought an instant response. Before Merl could force a kiss on her, Gordoc was in the room and had him by the scruff of the neck.

"Even among us poor folk, your lordship, a lady's 'no' means 'no,'" Gordoc said, giving Merl a shake.

Nerul appeared at the tent flap, his expression furious. Ramil stood behind him, fists curled.

"Brother," barked Nerul, "you forget yourself and carry your intrigues too far. Under my roof, the Princess Taoshira is entitled to her privacy and certainly to be spared such ungentlemanly treatment. Leave her in peace."

Dumped on the floor, Merl straightened his clothes and stalked from the room.

Nerul turned back to Tashi. "Forgive us, Your Highness. Merl has over-reached himself. His concern for you is his only excuse."

Tashi collected her dignity. "And I ask your forgiveness for anything that I have done that may have prompted him to hope where there was none."

Nerul gave a crooked smile. "I fear you are too kind to Merl. I know my brother well. He is experienced at this game and doubtless had you swimming into his net. Your decision to depart does not suit him. He thinks first of his pleasure, rather than his responsibility to his people. However, unlike him, I see the necessity and would like to offer you all assistance. Is there anything you require? I will give orders for packs of supplies to be made up. You leave as you came with your two horses?"

"And a mount, if I may beg one for myself. I do not wish to be a burden on my companions."

"Consider it done. Anything else?"

Tashi held her arms out, displaying her finery. "I was once told that you needed suitable clothes to ride a horse. Would you be able to find me something more practical?"

"We should disguise ourselves," Ramil added, stepping forward to take part in the discussion. He had been silent during the scene with Merl, fiercely happy to see his rival rejected by Tashi. "I think it best if I maintain my character as a mercenary from the south. Perhaps the Princess may condescend to take the part of my sister and dress accordingly."

Tashi wondered since when Ramil had felt the need to ask her to "condescend" to anything, but his idea was a good one.

"I would be happy to, sir, if such dress can be found," she replied with equal formality.

"And Gordoc here, if he wouldn't mind the indignity, could travel as our slave bodyguard. The desert dwellers are known to keep slaves like most of the people in those parts."

"Mind?" rumbled the giant. "Old Gordoc's skin is too thick to take offense. I'll be your slave, master." He thumped Ramil on the back, making him stagger.

"I will see to the disguises," said Nerul. "I suggest you get your rest, that is if you keep to your intention to ride at first light?"

"I do," said Tashi. "Time is running out."

"I will send messages ahead of you. If you would care to eat with me before you leave, I will give you as much advice as I can, maps too if I can find some suitable."

"Thank you, Your Grace."

Tashi dismissed them all with a bow. The three men retired from the room.

No sooner had Gordoc got Ramil alone than he dug him in the ribs. "Now you should be happy, young pup: she sent him packing and you have her to yourself again, just like old times."

"This isn't about her and me, Gordoc. This is state business," Ramil said stiffly.

"Go on, admit that you're pleased." Gordoc whistled to the crescent moon cheerfully.

Ramil met his friend's grin and broke into a smile. "All right, I'm pleased. For some mad reason, I'd prefer to be heading into danger with Tashi than leaving her to sit anywhere within a mile of Merl ac Mollinder."

"I knew it." The giant chuckled. "I knew it!"

Chapter 13

Seamstresses worked through the night to make Tashi and Ramil the long flowing robes of the Southern people. Tashi woke to find hers hanging on the screen in her chamber—a loose purple gown with a veil that covered her face with only a gauze to allow her to see. It was designed for protection against the fierce sandstorms of the desert, but it suited her purposes perfectly here in the cold north. Wearing a pair of long leather gloves, she would be completely hidden.

Having completed her rituals, she arrived at breakfast to find the table more crowded than she had expected. In addition to Nerul, a chastened Merl, Ramil and Gordoc were Professor Norling, Melletin, and the dark-haired woman Tashi had once glimpsed on the practice fields. The men rose on her entrance. Nerul conducted her to the chair at his right hand.

"The robes are perfect," Tashi said, more like her old self than the formal Fourth Crown Princess of the last few days. "Please thank those who made them."

"My wife and her sisters were only too pleased to help." Professor Norling beamed.

Nerul passed Tashi a cup of hot kava. "I have given thought overnight to your travels and have some suggestions to make. The first is that you should take one of my people with you as a guide, at least for the part of the road that lies through Kandar. Melletin has volunteered. He says he owes you for the lesson you taught him on your first meeting."

Tashi furrowed her brow. "What lesson was that?"

Melletin grinned and touched his forehead. "To wear a helmet when attacking strangers."

Nerul smiled. "And if you would also accept the company of Yelena here, you will find she is most surprisingly accomplished in all matters regarding fighting."

Tashi remembered seeing the woman dump a much larger man in the dust so had no trouble believing him.

"I would be grateful to have the female companionship."

"And finally, our good professor has an errand in the Holtish capital, Tigral. If you would not mind including him in your party, it would save me sending another fighter away with him."

"Of course I would be delighted to have his company too, but would that not make our party suspiciously large?" asked Tashi.

Professor Norling shook his head. "I have thought of that, my dear. Melletin and Yelena will travel as man and wife, and will join us as chance acquaintances met on the road. That means it will be possible for them to travel ahead and check what lies before us where necessary. As for myself, I will be travelling on the invitation of the Horse Follower mercenary here to study medicine among his people." His eyes took on a distant longing. "Actually, that's something I've always wanted to do. It is a shame there is no time."

"No, Tadex," Nerul said with a fond look at the old man, "I need you to contact the network in Tigral. We have to know what steps Fergox is taking to protect his supply chain." He turned back to Tashi. "I thought this best because Fergox is still looking for you and knows that three are travelling together. Like this the pattern is confused. You can rearrange your party, arriving in different combinations at the settlements along the way, confusing any reports that might be sent back to him."

"I've also had my best students forge you some papers," Professor Norling added. "Passports and other supporting documents, that's if we meet a soldier able to read. Shocking lack of education throughout the Empire these days!" He subsided into a mutter of complaint.

"You seem to have thought of everything," said Tashi. "I am very grateful."

"Though I would wish to help you in any case, Your Highness," Nerul explained, "you are also an investment for us. If you can bring your country into this war now before it is too late for the East, then we might be able to turn the tide against Fergox and begin to reclaim our lands from him."

"I'll drink to that, Your Grace," Tashi replied, raising her cup to his.

The horses were saddled and ready for them outside the tent. Thunder was looking eager for the adventure and in excellent condition, well groomed and fed. The Inkar's warhorse, named Snowy by Gordoc, seemed more resigned, perhaps because he anticipated many weary miles carrying more weight than all the other mounts. Melletin's horse was a chestnut gelding, several hands smaller than the warhorses but matching them in fighting spirit. The mare Tashi had ridden was also waiting, as well as three more sturdy beasts, one loaded with the extra bags. From the cases of scientific instruments peeping out from among the food supplies, Tashi guessed that Professor Norling did not understand the concept of travelling light.

After the scene the night before, Tashi had not been expecting to escape without exchanging a few words with Merl, so she was prepared when he arrived at her side to help her mount.

"I apologize for my behavior yesterday," he said in a low voice. "I have suffered a sleepless night in bitter repentance."

"Then I forgive you, sir," Tashi replied, assuming her most regal air.

"I was serious when I said that I wanted you by my

side always. If our destiny allows us to meet again, I hope you will give me the opportunity to prove my sincerity."

Will he not take "no" for an answer? she wondered, secretly irritated by his persistence.

"Sir, I wish you and your brother all good fortune in your struggle, but do not look to such a time. I pray that you find your happiness here with someone else. I can offer you no hope."

"Then I will wait without hope, because I must."

With a final farewell to Nerul, the party headed out on the paths winding across the Fens. Tashi nudged her horse in line behind Melletin, trying not to think too much about what lay ahead, nor worry about the suitor she had left behind. Her inexperience as a rider helped as she spent so much time concentrating on her mare, Flake, that she forgot to fret. For some miles, they rode in silence through the freezing mist, each absorbed in his or her own thoughts. The cold was penetrating. Tashi had to keep flexing her fingers to stop them from turning to ice. Finally, Melletin signalled a halt in a clump of willows.

"This is a good spot—the last shelter before we reach the main north-south road."

Immediately, Ramil was at Tashi's stirrup to help her dismount but then walked back to tend to his own mount. Tashi chewed her lip, wondering how they could break this awkwardness between them. Before she could think of anything, Yelena came up to her and touched her discreetly on the shoulder.

"Your Highness, there's a place where you and I can go if you would like a private bush."

"Thank you." Tashi followed the Brigardian woman off the path and into the rushes. "But you must call me Tashi, Yelena," she called to the warrior's straight back.

The woman turned and grinned. Her front tooth was chipped, giving her a roguish look, and her blue eyes sparkled with mischief. "That's good. I was worried you were going to be all stuck-up and formal with me."

"No, that's only for the men," Tashi admitted, jumping over a streamlet.

Yelena yelped with laughter.

"I never feel more foreign than when trying to understand them," Tashi confessed.

"Join the rest of us, sister. They are strange creatures. No wonder your people put their women in charge. I've often thought things would've been different if men like Fergox had been kept in their place."

"Ah yes, but then you'd have women like the Inkar running things. She is formidable."

"True. I had forgot her." Yelena showed Tashi a clear place on the bank to wash. "But you speak as if you've seen her."

"I have. And Ramil even danced with her."

"You are joking?"

Yelena found the idea of this so hilarious that she roared with laughter and had trouble standing. She still had not calmed down when they returned to the men, causing the others to exchange quizzical looks.

"What's so funny, Yelena?" asked Melletin.

She shook her head, with not enough breath to string two words together.

"Women!" Ramil muttered to Gordoc, though his eyes were on Tashi who was caressing Flake with a secretive smile on her lips.

The travellers split up when they reached the main road. Melletin and Yelena were to scout ahead and ride back if there was trouble; otherwise they arranged to meet at the Yellow Dog, an inn on the border with Kandar.

"You have to be careful at the inn," Melletin warned. "The landlord is no friend to the resistance and a great enthusiast for the Empire. He's done very well by Fergox with all this traffic on the roads north."

"Is there nowhere else to stay?" Ramil asked.

"Why yes, indeed, but it is the last place Fergox's men would be looking for fugitives. If you brazen it out in the taproom there, they will hardly notice you. But ask for a private room for your giant and the lady. They will attract more attention and should keep out of the public areas. Yelena and I will fall in with you as if by chance. Professor Norling, I trust you will ensure they do not go astray?"

The professor flapped him away with his hand. "Of course, Melletin. I was travelling these roads before you were born."

The two fighters rode off on their hardy horses, urging them through the ice-covered ruts in the churned-up road. Tashi drew her veil over her face, now seeing the world through purple gauze. On the wider path, the four riders fell into pairs. Norling dropped behind with Gordoc and began to quiz him on his fitness regime, probing the secret of the man's exceptional strength. Ramil rode with Tashi, though he sat high above her, awkward for talking.

"Here, slacken the reins a little. Flake's mouth is tender and she's not comfortable," he said, noticing the mare fretting.

Tashi did as instructed, keeping her counsel behind the veil.

"You're doing well, for a beginner," he added, trying to strike upon a neutral subject.

"Yes, that is surprising, considering my teachers," she replied coolly.

Ramil believed himself reprimanded. They rode on in silence.

"I'm sorry about what I said to you the other night," he said at length, knowing the words had to be spoken sooner or later. "I should've realized that you and Merl weren't . . ."

"Yes?"

"Well, that you *weren't*."

"That is very well explained, Ram." She laughed. The sound made his stomach flip over. "And I'd like to thank you for the flower."

"Did you like it?" He wanted to ask if he had finally got something right.

"I'm afraid I sat on it." Her shoulders were shaking. He wondered for a moment what was so funny, then realized she was thinking of the dragonfly.

He joined in good-humoredly. "I'm afraid our love tokens are doomed."

That brought her up short. "Love token?" She glanced up at him, her eyes glinting through the veil.

He looked down at his hands. "Why? What did you think it was?"

"I didn't know. You'd just told me I made you feel bad."

"But you said that Blue Crescent men present them to their ladies."

"You listened to me? I mean, you were trying to be . . . ?" She floundered for a word.

"Sensitive. Yes, I, Ramil ac Burinholt, obviously well known for my cultural diplomacy, was attempting to be the ideal lover."

"But you don't like me . . . not like that!" Tashi protested. Her mind was trying to catch up with this new information. "Or are you merely trying to reopen negotiations on a marriage alliance?" she asked suspiciously. "Because if you are, I was going to argue with my sisters that they should offer our navy without that. I wouldn't want you to be yoked to someone you can't be happy with."

"Tashi, look at me."

"I am."

"But I can't see you through that veil."

"Then you'll just have to trust me."

Ramil smiled. "I wanted to give you the flower just as a boy would give a girl a present—not because you are a princess, or an ally, or for any of those reasons. It came with no conditions, no schemes, except perhaps the hope that you might like me just a little better."

"Then I accept it and thank you." Tashi felt a burst of happiness. She'd got it all wrong: he did like her.

"So what's next?" asked Ramil, feeling very pleased with himself.

"How do you mean?"

"What should a boy do now?"

"On the Islands, you'd write a poem in praise of my eyebrow," Tashi said teasingly. "Around here, you'd kiss me." She spurred her pony forward, leaving him wondering.

The Yellow Dog was a prosperous half-timbered thatched house strategically placed at the bridge over the river that formed the boundary with Kandar. As they rode up at dusk, the mullion windows on the ground floor streamed with light, indicating that the place was already bustling with visitors. Gordoc and Professor Norling took charge of the horses while Ramil negotiated for a private room for "his sister" to dine. The landlord was a fat, bald man with a sharp expression, his gaze flicking from side to side as he bargained, keeping an eye on the doings in the taproom. Ramil glimpsed Melletin and Yelena at a table, already embarked upon supper, but they made no sign that they knew the newcomers.

"You can have the room down the corridor, sir," the landlord said. "Though we're going to be pressed to find you a bed tonight. This lady—you say she's your sister?"

"Yes." Ramil adopted the superior air and the guttural accent of the Southerners.

"She'll have to share with someone, as will you, sir, with that old fellow you came in with. I'll see what I can do. A couple arrived just ahead of you. Perhaps I can sort something out with the lady."

"That would be acceptable."

"Your servant will have to make do with the barn."

"He will be happy with whatever I tell him to do."

"You know best, sir. Now I'll see to your supper."

Leaving them alone in front of the fire in the little sitting room, the innkeeper bustled out, shouting orders to his staff as he closed the door. Tashi reached to remove her veil, but Ramil shook his head and put his finger to his lips. He strode to the door and opened it suddenly, revealing the innkeeper bent double on the other side. Ramil pretended not to notice the man's odd posture.

"Where is my slave?" Ramil snapped.

"I'll send him to you directly, sir," the innkeeper said in a wheedling tone, backing away.

Ramil closed the door and sat down beside Tashi at the table.

"Sorry, but you'll have to stay covered," he whispered.

"We've heard he's Fergox's man. No doubt he's paid to spy on travellers."

"Oh well." Tashi sighed. "I rather like this veil. It allows me to be more myself somehow. I don't have to worry about what anyone's thinking."

"But that's exactly why I hate it. I've no idea what's going on under there."

The innkeeper soon returned with the supper on a tray, Gordoc behind him with the bags.

"Where is the doctor?" asked Ramil brusquely.

"He fell into conversation with some people, sir," Gordoc said, rather overdoing his performance by tugging his forelock. "Told you to eat without him. I'm to have mine in the kitchen."

"Off you go. But don't forget to clean my boots before you go to bed!"

Gordoc winked at Tashi as he left.

The innkeeper served a hearty supper of meat, cheese, and bread, washed down with ale. He watched bemused as Tashi's share disappeared under her veil.

"My sister is in mourning, sir," Ramil said, meeting his look. "Her husband served with me in the army but died at Midwinter."

"Beg your pardon, ma'am," the innkeeper said obsequiously. "My sympathy for your loss. But you, sir, you fought for the great Spearthrower?"

"Yes. I was part of the garrison at Felixholt. Too cold for my liking."

The innkeeper leant against the mantelpiece, settling

in for a good chat. "So you were there when the witch escaped then?"

"Indeed I was, to my great sorrow. My sister's husband was killed when that woman fled."

The innkeeper spat on the hearth. "Curse the demon. What was she like?"

"Ugliest girl you've ever seen." Ramil reached under the table and took Tashi's hand. "Glaring eyes like hot coals. Hair all stringy and colorless—not natural. Smelt of brimstone."

"Aye, that's what the others are saying. They can't find her—they think she's fled into Gerfal by now, but Lord Fergox says he's going to root her out and see she doesn't bewitch any more with her spells." He shook his head. "If I were Gerfal, I'd throw her back into the sea where she came from. She'll bring them nothing but bad luck."

"But bad luck for Gerfal is good luck for us, no?" Ramil suggested.

The innkeeper chuckled. "I suppose you're right, sir. Just ring if you need anything else."

Ramil sighed with relief when the talkative landlord finally decided to go, but he didn't get very far with his supper before Tashi swatted him in the stomach.

"Hot coals? Stringy hair?"

He laughed. "Shh! You know I was only saying what I had to say in front of him."

"But those words occurred to you—you must have thought them!"

Ramil scratched his head, knowing that he was probably damned whatever he said now.

"Well, your eyes can blaze when they're angry. I bet they're blazing now. And compared to us, your hair is pale—not that it doesn't have a most wonderful color. Um . . . stringy—well, you had been in prison for a while."

"Ram!"

"But you always looked beautiful to me." He put his arm around her. "May I?" he asked.

She nodded, wondering what he was going to do.

He leant forward and sniffed. "Not a hint of brimstone. Just mud and horses."

"What!"

"But I like horses."

"Ram, if you were thinking of making more attempts at winning my affections, I don't think this is the recommended practice in any part of the known world."

"So I still have a chance?" He pulled her snugly against him so she fitted in the crook of his arm.

"Not like this you won't. And don't forget, we are supposed to be brother and sister."

"Ah yes." He dropped his arm. "What a shame."

Tashi shared a bed that night with Yelena. They locked themselves in a little room at the top of the inn, leaving the men sleeping in a dormitory on the floor below.

"The house is packed with soldiers," Yelena said as she brushed Tashi's coppery hair for her. "Most are on their way north. It seems that Fergox is strengthening the garrisons on the road to protect his convoys."

"Yes, that's what I would do in his position," murmured Tashi as she took the brush and returned the favor for Yelena, sweeping the girl's long dark hair into a plait for the night.

Yelena yawned. "Looking at you, I forget that when you say these things, you actually do have men and navies and things to order. You look no older than my little sister. How old are you?"

"Sixteen."

"Then you're younger than she is! I find it incredible."

Tashi climbed into bed, pulling the covers up to her chin. "So do I. Every day. But what I find more incredible is that you can fight hand to hand like you do."

Yelena shrugged. "Takes practice, that's all."

"Do you think you could show me?" Tashi asked tentatively. "I've been in quite a few situations recently where I could have used some clever moves."

"Yes, like in Felixholt." Yelena nodded sympathetically.

"Actually, I was thinking about when Merl trapped me in the stables."

"Oh, I see." Yelena hid her amusement. "In that case, we'll start tomorrow as soon as we're clear of here. I think I'll enjoy that—my first pupil and she's a princess."

"Goat-girl turned princess," Tashi amended. "That sounds a bit less exalted."

Yelena poked her in the ribs. "Don't spoil it. I want my friends to be jealous."

Chapter 14

Early the next morning, the travellers arrived at the crossing point into Kandar. Melletin advised that this was the best time: the soldiers would be tired and hungry after a night's watch, not wanting to stand about in the grey morning questioning strangers. To add further to the distraction, Yelena wore her skirts tucked over her knee and carried a pannier of bread purchased from the inn's kitchens, her job to engage the men in flirtatious conversation while her "husband" looked on resentfully.

Ramil, Tashi, Gordoc, and Professor Norling crossed the bridge without incident, leaving Melletin and Yelena to their noisy argument in front of the fascinated guards. Hearing a bird call beneath her, Tashi looked over the parapet to see a white gull fishing in the river. The waters rushed beneath the stone arches seeming to drag the bridge with them as they hurried on to the ocean. The River Kand was deep, swift, and strong here. She remembered from her geography lessons on

Rama that it flowed out of the heart of Kandar, from a land of hills and forests. Wild animals abounded in this difficult terrain—wolves, bears, and great shaggy bison making their home in the densely wooded interior. The Inkar's people were not so flourishing. They lived a marginal existence: the nobles clinging to their castles on the crags, the peasants scratching what crops could be coaxed from the reluctant soil, fearful of the forests at their door. Only the flood plains to the east with their rich alluvial deposits offered any hope to the farmer, but these lands had been sequestered by the Inkar and turned into slave plantations, displacing the original inhabitants.

"It's a sad place now," said Professor Norling to Tashi as they passed through the first sorry-looking settlement, children in inadequate clothes running along at their stirrups to beg. He threw them some coppers. "The Inkar's grasp of land management and social rights is weak to say the least. She's running a poor land into destitution, battening a huge army upon it like a parasite upon a frail host."

On hearing the jingle of harness behind them, they turned. Melletin and Yelena were fast catching up, both grinning broadly.

"How did it go?" Ramil called.

"Would you believe it: he threatened to lock me up in his mother's house if I didn't behave!" exclaimed Yelena, sticking her tongue out at Melletin. "I threw a roll at him and he clipped me around the ear. The soldiers were all about to beat him up when I burst into tears and begged his forgiveness. We had a passionate reconciliation and went on our way with their good wishes for our marital harmony."

Melletin rubbed his lips. "Where's the next check-point, Yelena? I can't wait to do that again."

"Watch it, sir: I'll report you," Yelena threatened, but she looked very pleased all the same.

Melletin estimated that it would take them at least a week to cross Kandar. They rose early each day to make the most of the short winter daylight, taking the road that cut through the thick forest. Riding was uncomfortable as they trudged in sleety showers and gritted their teeth against the cold winds. There were few people on the road, apart from convoys of soldiers. Whenever these were spotted, the travellers left the highway and sheltered in the trees until they had passed. Ramil was thankful they had a guide who knew the country so well. Melletin seemed to have a sixth sense for anticipating trouble and unerringly led them to shelter at the end of each day. None of them fancied spending a freezing night outside with the wolves and roving soldiers for company.

Five days into their journey, Melletin called a halt on a ridge looking down upon a forest valley. Outcrops of rock reared above trees like islands in a green ocean.

"We've reached the wild zone," he explained.

"You mean what we've passed through wasn't the wild zone?" Tashi asked. The forest pressing on either side of the road had looked very savage to her.

"I mean the ungoverned part—the resort of bandits and other desperate folk. Some of them are friendly to the resistance, but some, I regret to say, are friendly to no one."

"And how will we find out?" Ramil asked. "Before or after they've attacked us?"

"There's a secret sign. If they approach us, we'll find out soon enough if they recognize it. Look to your weapons and keep alert. I would bet my sword on someone waylaying us before the end of the day: we are too tempting a target to be neglected."

Before mounting again, Tashi collected a pouch full of stones and prepared a sling. She stayed close to Gordoc as the horses took to the road.

"Don't worry, my pretty, I'll make sure no bandit touches you," he said cheerfully.

They trotted on for hours, seeing no sign of man or beast. By noon they had entered a particularly dark, dense region of the forest. Ramil watched the trees nervously. The road surface was broken up, tree roots creating havoc with the stones that had once been set smooth in the ground. Ramil decided that if he was commanding a band of robbers, he would think this an excellent place for an ambush because the riders would have to mind where they were going and be unable to keep a constant watch.

As if obeying Ramil's thoughts, a man dropped out of the trees ahead of Melletin and held up a hand. He had a coarse lined face with a rough black beard and moustache; his clothes were ragged and patched.

"Good people, you have neglected to pay the toll!" he called.

Six more men dropped from the trees around them and three emerged from the bushes at the rear. One threw the leader a stout staff, which he caught and held out, blocking the way forward.

Melletin raised his fist to his chest, fingers circled in an O.

"We are friends, sir, and only wish to pass in peace."

The man took no notice of the sign. Ramil's hand moved to his sword.

"There is no peace to be had in Kandar. You must pay the toll."

Melletin dropped his hand casually to rest on his hilt. "And what may that be?"

The bandit scratched his chin, looking the party over. "Your horses, goods, and weapons." He caught sight of Yelena. "And perhaps the girl too."

Yelena gave a disgusted snort. "Just you try," she muttered.

"If you want that much, then you'll have to fight us for them," said Melletin, swiftly drawing his sword.

The bandit leader raised his staff to meet the blow. A man swung from the trees to knock Melletin from the saddle. Like a squall blowing up out of nowhere, the skirmish became intense and confused: swords meeting staffs, men swarming from the trees. Gordoc and Yelena flanked the Princess in the rear while Ramil and Melletin took on the main attack. Tashi felled one man with a slingshot as he was about to stab Melletin in the back. One bandit already lay in the dust, killed by a kick from Thunder.

"Keep away from the horses!" yelled the leader, realizing too late that these were trained for combat.

Professor Norling had drawn a cane from his waist-band and was belaboring a bandit around the head as he tried to make off with the baggage horse.

"Not my instruments!" he shouted in outrage.

Tashi didn't see what happened to him next because Gordoc barged in front of her, cutting off an attack by three staff-wielding men. She heard a shriek from behind and turned to find Yelena being pulled from the saddle by two assailants. One Tashi struck with a stone but she had no time for a second as a man dropped from the trees, knocking her to the ground with him on top of her.

"Let's see what we've got under here!" He reached for her veil and pulled it off. "Another pretty wench!"

He got no further—a foot kicked him in the jaw, catapulting him backwards. Yelena stood over Tashi, crouching in combat stance, her own attacker a crum-pled heap on the road. Tashi scrambled to her feet and positioned herself behind Yelena, swinging her sling, searching for the next mark. Ramil was fighting two men—one fell to a stone, the other he ran through with an efficient swipe.

"Retreat! Retreat!" shouted the leader.

The bandits who could still walk stumbled off into the trees, dragging their wounded with them. That left four on the ground: one killed by Thunder, one by Ramil, and two crushed by Gordoc's bare hands.

Ramil limped over to the girls, sword still bloody.

"Are you all right?" he asked anxiously, stabbing his blade into the ground so he could hug Tashi.

"Yes, thank you, sir," Yelena said with a grin. "Thank you for being so concerned about me."

She did not stand uncared for long as Melletin was soon at her side asking the same question. Professor Norling and Gordoc swiftly caught the horses and brought them to the girls.

"We'd better get going before they come back," said Melletin. He grimaced at the bodies lying in the road. "What a waste—half-starved, desperate, now dead. The Inkar has a lot to answer for to her people."

They reached the border between Kandar and Holt three days later. All were heartily sick of forests and looked forward to the open plains of Fergox's land, though they knew they would soon miss the cover the trees had provided. Melletin showed Tashi and Ramil a map, rolling it out on a log at their final stopping place before the checkpoint.

"Tigral is way down to the southwest," he said, pointing to the capital on the shores of the Inland Sea. "We have a choice, risk going straight for it—it is the most direct route but it's also the most dangerous. The lands between are rich. There are plantations, vineyards, big towns and cities: in short, lots of people on the road. If we go south we can skirt round to the sea by the desert region, not going into the sand zone, but keeping to the edge. It's a longer, tougher road but perhaps safer."

"Longer, tougher, and safer sounds good to me," said Ramil.

"But we don't have the time to go so far out of our way," argued Tashi.

"We'll have even less time if we end up in one of Fergox's prisons," Ramil countered.

"But what good is my country's aid if it arrives too late? It's already February and we still have weeks of travelling ahead of us. The thaw will come in late March or April and it will take my navy at least a month to sail to Gerfal."

"You speak, Tashi, as if Gerfal will not last beyond that time. We will put up a stiff fight if I know my father. I would not expect the battle to be over in a few weeks—we might even last the summer."

"And then there's the resistance harassing Fergox from the rear—he'll be made to regret he's stretched his supply lines so far," added Melletin.

"So you both favor the longer route," Tashi said, her arms folded across her chest.

"Yes, I do," said Melletin, rolling up the map.

"I do too, Your Highness," seconded Ramil, his hands on his hips.

But would it give them enough time? Tashi fretted. She closed her eyes for a moment, seeking wisdom in a silent prayer. Their mission was in the Goddess's hands. If She wanted them to succeed, the Mother would make it happen by Her own means.

"I will follow your advice unless we see a clear sign that we have chosen ill," she said. "Then all I ask is that you be open to a change of plan."

"Of course," said Ramil, rather pleased to have won this first battle of wills. "I'm open to any suggestion of yours."

Tashi pelted him with a twig. "Don't: you sound like Merl when you talk like that."

Ramil put his hand over his mouth, feigning horror. "I will not speak another word."

"Good." Tashi smiled.

Melletin proposed that they reorganize their party so that they no longer resembled the same group that passed the border a week ago.

"In case the alarm has been raised since and they are on the lookout for us," he explained.

He suggested they fall into pairs: the girls together, posing as two servants off to find work; Ramil and the professor on their errand to the south; he and Gordoc as slave overseers, heading to the plantations around the shores of the Inland Sea.

"We'll stick close together, but make no sign we are acquainted. The girls should go ahead so that they get through first. We'll follow close behind to be there for any trouble."

"Don't worry, my dears," said the professor gallantly, "I'll rescue you from any difficulties."

Yelena laughed and kissed the old man on the cheek. "Of course you will. I don't know why we bother with these other men, do you, Tashi?"

"But they are decorative, aren't they?" the Princess replied archly. It was fun to have a girl with whom she could gang up against the boys—she'd never had a friend like that before. "They give us something to look at on the boring stretches of the road." She let her eyes linger on Ramil, who appeared very warm all of a sudden.

Yelena swung herself into the saddle. "My, my, Princess, I didn't know you could flirt."

"I'm learning from a master—or should I say mistress—of that art," Tashi said with a bow.

The girls trotted off, their joking tone replaced by seriousness once they were out of sight and had rejoined the road.

"Do I look all right?" Tashi asked, touching her hair nervously. She felt exposed after the days spent looking at the world from behind a veil.

"I suppose you don't mean 'How do I look in this?' You're wondering if they'll recognize you. No, sister, they won't think you're a princess, not dressed like a peasant and with hair that cries out your Brigardian ancestry."

"Good. So will they let us through?" Tashi checked she still had her new set of forged documents safe in her saddlebags.

"Let me do the talking and be prepared to bat your eyelashes at them. I don't think they'll see us as a threat—light relief maybe from their boredom, but not a threat. You can be thankful that men always underestimate us women."

The two girls arrived at the checkpoint and joined

the queue moving slowly forward. There were plenty of other refugees from Kandar, all hoping for a better life in the big cities of Holt.

The border guard peered out from his box at Yelena and Tashi when they reached the front of their line. He brightened up and smoothed his moustache.

"Well, ladies, what brings you here?" he asked, unrolling their documents.

"Off to Tigral, sir," Yelena said, bathing him in the full glow of her widest smile. "We hear there's work to be had for a pair of willing girls in the big houses."

"I'm sure you'll have no difficulty finding a place," he said, stamping their papers with a flourish. "But you'd best find some company for the road." He leant forward and said conspiratorially, "All sorts of bad types on the move—soldiers, slavers, and now there's a rumor there's a witch of some sort on the loose."

"Save us, sir!" Tashi gasped, touching her forehead in the sign she had so often seen in her vicinity. "I hope we don't run into her!"

"So do I, my dears, so do I. Travel well!"

Keeping a straight face, the two girls prodded their horses forward. Yelena allowed herself to laugh only when they had ridden through the border village. She then aped Tashi's expression of horror. "Oh, save us, sir, save us!" she said in a high voice. "You should have joined the players, Tashi; you're a natural."

The girls found a secluded corner not far off the road and passed the time practicing the combat techniques Yelena had been teaching Tashi over the past week.

The men seemed to be taking a long time to catch up. The girls were just beginning to get anxious when they heard the sounds of heavy horses. They ran to the edge of the road and waved down their friends. Professor Norling was in a high dudgeon, his protests already vocal before he reached them.

"They strip-searched me!" he burst out. "Me! Old enough to be their grandfather and they made me stand naked in the road, my things all unpacked in the mud!"

"They were only doing their job," said Ramil wearily. He had evidently had much of this complaint to endure since leaving the border. "They're looking for enemies— you must admit they had a point."

"Point! To make the four of us—and those other men—stand in our birthday suits for all to see!"

"Shame we rode on so quickly," Yelena murmured to Tashi.

"I trust they did not subject you to the same indignity?" Ramil asked the girls delicately.

"No, the guard was most helpful. Told us to beware of bad sorts on the road and waved us on our way," Tashi replied.

"I'm pleased for your sake, my dears," said Professor Norling, "though I still think it very unfair."

"Very stupid, you mean," Melletin muttered to Ramil. "I mean, who would you prefer to search?"

Ramil did not have to think very long about his answer.

Riding through eastern Holt, Tashi was surprised to find it a beautiful country. Having met Fergox, she had expected it to reflect his character: harsh, warlike, and uncompromising, but instead it was a gentle landscape of meadows just awakening to the early southern spring; flocks of sheep and goats out to pasture, well tended vines and olive trees. The villages looked prosperous: houses with terracotta roofs and white-washed walls nestled together around the village temple. But there were jarring notes: at many crossroads they came across the bodies of Fergox's enemies, hanging in chains from scaffolds; the temples in the villages were decked in red war banners and the steps sprinkled with blood from recent sacrifices. Despite this, Tashi could not rid herself of the impression that Fergox's influence did not run deep, that if he was no longer in power, the people of this land would not find it difficult to return to a more peaceful existence.

She expressed this view to Professor Norling, who was riding with them until the road divided, one branch to Tigral, another continuing to the desert regions.

"Yes, my dear, eastern Holt has a rich culture of its own—not at all warlike. Fergox has his power base in the harsher mountainous west. His own people come from there. They are a seafaring nation, making up for what the land lacks with raids on more fortunate countries. But I'm sure you are very familiar with them because they form his pirate fleet. I would advise you to steer clear, if you can, on your journey home."

They passed a line of workers preparing the soil for sowing.

"But look there, child," Norling said, pointing with his cane. "That reminds us that the beauty of this land is founded on rottenness. The fields are tilled by slave-labor, the mines worked by these same poor captives; even the poorest houses of the freeborn have their little slave to cook, clean, and mind the children."

Tashi looked back at the workers and noticed that they each wore an iron collar.

"How can the people bear it?" she asked.

"The slaves, of course, have no choice. Most are taken from lands subject to Fergox, inferiors in the eyes of the Holtish people. As for the inhabitants, those that have a conscience about such things claim slaves are well looked after, part of the extended family. They predict the collapse of the Holtish economy if the slaves were liberated. Most owners don't worry too much about excuses—they just count the benefit to themselves."

"Well, I think it an abomination," she said angrily.

"And so do I." He fixed her with an acute look, reminding her that beneath his genial exterior was a razor-sharp mind. "And maybe you can do something to change it if you help defeat the warlord."

Chapter 15

They bade farewell to Professor Norling where the road divided, seeing him safely attached to a party of pilgrims heading for the Great Temple of the Warmonger in Tigral. Three days later, as they travelled down the road to the south, Flake cast a shoe. Now far beyond Melletin's knowledge of the land, the five travellers debated whether to turn back to the last village or ride on in hopes of finding another forge.

"I'd hate to retrace any step of this weary road," Melletin said. "I could ride ahead with Flake and find a smith if Tashi would not mind riding pillion with one of you."

"She is welcome to ride with me," Ramil said quickly. "We've shared a saddle before."

Yelena grinned at Tashi as the Princess mounted in front of Ramil.

"Hey, Melletin!" Yelena said, a twinkle in her eye. "How about having some company on your errand? We don't know what lies ahead and you could do with some backup if there's trouble."

"Good thinking," replied Melletin, oblivious to the girl's hidden agenda. "Big man, would you come?"

"No, I . . . " Gordoc began, then caught Yelena's eye. "I mean, yes, I'll watch your back for you."

Melletin, Gordoc, and Yelena rode off quickly with Flake trotting riderless in tow.

"Did she do that on purpose?" Ramil asked Tashi as he saw Yelena give them a final jaunty wave.

"I think so," Tashi admitted. She leant back against him, conscious that they hadn't sat this close since they had begun to understand each other's feelings. They rode on in happy silence, taking delight in the opportunity to be together. It gave Ramil the chance to build up his courage for what he had wanted to say for some time.

"Tashi, you know I love you, don't you?" he said sofly in her ear.

She smiled: trust the son of a Horse Follower to woo in the saddle.

"I thought we were already betrothed."

"You broke it off, remember." He kissed the top of her head.

"Oh yes, I suppose I did. I'm sorry about that."

"I didn't deserve you. I don't deserve you now."

"Well, as long as you know that." She turned and gave him a mischievous smile.

He traced the line of her lips with his forefinger.

She felt in her pocket and pulled out two tiny paper models. "I've kept them safe. You'd better have this one back." She gave him the dragonfly. "I improved it a little when your attempt unfolded, but I haven't touched the horse: I like it just as it is."

"I promise to take care of it."

"And I'll take care of yours." She settled back against him, the paper horse held carefully in her hand.

Ramil smiled down at the copper head beneath his chin, knowing that he never wanted to be apart from her again.

That night the travellers decided to camp under the stars. They were approaching the warmer climes of the desert and no longer needed a roof over their heads at night. Added to this, Melletin reported that the village inn was hosting a party of slavers from the south, their captives shackled in the barn, and no one wanted to come to their attention. They rode through the village with their heads down.

Finding a likely camping spot in a bend in the river, Yelena and Tashi went off to bathe, leaving the men to make the fire. The horses strayed on the bank, picketed in reach of the water.

"So, Ram," said Gordoc, skewering some goat's meat on a stick to roast, "do I have to thump you?"

Ram shook his head. "Only very gently. A light pummelling. Or you could congratulate me: our marriage alliance is back on."

Melletin clapped him on the shoulder. "Lucky man."

Gordoc assumed a stern, fatherly expression. "And, young Prince, what are your prospects? Can you keep my girl in the manner to which she has become accustomed?"

Ramil laughed. "I hope I can do much better than that. So far, all she has known with me is prison cells and tents. As for my prospects, touch and go at best, but I don't think she minds."

"Yes, and it's not every girl who comes with a navy attached," added Melletin.

"Or so we hope," said Ramil, placing the skewer he had prepared for Tashi over the flames.

They fell silent, listening to the delighted shrieks and laughter of the girls splashing in the water downstream. Melletin had a thoughtful expression at all this talk of marriage.

Suddenly, Gordoc nudged Ramil. "Look sharp, Ram, we've got company."

The three friends reached for their weapons and turned to face the road. A cart drew up, driven by a dark-skinned man wearing the loose robes of the south. Eight others of all nations jumped out of the back; the only thing they had in common was that they were heavily armed.

"Here they are!" called the man. "I told you I saw them ride this way."

The newcomers swarmed down the bank, making straight for the fire. Ramil stepped forward.

"Peace, friends," he said. "How may we help you?"

The cart driver returned the gesture. "If you would like to put down that shiny blade of yours and come with us, that would be a start."

"The start of what?" Ramil held the sword in guard position, shifting his weight, ready for an attack.

There was another round of laughter from the river. The stranger nodded to three of his men. "That's the girls. Go get them."

"No!" shouted Melletin and Ramil together, springing forward to block the path, but the other men were upon them, forcing them back with spears and swords.

"Tashi, Yelena, run!" boomed Gordoc. He lashed out with his fists at the men dancing around him using whips and chains to hamper him.

Frightened, the horses pulled on their pickets, scattering from the flailing swords.

Ramil cursed. The slaver had planned this well. He let his men engage the three travellers in battle but only so as to keep them from going to the assistance of the girls. He must have gauged their strengths earlier and knew he would lose fighters if they went to disarm the giant and his two companions.

Bursting with fury, Ramil fought, desperate to reach Tashi. Every time he tried to break through, a man would attack from behind, forcing him to turn and defend himself. Once he had the advantage over that assailant, another would step in, starting the fight all over again. These were no novice soldiers like those at Nerul's camp; these were hardened overseers, disciplined and used to controlling those who were stronger than them. He gritted his teeth and fought on. He had to reach her, he had to.

On the riverbank, Tashi had just finished dressing when she heard Gordoc's shout. Nearer to the camp, Yelena was bent double, tying her shoes. Immediately, the warrior-girl sprang up, casting round for something to use as a weapon, but three men burst out of the trees and knocked her flat before she had a chance.

"Run!" Yelena screamed, fighting like a wild cat with the man who grappled for her arms.

Terrified, Tashi fled. The river was swifter here, channelled between two high banks. Water foamed around rocks. She had nowhere to go but along the river's edge, crashing through bushes, stumbling over stones, her breath tearing at her lungs in harsh gasps. Feet pounded behind her. Men cursed as the brambles snatched at their hands and legs, but Tashi was unaware of the scratches. The ground rose under her feet; she ran up the incline and emerged into the open, finding herself right on the very edge of a curving river bluff. The brown water flowed rapidly some ten feet below. Her two pursuers divided to approach her from either side, like dogs rounding up a stubborn sheep. The biggest one, who had a shock of matted black hair and a gap-toothed grin, held out his hand and beckoned her.

"That's right, sweetheart. Nowhere to run now. Come along and you'll not get hurt. We don't mark the pretty ones, do we, Garth?"

"No, Mol, we don't. Treat them fine, we do." The

smaller man, no more than a boy really, slipped a rope from his belt and made a loop.

Tashi took a step closer to the edge. They stopped moving.

"That'll do you no good, girl. The river'll mash you up and spit you out drowned dead," Mol said. "But with us, we'll find you a nice kind master who'll look after you. You'll live very comfortably—better than most."

Tashi called silently on the Goddess. *I can't get taken now—I'll never reach my people in time to save Gerfal,* she pleaded.

Then don't get taken, came the answer.

There was no choice. She knew what she had to do, but she wasn't sure if her faith was strong enough to believe she could.

"As the Goddess wills," Tashi muttered, knowing there was only one way to find out.

She slowly raised her hands. The men relaxed, thinking she was about to come to them.

"All right, I surrender," she whispered. "I'm sorry, Ram."

Giving up her life to the Mother, Tashi turned and jumped. She heard a snatch of a cry behind her, but then she plunged into the water and went down, whirled away on the current.

Ramil fought on until he saw Yelena hustled into the camp, a knife at her throat. Her attacker had a black eye, but he'd managed to rope her wrists. The leader of the slaving party whistled and the other men fell back.

"Now, my friends, you have a choice. If you fight on, I'll have to kill this girl. Surrender your weapons and we'll treat you all fairly."

Melletin was the first to drop his sword. Ramil followed and Gordoc let his hands fall to his sides.

"Excellent. A slave that sees reason is worth his weight in gold." The leader turned to the man still holding Yelena. "Where are the others?"

"Gone after the other one."

"You two, round up the horses. Kinto, shackle our newest acquisitions."

Ramil watched the path from the river with sick apprehension. He barely noticed the iron collar being bolted to his neck and manacles clamped to his wrists.

Finally, two men emerged from the bushes. They were alone.

"Where is she?" barked the leader.

"She jumped," Mol said with a shrug. "Straight into the river and never came up again. Rather die than be a slave, even though I told her we'd treat her nice."

Ramil felt something snap inside him. It was as if all the strength had gone from his body. He collapsed to his knees, empty.

The southerner sighed with regret. "Well, you can't catch them all. Never mind. Let's get these back to the barn. We deserve a drink. I'm paying!"

The slavers cheered and herded their captives onto the cart. Five horses followed in a string. Thunder had not been caught; last seen streaking away to the south, sparks flying from his hooves on the flinty ground.

No one dared say anything to Ramil. Gordoc was moaning softly to himself, clenching and unclenching his hands. Melletin hugged Yelena, who was weeping on his shoulder.

Disaster had come upon them so quickly. One moment he had been joking about the future and cooking Tashi's supper, the next he was a slave and she was . . . Ramil could only think of what the man had said. She would rather die than be a slave. Yes, that was Tashi: the proud princess, unbroken to the last, his darling, brave girl.

And she might still be alive.

This thought was a torment because it allowed him a bitter hope. If it was true, then she was alone some-where out there, without him. How long would she survive?

He dug his nails into his palm, drawing blood. He was hurting so much inside he had to make his body suffer. If he hadn't been shackled, he would have hurled himself from the wagon. A big hand clamped down on his wrist, chain rattling.

"Don't," Gordoc said. "She wouldn't want it."

Ramil turned and buried his face in the giant's shoulder, his body racked with dry sobs.

The next few days passed in a dark blur for Ramil. He was aware of little but his grief as the chained slaves marched north in the wake of the slaver's wagon. Gordoc switched his protection from the missing Tashi to the immediate needs of Ramil, making sure he drank and ate, keeping him on his feet when he sank with despair. Weak slaves met with no mercy. The whip saw to the slow ones; the knife to the feeble. The slavers were in a hurry to make it to the market in Tigral by the turn of the month so kept up a punishing pace.

Yelena had been separated from the men and now rode with the other female slaves in the wagon. The slavers were keen that the women arrived looking presentable, as premiums were paid for healthy house girls. Appearance for the men was less important as most were destined for the mines. A few whip strokes would make no difference in price. Strength was the main quality prized and the slavers had high hopes for the big man they had captured, sure he would break all records this year when put to auction.

They reached Tigral at the end of the second nightmarish week. Ramil barely stirred himself to look up at the walled garden city rising out of the coastal plain. The Inland Sea curled around the rose-colored stone of the walls, ships at anchor in the ports. Fergox's palace stood in the center on the top of an artificial mound, the work of previous generations of slaves. It was painted gold and twinkled in the sunlight—a palace built primarily for pleasure rather than defense. His wives lodged here, each with her own pavilion and garden. Lemon and orange trees shaded the broad avenues of the rich men's houses. Cherry trees bloomed exuberantly in the courts of the Great Temple, white petals falling in drifts, covering the bloody gutters that trickled in constant sacrifice to Holin.

The slaves only glimpsed this other world before they were ushered to the holding pens down by the port. The women were escorted to a shed but the men were held in the open. The cages were already full of captives and space was bitterly contested but somehow no one saw fit to challenge Gordoc for his corner, allowing Ramil and Melletin to sit unmolested at his side. The pen smelt of unwashed bodies and human waste. Those who had already been here a week scratched blank-eyed at their scabbed knees, only rousing when the food was poured into the trough at the entrance. Flies buzzed, settling in clouds on mouths and eyelids.

No longer able to bear his thoughts about Tashi, Ramil turned his mind to his father. Lagan would weep to see his son here. But Ramil knew that many more Gerfalians would be joining him in the pens very soon now that their mission to bring the Blue Crescent navy into the war had ended in disaster.

I've failed them, he thought. *My father trusted me to do what was in the best interests of my people, but I failed.*

And what has my life been about really? Ramil wondered. *I've reacted to events, never initiated any action I can be proud of—except the escape.*

He thought about what he had told Tashi when she had been at her lowest ebb. He had said to her that maybe the Goddess had put her there because She wanted her to follow a strange path. They had been glib words from someone who had not known her depth of suffering. Ramil knew that his own faith was a sorry affair compared to Tashi's—a lazy belief in some benign Father God, a creator who had always been on excellent terms with the ac Burinholts like a jolly old patron. There was little for him to hold on to now that he had reached his own nadir.

So do I give up? he asked himself. *Not listen to my own advice to trust that there is a plan?*

If there is a God behind all this, it looks like a pretty rubbish plan to me, his cynical side chipped in.

But what would Tashi want me to do?

No sooner had he framed the question than he knew the answer. She would want him to trust his God; she would expect him to do his duty. He could not honor her by dying here in the filth with a whimper.

If this is where I am supposed to be right now, Ramil thought, *then I have to find a way to serve the interests of my people. I don't stop being a prince just because I'm in chains.*

Ramil sat up, the light of battle re-ignited in his eyes.

"Right, Gordoc, Melletin," he said, "we've got work to do."

The river washed Tashi up on a sandbank two miles down from where she had jumped. She was barely alive, her spirit wandering between this world and the Peaceful Gardens of the Mother. But it appeared the Goddess did not want her company just yet: She sent Tashi back so that the girl returned to consciousness, coughing and vomiting river water as she lay on her side.

Tashi stayed where she was for a long time, hearing the water chatter by over the stones, and the night chorus of crickets squeak in the long grass. She didn't want to think because thinking meant admitting that she'd lost Ramil and her other friends. She'd left them with the slavers and there was nothing she could do for them—nothing she could do for herself.

To punish her body for being alive, she sat upright. Her hair hung over her face in pale threads, the dye washed from it after her dousing in the river.

It's stringy, she thought, and burst into tears. She hugged her body, missing the warmth of Ramil who had held her to him only hours ago. She touched her lips, trying to recall the feel of his mouth on hers, but she was cold and bruised, her face swelling out of all recognition since her passage through the rapids.

Long slow minutes of darkness passed. Then a horse neighed from the bank. Tashi looked up and saw Thunder standing there, clearly wondering what she was doing sitting in the wet. She thought for one wild moment of hope that he might have Ramil on his back, but he was alone, the picket rope trailing from his bridle. Even so, she was relieved to see a friendly face, if not a human one. Tashi crawled out of the shallows and pulled herself onto the bank. Teeth gently pulled her up by the back of her tattered tunic.

"Thunder!" she said, falling against him when she reached the top. "Thank you."

Her shaking hands explored his back. She touched a saddle and bags, then a bedding roll. Ramil had not taken them off, which was unexpected because he usually saw to the horse before himself. She then remembered that he had promised he'd have her supper waiting for her when she returned from her wash. He must have rushed to start cooking, for once leaving the horse till later. She took off the blanket and wrapped it around her shoulders, then opened the bags. They were full of Ramil's gear. The familiar smell of his shirts was heart-rending and wonderful at the same time. She slipped out of her own wet things and dressed herself in his spare clothes, closing her eyes and trying to imagine that he was with her.

"Well, boy, what next?" she asked the horse.

Thunder nudged her with his soft nose, inviting her to mount.

"I'm not as good a rider as Ramil. You'll have to do all the work," she said wearily, hauling herself into the saddle. The slaver had said the river would mash her and he had been right. Every limb cried out with pain as she moved.

Thunder trotted smoothly back up the road.

"Which way?" she wondered.

Thunder made up her mind for her. He headed south, smelling the horse pastures on the desert's edge.

273

Tashi slumped over his neck, letting him take her where he wanted.

The miles passed by but Tashi did not notice. She only woke up when she hit the ground. In her exhaustion, she had fallen asleep and rolled off Thunder's back. He nuzzled her in puzzlement, wondering what his rider was doing on the road. Groaning, she stood up, her whole body shaking.

"I've got to sleep," she explained. "This will do as well as anywhere else."

She led him off the side of the track, down a dry ditch and behind a tumbled wall. It was shelter of a sort, and she could go no further. Thunder stood guard while the pale human slept, her sleep broken with bad dreams. He heard his master's name on her lips and knew she was missing him too. He scared off the wild dog that came sniffing around and stamped on a snake that slithered out of the wall when the sun hit the stones. Still the human foal slept.

The sun was high in the sky when Tashi opened her eyes, though it had turned into a cloudy day and a damp warm rain was falling. If anything she felt worse now that the numbness had worn off. Her body was battered and bruised, her spirit too. Only determination kept her moving. Swathing herself in Ramil's spare cloak, she returned to the road and doggedly set off once more.

Over the next couple of days she saw few people, and those she did see galloped past. Tashi did not want to risk speaking to anyone. The landscape was changing. The meadows and fields were giving way to treeless plains. The only things that flourished here were tough grasses and low scrubby bushes spiked with thorns. Even the road seemed to peter out, becoming little more than a hint of a track through the waving grass. Thunder raised his head and let out a whinny of joy: this was his land, the home of the horse. He darted forward, lengthening his stride, feeling the little human tighten her grip with her knees. His dark mane rippled behind him, as did hers, streaming gold. They abandoned themselves to the pleasure of the race, with no idea but to run until their breath failed them. Tashi had tears on her cheeks as she remembered Ramil shouting to her on the first ride "Don't you love the speed!" Now she knew what he meant.

This was how the Horse Followers first saw Princess Taoshira racing across their pastures. The leader of the scouting party called a halt on the ridge and watched silently as the girl and the blue roan streaked across the grass. Finally, the horse slowed, tiring after its long canter. The leader signalled his men to move out and they galloped down the hill to meet the strangers.

Tashi heard the thunder of their hooves before she saw them. She sat up straight in the saddle, too weary to be afraid. The horsemen made a fearsome spectacle: their dark purple robes flowing, their swords out.

Well, if they cut me down, at least it will be a swift end, she thought with resignation.

The leader, a wiry black-skinned man with a gold ring in his earlobe, galloped his men around her, then drew to a halt, a line of fighters barring her way forward. He pointed his sword at her throat.

"What does a pale girl do riding on a horse fit for a prince?" he asked in Common.

He had not been fooled by her lack of skill, Tashi thought sadly.

"The horse does belong to a prince, but we have lost him," she replied, trying to hide her trembling hands under the long cuffs of Ramil's shirt. "Thunder lets me travel with him for a while."

The man examined the girl closely: she was injured and weak. It would be the work of a moment to take the mount from her. The horse, as if sensing his thoughts, reared up, almost unseating Tashi, flailing his hooves in the direction of the leader. It appeared the horse would not be so easily parted from its rider; this called for a change of tactic.

"Who are you and where are you going?" the man asked imperiously.

"I'm Taoshira, the Fourth Crown Princess, also known as the Blue Crescent Witch, and I'm going home," she said, beyond caring what they thought of that.

What they thought was that she was joking. Laughter rippled through the line of riders.

"I like your imagination, girl," the leader said. "Come, you ride with us while I decide what to do with you."

"That is not your decision, sir. My fate lies in the hands of the Goddess."

He gave her a crooked smile. "Then maybe I'm her instrument." He reached down and took the picket rope still tied to the bridle. "Follow me."

Chapter 16

As they rode, Tashi tried to stay awake this time. Falling from the saddle in front of these men did not seem a good idea: they'd probably just leave her on the ground, taking Thunder with them.

"What is your name, sir?" she asked the leader.

"Zeliph of the Horse Followers."

"And am I your captive, Zeliph of the Horse Followers?"

"I have not decided. We return to my tent. There you will tell me your true name and your story. Then I will decide."

Tashi accepted that there was nothing more she could do. The scouting party travelled over the feature-less steppe with an unerring sense of direction. Once they gave a shout in unison, greeting a herd of horses galloping free the other way, but they did not stop. By late afternoon, they approached a collection of white tents pitched by a pool. Beyond lay the first dunes of the true desert, golden in the setting sun. As Tashi watched, the light changed and they flushed blood red.

Zeliph reined in the horses outside the largest tent. Tashi slid stiffly from the saddle and almost continued going to the ground but caught herself on the stirrup. Zeliph whistled and a young boy bobbed out of the tent and took the horses.

"He'll be well looked after," Zeliph assured her, seeing Tashi's worried frown.

Tashi hadn't doubted that, but she was thinking if she would ever see Thunder again.

Not bothering to welcome her to his tent, Zeliph took the saddle bags inside and upended them on the rug. He picked through the shirts as if looking for some clue to his guest's identity.

"Men's clothes, not yours," he said, stating the obvious.

Tashi nodded.

"Did you steal the horse?" he asked bluntly.

"No."

"But he doesn't belong to you?"

"No." It was clear Thunder was the only thing this man was interested in.

"Then who does he belong to?"

"That's a difficult question." Tashi was feeling light-headed and very tired. "May I sit?"

He gave a curt nod.

"I suppose he belongs to Fergox Spearthrower, but Ramil liberated him when we escaped from Felixholt."

She wondered faintly when was the last time she'd eaten properly. She'd survived on a canteen of water and scanty rations since her plunge in the river.

The man was oblivious to his guest's distress.

"Ramil? Ramil ac Burinholt? Zarai's son?"

Tashi nodded. "I'm sorry, but I think I'm going to . . . " She didn't complete her sentence, as the world suddenly turned sideways and she passed out on the cushions. Alarmed, Zeliph called his wife to assist him. Together they carried the unconscious girl into the women's quarters at the back of the tent.

His wife did not stop berating him. "What were you thinking of?" she scolded. "Questioning the poor child like that? Can't you see she's been through an ordeal?" She flapped him out of the room and efficiently set about nursing the stranger, stripping off her rags, washing her cuts, putting ointment on her bruises, and finally burning a feather under her nose to rouse her.

Tashi opened her eyes to see a dark brown pair gazing down on her.

The woman touched her chest. "I'm Larila."

"Tashi," she replied, touching her own chest. She then realized she was naked under her cover. "Where are my things?"

"I have sent them to be washed."

The girl burst into tears, clutching the blanket to her chest. "Don't do that! They won't smell of him anymore if you do that."

"It is too late. They have already gone," Larila replied, wondering at this irrational response. Was the child mad?

The girl turned her head to the pillow, her shoulders heaving, and refused to answer more questions.

Ramil chose to look upon his situation as a war and plan his strategy accordingly. Sitting in the filth of the pen, he was in retreat and had to move on to the attack. His greatest and only strength was that many others shared his predicament. All the slaves penned for the sale the following day would be potential recruits. There was no advantage in waiting for a better opportunity because he was unlikely to find one. But he had to allow for some being too fearful to get involved and others that might see it in their own interests to betray any conspiracy to the masters. The captives had no weapons but their bare hands and chains. Looking round the slave market with its guards and whip-bearing overseers, Ramil knew that the first task would be to break out of the pens and hold a defensible area of the city, before he could get involved in more ambitious plans. Ramil had already set upon Fergox's palace as his ultimate target. Like a flea biting a man in armor, Ramil's hope was that he would distract the warlord from his fight with Gerfal by attacking his soft part underneath.

"Send out the whisper," Ramil told Melletin, "starting with all Brigardians in the pens. Tell them the Dark Prince who escaped Fergox has come to lead them—"

"But you're in the cage with them," Melletin pointed out.

Ramil shrugged. "They don't need to know that. Keep it vague and majestic. See if the ones who have been here longest know who we can trust. There's bound to be a few slave rats among us. We'll make our move during the sale once we're out of these pens."

Melletin nodded. "And what's the sign?"

Ramil looked at Gordoc. "Our new masters are so proud of their big man that they haven't stopped to ask just how strong he is. Gordoc, I've seen you bend bars in Felixholt. Do you think you could break our chains?"

The giant looked down at the hefty links shackling his hands to the collar around his neck. "I'm not sure. But I could certainly break that pretty necklace of yours. The bolt's the weak point."

"That will do. With the ring attached to the chain, I'll have a useful weapon to swing at someone. So the sign is when I take my collar off and attack." Ramil smiled wryly at the ease with which he made that suicidal statement. "We'll only win if we have over-whelming numbers. Everyone has to join in or this'll be the shortest slave revolt in history."

Under the cover of darkness, Gordoc slipped his stout fingers inside Ramil's collar. It felt like being throttled, but then the strong man pulled and the collar snapped open.

"Thanks," croaked Ramil, rubbing his neck. He then replaced the neck ring, securing the broken hinge with some cloth ripped from his shirt. "I hope they just think I'm trying to stop it from chafing."

Gordoc moved silently on to the other men in the pen, starting with Melletin. All the slaves, bar one, had agreed to join the revolt. The exception, a thin mad-looking man who was a defrocked priest of Holin, had been too crazy to trust with the secret.

As dawn approached, Ramil gazed at the men crouched around him: his first army. He knew that he was probably leading most of them to their deaths. The whole plan had only the barest chance of success. But he made no apology for the attempt.

"I'd rather die than be a slave," he murmured, thinking of Tashi's desperate plunge into the river.

"What's that, Ram?" rumbled Gordoc.

"We'd rather die than be slaves, wouldn't we, my friend?" Ramil said with more confidence, knowing that his men were listening.

"That's right." Gordoc laughed. He seemed untroubled by the enormous risk they were about to take. "What about you, my brothers, is that what you think too?"

The men grinned at each other recklessly, eager eyes shining in the darkness of the cage.

"Aye, big man, we're with you and the Dark Prince," said a man from Kandar. "We'll give Fergox a bloody nose before we're done."

The market began mid morning. In the shade of a pink silk canopy with gold tassels, rich merchants, farmers, and mine owners lounged on chairs, conveniently close to the block on which the slaves stood for display. The slaves were hustled from their pens lot by lot. The majority of those who had already been sold waited to one side with their new masters—good news for Ramil because it meant potential allies were in the open. Finally, it was the turn of Ramil's slave masters to bring out their wares. They started with the women.

"Now here's a sweetener to open bidding," the southerner called, prodding a mother carrying a baby onto the block. Ramil made a mental note that he would have to do something to protect the women and children in the battle that would follow. He murmured to Melletin, who nodded and passed on the message.

The mother went for a good price to a family needing a wet nurse and was led away. Next onto the block was Yelena. Rather than treat the block as humiliation, she stared around her with a scornful look like a queen on her throne. The slaver prodded her with the end of his whip.

"A house girl, fresh caught and spirited, a pretty addition to any household."

Bidding for Yelena was intense. Two merchants had their eyes on her and drove the price up. The southerner was clearly delighted when he finally closed the bidding at a hundred heralds. Ramil watched anxiously as she was led from the block to her new master under the canopy. The merchant pinched her cheek and said something to his neighbor as she glowered at him. Ramil was relieved to see Yelena being told to wait behind her new master; they would have had little chance to find her later if she'd been led away now.

The women all sold. It was now the turn of the male

slaves. Ramil had been hoping to be one of the last so that most of his men would be out of the pen; instead, he found himself hauled out first. He made a rapid change in plans: he would have to allow himself to be sold before he gave the signal.

The southerner propelled Ramil up to the block.

"Another top quality slave, ladies and gentlemen. Strong fighter. Healthy. Biddable. Suited to be a body-guard or bath-house attendant."

A lackluster bidding began, not enough to satisfy the man's greed. He ripped open Ramil's shirt and slapped his well-muscled torso as if he were no more than a side of meat.

"Come, ladies, we can't waste this young man in the mines. Think what a pleasure it will be to have this lad carry your fan for you when you go visiting. You'll be the envy of all your friends."

The bidding picked up and Ramil was finally sold to a rich elderly woman in a dress of lurid green silk. She giggled with her companion when Ramil was pushed before her. After ogling him closely, she ordered him to wait behind with the other new house slaves.

Ramil made sure he was standing next to Yelena.

"I feel a fool," Yelena muttered, glaring at the velvet back of her new master. "But what he doesn't know is that he's just bought himself a trained assassin. He's in for a shock."

"The shock will come sooner than you think, Yelena," Ramil replied, watching the block as more of his men were sold to the mine owners and herded to one side. "We're going to kick up a little dust in a minute. Be ready."

Yelena's eyes narrowed. "I'm with you, brother."

The final slave to be brought out of the pen was Gordoc. An excited murmur ran through the bidders.

"Now, ladies and gentlemen, last but not least, I present to you our greatest prize!" declared the slaver. "As strong as an ox, he'll do the work of ten men."

Gordoc stood up proudly and thumped his chest. The slaver stepped back, delighted that his catch was playing to the audience.

"Would you like to see how strong I am?" Gordoc roared.

"Yes!" shouted back the merchants, all grinning at this unexpected display. Slaves rarely gave such good value.

"Then I'll show you." Gordoc glanced at Ramil, who gave him a nod. Gordoc tugged the chain that looped between his manacled wrists and collar until he had enough slack in his right hand. He then folded it over his fist. Taking a couple of breaths he began to pull, the muscles bulging in his arms, veins standing out in his neck as he strained. The crowd shouted encouragement and cheered until finally the links broke and Gordoc stood there with his hands free, chain dangling in two pieces. The merchants burst into spontaneous applause which gradually petered out as they realized they now had a giant man standing in their midst unshackled.

"Er . . . shall I start the bidding?" quavered the

slaver, giving Gordoc a wary look. "Who'll give me two hundred heralds?"

At that moment, Ramil ripped off his neck ring and sprinted from behind the merchants. He vaulted onto the block to be caught up by Gordoc and lifted onto his shoulders. The big man steadied Ramil's legs so he stood high above everyone. The Prince swung the collar two-handed in the air.

"Ironfist has shown that we are strong. We'd rather die than be slaves!"

With a head-cracking swoop of the collar, Ramil struck the slaver, dashing him to the ground. Confusion erupted in all quarters as the men from Ramil's pen swung their collars with deadly intent. Guards rushed to subdue the ringleaders only to find themselves attacked by slaves on all sides of the market. Chains were used to throttle guards; soldiers were overwhelmed by the weight of numbers as men threw themselves on sword arms. Those still in their pens howled and clashed the bars. Onlookers screamed as they tried to escape the crush. Melletin and his Brigardian recruits formed a barrier around the slave women with young children, defending them from the stampede. The rich merchants turned to flee but found a determined-looking slave girl standing behind them armed with a pole ripped from their canopy. She cracked one man over the head as he lunged for her. He went down and did not get up again.

"Stay where you are!" Yelena warned the rest, holding the pole like a staff. Two other house girls appeared at her shoulder, one carrying a hefty parasol, the other brandishing a copper pan.

A merchant barked an order to his bodyguard to force passage through, but Yelena poked the man in the ribs with the butt of her pole.

"Are you his slave?"

The bodyguard grunted a "yes," uncertain what to do.

"Then join us, brother. It's your chance to be free."

"Kill the slave filth!" screamed the merchant, thumping his guard on the back.

Yelena pouted, keeping eye contact with the man. "That's not very handsome of him."

"If you don't do your duty, I'll have you flogged!" the merchant spat.

With a roar, the bodyguard spun and knocked his master flat out. The other merchants yelled and scrambled to escape over the rail that had separated them from the common people, but Yelena and her girls brought the canopy down on their heads, trapping them beneath.

Ramil had disarmed a guard with his collar and now had a sword to fight with. Hampered by having to wield it with a loose chain and collar attached to his wrists, he still managed to defeat those swarming towards him. His feet slipped in the blood spilt on the cobbles but he fought on. Injured slaves and overseers groaned on the ground; bodies lay sprawled in the dust. Ramil fought with desperate efficiency. He knew they had to bring this phase to a close before the regular soldiers arrived; bells were already tolling the alarm.

His makeshift slave army would not stand a chance against a disciplined attack.

Finishing off his last assailant, Ramil shouted instructions: 'Gordoc, get some men and build barricades across the main roads into the market. Melletin, release the other slaves from the pens! Yelena, put the hostages in the empty cages.'

"My pleasure!" she replied, rapidly organizing the slave girls who had gravitated to her during the fight.

Ramil could not help smiling when, out of the corner of his eye, he saw her pinch the cheek of her master and prod him over to the pen.

Keys were liberated from the fallen slavers and manacles undone. When the bodies had been piled up, twenty slaves had been killed and thirteen overseers. Saying a prayer for the fallen, Ramil wiped the sweat from his brow, knowing that they had got off lightly on this first attempt. Now the challenge was to keep what they had gained and build upon it. The market offered little in the way of defensive positions. The shed where the women had been housed would do for the wounded but he couldn't afford to get boxed in. He quickly reconnoitered their situation. Gordoc was making good progress with the barricades, piling up carts and crates across the entrance. Weapons that had been in the hands of the oppressors now were distributed among the slaves.

For the slave army to survive, he would need discipline and organization. Already he could see a broad-shouldered slave arguing with Melletin for preventing him from killing his old master.

"My friends!" shouted Ramil, jumping back on the block and clanging his sword against a shield. "Listen to me! Fergox's soldiers will be here very soon and we must make preparations for our defense."

"Who put you in charge?" growled a stocky man, his face showing the sign of many strokes of the lash. "We're free. We should take what we can get and run for it!"

"If you do that, they'll hunt you down and you'll be standing back here next week or hanging at a crossroads!" Ramil replied. "They expect us to act like mindless slaves, weak because we act alone, scattering when we come up against opposition. I say we should act like free men and choose to fight shoulder to shoulder."

Yelena strode forward with a party of girls at her back.

"And free women, Prince," she shouted. "We're with you." She slapped the stocky man on the chest scornfully. "Are you lot so spineless that you'll flee at the first sign of a real fight?"

"You heard the ladies," said Ramil. "Fergox has soldiers, but they only fight because they're paid to do so. Every house in this city has slaves who'll fight for their freedom. We've more allies than we can count if we see what we've started through to the end." He held the gaze of the objector. "But I don't want people I can't trust at my back. If you're with me, good; if you're not, you'd better run because it's going to get very hot around here very soon."

Melletin jumped up on a barrel beside Ramil. "Brigardians, are you with the Dark Prince?"

"Aye!" shouted his countrymen.

"What about you other men?" Ramil asked, looking across the crowd of faces drawn from all parts of the Empire.

The slave who had challenged him took one look at Yelena, then raised his hand. "I'm in. It seems you might know what you're doing after all."

Ramil grinned. "I can't promise that—but I can promise that I'll buy you a drink if we're still alive by the end of tomorrow!"

This met with a cheer and a laugh.

"Now I can't talk to all of you. Form yourselves into your pen groups and appoint a leader. He or she will be your commander. Send them to me. Melletin, can you and the Brigardians stand guard while we get this rabble sorted?"

"Aye, Captain." Melletin ran to the main barricade, swiftly organizing his men to defend all approaches to the market. Ramil was thankful he had such a seasoned resistance fighter on his side; Melletin knew exactly what to do. Search parties were sent to clear any hostile forces from the buildings surrounding the square and a watch established on the upper floors to give warning of any attack.

Ramil was thinking fast. He now had a new advantage he hadn't anticipated, thanks to Yelena's swift action to take the merchants hostage. He approached the pen where they were being held. His merchant-mistress spat at his feet. Ramil ignored her, looking for someone who showed more presence of mind.

"Is anyone here fit to deal with me?" he asked in his most regal tone.

"Fit to deal with slave trash?" howled the old woman, her priceless silk dress now smeared with dirt. "I think not."

Ramil gave her a humorless smile. "Dark Prince, I think you'll find is a more accurate term, madam. But, ladies and gentlemen, I haven't got all day. Who shall speak on your behalf?"

The merchants exchanged a few shifty glances, then a man wearing the chain of a city guild leader stepped forward.

"I will treat with you," he said stiffly. "Know now, slave, that if you surrender, I will see that you are dealt a merciful death. Your allies will be spared but returned to their masters for punishment."

"That is very generous of you," Ramil replied with an ironic bow. "But I think you do not understand your position. I am the one offering you mercy. Send a message to your houses that we will accept a ransom of a hundred thousand heralds for each of you. If the city guard try to attack us, then sadly you will be executed before they can reach you."

"You would not dare!" exclaimed the guild leader.

"Me? No. I have no taste for taking lives. But if I see the troops coming for you, I will not stand between you and your old slaves. If you were merciful masters, then maybe you have nothing to fear; if not, then . . . " He left the sentence hanging, letting them imagine what their people would do to them.

The guild leader struggled with his outrage for a moment but then jerked his head in a nod. "We will send the message. But I cannot be answerable for the reply."

"And I cannot be answerable for the slaves you have nurtured in your households. We are well matched."

Ramil strutted away, pretending more confidence than he felt. He had no intention of allowing even these people to be cut down in cold blood. However, he saw no advantage in letting the old masters know this; they deserved to sweat a little.

"Now, where are my commanders?" Ramil asked, rubbing his hands together in anticipation as he rejoined Gordoc. The big man was outside, surrounded by a dozen men and women, backs straight and eyes aglow with a combative light for the first time since they had been taken into slavery. It took Ramil a second to realize something: he was actually enjoying himself.

Chapter 17

Zeliph lost patience with his silent guest after two days. He was eager to settle the matter of the horse's ownership so he could claim it for himself. Thunder was the kind of mount a rider in the Horse Followers would sell all he possessed to own. Ignoring his wife's protests that the girl was still unwell, he marched into her chamber and dragged Tashi from the bed. He brought her, still trailing her sheet, into the main part of the tent in front of a meeting of tribesmen. She was clad in one of the men's shirts, from which she had refused to be parted to put on more suitable women's robes, and her legs were visibly trembling with weakness.

"As headman, I ask the tribe to give me the blue roan as a prize," declared Zeliph. "This girl says the horse is not hers and she is clearly not fit to own it any more than the clothes she wears. Therefore the stallion should go to me as I caught him on our pastures and brought him here." He sat down as if the matter was done with.

Silence fell for a moment, broken only by the swish

of fly whisks as the men brushed the buzzing nuisances away.

"But what of the pale girl: what will you do with her?" asked an old man seated near Tashi.

Zeliph shrugged and gave a languid wave to the door. "She can come or go as she wishes. She is touched in the head and talks nothing but nonsense when she talks at all. She is of no account."

"But where am I to go if you take my horse?" Tashi asked, her voice so quiet it was barely audible.

The old man cupped his ear. "There, Zeliph, she's clever enough to understand that you're taking from her. Are you sure she's touched?"

"What does it matter? She's a stranger and a woman—she's nothing to us. She can walk home if she must, unless one of you wants to offer her a place in your tent. I've had enough of her in mine."

"I'll offer her a place if your hospitality is so deficient," said a new voice in the entrance. The men looked up and hurriedly rose to their feet, bowing low.

Zeliph's face wrinkled in a worried frown as the newcomer swept in to take a seat next to him. The visitor was an old man with white curly hair and ebony skin, at least six feet, broad-shouldered and still strong despite his years. On his right index finger he wore a gold ring shaped like a running horse.

"Umni Zaradan, you are welcome to my tent," Zeliph said, bowing again.

"But this stranger is not," the man replied, his eyes fixed on Tashi, "even though she brings word of my grandson, Ramil ac Burinholt? Why did you not send for me when she first mentioned his name?"

"A wild claim, sir," blustered Zeliph. "How can this . . . this pale westerner know anything of him? She probably just heard the rumors and spun her story accordingly."

Tashi returned the gaze of the man who claimed to be Ramil's grandfather. She had no need to be convinced of his identity because the family likeness was strong. He was much darker than his daughter's son, but they shared the same brown eyes and stubborn chin.

"Tell us how you know Ramil, child," the man said in a kindly tone, "and let us see if you are a liar as Zeliph claims."

Tashi wrapped the sheet around herself protectively. "I'm betrothed to your grandson, sir."

He raised an eyebrow sceptically.

"I am the Fourth Crown Princess of the Blue Crescent Islands. Ours was a marriage alliance but it . . . er . . . went rather off course." Tashi thought that this was probably an understatement. "We were abducted by Fergox Spearthrower but managed to escape at Midwinter. We were travelling to my home with some companions but it all went wrong again." She stopped. The hostility in the room was palpable. She could not continue so painful a subject if they were just going to pour scorn on her, trampling on her already bruised feelings.

"I believe you are from the Crescent Islands—your hair at least says this is so," Zaradan said coldly. "But if you travelled with my grandson, where is he and why do you have his horse and"—he gestured to the shirt—"what look to be his clothes?"

"Ramil and our friends were taken by slavers on the road near the river," she explained.

Zaradan's eyes narrowed. "But you escaped?"

She nodded, looking down. He had put his finger on the guilt she felt at having survived.

Zeliph sensed that Zaradan's suspicions were roused and hurried to widen the breach between the tribe and the stranger. "How can a defenseless girl escape when a fighter like Ramil ac Burinholt gets taken?" Zeliph asked the men. "I do not believe a word of it. More likely she betrayed them, then ran away with his horse."

"No!" Tashi said indignantly, curling her fists. "I do not know how the men of the Horse Followers behave, but I would never sell my friends! Yes, I ran, but only because we were outnumbered and I had no choice." Tashi turned to Zaradan. "Sir, if you love your grandson, please believe me when I say that I only left him because I had to. Ramil knew that it was my duty."

"Oh?" Zaradan asked guardedly, stroking the bridge of his nose. "And what duty was that?"

"I must return to my people in the Islands and ask them to declare war on Fergox." Tashi knew it sounded like a big claim for a young girl to make in this circle, but she continued, "If our fleet does not reach Gerfal in time, then King Lagan will be defeated. Ramil will have no kingdom to inherit. He would have wanted me to escape, I'm sure of that."

Zaradan arched his fingers together. "I had heard

that Fergox lost two prisoners at Midwinter—the Dark Prince and the Fair Witch, they are calling them. I did not realize the prince in question was my grandson. That makes you the witch."

She nodded. "That was the kindest of the terms Fergox's people called me. But I'm not really a witch, if you are wondering."

Zaradan frowned. "What proof do we have of that but your word?"

"If I were a witch, would I be sitting here with nothing but a borrowed shirt, begging for the return of a horse I do not even claim to own?"

Had he smiled? Tashi could not be sure for the expression was gone, replaced by a determined frown.

"Ah, yes, the horse. I fear nothing can be resolved until that is settled." Zaradan stood up, having reached a decision about her. "It is your right to claim it through trial by combat or trial by ordeal. I'm sure, in fairness to our host, Zeliph would have mentioned this to you eventually."

Zeliph gave Zaradan an ugly look.

Tashi did not like the sound of either option. "But, sir, as I said, I do not claim Thunder. He belongs to Ramil, if anyone."

Zaradan gave her a penetrating look. "So you do not care enough for my grandson to protect his horse for him?"

She realized he was posing this as a test of her veracity. It went far beyond the question of who got to ride the blue roan.

"I would protect anything or anyone that belonged to Ramil with my life," she replied steadily.

"So what is it to be?" Zaradan glanced over at Zeliph, who was reaching for his sword.

Tashi had a sickening recollection of her warrior lessons in Fergox's court. "I am no fighter, sir. Surely, the Horse Followers do not expect young girls to face seasoned warriors?"

"The ordeal it is then. Are you content, Zeliph?"

"Yes, Umni. But what ordeal do you choose? Fire-walking? Desert endurance? Running the gauntlet?" Zeliph sounded ready for anything to prove his worth to own the prince's horse.

Zaradan gazed at the ashen face of the girl who claimed to be his grandson's betrothed.

"Horsemanship. The one who shows the most skill with the roan shall keep him."

Tashi dropped her chin and shook her head, knowing she'd already lost Thunder.

"I'll go first!" declared Zeliph eagerly.

Thunder was brought from his paddock to the space in front of Zeliph's tent. The tribe crowded around their headman, calling out encouragement and praise. Tashi stood to one side, supported by no one. Zeliph leapt on Thunder's back and executed a series of beautifully judged turns and jumps, concluding his performance by making the stallion rear in front of Zaradan. He slid nimbly from the horse's back, exhilarated by his own prowess. Tashi had to admit he knew how to bring out the best in the stallion.

"Let's see what the girl can do!" Zeliph mocked. "I'll wager she can't even climb in the saddle."

The men laughed.

Resigned to defeat, Tashi moved forward, remembering how Ramil had always approached his horses. She stood in front of the great warhorse and waited for Thunder to notice her. The stallion bumped her gently with his nose, and they stood head to head for a moment.

"I'm sorry, Thunder," she whispered, "I don't want to lose you but I'm just not a very good rider."

Then don't ride, came a prompting in her head.

It was worth a try. If she didn't get trampled, she might make her point.

"Any man who wants Thunder will have to separate us," she said aloud, and sat down between the warhorse's front hooves. He bent his neck and nuzzled her hair, standing over her as if she were his foal.

"This is ridiculous!" snarled Zeliph, striding forward to take the bridle. "I'll show her who is the horse master!"

Protecting his charge, Thunder flicked his head clear, then snapped his teeth at the man's arm. Zeliph tried to mount him, but the stallion sidled away, all the time keeping Tashi beneath him, out of reach. Tashi tried not to flinch as the hooves stamped around her. Desperately, Zeliph threw himself in the saddle. Thunder bolted clear of Tashi, then bucked until he had unseated the Horse Follower. Job done, he trotted back to stand over the girl as if nothing had interrupted them. Outraged to be humiliated before his tribe, Zeliph approached from behind but Thunder was wise to his game. The headman received a sharp kick to the stomach and ended doubled up, clawing at the sandy earth in agony.

Zaradan clapped his hands. "Enough! It is clear the stallion prefers the girl over Zeliph. They stay together."

Zeliph hobbled over and spat at Tashi. "You favor the claims of a bare-legged girl over a tribesman? Are you mad?"

Zaradan's face became stony, his dark eyes flashed. The men murmured at Zeliph's audacity. "Take that back or I'll cast you from the tribe! No man questions my judgment as long as I am Umni." He reached for a curved knife tucked in his sash.

Zeliph knew he'd gone too far. He touched his lips and then his heart. "I repent of my rash words."

The Umni of the Horse Followers released the knife hilt. "Then they were not heard," Zaradan said formally, touching his ears then heart.

Zeliph kicked the flap to his tent aside and disappeared without looking back at his lost prize.

"Come, child. You will not be welcome here any longer," Zaradan said to Tashi, gesturing to Zeliph's household.

Tashi got up and patted Thunder on the neck. "Thank you," she whispered.

"My tent is half a day's ride away." Zaradan frowned at her appearance, bare legs showing beneath the shirt. "Do your people really choose to dress like that? It is not suitable for the desert."

"No, sir. I was taken from my bed," she added defensively.

"If you are to be my grandson's wife, I cannot allow you to ride in this fashion. You there!" He pointed to one of the men. "Fetch the girl a robe."

The man hurried off and returned with an old grey scrap of cloth.

"I see Zeliph is feeling generous," Zaradan said ironically, wrapping it around her. "He's headman here and I'm afraid you have just made yourself very unpopular."

Tashi wrinkled her nose. "I'm used to it."

"Come then. Let's ride."

Zaradan's tent was larger than Zeliph's, but like his it had separate quarters for men and women. The interior was brightly decked with rugs and hangings all with the horse motif. It was cool in the tent, thanks to the kilted-up sides that allowed a breeze to keep the air moving. Zaradan left Tashi in the care of his son's wife, a shy woman who responded to her attempts to make conversation only with nods and nervous laughter. Two big-eyed girls hung at the entrance, staring transfixed at the strange-looking foreigner. The woman offered her a fine turquoise tunic, decorated with seed pearl, and loose-fitting trousers. She then brushed Tashi's hair for her, murmuring to her children as she admired the color.

Zaradan invited Tashi to dine with him that evening, an invitation she accepted with trepidation. She had realized that he must be some kind of king among his people as Ramil's mother had been referred to as a princess. Yet it appeared that the notion of kingship here was different from any she knew; what she had witnessed at Zeliph's tent suggested Zaradan was more like a chief of a series of subordinate tribes with fluctuating loyalties. Ramil had never mentioned his grandfather, so she did not know how Zaradan would regard her presence here.

When she entered the men's side of the tent, she found the Umni was not alone. A man in his middle years, of similar build and coloring, was reclining at the table at his side. Both rose as she approached.

"This is my son, Resphir," Zaradan said. "And this girl appears to be Ramil's betrothed, though what her true name is we have not yet established."

"Ramil calls me Tashi," she replied, bowing Crescent-style to the two men. Zaradan waved her to a cushion and offered her a plate of meat and couscous. She helped herself to a small portion, not feeling very hungry. She sipped nervously on a tiny cup of mint tea.

"Where is Zarai's boy?" Resphir asked her bluntly before she could even swallow a mouthful of food.

"He's . . . I'm not sure. He was captured, I think, about three days' ride south from where the road divides to Tigral." An idea occurred to her. "Can you help him? Do you know where they would have taken him?"

"The slave market in the city, that's plain enough," said Resphir with a frown. Tashi had the impression he did not approve of her. "I told you, Father, that you should never have allowed Zarai to marry that Gerfalian. Her child in slavery—it is an insult to the whole family."

Tashi felt a rush of annoyance. It was easy for him to criticize when he hadn't been the one fighting for his life. "It was hardly Ram's fault!" she protested. "I don't know how many came for us, but there were three alone after the other woman and me, so they must have come in force. No man, not even Resphir of the Horse Followers, could've escaped them."

Zaradan held up a finger to stop her tirade. "But you have not yet told us how you avoided the indignities of being auctioned in Tigral."

Tashi pushed her plate away. Once again she was being made to justify her choices. "I jumped in the river."

"I do not believe you could have done that and survived," said Resphir dismissively.

"Would you like to see the scars?" Tashi asked. "Because the river was not kind to me and left plenty of marks." Tired of being doubted and scorned, she turned to Zaradan. "I don't know what you think I am doing here, sir, but for some reason our paths have crossed. You have a choice: either to believe me and aid me in my mission, or thwart me and make Fergox Spearthrower very happy."

Zaradan crumbled up a piece of bread as if he had not heard her. His face was impassive.

"All right," she said in exasperation, "even better, hand me over to the warlord. He'll either make me his fifth wife or burn me at the stake, but never mind that! You'll be able to disappear into your desert knowing that you did not lift a finger to save the land your daughter loved, nor the woman Zarai's son chose."

"You are passionate, little one," said Zaradan calmly.

Tashi felt like throwing her plate at him. "I think you would be too if you had been been kidnapped, shot at, beaten, accused of witchcraft, and I don't know what else for the last few months."

"And you've fallen in love."

This brought her up short.

He smiled. "I would have made a sorry use of my years on this earth if I could not tell when a young girl is in love. It always gives them a certain sparkle." He fluttered his fingers in the air. "So what do you want from us, O lover of Ramil?"

His tone made her outburst seem childish.

"I . . . I want to take a ship home. And I want you to help Ramil because I cannot," Tashi said, feeling her cheeks burn. Zaradan made her feel all the inadequacy of her own sixteen years against his decades of experience.

"I think we can do that," said Zaradan with another smile. "Now eat your food. My grandson will not want a scrawny wife in his bed when we get him home."

Chapter 18

The slave revolt acted like a spark to dry tinder. By the end of the second day, Ramil had more recruits than he could easily accommodate in the makeshift barracks around the square. Slaves were simply walking out on their masters and presenting themselves at the market to have their chains struck off. Nursemaids left their charges on their mistresses' doorsteps, cooks abandoned the stoves and let the bread burn, gardeners picked up their shovels and headed to the harborside.

Ramil's pretense that this was all about ransoms for the rich people had worked. What he feared most—an immediate assault by trained soldiers—had not material-ized as the influential families were concerned for the lives of their hostages. The authorities held back from a counter-attack, believing the slaves could be bought off, separated, defeated in dribs and drabs, then executed at their leisure. They were already devising a spectacular demise for the ringleader, something to make all slaves in the Empire tremble. But Ramil was not worried about their plans; his main problem was keeping his troops focused: too many yearned for revenge and had no vision beyond making the masters suffer. He needed something to hold them together and raise their spirits before he attempted to take more of the city. Sitting in the market, watching the ships at anchor down by the water only a few streets away, he thought he had the solution.

"So, Melletin, what do you think about taking on the pirate fleet?" he asked casually at breakfast.

The Brigardian choked on his mouthful.

"They're sitting there like fat ducks," Ramil continued, gesturing to ten vessels tied up at their moorings. "It would be a brilliant stroke if we could sink them."

"But what about the galley slaves?" Melletin pointed out once he had found his voice. "We can't just burn them—we'll be roasting a lot of innocent men if we do that. And if we just march upon them, the sailors will massacre us from their decks."

Ramil shook his head. "You're thinking like a soldier. I'm thinking like a devious slave trying to get even with his master."

Melletin laughed. "Are you, Prince? So what's the big idea? I assume you have one or you wouldn't look so pleased with yourself."

"I think this is a job for the girls."

At dusk, mist rolled in from the Inland Sea, wrapping the port in its featherlight embrace. A gaggle of pretty dockside girls sauntered up to the fleet at anchor. Two approached the gangplank leading to the flagship, the *Bloody Spear*. A bored sailor standing guard peered over the side and made out the comely form of a black-haired girl. She had a dark-skinned companion swathed in a veil hovering shyly at her shoulder.

"Hey, gorgeous!" called the girl, raising her skirts to flash a shapely ankle. "Need some company?"

The sailor glanced behind him. "Sorry, sweetheart, not allowed to have visitors on board. Not with all the trouble yonder."

"Aw!" said Yelena. "Those cursed slaves are ruining our fun—everyone is saying the same." She minced a few steps up the plank, her friend following. "But I wouldn't have thought you would be a spoilsport."

The sailor scratched his head. "What about my boss?"

Yelena put her hand on the rail. "Don't worry about him," she said breathily. "My friend will see to him."

The veiled girl nodded and dropped onto the deck. She was surprisingly tall for a woman, but then the sailor knew that Captain Jirk liked an armful. He beckoned the pretty one towards him.

"He's in his cabin," he told the dark-skinned girl. "Say I sent you with my compliments."

The second girl padded off in a rustle of silk and cloud of cheap perfume.

"Now, what about you, my lovely?" the man said, reaching eagerly towards Yelena to pull her into a hug. But he never touched her. Everything went black and he ended up headfirst in the water with a quiet splash. Yelena ran across the deck and swiftly despatched a second sailor on watch. A muffled cry came from the captain's cabin—Ramil emerged wiping his sword on his dress.

"Don't do that!" said Yelena. "You'll ruin the material."

The two "girls" crept down the ladder to the lower deck. The smell of the pit holding the galley slaves was worse than the pens in the market. Four sailors were playing cards on an upturned box while their slaves slept over their oars. Yelena approached, swinging her hips provocatively.

"Hello, lads, looking for some fun? My friend and I, we're full of surprises."

A big bald-headed man nudged his card partner. "Things are looking up, Toburt. The captain's sent us a present."

A bell outside began to sound the alarm. Yelena and Ramil exchanged a glance: one of the attacks must have been spotted. Oarsmen stirred in their seats. Thinking quickly, Yelena grabbed on to the big man's arm, pretending to quiver with fear.

"What's that?" she gasped. "Don't tell me the filthy slaves are making more trouble! Oh no, what's going to become of us?"

There were yells and cries outside. Toburt and the other two men grabbed their swords and disappeared up on deck. The bald man hung back a moment to pat Yelena condescendingly on the rump.

"Stay here, darling; I'll go sort it out and be back to look after you."

"Perhaps I should look after you now," Yelena said, moving in closer.

The man grunted and fell back, clutching at the dagger slipped between his ribs, his eyes wide with surprise.

Yelena rubbed her bloodied hands on his shirt with disgust as the slaves cheered and rattled their chains.

"I hope he deserved it," she said wistfully as Ramil unchained the first bank of slaves.

The first oarsman limped forward and kissed her hand. "He did, miss, a nasty brute. Even his wife'll thank you."

Ramil put an arm around her. He knew how she felt. Taking a life in cold blood like that made you feel no better than the enemy.

"I'm sorry, Yelena. Perhaps I should've come up with a different plan," he said as the slaves rushed the ladder, sweeping the remaining sailors out of their path.

Yelena straightened her shoulders. "No, Ram, it's what I was trained to do. I'm saving far more lives than I'm taking—that's the main thing."

Ramil kissed her brow, honoring her courage. "Come then, let's see how the others have fared."

From the evidence of the dockside, the operation had largely gone to plan. One ship had rumbled the fake "girls" and put up a fight, but that was soon ended by an influx of slaves freed from the other ships. Ramil watched with satisfaction as the freed men set about firing their former prisons. They knew exactly

310

what to do, doubtless having dreamt of such a day for years. It seemed only right that they should have the pleasure.

March had arrived and with it the spring. The meadows and forest were bursting with blossom but no one greeted it with joy. Each petal that unfolded was another step nearer to invasion. King Lagan had done everything he could think of to prepare. Wardens had formed into bands of fast-moving raiders, ordered to harass Fergox's army as it marched through the forest, but Lagan knew that the major battle would happen outside the walls of his city. That was where the war would be decided.

Lady Egret, now one of the King's counsellors, approached him on the battlements one sunny morning as he stared out across the ocean. The twenty Blue Crescent ships were still moored in the harbor. They had defended Falburg from pirate raids, but Lagan wished heartily that the alliance had gone ahead as planned.

The King turned on hearing the distinctive tap-tap of her cane. Lady Egret was smiling.

"Good news, my lady?" the king said, guiding her to a seat. "I could do with some."

"Yes, I think it is good," she said, lowering herself carefully onto the bench. "Duke Nerul reports that Fergox has handed over command of his army to Junis and is returning with all speed to Tigral."

This news was so unexpected; Lagan was aware that he was gaping in a most unkingly fashion. "And this is certain?"

"As certain as my bones ache every morning," she replied with a smile.

"And does the duke say why?"

"There is a full-scale slave revolt in Tigral. Beautifully timed, I may say, thank the Father."

Lagan rubbed his hands. "I could not have ordered it better myself. I don't suppose you can add icing to this cake of news by giving me word of Ramil?"

She shook her head. "I'm sorry, Your Majesty. All I know is that he and the Princess headed south, attempting to reach the sea and sail to the Islands that way. Perhaps you should look to the ocean for news of him now, not to Brigard."

The King nodded. "Thank you, lady."

"No more proposals of marriage today?" the old woman said with a glint in her eye as she rose.

Lagan put his hand to his chest. "Having heard your warning, I am too afraid of Lord Egret to dare to importune you."

She chuckled. "Ah, would that I were young again and then maybe I would make my lord jealous. Sadly, those days are long gone." She bent her head to him and hobbled away, a distinct spring in her step.

Zaradan escorted Tashi to the southern shores of the Inland Sea. The way lay through the pastures of the great herds, jealously guarded by the desert people. Without the Umni as her guide, Tashi would have been stopped before she had gone very far. As it was, they rode through the tent villages and were made welcome each evening by a different headman.

"My grandson's betrothed," Zaradan would say with a regal sweep of his hand to Tashi, now well hidden under purple desert robes. This was enough for her to be accepted.

In the hours spent together in the saddle, Tashi grew to admire the old man. He was no friendly soul like Lagan, ready with a hug and a word of encouragement, but harsh and indomitable, rather like his land. Yet he had a kindly streak and a respect that showed in his dealings with her. He had begun to call her "daughter," as if he considered her already married to Ramil—a bittersweet title for Tashi, not knowing if she would ever see him again.

At the port of Tarqui, a ramshackle town of white houses and wind-blown palms, Tashi realized she had reached the point where she would have to leave the stallion behind.

"Umni," she said as they dismounted on the harbor, "please take Thunder for me." She handed him the reins. "Keep him for Ramil."

Zaradan touched his head then his heart. "I promise to deliver him to my grandson."

Tashi took off her light saddle bag, containing Ramil's shirts and her old clothes ruined in the river, then said her farewells to the horse.

"If you find Ramil," she told Thunder solemnly, "take care of him for me."

The horse bumped noses with her, then butted her gently away.

Zaradan sent a man ahead to scout the dockside. No Empire ship would be safe for Tashi; it would have to be a trading vessel from another nation, like the neutral lands to the south or the Ice Archipelago. Tashi waited patiently, watching the seabirds diving for the scraps thrown to them by the fishermen gutting their catch. The man returned swiftly.

"Umni, there is a Blue Crescent trader in the harbor!" he declared. "They said they'd take on a passenger."

Tashi felt her heart leap. Finally, the Goddess was smiling on her.

"Well then, let us negotiate your passage," said Zaradan, offering her his hand. "It will be interesting to have proof of your identity from a countryman."

"Countrywoman, I expect," Tashi corrected him, hurrying towards the square-sailed boat with a feeling of coming home.

The return to her people, however, did not proceed smoothly. Uniloma, salt trader from Phonilara, refused to believe Tashi's claim that she was the Fourth Crown Princess, even when she removed her desert veil and showed her blonde hair. Instead, the hard-bitten old trader called the Goddess's curses down on the head of the girl who could make such a sacrilegious assertion.

"I've seen the Fourth Crown Princess," Uniloma declared. "She was on her barge heading off on some grand voyage. Beautiful she was: so poised and calm, face white as it should be, hair veiled."

"But that was me!" protested Tashi from the dockside. "I was sitting on the Throne of Nature wearing an orange sash."

"Any fool knows what the Fourth Crown Princess wears. That proves nothing. You don't behave like an Islander, young miss; you look like one, but you're acting like an Easterner."

Tashi opened her mouth to refute this but then closed it again. It was true: her countrywomen would hardly recognize her these days as she had become so emotional. Her behavior was indecent by Blue Crescent standards.

Zaradan stepped in. "So you say this girl is an impostor?"

"I can't see how she can be anything else," Uniloma stated resolutely.

"But, by your admission, she is an Islander. Will you carry her to Rama? I will pay you well for your trouble."

"As long as she does not come up with any more nonsense like this, I'll take her." Uniloma's eye was on the purse at Zaradan's waist.

Zaradan nodded and dropped a bag of coins into the woman's wrinkled palm. Tashi turned away, humiliated. A cloud covered the sun and the water turned grey.

Small waves chopped at the jetty. Everything looked bleak and colorless. She felt a pressure on her arm and found Zaradan at her side. He bent and kissed her on the brow.

"It took me a while but I believe you, daughter. Captain Uniloma will too when she realizes that people, even crown princesses, can change. You've become more yourself, that is all."

"Thank you," she whispered. "Thank you for having faith in me."

"And you, my daughter, have faith that I will help Ramil. And when I see him, I will tell him where he can find you."

It was a slight hope he offered but far better than nothing. Tashi nodded and bowed a deep Blue Crescent bow to a king. She then picked up her bag and boarded the ship. Uniloma was ready to sail, having loaded her cargo. Tashi kept out of the way as her countrymen cast off and turned the boat westward. The southern shore with its little ports and rocky inlets dropped below the horizon, leaving only the golden glow of the distant sand dunes to hint at the presence of land.

On the journey home, Uniloma and the rest of the crew watched their passenger suspiciously. The girl said very little, but they were surprised to see she knew the rituals of the Goddess and followed them faithfully each morning and evening. It was clear that she found great solace in this task; her face was calm and content as she completed the prayers with skill and no fuss. A whisper of doubt crept into the captain's mind.

"Where did you say you were from, girl?" Uniloma asked gruffly one morning. The vessel was far out to sea, giving a wide berth to the coastline of western Holt and any bold pirate vessel.

"From Kai."

"And your name?"

"Taoshira." Tashi did not risk giving her title again but neither was she going to lie.

Uniloma clucked in irritation.

"My family and friends call me Tashi."

"I'll call you Tashi then. I'm not using a princess's name for you."

Tashi sighed. There was no point arguing. The truth would come out when they returned to Rama. It would only be an unseemly squabble if she pressed her claim here.

That's if anyone recognizes me, Tashi thought glumly. *I'm not sure I'd know me either. I might have to stand naked before my servants to prove my point.* She smiled at the idea. *No, I'm definitely not the same person if I can laugh about that.*

After two weeks at sea, Rama appeared on the horizon, the familiar mountain rising from the Sapphire Ocean with the city on its slopes in a patchwork cloak of green, gold, and white roofs. Tashi leant on the rail, wishing away the final miles, relieved that she had made it home in good time. The long journey through Brigard, Kandar, and Holt now seemed almost like a dream as her life joined full circle with the girl who had sailed unwillingly for Gerfal only a few months before.

Uniloma wanted no more to do with her dubious passenger once they had cleared customs. Dumped with her bag on the dockside, Tashi hesitated as to her next step. There was no barge waiting to meet her, no guard of honor. The porters jostled her, the sailors ignored her, and the street vendors took one look at her frayed shirt and Southerner robes and left her alone. Tashi realized she did not know how to get from the port to the palace. In the past she had always been carried in state, having to make no decisions herself. The palace shone above her, walls golden in the setting sun. Its green curved roof, decorated with dragon and lion gargoyles, glowed like polished jade. Down here in the dirt of the harborside, it seemed impossibly far away, like an enchanted palace from legend. Tashi understood why Uniloma refused to believe that a flesh-and-blood girl could be the same creature as the untouchable Fourth Crown Princess. Stripped of her trappings of rank, she was an unimpressive creature.

Well, thought Tashi, shouldering her pack, *it's about time the rulers of the Blue Crescent Islands got a bit closer to their people. I sat on the Throne of Nature: I've just become more natural, that's all.*

She set off up the hill following the line of the canal.

In the twilight, the big bronze gate of the palace loomed above Tashi, oppressive and closed.

What now? she wondered. *How do people get in to see us if they need to?* She had never asked herself this before, accepting that there was a line of officials between her and the public who filtered out the timewasters and the frivolous, in fact dealing with everything but the most crucial business.

She knocked on the door.

A little window jerked open and a man put his face to the grille. "Palace hours are between nine and six. Come back tomorrow." He slammed it shut.

Tashi knocked again.

The man reappeared. "Are you deaf? We are closed to the public."

Tashi jammed her fingers in the gap, yelping as he tried to squeeze it shut.

"You must listen to me. I am Princess Taoshira, the Fourth Crown Princess, and I'm going to sit here until you let me in—or summon someone to check my claim." Tashi removed her bruised fingers and the doorkeeper banged the portal shut.

Bells in the palace began to ring: it was the time of the evening service. Disheartened by this final obstacle, Tashi slumped down against the door and began to pray. She heard the grille open again but carried on.

An hour passed. Two soldiers came out of the palace.

"You've got to move," the woman officer said, poking Tashi with a pike. "You can't sit here all night."

"I'll sit here until someone comes to find out if I'm telling the truth," Tashi replied defiantly.

The officer gave a tired groan. "And that is?"

"That I am Taoshira, Fourth Crown Princess."

"Good try, love, but if you want a free bed for the night I'd set your sights a bit lower." The officer chuckled. "I don't want any unpleasantness, just move along."

"You'll have to arrest me if you want me to move," Tashi said steadily, "because I have no other way of proving my claim but to wait until someone in the palace comes. Send for the Mistress of the Royal Chamber, or any of her assistants, but please do not mistake me: I am neither mad nor a fake. Just well travelled."

She closed her eyes and leant back against the bronze panels of the gate, wondering what the guards would decide.

"Wait here," the officer said, motioning to her colleague, and disappeared back inside. She returned five minutes later with the Under Mistress. Tashi could hear her apologizing for the inconvenience as she guided the lady to the gate.

"It's probably nothing—just a silly girl playing a joke on us—but I thought it best to ask you."

Finally, her luck had changed for the better. Tashi opened her eyes, looked up and smiled at the elaborately gowned palace servant.

"Hello, Fa Rinira."

For the first time in her life, the Under Mistress screamed.

The Crown Princesses called an emergency meeting as the palace simmered with the astounding news. The Fourth Crown Princess, last heard of in Gerfal, had turned up like a beggar at the gate. Rumors had placed her in Fergox's prison, a convert to the worship of Holin, dead, lost in Brigard; but no one had expected her to find her own way home. On the urging of Korbin, the Third Crown Princess, a month ago they had even begun deliberations on how to replace a princess who was only missing and not deceased, thinking this would call for a new ritual and a vote. Now all this was thrown into confusion.

Tashi sat in the Hall of the Floating Lily waiting for her sisters to assemble. Her throne was in Gerfal, so she made do with a wooden stool. The throne had never been very comfortable in any case. She could sense people coming to look at her, peeking out behind the pillars. By the standards of the court, the mood was tempestuous. Fans were flapping nervously; brows furrowed.

The three Crown Princesses came in together. Tashi guessed they had been in the antechamber, conferring as to how to handle her return. She rose and bowed, proud to be standing before them in her travelling robes and Ramil's shirt, wanting them to see her as she was after the journey they had sent her on.

"Fourth Crown Princess, we rejoice to see you back among us," said Marisa, the First Princess, though her eyes were full of doubt and tone far from welcoming. "We expected you to return married with your husband, but you stand before us alone. How is this possible?"

Tashi looked to her ally, Safilen, the Second Princess, and saw that her eyes were glistening. Had she been crying? With joy or sorrow to see her back? Korbin was her usual inscrutable self.

"The Goddess chose another path for me to the one we elected," Tashi said quietly. "Tested by many trials, the alliance stands. I have come to ask that we defend our friends, the Gerfalians. The man responsible for my abduction, insulting our entire nation in doing so, stands at the borders of King Lagan's land. I move that we send our fleet to Gerfal's aid."

The Third Crown Princess raised a finger. "It is too soon to talk of such things when we do not understand what has happened to you. You are not married to the Gerfalian Prince?"

"No."

"The Gerfalians let you be taken by Fergox Spearthrower?"

"They failed to prevent it, yes. Prince Ramil was also abducted."

"And are the rumors true that you wavered in your faith before the whole of Fergox's court?"

Tashi felt the question like a blade at her throat but had no intention of pretending she was better than she was, whatever the consequences. Her journey had stripped her of the desire for such artifice.

"I did."

The hisses of collective censure buzzed in the room, but Tashi felt she was beyond shame now. The events in Fergox's court seemed to involve a different person.

Korbin regarded her coldly. "You are not worthy to stand here."

"Then I kneel." Tashi sank to her knees. "I have never been worthy; I have been taught this by bitter experience. I am a goat girl from the smallest island made princess through bribery and corruption. But I say to you, sister, that none of us are worthy of the Goddess. She chooses the most unexpected instruments to do her work—even warlords, even goat girls."

Tashi turned to Safilen and saw that she was nodding.

"I know it is not our way to show emotion and I am showing my feelings now, but you sent me on this journey and should not blame me that I come back changed. I cannot pretend that none of this matters to me or hide my feelings from you all. You should at least listen to what I have learned as, believe me, I have suffered to gain this knowledge."

She paused, waiting for permission to carry on with her plea.

The First Crown Princess inclined her head. "Continue, sister."

Tashi knotted her fingers together in her lap. "I have learned that the Goddess wants us to risk ourselves in her service. Her love is not just for the Islands but for the Easterners too. If we do not help defend these people, we will condemn them to Fergox's rule. I have seen it and it is founded on rottenness and cruelty. If we do nothing, we also condemn ourselves. Fergox will turn his eye on us and destroy our culture, just as he tried to destroy me."

Tashi stopped, her throat too tight to continue. She felt angry with the Princesses sitting there so calmly when she was living through such a maelstrom inside.

In the silent cloisters, water tinkled from a fountain into a pool, the ripples rocking the lilies.

I'm like the fountain, merely rocking them in their complacency, Tashi thought bleakly, gripping her knees to stop herself from clenching her fists.

Marisa spoke: "We know that our safety and that of Gerfal are connected, but we must be able to trust them as an ally before committing our navy. That was the reason for the marriage, an unbreakable bond between our two nations. Yet this did not take place and you sent word that you were returning unmarried. Why should we trust them now?"

Tashi held up open hands in despair. Her passion was not swaying them and she was running out of reasons. "Because the King is a worthy man—because his son risked his life to get me home—because, despite what I said a few months ago, Ramil and I are pledged to each other." She raised her eyes to meet the First Crown Princess defiantly. "Because I, Taoshira, the Fourth Crown Princess, trust them."

Marisa nodded, giving nothing away. "Then, sisters, let us vote. Shall we send our fleet to the aid of Gerfal?

Cast your color to the floor: on my right for yes, on my left for no."

Tashi reached for her voting sticks but, of course, she had no throne and she had transferred her rights to the Second Princess. Korbin saw the gesture.

"We have not said the ritual to return Taoshira her vote in matters of state; neither has the question of her fitness to rule been satisfactorily resolved," Korbin announced. "There should at least be an inquiry into her conduct at Fergox's court. She will have to abstain if we make the decision now."

"Do you still wish us to proceed, Taoshira?" Marisa asked.

Tashi looked down at the lily mosaic, seeing the lines rather than the whole picture. She remembered the body of the priest sprawled in front of her in the temple and the shame of her time in the hands of the priests of Holin. She had no idea how merciful or understanding her sisters would be when she told the detail of that story.

"I wish for no delay," she declared. "I trust my sisters to make the right decision." She looked meaningfully at Safilen, the only one so far not to have spoken.

A bell rang. The First Crown Princess closed her eyes and cast her vote to the right.

"I say we should send our navy."

The bell rang again and the Third Princess threw her stick to the left.

"I say we should defend our home waters, not leave ourselves exposed to the Pirate Fleet."

The Second Crown Princess held two sticks in her hand. She kept her eyes open as she cast her votes, looking unflinchingly at Tashi.

"I say that sound policy points to helping our allies; our sister's love for these people confirms it."

Orange and green sticks tumbled down to join the white of the First Princess.

"Then it is decided. The fleet will be despatched immediately," announced the First Princess.

Tashi sank down, the tension gone from her body. She had done it: she had fulfilled her promise to Ramil.

If Korbin was disappointed, she hid her dismay well. She rose. "It will be my task, as the one responsible for the dispensing of justice, to undertake the inquiry into the recent conduct of Taoshira. We must discover if she has broken any of her vows and investigate the validity of her election."

"It is your right, sister," said the First Princess gravely.

Safilen frowned.

"Then Taoshira of Kai must be confined for a period of reflection and examination in the Goddess's Enclosure while I complete the investigation," Korbin continued.

Tashi had been expecting something like this, but confinement to the Enclosure was an unheard of step. Only maidens and single men dedicated to a lifelong silent worship of the Goddess were allowed there. It was the most sacred place in the temple complex within the palace walls. To send her there without being one of the devotees was to isolate her completely.

"But why treat our sister with such harshness?" objected Safilen, anger flashing in her eyes. "What has she done to be kept imprisoned? For that is what you are proposing, is it not?"

"I do not know what she has done. It is the purpose of the inquiry to find out. I am merely thinking of the security of the Islands," the Third Princess said calmly.

"I think my honored sister doubts my loyalty," Tashi said in a weary tone. "She is wondering if Fergox has made me into his creature. I will submit to the inquiry. I ask nothing for myself now that my mission to aid Gerfal is accomplished."

"Then lead our sister to the Enclosure and see she is suitably accommodated," Marisa instructed Korbin. "We will hear the results of your investigation at the New Moon."

The meeting broke up. Numbly, Tashi followed the dark robes of the Third Princess along the corridors. She could hear the bustle of messengers running through the courtyards, the murmur of people spreading the news about the decision to send the fleet and the disgrace of the youngest princess. It was a bitter homecoming. Palace servants peered at her from behind doors, speculating as to what taint she brought with her: loss of faith, deceit, treason? Tashi knew in her heart of hearts that she no longer belonged here. She had grown too rebellious for her role in the state administration. They might judge her guilty and cast her out, but even if she regained her position, she would only break the system of government like an ill-fitting cog in a machine. Perhaps the Third Princess sensed this and knew the real danger.

Korbin stopped at the door leading into the Silent Courtyard.

"Please do not mistake me, Taoshira," the Princess said stiffly. "I am driven by no personal animosity towards you and think only of our nation."

"I understand." Tashi bowed.

"I will attend on you tomorrow to begin our inquiry. Use the time to pray and reflect on your errors if you have committed any."

"Many. All the time," Tashi admitted with a slight smile. "But then don't we all?"

She stepped through the gateway, not looking back.

Chapter 19

In the slave market shed, Melletin spread a map of Tigral out on a table.

"We're here," he said pointing to the port district. "When the troops attack they are likely to try to surround us and wear us down with crossbows and archers posted on these vantage points." He indicated the tall houses up the hill with roofs overlooking the square.

Ramil sat cross-legged on a crate, his commanders around him.

"Well, we've known all along we can't stay here. If I were them, I'd also attack from the sea, opening up a fourth front. We'll be squeezed to death if we try to defend this place. What would be the most defensible spot in Tigral?"

"That'd be the palace—it's got walls all the way around it," said a local man.

"Then I suggest we move headquarters to more comfortable accommodations," Ramil said with a grin.

"But, brother," said one of the Brigardians, "we can't just go marching up there and knock on the door!"

"Oh, I wasn't thinking of knocking. Remember, my friends, Fergox has sent his army to the border; the garrison here will be at its lowest for years. The city authorities will be demanding their assistance to crush us rebellious slaves. What I had in mind was something to force their hand and empty the palace of the fighting men. If we could bait them to attack us at the market, we could take advantage of their distraction and some of us can use it to enter the palace."

Melletin rubbed his chin. "But that would be suicidal for those left down in the market. Why not divide our forces and start lots of minor disturbances all over the lower city? Let's get the authorities chasing their tails. We can then, on an agreed signal, melt away and all make our way to the palace."

"I like it." Ramil rubbed his hands together. "Now I know why my father has counsellors—to do the thinking for him."

"I'm thinking like a bandit, Prince, not a counsellor," Melletin explained.

"But the success of this particular bit of banditry would depend on the discipline of our troops," Ramil pointed out. "It would be a disaster if they disappeared and never showed up again. I don't fancy trying to hold the palace on my own."

"Some of them will desert," said a commander from among the galley slaves, "but the majority will stay with us—at least as long as they think you offer them a better future."

Future? Ramil hadn't been thinking that far ahead,

but the men needed to know he would see this through to the end. It was his duty to do so. He couldn't expect them to risk their lives as he did in the hopes of helping a distant Gerfal.

"You can tell them that if, with their aid and if God wills, we win the city, there will be no slavery, but neither will there be a bloody revenge. I'm not here to reverse matters so that slaves become masters and masters slaves. I'm here to rewrite the rules completely."

The galley man displayed the sores on his ankles where his chains had eaten into his flesh. "No man should be a slave. I hope, young Prince, you live to bring in your new order."

"So do I, my friend, so do I."

Preparations were set in motion to split Ramil's army into divisions charged with causing trouble in the different quarters of the city. Melletin and his Brigardians volunteered to take on the toughest assignment, the fort down at the harbor. Yelena and her volunteers chose the food markets. Gordoc said he would stay with Ramil and a party of a hundred hand-picked men who were going straight for the palace.

"We move out at first light," said Ramil, "so everyone get some rest."

"What about our guests?" asked Yelena, gesturing to the caged merchants. "If we're abandoning this position, what shall we do with them?"

"Kill them," suggested a man from Kandar running his thumb down the edge of his knife.

"Now, now," said Yelena, batting him playfully on the arm, "none of that. After all, I've got quite fond of my pet master and wouldn't like to see him hurt."

"And neither do we want to start the day with revenge killings," Ramil added. "If they are guilty of crimes against you, they should be given a trial, but unfortunately there's no time. No, I think the best thing to do is to leave them here. They have served their purpose. Once we move, either we'll be strong enough to defend ourselves or we will have failed and they become irrelevant. Besides, I imagine we will have plenty of new hostages to handle if we get as far as the palace."

This comment met with a general murmur of assent.

The meeting was on the point of breaking up when Jules, one of Yelena's troops, entered the shed at a run.

"Prince, there's a man here who wants to speak to you," she announced breathlessly.

"One of the merchant families come to bargain, I expect," Ramil said with a groan. He had suffered these embassies repeatedly over the past week. "I swear they are trying to wear me down so I drop my price."

"That's merchants for you," said Gordoc with a shrug.

"He's not a merchant; he's—" Jules began.

"Let me through, let me through!" Professor Norling forced his way past the guard and marched into the shed. "Ah, it is you! I thought as much when I heard the rumors of a dark prince being in residence. What foolishness made you a slave, eh? See what happens when I leave you children to your own devices!"

"Professor!" Ramil leapt up and embraced the doctor. Then Gordoc thumped him on the back, Melletin shook his hand vigorously, and Yelena planted a kiss on his blushing cheek.

Smiling at this welcome, Norling looked round the room. "And where's our little princess?"

Melletin shook his head, trying to warn him off the subject. Ramil closed his eyes; in the tumult of the past days, he'd managed not to dwell too much on Tashi's fate. Yelena whispered in the old man's ear.

"I see." Norling coughed awkwardly. "I'm more sorry than I can say."

Ramil braced himself; he could not slide back into paralyzing grief again. If Tashi were dead, he would soon be joining her if he didn't focus on the task at hand, and she would never forgive him.

"I take it, Professor, this is not only a social visit?" he asked, his voice almost normal.

"No, of course not. I've come to ask why on earth you haven't called on me before now?"

Ramil took a step back. "Er . . . well, we've been a bit busy, Professor."

"I can see that for myself. I had a terrible job getting here: they've ringed you off with troops five men deep. I had to crawl through the tunnels and some of them are in a disgusting state." Norling sniffed his robe with a doubtful look. "But why you did not think to ask the resistance for aid is beyond me. We can be immensely helpful to you."

Ramil struck his forehead with the palm of his hand. "Stupid! I should have been drowned at birth," he muttered.

"Oh, I wouldn't go that far," said Norling generously. "I don't think it's too late. In fact, I'd say that you've managed very well without me."

"So, what can you do?" asked Melletin, pulling up a barrel for him to sit on.

"Firstly, I can move your men around the city for you undetected—that's if you don't want to fight your way out of here."

"I'd prefer not to," admitted Ramil.

"Then my people can show you the tunnels under the city. The resistance have been using them for years to pass unnoticed and to smuggle people in and out."

"Thank you, that is most timely."

"And there's more. I bring news that is both good and bad."

"Yes?" Ramil looked puzzled.

"Fergox is on his way back."

Ramil slapped his thigh. "Brilliant!"

"For Gerfal perhaps, Prince, but not for us," Norling said soberly. "He's pulled back two thousand men and is making for us at high speed. And you can bet that he will not be in a very loving mood when he gets here. It's not just you slaves that need to be worried: it's every man, woman, and child in Tigral now. You can expect him within a fortnight, maybe earlier."

"Then we'll be ready for him. He won't recognize his capital when he gets back." Ramil stood up and shook each of his commanders by the hand. "There's no time to lose. We're moving headquarters. Take your men out of here under the cover of darkness—the professor will show you the way. We attack at dawn. I'll see you all in the palace tomorrow night. Don't be late to the party or I'll have to start without you."

Ramil watched his men file out, wondering just how many of them he would see again.

At dawn, bells began to ring all over Tigral. The meat market was on fire, the smell of frying pork wafting enticingly over the lower city. Traders shut up shop and kept their families inside as the streets descended into an anarchy of looting and burning. The Guild Hall went up in flames. Next came the news that the fort was under attack; the Shoemakers' Street was reported to be a running battle between the watch and rebels, animals released from their pens adding to the confusion.

The officer in command of the troops surrounding the slave market waited for orders from the City Guild. In contrast to the rest of the capital, the market was eerily calm. Eventually, a messenger arrived from the city authorities.

"You're to take your men to restore order in the Cloth Market!" the man gasped. He'd run all the way from the burning Guild Hall and inhaled far too much smoke.

"But what about the slaves?" the officer asked, gesturing towards the barricaded market. "You won't want them escaping and adding to the riots."

The messenger shook his head in disbelief. "They're already out. Surely, you realize you're guarding an empty cell?"

The officer gulped, anticipating the court martial already. Knowing he would be blamed if this was a ruse to let the slaves escape, he decided quickly that he was not going anywhere until he had seen the evidence with his own eyes. He gestured roughly to his lieutenant.

"We're taking the slave market back and then proceeding to the Cloth Market," he announced, sounding more confident than he felt.

With a heroic cry, he led his men over the barricades, bringing much noise and swinging of weapons, only to be met with stony silence.

"You and you, search the buildings!" he barked, pointing at two of his most reliable officers. He could feel his authority ebbing away in the scornful looks of his men. "The rest of you, form up. We are going to teach those filthy slaves a lesson."

Yelena, lying on a roof top of a nearby house, grinned as the merchants were led out of their cage, blinking as they stepped into the sunlight. She blew a farewell kiss to her pet, then slithered out of sight.

The resistance network had a back door into the palace, thanks to the offices of a sympathetic cook in the massive kitchen complex. So many people came and went to supply the appetite of the court that an extra delivery was not likely to raise suspicions. Ramil, Gordoc, and two men waited outside the walls, sides of stolen meat on their shoulders, their weapons hidden in the carcasses. A guard came to check them over.

"Delivery for kitchen, sir," said the cook, a little man prone to sweating when nervous, as he was now. Ramil wished the man would stop wringing his hands; he would give them away if he carried on like that. "I'm making the First Wife's favorite for a dinner party. She's particular about wanting it fresh."

The guard body-searched the butcher's boys before waving them through.

"Don't expect her party will be going ahead," the guard grumbled, "not with all that trouble down in the city."

"In that case, sir, I'll bring it to your mess," babbled the cook, rather too keen to please. "Must hurry. Lots to do."

He ushered the four rebels into a pantry and waited while they pulled out their swords.

"Thanks, my friend," said Ramil, shaking his hand. "Keep your head down. It's going to get interesting in here."

They had chosen the northern gate. As most of the trouble was happening to the south, Ramil guessed all eyes would be turned in that direction. They ran swiftly and silently through the slave quarters. Though they were seen by many of Fergox's household, no one stopped them. Most just turned their eyes away, having learned that it was best not to notice, but a few more adventurous souls grabbed makeshift weapons and ran after the rebels, poised to defend their backs.

Ramil paused in the shelter of a doorway opposite the gate. He glanced out: there were five guards, armored and alert. He leant back, taking a pause before the plunge.

"Do you remember Tashi dancing before those guards at Felixholt?" Ramil asked Gordoc.

"Aye, Ram."

"Of all the stupid, brave things to do! I was so angry with her."

"So was I. She could be very stubborn."

"For her then."

"For her."

The two men launched themselves across the court-yard, unaware that they now had twenty slaves behind them in addition to their back-up of two. The soldiers grabbed their weapons but too late. Slaves smashed them over the head with logs, buckets, anything they could lay their hands on, as the rebels ran them through with swords. The skirmish was bloody but brief. Clearing the bodies to one side, Gordoc opened the gate with a heave and the men waiting outside rushed in.

"You know your targets!" Ramil shouted, abandon-ing stealth. "Attack!"

Half the slaves swarmed up the walls, engaging the soldiers in close combat. Ramil led the rest towards the main palace buildings. Arrows whizzed overhead. A man on his right fell with a grunt. Surprise gave the slaves a huge advantage. Ramil took out the captain of the guard on the steps of the throne room while Gordoc saw to the man ringing the alarm. The big bell stopped tolling.

"Is that it?" Ramil asked, wiping his brow. It had all seemed so sudden. He had expected more resistance. Unknown to him, in the other buildings of the palace complex, word had gone out and slaves had quietly slit the throats of the men-at-arms. Few had been left to defend Fergox's throne. Like Tigral itself, years of abuse had made the palace ripe for picking.

Gordoc and Ramil shoved the double doors open.

"I never did like Fergox's taste," Ramil said with a curl to his lip.

The high hall was decked in red cloth, falling in swaths to the ground like rivers of blood. The ceiling was held up by black pillars rising out of a black marble floor. A gold throne sat under a canopy at the far end. But the hall was not empty. Standing on the steps to the throne was a grey-haired woman dressed in a gold silk robe. Three children clung to her skirts. Ramil glanced at Gordoc, who shrugged, as surprised as him. They expected everyone to have fled by now.

Ramil advanced, sword still drawn. He had learnt from Yelena never to underestimate a lady.

"That's right, slave scum!" the woman said, clutching her children to her. "Run me through in cold blood!" She wrenched aside her robes, inviting the killing thrust.

Ramil put his sword point on the floor and leant on the hilt.

"I have no intention of doing any such thing, madam. Who are you, pray?"

The woman looked a little confused to have her dramatic gesture rejected but she did not give an inch.

"I am the First Wife of Fergox Spearthrower. I ask no mercy for me or my children. Kill us now, rather than subject us to the mockery and disgrace of being prisoners of slaves."

Ramil bowed, now understanding exactly with whom he was dealing. "Honored to meet you, madam. I have heard about you from your husband."

The woman laughed wildly. "You? You've heard of me from the Emperor? I think not."

"I did, when guest of your husband in Felixholt. He was planning to dispose of you, if I remember, and replace you in his affections with a younger woman."

The First Wife spat. "The witch!" She had obviously heard the rumors.

"In your place, I would reserve my anger for the husband, not the unfortunate woman of his choice. Anyway, I can assure you that he will not be marrying her." Ramil spun his sword on its tip, wondering what he should do about Fergox's family. The First Wife would make a terrible hostage if Fergox wanted her dead—and Ramil had an inkling that he could not live under the same roof as her for long.

"You claim he was going to get rid of me?" The woman hugged her eldest daughter to her side. "He wouldn't dare!"

"I'm afraid he would." Ramil sighed. "I wish no harm to come to any innocents caught up in the transfer of power. But neither can I leave you to cause trouble for me." He had a sudden idea—brilliant if he could negotiate it. "I would like to offer you the choice to go into exile—you and the other wives."

"Exile? Exile where?" The woman frowned.

"The Blue Crescent Islands. I understand they give shelter to women in their temples and treat them much better than here."

The woman looked aghast. "You would send me to that island of witchcraft and demon worship?"

"Or would you prefer to stay here as a slave captive and await your loving lord to rescue you? He was talking to the royal axeman about your neck last time I saw him."

The First Wife glowered. "It seems I have no choice. I will go into exile, but return triumphant when you meet your doom."

"Quite so. I'm glad you have seen reason. I suggest you leave as soon as I can arrange passage as I fear you won't like the changes I'm about to make to your domestic arrangements." He bowed, waving her in the direction of her pavilion.

With a flounce of her skirts, the First Wife swept out.

"What a woman!" Gordoc sighed appreciatively as he watched her disappear in a swirl of indignant silk.

The interrogation of the Fourth Crown Princess took place in a plain white room near the Silent Court, the Third Princess on one side of a grille, Tashi on the other. Tashi sensed that her answers did not satisfy her inquisitor. Court scribes hovered in the background taking notes. Scrupulously keeping to the truth, Tashi admitted that Fergox had told her he had paid for her election and bullied her into doubt for a short while. Korbin seemed less interested when Tashi explained how she had regained her faith and rediscovered the beauty underlying the rituals.

"I fear, my sister, your election was tainted from the beginning," the Third Princess announced at the end of the session. "You are blameless in this, but it undermines our system of government if such things are left to stand."

"Perhaps," said Tashi, but then she recalled how the Princess before her represented the most powerful family on Rama. "However, all of us were elected through a system open to human greed and ambition. We have to trust the Goddess's hand is upon the process."

"You are not comparing your case with mine and my sisters', I hope?" Korbin asked primly, fluffing up her robes like a cat with her fur on end.

"Actually I was. I'm sorry if you find that offensive."

The Third Princess twitched her skirts round as

she walked out of the room, not deigning to give a response.

Well, that went well, Tashi thought bitterly, tapping her fingers on the table.

The new moon rose over an expectant Rama. The fleet was already far away on its journey to Gerfal, but the people were more interested in the drama close at hand. Tashi's grandmother, the matriarch of the family, had come to court to hear the Third Crown Princess's findings. She had not yet been allowed to see her granddaughter, but had been given a place in the front of the audience for the hearing. The old lady sat grim-faced. If the rumors were true, then their girl had failed them all in a spectacular fashion.

When Tashi was led into the Hall of the Floating Lily, her grandmother was the first person she saw. She had managed to remain calm until this point, but the sight of the matriarch's disapproving expression made her hot with shame and fear. The awareness that she was displaying her emotion made Tashi feel even more wretched. Now she understood the function of all that white paint.

The three Crown Princesses were already seated. In the space usually occupied by the Throne of Nature, someone had found her a plain wooden chair. Tashi sat down quickly, wishing she could make herself invisible.

A bell rang and the Third Princess rose.

"Taoshira of Kai, I have investigated the matters concerning your fitness to rule and will present my conclusions. Firstly, my sisters join me in regretting the ordeal you endured in Gerfal and your subsequent incarceration. We are aware that this would test the strength of any of us. However—"

Tashi flinched at the "however." She guessed that it boded ill for her.

"Two concerns remain. The first is that you publicly doubted the Goddess, undermining the reputation of our creed before the eyes of the world. This is contrary to your vows of office in which you promised to defend our faith until death."

Tashi pressed her lips together. So Korbin expected her to die rather than waver a fraction. If so, then she could have no conception of what Tashi had endured and how death would have even been welcomed by her. Only Ram had saved her from throwing her life away.

Ram.

I must be strong for Ram, she thought, and raised her chin.

"The second concern," continued Korbin, "admittedly beyond your control, is that it has emerged that your election was flawed. The Chief Priest on Kai is now under arrest while this matter is investigated. This fact, coupled with your weakness under trial, suggests that you should never have been chosen for the role you now occupy. The Goddess's will was not followed when you were erroneously instated as Princess."

344

Tashi put her face in her hands, not wanting them to see her shame. She had never felt worthy, now this was publicly confirmed.

"The procedure in this case is clear. The election is to be declared null and void and a search for the correct candidate to be instigated."

The Second Crown Princess raised her hand.

"Yes, sister?"

"Are we not to vote on this?" Safilen asked, her voice tight with anger.

Korbin shook her head. "We cannot vote to uphold a corrupt election. We have no choice but to reject the false one and quickly find a replacement."

So that was it: they were casting her out. Abruptly, Tashi got up from her seat and turned to go. There seemed no requirement for her presence any longer and she had no stomach to sit through deliberations on the unfortunate girl to succeed her. At least now she could return to Holt and search for Ramil. That's if he still wanted her when she found him.

"Taoshira, you are not free to leave," the Third Crown Princess said severely.

"I would've thought you would be pleased," Tashi said quietly, standing with her head hung.

"Anyone who has held the office of Crown Princess cannot simply walk out and rejoin society."

"Then I'll go somewhere else, away from the Islands." Tears were running down Tashi's face. She brushed them off, angry at herself for her weakness.

"But, I repeat, you are not free under law to do so. You must return to the Silent Court and live out your days in the seclusion of the temple."

Tashi spun round to stare in horror at Korbin. "I cannot—I will not believe that this is the Goddess's will for me! You take away my position, my self-respect, and now my last chance to find happiness. I beg you to show mercy."

"Child," the First Crown Princess intervened, "there is no happier being than one who has chosen to serve the Goddess in the Silent Court."

"But I do not choose it—not now, maybe not ever." Her voice cracked with panic.

"Sisters," implored Safilen, "is this necessary? Taoshira has been tested enough. Why not let her be free on her own terms?"

"Because that is not the law," Korbin said resolutely. She turned back to Tashi. "But you may bid your family farewell before returning to the Goddess's Enclosure for the last time. There is no law against that."

Tashi stood for a moment, feeling as if her heart was crumbling into pieces inside her. She had nothing left to live for, no hope of rejoining Ramil, no future. Fergox had been cruel, but this was a trial beyond any she had endured. Mechanically she walked to her grandmother, knelt, and kissed the hem of her robe.

"Sorry," she said briefly, then left with her escort, no longer caring what became of her.

Chapter 20

Fergox's troops had a miserable time marching as fast as they could endure from their camp on the borders of Gerfal to the capital, Tigral—a journey of hundreds of weary miles. The wagon train was ambushed in Brigard. Stragglers were set upon by bandits in Kandar. By the time they reached the open plains of Holt, they were all itching to be home and take their revenge upon the slave rebels who had caused them to miss the conquest of Gerfal.

Riding at the head of his army on his second-best horse, Fergox knew he was paying for his mistake of pushing ahead with expansion while neglecting the lands he already owned. He took the lesson philosophically. Perhaps this slave revolt was a timely reminder. Once the revolt was crushed and the ringleaders disposed of, he would have to impress his rule more firmly on his people. He pondered the punishment of killing a tally of all slaves across the Empire, even those who took no part in the rebellion. If he killed one in five that would reduce his workforce, but he could make sure that only the least valuable were chosen to bear the penalty. Yes, that would be fitting and stamp out any embers of revolt. As for the one they called the Dark Prince, some jumped-up slave currently lording it in the palace, he would be executed very slowly in the slave market where he belonged.

Fergox camped at the last crossroads before the city walls and summoned his commanders. In the last few miles, his forces had been swollen by those who had escaped from the city. They brought with them tales of the ferocity of the galley slaves and the widespread unrest. Most of the rich families had fled—if they hadn't been murdered in their beds by their own servants. The middling folk, the shopkeepers and the tradesmen, had stayed to look after their property, making peace with the slave rulers, but the rich merchants predicted it wouldn't last.

Fergox executed the officers who had been in charge on the day when the palace fell as a reminder to the others what was at stake. He then ordered his troops to form up in their ranks, ready for the onslaught.

"We're facing a rabble army that has been fortunate enough to meet with general incompetence from those whose blood now stains the crossroads," Fergox said, gesturing to the headless officers thrown ignominiously to one side. "We'll pass through the city like a cleaver through a carcass and retake the palace. Any civilian on the streets may be counted an enemy and treated accordingly. When we have attained our objective, you may teach the citizens of Tigral a lesson and reward yourselves for your loyal service to me."

The soldiers thumped their shields. It was rare that Fergox gave them free rein to take plunder after a victory.

"Now ride out!"

The army jingled into action: the infantry marching in tight squares of fifty men, the cavalry sweeping along behind. Fergox had no interest in retaking his capital street by street. His plan was to capture the center of power and then assert his authority over the rest. The slaves would probably crumble at the first sign of real soldiers. They could not possibly have any experience or training to match. He wouldn't be surprised if he was able to stroll in and win just by the terror of his presence.

His views seemed to be confirmed by finding the city gates wide open to receive him. There appeared to be no one mounting a defense—surprising because at the very least he expected the most hardened slaves to try to prevent him from entering. He sent a division of his elite cavalry troops ahead. They clattered over the cobbles, through the gate and into the square beyond. All the shutters on the houses edging the plaza were closed, apparently abandoned. Normally this area was dominated by an equestrian statue of Holin, which looked uncannily like Fergox sitting upon his stolen blue roan warhorse. Today the god had been dismounted, leaving the rearing horse riderless.

Cautiously the cavalry rode on, alert for any sign of resistance. The commander sent outriders ahead to tell them what lay around the bend in the road. They didn't come back. He was about to send word of this to Fergox when a sound behind him made him turn in his saddle. The old portcullis, unused for years, crashed down, dividing the cavalry from the main body of the army. A huge man stood by the gate holding an axe, having just severed the portcullis rope with one mighty stroke. Before the commander could give an order, the shutters on the houses flew open and missiles rained down on the riders. They were caught in an ambush.

"Ride on!" shouted the commander, knowing he had to get his men out of this deadly valley. The horses clattered along the street, men falling from their saddles sprouting arrows from their backs. They rounded the corner to come face to face with a barricade bristling with pikes and sharpened sticks. The commander tried to force his way through but his mount perished, driven onto a spike, and the commander was trampled where he lay.

The massacre was soon over. Melletin grimaced as he surveyed the results of his plan: it had worked perfectly but the aftermath was ugly. Horses scattered in riderless panic until caught by rebels and quickly led away. The bodies of the men with scarlet threads in their beards and the mounts that had perished were dragged off the streets to be buried later.

"First win to us, I think," Melletin said to Gordoc. "Take word to Ramil. Tell him Fergox is going to be really mad now."

Fergox had no commander to punish for the fiasco as not one of his elite troops returned. He'd underestimated the slaves, he admitted to himself. Someone knew what he was doing. This put Fergox on his mettle. He still had nearly two thousand men and knew the city well. He was not really concerned.

"Commanders Horg and Finuil, take your men and enter by the East Gate; Minol and Kay, yours is the West Gate. I will lead the rest by the North Gate, making straight for the palace. It appears this rebellion has a thinking head; we have to cut that off before it can be crushed."

Fergox gazed up at his beautiful palace, home of his wives and younger children. The slaves had probably killed them already as they had made no attempt to bargain with the lives of their hostages. He had already decided that he would not treat with the rebels. He had grown-up sons in his army—enough to ensure his succession. Though it angered him to lose any child of his blood, he knew they were a weak point if he allowed himself to become sentimental. As for wives, they were replaceable.

Fergox crushed his reins in his fists. *I'm angry*, he thought in surprise. He had been in command so long, used to people doing his will without question; he had not been defied for years and now it had happened twice since Midwinter. The strength of feeling reminded him of the early days when his reckless passion for conquest had driven him to turn himself from small bandit lord to ruler of the known world. He relished the merciless rage for a moment, like a rider enjoying the speed of a galloping horse, before giving his commanders a chilling smile.

"What are you waiting for? I want the heads of all the rebels at my feet by nightfall, but make sure you save the Dark Prince for me."

King Lagan watched from outside the walls of his city as Fergox's sister, the Inkar Yellowtooth, led her troops from under the cover of the trees. His spies had reported their numbers, but seeing the rank upon rank of men march onto the green meadows of his land, he felt his heart constrict in his chest. He had delayed them as long as he could, sacrificing many of his wardens in desperate skirmishes in the forest, but now the invaders were here.

Lord Taris with his son behind him, both in full battle armor, rode up to the King.

"We are ready, Your Majesty," Taris said.

"It's going to be tough," Lagan replied, wiping his brow with his leather gauntlet.

"Yes, sir. But without Fergox's cool head to guide them, we have a chance."

"Not much of one."

"No, but still."

Lagan smiled.

A helmeted man on horseback, followed by twenty others, trotted forward from the city. His armor was in the old style, embellished with swirls of bronze inlay.

He paused before the King and bowed, then flipped his visor up, revealing an old face with fierce blue eyes.

"Lord Egret and the Brigardian exiles reporting for duty, Your Majesty."

"Ah, so you're Lord Egret," said the King, touching swords with the man in greeting. "May I say that your wife is a treasure?"

"You may, sir. And I'm here to defend her and all those of our nations who cannot fight."

Lagan thought the old man looked as if his fighting days should be over too, but there was a steely glint in Lord Egret's eye that forestalled such comments.

"You are a very welcome addition to our forces. Take your orders from Lord Usk, please, and fall in on our right flank."

The Brigardians trotted away with the Prime Minister's son in the lead. Lagan paused to admire his army spread out across the field: so many young lives and brave hearts about to plunge for the first time into the messy horror of battle. It was one small mercy not to have to worry about Ramil being among them.

The Empire herald galloped across the battlefield with a white flag. He reached King Lagan and bowed.

"The Inkar Junis wishes to parley," he said briskly. "She wants to offer terms."

"I'll hear her, but the only terms I'll accept are unconditional withdrawal," Lagan replied.

The herald nodded and turned his horse to take the message back to his mistress.

"Are you coming with me?" Lagan asked Taris.

"What? To see your old sweetheart?" The Prime Minister chuckled. "I wouldn't miss this."

The two men rode forward to meet the Inkar halfway across the meadows that separated the two armies. She approached them alone, making a fearsome sight as she galloped towards them, the feathers on her helmet fluttering in the breeze.

"Junis." Lagan bowed as soon as she reigned her horse to a standstill. "It is always a pleasure to see you. But why come in such warlike fashion?"

The Inkar frowned, disliking what sounded very much like mockery.

"Surely two old friends should not meet like this?" continued Lagan. "If all my men hadn't been so busy defending my nation, I could have thrown you a nice little ball. I seem to remember you liked dancing."

Junis bared her yellowed teeth at him. "I danced with your son at Midwinter, did you know that?"

Lagan smiled grimly. "No, I did not know he had that pleasure."

"And where is the stinking horse thief? I'll make him dance when I've killed you and all your little fighters and flushed him from his hiding place. You've not a hope against my army. You're outclassed and outnumbered."

"Outnumbered, perhaps," said Lagan, stroking his beard. "But not outclassed. I see that your diplomatic skills are still as strong as ever, Junis."

She snapped her fingers at him. "That to diplomacy. I do my business by the sword."

Lagan sighed and looked at the skies as a relief from her vindictive face. A strong wind blew in from the sea, and the clouds were moving rapidly like hosts of white soldiers driven to assault the land. Junis had betrayed the fact that Ramil had not been recaptured, another good thought to cherish on this terrible day. This desperate battle did not seem so hopeless if Ramil survived somewhere in the Empire.

"Your herald mentioned terms," he prompted her.

"Yes." She licked her lips. "If you surrender the city, I will spare the civilians, take your soldiers into slavery or recruit them to my forces, and see to it that you are given a dignified death. Your daughter will live as a guest in my house; your son, unfortunately, will not."

"Very generous," Lagan said in a hollow tone. His eye was caught by a glimmer out to sea on the horizon. A tiny white sail appeared, followed by others, until the whole ocean seemed to be covered by a flock of birds come down to rest on the waters. "I don't believe it!" he murmured.

"You had better believe it," said Junis, "because it is my final offer."

Cheers and bells could now be heard in the city. The Blue Crescent ships already in harbor fired a salvo that echoed from the walls.

With an upsurge of hope, Lagan turned in his saddle and snapped his fingers. "That to your offer, Junis. I reject your terms. Look to the ocean. You should be thinking what terms you might accept from *me*." He spurred his horse to retreat.

With a scream of fury, Junis galloped back to her troops and ordered the attack. Her infantry advanced, tight ranks of soldiers in red tunics crawling like ants over Gerfalian land. Lagan signalled his own men forward.

"You fight for your homes and your freedom!" he shouted, riding along the lead edge brandishing his sword. "Charge!"

The cavalry swept forward, driving into the pike-bearing infantry as battle was joined on the flower-studded meadows. Soon the spring blooms were trampled under boots and hooves, the ground wet with blood. Men cursed; horses screamed. Lagan's forces were hard pressed, pushed back to the walls by wave upon wave of Empire soldiers. Lord Taris fell as he defended the gates. Ramil's cousin, Hortlan, was trampled when knocked from his horse. The King fought by his standard bearer, aware that his knights were dying around him. Lord Usk went down, wounded by an arrow. Lord Egret killed Junis's second-in-command only to die on the Inkar's sword. Lagan spurred his horse forward to meet her in battle. She yelled with delight as she saw him charging towards her. Their swords met with a clang, sparks flying.

A shout went up from the harbor.

"For the Goddess!"

Now under new orders, hundreds of Blue Crescent

sailors from the ships that originally came with Tashi rushed to the relief of Gerfal. More warships arrived, disgorging their cargo of fighters onto the harborside. Armed with swords and long knives, the Westerners hacked and slashed their way through the Empire's infantry. An elite force of riflemen took up position on high ground to fire upon the invaders. Cannon boomed from the decks, shot sailing overhead to pound the Inkar's reserves.

"Witchcraft!" shrieked the Empire soldiers as comrades fell to invisible missiles, which left circular bloody wounds. Some turned to flee only to be shot in the back.

In the midst of battle, Lagan and Junis exchanged arm-jarring blows. She caught him with a swipe, cutting his cheek to the bone. He replied with a slash that smashed into her left arm, leaving it hanging useless, blood spurting from the wound. Junis stared down at her arm in mild surprise.

"Lagan," she said faintly.

The King struck, killing her with a blow to the head.

"Sorry, Junis," he said as the Inkar fell from the saddle. "These are the only terms I offer."

Reports from all over Tigral reached the rebel headquarters in the palace throne room. East Gate had fallen but the galley slaves were holding their own at the barricades in the Cloth Market. West Gate still survived but the Brigardians were taking heavy casualties. No one had tried South Gate again.

Ramil paced the room restlessly. He knew their fortunes were balanced on a knife edge. The only way they could win was if he could take out the Spearthrower himself. He was relying on Fergox's pride to bring him to the palace. He just had to hope the warlord would take the bait.

Yelena dashed in, her face shining with excitement.

"The old goat's at the North Gate. What shall we do?"

"Let them through but keep out of sight. Are your soldiers posted all round the walls?"

She nodded.

"Remember, Yelena, we mustn't let them out of the palace but pen them in here until I've finished with Fergox."

Yelena nodded, then darted forward and kissed him on the lips. "That's for Tashi."

Ramil smiled, touching his mouth. "You're a wicked woman, Yelena. Melletin's going to have his hands full with you."

"I hope so!" she called, returning to her position outside the throne room.

Ramil gave orders for his assistants in the command center to fall back out of sight into the robing room. He checked that the archers were up in the rafters, bows trained on the doors, and then took up his post on the throne, sword across his knees.

As anticipated, a few minutes later the doors were thrown back and Empire soldiers poured into the room, fanning out to the edges to take up defensive positions. A man appeared in the doorway, hands on hips, gazing straight down the hall at Ramil. He drew his sword and marched forward confidently.

Ramil rose and bowed.

"Hello again, Fergox."

A soldier rushed towards Ramil, his sword raised. An arrow flew from the ceiling and brought him down sprawling at the Prince's feet. Fergox glanced up once into the roof, but continued advancing.

"Ramil ac Burinholt. I confess that I'm surprised to see you here. I thought you had scurried home to Gerfal," Fergox said coldly as he reached the bottom of the steps. "Though perhaps I should have realized that no ordinary slave could have got so far."

Ramil held out his sword to stop Fergox from coming any closer. "If you bothered to investigate your own subjects, you'd find out that there is no such thing as an ordinary slave."

Fergox raised his sword. "How touching. But tell me, before I kill you, what have you done with my little Tashi?" He took a swipe at Ramil, no more than a probing of his guard. Ramil blocked it and swung away.

"She is not your Tashi and never was."

Fergox smiled. "You've warmed to her, I see. That makes it all the more perfect a revenge when I kill her. I'd like to keep you alive so you can watch me do it."

Ramil swung but Fergox jumped back out of range.

"In fact, I hope you've got her hidden away somewhere in the palace for me to hunt down," the warlord continued. "I have some unfinished business with her which I'm looking forward to settling."

Ramil brought his sword round in a high strike; Fergox blocked so that they were face to face, wrestling for an advantage.

"She's not here," Ramil hissed. "She's dead."

It was the first time he'd admitted this aloud and he felt a yell of fury inside. This man had brought about the death of the woman he loved. Ramil launched himself into an attack for real, entering into a glittering pattern of thrusts and strikes. Fergox's eyes widened with surprise but he matched Ramil, parrying each blow efficiently, experience telling him to let his opponent tire himself. Sweat ran down Ramil's brow, his breathing fast, his muscles singing with the strain.

Fergox gave ground until he had his back to a pillar swathed in red cloth. With a swipe he cut the cord and the cloth fell down in folds, burying Ramil's sword. Before the Prince could get it free, Fergox thrust at his heart. Ramil dived, feeling the blade nick his left arm. He rolled, now weaponless, his sword still caught up in the cloth. A soldier behind him moved forward to finish him off.

"Leave him!" barked Fergox. "He's mine."

Ramil sprang to his feet and sprinted back to the throne.

"Pathetic!" Fergox laughed. "Still clinging to power, are we, Prince?"

Ramil kicked the chair over and picked up a short spear from among the weapons he had hidden there. He levelled it on his shoulder, knowing he had only one shot before Fergox ran him through. The warlord charged, mouth open in a yell. Ramil threw his spear. It struck Fergox in the throat, above his breastplate, cutting off the cry.

"We never did finish best of three, did we?" Ramil said.

The warlord staggered, then stopped, the sword clanging on the floor as his arms lost all strength. He swayed, then fell backwards, a look of shock on his face.

With a shout of fury, the soldiers rushed forward to avenge their commander. Ramil swept up Fergox's sword and leapt back on the dais to defend himself. A soldier swiped at his legs, catching him on the calf. Ramil cut him down with a back stroke. His slave supporters burst from their hiding place in the robing room; arrows hissed from overhead. Bloody confusion reigned as fighters exchanged blows and some cut down their own side in mistaken frenzy. When Ramil was finally able to lean on his sword, surrounded by the dead, he saw that he had lost many of his men, including the surly man who had challenged his authority on that first day in the market. He had turned out to be a fierce and loyal fighter and left a family in eastern Holt. Others lay there, each with his own history, united only by their belief in Ramil's promise to offer them a better life.

Ramil bowed his head in respect, vowing to fulfil their expectations if he survived the day, then limped to the door.

"Toll the bell," he ordered one of his men.

The great bell of Tigral began to boom—the pre-arranged signal that Fergox was dead. Ramil thought he could hear faint cheering around the palace. He stepped through the open door and looked down into the courtyard.

The killing had gone on here too. As ordered, Yelena and her troops had engaged the army as it entered the courtyard. The rebels had been losing ground against the best-disciplined of Fergox's soldiers when a mass of purple-robed horsemen had appeared out of nowhere, sweeping through the North Gate. Galloping into the courtyard, they had been like a scythe through corn, cutting down the warlord's men. A small band resisted, fighting back to back surrounded by the bodies of their comrades, harried from all sides by slave fighters and the ruthless men of the Horse Followers.

Ramil gave a shrill whistle. Gradually, the rebels heard the signal and stepped back, their weapons red with blood.

"Soldiers!" Ramil shouted, brandishing the warlord's sword. "Fergox Spearthrower lies dead on the steps to his throne. This battle is over. Put down your weapons and I will be merciful. Carry on fighting and it will be to your deaths."

One soldier howled with rage and threw himself at the large chieftain of the Horse Followers. Before he even reached him, the soldier died with a kitchen knife in his back, thrown by the resistance-friendly cook. This seemed to convince the others. They dropped their weapons.

Ramil nodded. "Good. Yelena, take the prisoners to the barracks."

The Dark Prince gazed around his kingdom. What a way to start his new order: men lying in bloody heaps, limbs severed, the wounded groaning.

The wounded. The thought prompted him back into action.

"Sir Cook!" he shouted to the knife thrower. "Can you gather some men and see to the wounded, please? Tell Professor Norling that we treat friend and foe alike."

Professor Norling jumped down from the wall, where he had been expertly firing a crossbow for the last half hour, and rolled up his sleeves.

"Professor Norling wouldn't let you have it any other way," he muttered.

The chieftain dismounted and walked up to Ramil, leading a familiar blue roan by the bridle. The prince thought that in his exhaustion he might be hallucinating: *Thunder here? But how?*

"Greetings, Grandson. I haven't seen you since you were a baby and I must say you've turned out well." Zaradan gestured to the conquered palace. "A credit to your family. My daughter, Zarai, would have been proud."

"Thank you, Grandfather," Ramil said faintly, remembering the tales of his mother's father, the Umni of the Horse Followers, and of his presence at Ramil's naming ceremony. What he was doing here now Ramil could not even begin to guess. "Your decision to come for a family reunion was very well timed."

Zaradan smiled, his white teeth gleaming. "That wasn't my idea. I am here merely as a messenger. Tashi sends her love and returns your horse."

Ramil swayed with shock at this news. Zaradan let go of Thunder's reins and caught his stunned grandson to his chest, feeling him shake with laughter mixed with sobs.

Thunder trotted forward and gave Ramil a nudge with his nose, checking his rider was all right.

"Oh yes, Tashi told him to take care of you," said Zaradan, laughing. "Not my idea either."

Chapter 21

Two weeks into Tashi's sentence, the peace in the Courts of the Goddess was disturbed by the arrival of exiles from Holt. Four women and assorted children had been accommodated in the pilgrims' quarters in the palace, separated from the devotees only by a grille. Tashi watched them closely as they moved among the pilgrims, keeping themselves aloof from the Islanders. They appeared to be led by a formidable grey-haired woman dressed in white mourning robes and took no part in the worship in the Enclosure.

Of course if they were from Holt, they would no more worship the Goddess than a goat, Tashi told herself. But what were they doing here? And why had the Crown Princesses decided to lodge them somewhere that must be offensive to their Easterner sensibilities?

Her obligation of silence prevented her from asking. Each day for a week she lingered by the grille, hoping to have her curiosity satisfied.

Strange, it was the first time she had felt anything

but despair since being sentenced to spend the rest of her life here. They represented to her a link to the outside world—to the land where she hoped Ramil still lived. And from what she gathered from the twitter of voices around the white-robed woman, the Holtish exiles were bitter, complaining about everything from their beds to the food, deeply suspicious of the intentions of their hosts.

Her silent observation did not go unnoticed by the four women as they sat over their desultory attempts at embroidery. On the eighth day, their own curiosity got the better of them and the grey-haired one strode forward to the grille to challenge the young woman hovering there.

"What do you want?" she snapped.

Tashi took a step back and shook her head.

"Come to gloat over our fall?"

She shook her head vigorously; she had meant no disrespect.

The woman narrowed her eyes. "Who are you?"

Tashi put her finger to her lips to signal that she could not speak.

"Goddess got your tongue?" sneered the woman. "I expect they've cut it out. I heard they do that here."

"My tongue has not been cut out," Tashi replied, stung to defend her faith. "I have a duty of silence."

"Which you have just broken," the woman declared triumphantly, glancing back at the other women.

It was true, Tashi acknowledged. She had failed the

first test of the obligations imposed on her, just as she had failed at everything else. There was no surprise in that; hardly any shame, as she was already as low as she could get.

"Yes, I have failed," Tashi agreed humbly. Now that she had broken her silence, she might as well satisfy her curiosity. "Who are you?"

"You have not heard?" The woman seemed displeased not to be recognized.

"No, I'm not allowed out. I am a pris—a devotee." The woman was not fooled. She moved closer to the grille to stare at the fair-haired girl.

"A prisoner? You are like me then, though they call my incarceration 'hospitality.' What did you do, child?"

What had she done? Everything—nothing. "I broke my vows. And you?"

The woman smiled grimly. "I married the wrong man."

"Can you not divorce him?"

"He is dead—and his Empire another's."

Tashi felt a swoop of alarm. Even in the enclosure, all had heard of the fall of Fergox and given thanks for his defeat. She now knew who she was speaking to and could guess who the other three women were. But what strange paths had brought them to Rama she could not fathom. She had to get away from them before they found out about her.

"I'm sorry for your loss," she whispered hastily, and backed away.

"No, stay!" commanded the First Wife. "You are the first Islander to speak civilly to me."

"I can't, I'm sorry." Tashi walked quickly back to her cell, determined to stay away from the grille in the future.

The First Wife was not a woman to let her desires be ignored. The fair-haired oath-breaker intrigued her and she wanted to talk to her again. The girl was more like an Easterner than any of the Islanders the wives had met since disembarking from their ship.

The Etiquette Mistress had been appointed as liaison between the Holtish exiles and the Blue Crescent court. The Crown Princesses had agreed to shoulder the burden of protecting the warlord's family as a goodwill gesture towards the new ruler of Holt, but no one was happy to have the wives in the palace. The Etiquette Mistress met the women once a day to check that their reasonable demands had been granted and their unreasonable ones dealt with diplomatically. She had naturally refused the Holtish exiles' request to be given a place to pray to their own god—worship of Holin in the palace: unthinkable! The Crown Princesses were seeking more suitable accommodation for the exiles, somewhere where they could do no harm, but the population were hostile to having Fergox's family settle among them and so far no suitable solution had been found.

The First Wife listened impatiently to this explanation. She drummed her long fingers on the table as the

Etiquette Mistress apologized to her with the elaborate courtesy of the Islands.

"So, we are to remain your prisoners," the First Wife rapped out.

"You are free to go out with an escort—for your own safety," explained the Etiquette Mistress evenly. "We keep no one prisoner."

"No?" The First Wife pounced on this admission. "What about the fair-haired girl in the Enclosure—the one with purple robes?"

The Etiquette Mistress's eyes glinted. "You spoke to Taoshira?"

"Who?"

"She spoke to you?"

The First Wife could hear the barely suppressed rage in the woman's voice.

"Yes, we spoke. Briefly," the First Wife said coolly.

"That should not have happened."

"But it did. I am interested in her. Who is she?"

The Etiquette Mistress swallowed, debating whether she should answer. If the First Wife did not hear it from her, she could winkle it out from any palace servant.

"She is the disgraced Fourth Crown Princess."

"The witch!" exclaimed the First Wife in disgust.

The Etiquette Mistress did not correct her, pleased that she had taken the news so ill. She would not be seeking Taoshira's company again, the Mistress thought smugly.

"Is there anything else, my lady?" the Etiquette Mistress asked.

"No. I've heard enough." The First Wife strode from the room, clenching her fists.

The first Tashi knew about her visitors was when someone grabbed a fistful of her hair and dragged her from her bed. Her room was pitch black, the floor cold; it was still the middle of the night.

"What—!" she gasped, dazed with sleep.

The hand let go. Tashi sensed that there was more than one person in the room.

"You evil witch!" snarled a woman's voice.

Tashi panicked. "Guards!" Further cries were cut off by a hand over her mouth.

"You caused the ruin of us and our families," continued the First Wife, "and you will pay for that."

Tashi wanted to say that it was none of her fault; that Fergox deserved to die; that it was madness to invade the Enclosure and attack a devotee; but the Second Wife had gagged her with a silk scarf and bound her wrists and ankles.

"You have humiliated us; now we will do the same to you," announced the First Wife gleefully. "First we will cut off that hair that so bewitched him, and then mark that perfect skin of yours so no one will forget what you did."

Terrified, Tashi struggled in earnest, kicking with two feet at the woman crouching by her legs, propelling herself backwards against the washstand. She struck with her fists at the First Wife, knocking a knife from the woman's grip. Rolling over, she upset the dented bronze fingerbowl at her bedside; it fell to the ground with a reverberating clang.

"Oh no: you don't escape again!" panted the First Wife, grabbing Tashi's arm to pull her back into the center of the circle.

Feet pounded in the corridor outside. A fist thumped on the closed door. The four wives froze.

"Devotee Taoshira, are you all right?" bellowed the guard.

Tashi screamed through her gag, a strangled sound but enough to alert the man that something was wrong. The door flew open.

"What in the Goddess's name is happening here?" he exclaimed.

The First Wife kicked the knife out of sight under the bed and moved calmly to the entrance.

"We were just paying a social call on our sister here," she said. "We'll return to our beds now."

"Social call? In the Enclosure? At midnight?" spluttered the guard. "Why is Devotee Taoshira tied up and gagged?"

"We didn't want her to break her vow of silence again." The First Wife's eyes were cold as she looked at her victim.

Another guard appeared at the door. She quickly removed Tashi's bonds and helped her to her feet. Tashi was shivering with shock.

"I will have to report this to the Third Crown Princess," said the first guard. "Wait here."

Leaving them under the close watch of the other guard, he sprinted off.

Tashi stood to one side, rubbing her arms. The eyes of the four wives were on her.

"The penalty for attempted murder in the Islands is death," she said quietly as if to no one in particular.

The First Wife pursed her lips. "You know we had no intention of killing you."

That wasn't what it had felt like, being at their mercy. Tashi remembered all too well the ease with which Fergox's people had shed blood.

"Even if you tell that lie," continued the First Wife haughtily, "we are caught in a living death as it is. What do we care? Anyway, your people would not dare execute us on your word."

That is probably true, thought Tashi, not that she sought anyone's death. The diplomatic consequences would be huge: the new ruler of Holt, whoever that was, had sent the women here for safety. It would be easier to disregard the testimony of an oath breaker.

But she deserved better than this. Tashi straightened her spine and dropped her hands by her sides. She had been punished enough for her real faults and should not now be made to answer for the sins of another. Enough of submission and apologies.

Tashi faced the First Wife and took a step closer. "I am not your enemy. I did not seek marriage with Fergox, but fled at the first opportunity. You avenge yourselves upon the wrong person. He was to blame for his own downfall, and therefore yours."

The First Wife's eyes narrowed, her face ugly with rage. "Don't you think I know this, witch? But he is gone and you are left: the favored one—the wife with whom he was going to replace me! You must have bewitched him—everyone said so."

Tashi felt her anger rising. "When did I do that? And how? Do you mean I did so as a child when, thanks to your late husband, I was chosen as Fourth Crown Princess? Or perhaps when I was being beaten by the priests of Holin? When exactly did I have a chance to do this? If I had enchantments, I would have chosen an easier path, believe me."

The First Wife met Tashi's stare and held it. "I was right. You are not like the other Islanders," she announced with a curl of her lip.

"I think you mean that as an insult," Tashi said proudly, tilting her chin up, "but I take it as a compliment. This is the way the Goddess has made me. It is what I am."

There was a rustle at the doorway and Korbin swept into the room, showing no sign that she had just been roused from her bed: her hair veiled, her robes smooth.

"Devotee Taoshira, what of your vow of silence?" the Third Crown Princess asked.

As if that was the most important crime of this night!

"I'm afraid, Crown Princess, that my vow shattered when I was dragged from my bed by my unexpected callers." Tashi knew her tone was mocking but she felt so angry with them all.

"Ladies, perhaps you did not understand, but this part of the palace is out of bounds to all but the devotees," Korbin said sternly.

The First Wife smiled. "Then why not lock the doors?"

"Because all remain here voluntarily and no one else dare disturb the Goddess's worshippers." No one else but rude Holtish heathens was the implication.

"Then I apologize for our intrusion. We will retreat." The First Wife made as if to leave.

"Wait! What were you doing here? And why did you bind the devotee?"

The First Wife looked at Tashi, daring her to tell the truth. Korbin turned to her as well.

"Devotee Taoshira, do you have an explanation?"

Tashi kept her mouth closed. If she accused the wives she would be giving her nation a diplomatic headache, perhaps even risking war with the new authorities in Holt about whom next to nothing was known. How would they react?

"You may speak," snapped Korbin, showing more emotion than usual.

"Oh, heavens, girl, you can tell her," interrupted the First Wife, riled by the dignity of her rival. She had expected the girl to blab and weep; instead she stood there like a little queen, above the insults offered her. "We came to cut off her hair and mark her face, is that clear enough for you?"

Korbin took a shocked breath. This confession plunged them all into a nightmare of consequences.

Tashi knew she had to do something. "My dear friend," she said with an attempt at warmth in her tone as she smiled at the First Wife, "you take the jest too far. Your Highness, we were merely . . ." She struggled for an explanation. "I boasted to my friends that I was scared of nothing, so we made a wager that they could not frighten me. I must admit they won; I was sincerely terrified when they swooped in on me."

All four wives stared at Tashi with undisguised amazement but Korbin frowned.

"You pass your time in the Enclosure playing games, Taoshira? Have you no respect for this place?"

"It seems not, Your Highness. I'm sure you can believe that of me as you know what I'm capable of. Perhaps it is these ladies who are acting out of character? Maybe if they were given a home that was less of a prison and a place for their own worship, they would not fall prey to the temptation to pass their time with such frivolous bets."

"Are you telling me what to do, devotee?" Korbin said with a frigid tone.

"No. I was only reflecting that on my ill-fortuned embassy to Gerfal, the host nation allowed me the freedom to worship in our way even though it was an abomination to them. I was wondering why we were less generous and forced strangers into the heart of a temple they despise, with people they do not trust. It is almost as if we are driving them to cause trouble."

Tashi turned her back on them all. "If you do not mind, I'm tired and wish to sleep."

Bending gracefully, she scooped the knife from under her mattress and passed it to the First Wife.

This gesture revealed what everyone suspected: that she had lied about the reason the wives had come to her and had done so to protect them from punishment. But there was nothing more to be said if she did not change her story now. The four exiles retreated under guard.

Korbin lingered for a moment, fingering the door handle.

"Why?" she asked simply. "Why lie for them?"

"You never understood me, Korbin," Tashi said. "Think what you like, but having just escaped one war, I do not want to provoke another."

The next week, a villa was found for the wives, complete with a place for a temple where worshippers of Holin could gather as long as no human sacrifices were made. Peace returned to the Goddess's Enclosure.

Two months after the incident in Tashi's room, the new ruler of Holt sent word to the Blue Crescent court that he was coming to conclude negotiations on a marriage alliance with the Fourth Crown Princess. He apologized for being unable to come any earlier as he had a kingdom to subdue after the tumultuous fall of Fergox. He wanted to be confident that it would remain peaceful in his absence while he left it in the hands of his viceroy, Zaradan of the Horse Followers, for a few weeks. He signed himself Ramil ac Burinholt.

The Crown Princesses, including the newly elected Fourth Crown Princess who had replaced Tashi, met in closed session. The first decision they took was to agree to see the young man on the terms he himself had proposed.

"Though the Fourth Crown Princess is too young to marry, we can agree to the betrothal," said Marisa, nodding to the shy twelve-year-old of impeccable matriarchal lineage from Kai. "She can marry him in a few years."

"I do not think that is what the Prince has in mind," warned Safilen. "He thinks he is marrying Taoshira."

Korbin stroked her blue robes as if to soothe herself. They all knew they were taking a risk allowing him to set foot on Rama, but for peace with Holt this was a price worth paying.

"The Prince is a ruler. He wants a political alliance with us to consolidate his fragile hold on the crumbling Empire. He will compromise," she declared. "He will want to repay the favor we did him by taking the exiles off his hands."

"You underestimate the strength of his bond with Taoshira," Safilen objected, her patience with her censorious sister worn to the bone.

"But she is beyond his reach, dedicated to the Goddess," Marisa pointed out. "The priests are very pleased with her devotion and say she is much quieter since the Holtish exiles left. I think we can safely say that the episode in her life with the Gerfalian prince is closed."

"With love, nothing is safe," muttered Safilen, wondering if Marisa had ever really loved anyone in her long life of selfless service to the nation. If she had, she would not be so complacent. "But let us see him and find out which of us is right."

Ramil found the journey in the royal barge a torture. He wanted to run along the banks, vaulting the fences until he burst in upon Tashi and swept her up in his arms.

But I'm in her territory now, he reminded himself. *I mustn't upset my hosts.* Instead he behaved himself, sitting in the chair provided for him, waving to the crowds on the bank who had gathered to see the Dark Prince, killer of Fergox, new ruler of the Holtish Empire.

The Etiquette Mistress, whom he remembered from Gerfal, met him at the door. Ramil greeted her like an old friend, completely forgetting she disliked him.

"This way, Prince," the woman said with a low bow. "The Princesses are waiting in the Hall of the Floating Lily."

Ramil followed her down the corridor, barely taking in the beauty of his surroundings with its delicate tracery, silk hangings, and hidden gardens. He entered the hushed chamber, seeing the four Princesses ahead of him, seated on their thrones, resplendent in robes of blue, green, white, and orange. All had the same white faces and veiled hair he remembered Tashi wearing. He was a little surprised that the smallest of the four, on the Throne of Nature, had not turned to show him some sign of recognition, but then maybe Tashi was also trying to behave. The thought made him smile.

Ramil reached the edge of the circle of thrones and swept a low bow, feeling his moment of triumph had arrived.

"I come, Your Highnesses, to claim the hand of the Fourth Crown Princess." He turned to Tashi, expecting to see an answering glitter of joy in her eyes, and found himself staring at a stranger. "But where is the Fourth Crown Princess?" he asked, suddenly realizing that something was very wrong.

"This is the Fourth Crown Princess," Korbin said steadily.

"Then what has happened to Tashi—to Princess Taoshira?" He could feel his heart pounding.

"Taoshira was obliged to join the devotees of the Goddess in the Silent Court," replied Marisa. "She is no longer a crown princess."

Ramil's brain struggled to catch up with this news.

"Her election was discovered to have been flawed and her behavior unworthy of her office," added Korbin.

Ramil took a step towards her. "Are you telling me that you threw her out? After all she did for you and for my people?" His rage hummed in his ears, his diplomatic skills deserting him. "She was beaten and tortured by Fergox's priests for defending your Goddess, all the while behaving with dignity and courage, and yet you say she is not worthy!"

"She denied her faith," Korbin said firmly.

"She had a moment of doubt. Do you have hearts beating under those robes of yours? I would like to have seen any one of you do better in her shoes—oh, but I forget, she wasn't allowed any! She stood barefoot in front of the Inkar of Kandar as that woman tried to kill her and Tashi still refused to fight for Holin—that was the strength of her faith!"

Silence fell in the chamber as Ramil struggled to control himself.

"Where is she?" he hissed.

"You cannot see her," said Marisa, frowning at this outrageous display of emotion. "She is in the Goddess's Enclosure."

"I'm seeing her if it's the last thing I do. Send your guards to cut me down if you wish, but I didn't come all this way for nothing." Ramil moved towards the door.

"What you propose is sacrilege!" Marisa objected. "We refuse to allow any more invasions of the Enclosure."

"Then bring her here to me. One way or another, I'm seeing her." Ramil clenched his hand on his sword hilt and stared down the eldest Princess.

"I say we should let him see her," Safilen said gently. "Let the Goddess punish him if it is wrong to do so. Far better that than to start a war with a man who killed Fergox Spearthrower."

Reluctantly, the First Princess nodded and summoned a priest. "Bring the Devotee Taoshira here at once," she ordered.

Ramil paced between the thrones of Nature and Justice, making both occupants very nervous. The newest Princess could not hide her fear as the man they said was to be her husband fumed beside her. Then a door opened at the far end of the chamber and a little procession of priestesses entered, a fair-haired girl in their midst. Ramil held his breath: it was her. He could hardly believe it.

The devotee looked up and saw him standing in the middle of the chamber.

"Ram!" Tashi cried. Breaking with all conventions, she pushed through the priestesses and sprinted the length of the hall. Reaching him she wrapped her arms around his waist, burying her face in his neck. He hugged her tight, stroking her hair and kissing it.

"Excuse me, ladies, your devotee and I have some catching up to do," Ramil announced, lifting her up and carrying her out of the chamber. He blundered through the corridors until he found a quiet garden and ducked into an arbor, hidden away from anyone pursuing them. He lowered Tashi onto the bench and sat opposite her, just staring. He reached out and brushed her cheek.

"I thought you were dead," he said.

"I have been," she replied, marvelling to see how well

he looked. "Slavery becomes you."

He laughed. "Actually I'm not a slave. I've come to offer you Holt as a wedding present. They've made me their king and the position is vacant for a queen. So, what do you think?"

Tashi shook her head in amazement. "Is this one of your jokes, Ram?"

"No, my love, I'm deadly serious." He looked at her more closely and saw that she was wearing one of his shirts and robes of the Horse Followers. "I can see that you have as many tales to tell as I do, but mercifully we have the rest of our lives to hear them. Just say that you'll be mine—that'll do for now."

Tashi felt the huge weight of despair settle on her. What he was asking was impossible for so many reasons. It was like being at the bottom of a pit, able to glimpse freedom above but with no hope of escape. "But I can't, Ram. I'm a devotee now, not a princess."

"I don't want a princess—I want you." He put his arm around her and pulled her to him. "And what's all this devotee nonsense?"

"It's not nonsense. I've been sentenced for my failings. I have to make up for my broken vows with a lifetime of maiden service to the Goddess."

Ramil wrinkled his nose. "I don't like the sound of that—and I'm sure your Goddess doesn't either. You are not destined to be a maiden, Tashi." He kissed her brow but she drew away.

"I have no choice."

"Of course you have a choice. Your vow to me came first, remember? I'm not letting you break that." He stood up. "What do you have to do round here to get married?"

Tashi gave a weary laugh. He did not understand how impossible it was to break the Blue Crescent laws as if they were no more than cobwebs. "You find a priest, then the woman declares she wants the man as her husband, and he says if he agrees."

"Excellent!" Ramil rubbed his hands. "I was afraid there was some terrible ritual thing that would take hours."

Tashi shook her head. "No, marriage is regarded as a private matter and nothing to do with the state. But I'm in even less favor since I tussled with the First Wife." Ramil raised a curious eyebrow. "I'll explain later. What I'm trying to say is that you won't find anyone who'll dare marry us, if that's what you had in mind."

"I don't know much about your country, but the one thing I do know is that its priests are corruptible. I'll go and catch us one. You stay here."

His footsteps faded as he ran off back the way they had come. Tashi sat watching the dragonflies skimming over the pond in the garden, not daring to think, not daring to hope. Her life for the past weeks had been a desert. The only time she had felt even slightly alive was when she'd had to fight off Fergox's vengeful wives and that had only been temporary. Now Ramil had burst in upon her like a sudden storm. He was mad to think they could marry. He needed a political alliance to consolidate his new position; she was under a lifelong sentence.

But I prefer his madness to the sanity of my people, she admitted. What did the Goddess think?

The dragonflies twisted over the pool in a blur of flashing wings. The Mother would prefer their offering of love to each other than the desert of dry duty, Tashi realized.

"Here she is!" said Ramil, bringing a woman in a green robe into the garden.

Tashi fell to her knees in consternation. "Second Princess!" she gasped.

"Get up, child," Safilen said, making a beckoning gesture with her ringed fingers. "I've told this young man that I will hear your vows. Not a usual part of my duties, I know, but I understand from Korbin it is quite legal."

"Does she know too?" Tashi asked, aghast.

"Of course not. But I thought I'd better check before annoying her like this. We don't have long, so if you don't mind?" Safilen took Tashi's hand, smiling at the bewildered girl. "Do you, Taoshira of Kai, take Ramil ac Burinholt as your husband?"

"Yes, I take him," Tashi replied faintly, wondering what on earth she was doing.

"And you, Ramil ac Burinholt, agree?" The Second Princess grasped his wrist.

"Yes, I do," Ramil said firmly.

She placed his hand in Tashi's. "As the Goddess wills," Safilen proclaimed. "Well, that covers it, I think, though I apologize for not doing the full speech: I don't know it and it's rather boring."

"That's it?" asked Ramil, holding on to Tashi's fingers as if he feared she would slip away from him.

"Yes," said the Second Princess as she departed, "that's it."

Ramil ac Burinholt, King of Holt and heir to the throne of Gerfal, strode back into the throne room, bringing with him his dazed new wife. He bowed to the Crown Princesses.

"I apologize for leaving you so abruptly an hour ago," he said.

"It is forgiven," said the First Princess. "Now that you have spoken with the devotee, she will return to the Enclosure and we will return to our discussion of our alliance."

Ramil held on to Tashi tightly. Coming to her senses, she returned the pressure, gripping his fingers.

"Actually, your devotee is no longer suited to maiden service in the Goddess's temple as we have just been married," Ramil announced.

The courtiers rustled and whispered to each other.

"Is this true, Taoshira?" asked Marisa.

"It is, Your Highness," Tashi replied, tempted to make a run for it before she was arrested. Only Ramil's hand anchored her here. "I fear you will want to cast me out of the Enclosure."

"Who dared marry you?" asked the Third Princess, turning her eyes to her co-ruler as realization dawned.

"I did, sister," said Safilen, raising her hand. "Marriage under our law is a private matter and not something we put to the vote. I was quite within my rights."

Tashi began to laugh, realizing that she might, just might, be able to escape. "And as Prince Ramil has insulted you by choosing another wife than the one you proposed for him, you'll want to cast him out too," she suggested slyly.

"Oh, undoubtedly," murmured Ramil. "Do cast me out."

Safilen hid her smile with her fan. "Yes, begone, uncouth Prince," she said, waving him away.

"I obey," said Ramil, turning Tashi round and marching her from the room. "Excuse me while I abduct myself a princess."

"Uncouth!" snapped Korbin, glaring at Safilen. "They are both a disgrace."

Safilen rose and spread her fan, then leant down to her sister on the Throne of Justice.

"But uncouth is fun," Safilen whispered in Korbin's ear. "The Goddess laughs with us when we are happy, remember that. Come, sister." Safilen beckoned to the terrified new Fourth Princess. "I want to have a private word with you about love."

Ramil escorted Tashi aboard the flagship of his fleet of captured pirate vessels.

"I can't believe you just did that," Tashi said, reliving the moment in the Hall of the Floating Lily when Ramil had claimed her as his wife.

"What *we* did," Ramil said, squeezing her hand. "You Blue Crescent women can't pretend to be mere chattels of your husbands. I seem to remember *you* took *me*. A very novel way of marrying for us Easterners." He stroked her cheek. "I'm looking forward to finding out more about my rights later." He was pleased to see he had made her very embarrassed at the thought.

"I apologize it's not up to Crescent standards," he continued, leading her to his cabin through the ranks of grinning sailors. They whistled and cheered their new queen. "It's now manned by volunteers, but we've not had time to change the decorations."

The walls of the captain's room were covered with carvings of gruesome faces, buxom wenches, and graffiti. It was vile, but at least the sheets on the bed looked clean and the place smelt of pinewood. Ramil guided her to a chair and placed a paper dragonfly on the table in front of her.

"See, I kept it."

She pulled his horse from her pocket: it was an unrecognizable wad of paper after its dunking in the river. Her hand was shaking with a mixture of excitement and fear. Surely someone was going to stop them?

Ramil closed his fingers over hers.

"Don't, my love, it's going to be all right."

Tashi shut her eyes: everything was happening so quickly she felt as if she had left her common sense back at the palace. "Tell me what's been going on. I've been locked away from news—from everything—since I came back. How is your father?"

"Victorious, thanks to you. The Blue Crescent arrived in time to swing the battle in our favor. We suffered many losses but Gerfal did not fall."

"And what happened to Fergox?"

"I killed him." Ramil watched her anxiously. He knew he had rushed her into this marriage, but there had seemed no other chance to snatch her away from that oppressive court.

"Gordoc? Melletin? Yelena? The professor?"

"All alive. Gordoc is training my army for me—he's now General Ironfist and loves his uniform. He sends his love. Melletin is my prime minister and a very fine one he is too—I hardly have to do a thing. Yelena would have headed my government, but it appears that she and Melletin are due to have an addition to their family in the New Year so she suggested I pick him. I'm sure her turn will come. My grandfather is looking after Thunder and my throne for me while I go and find myself a wife."

Tashi put her hands to her cheeks. Yesterday she had been a disgraced devotee; now she was wife to the ruler of most of the known world!

Ramil hesitated, then continued.

"Duke Nerul is back in charge of Brigard. Merl has been injured in a duel with a jealous husband, but not seriously."

Tashi chuckled softly. "No more than he deserves."

"And I've sent Professor Norling to be the new Inkar of Kandar. I think in a few years they'll be the best educated of all our subjects."

"You have been busy. I am amazed and humbled. And definitely not worthy of you." She opened her eyes and turned them on him. "Thank you for rescuing me again."

Ramil pulled her onto his knee. "I was only returning the favor. You've rescued me more times than I can count. I need you with me, Tashi. I can't do this on my own. I want to be a good king and make Holt into a free country, where people can worship their own god—or goddess—and not be afraid." He put his hand on hers, pressed against her stomach. "I want lots of children to fill the palace with life and laughter." He kissed her neck. "But most of all, I want to be your husband and make you happy." He smiled. "I've got to get that bit right, or one of my generals will thump me."

Tashi stroked the back of his hand thoughtfully. "But, Ram, you must know that things are different now. I bring nothing to you—no position, no alliance."

"Hush," he said, kissing her lips, "just as well I married you if you're going to bring up all sorts of ridiculous things like that."

She pushed him away, hand flat on his chest. "But it's true."

"Oh yes, as you well know all I ever saw in you was your navy." Ramil rolled his eyes.

"I'm being serious. I'm not your equal now."

"No, you're far better than me. I'm still struggling to catch up with you. You'll make a brave, generous, kind queen: that's what our people need. They're lucky I've got such good taste."

She raised a sceptical brow.

"Look, Tashi, I'm not doing this as a favor to you; I'm doing it for me. I've known for months now that I can't live without you. Will you be so cruel as to deny me my happiness?"

Put like that, she knew she could not refuse. They'd have to risk failure together. Or maybe, with him at her side, even success? Tashi bent her head towards him.

"I love you, Ram."

"And I love you, my dragonfly princess."

The sounds of the ship leaving harbor filtered through from above. The room began to sway. Ramil met Tashi's eyes with a mischievous look. "Now, wife, we have a long voyage ahead of us with no interruptions, no affairs of state to sidetrack us." He brushed his fingers against the lacings at her neck. "Isn't it time you returned that shirt to its owner?"